BRUSH OF EMBERS
THE FIRESTORM DRAGON CHRONICLES

KIRA NYTE

Brush of Embers
Copyright © 2024 by Kira Nyte

All rights reserved. No part of this book may be reproduced in any form or by any electronic or mechanical means, including photocopying, recording, or information storage and retrieval systems—except in the case of brief quotations embodied in critical articles or reviews—without permission in writing from the author.

This book is a work of fiction. The characters, organizations, events, and places portrayed in this book are products of the author's imagination and are either fictitious or are used fictitiously. Any similarity to a real person, living or dead is purely coincidental and not intended by the author.

Edited by: Raina Toomey

Cover Design by: Daqri at Covers by Combs

Published by: Dark Illusion Publishing

BOOKS BY KIRA NYTE

Nocturne Falls Universe

A Dragon Speaks Her Name

A Dragon Gambles for His Girl

Merry & Bright, A Christmas Anthology

A Dragon's Christmas Mayhem (novella)

The Princess Protects Her Huntsman

Touched by Her Elven Magic

Touched by His Vampire Charm

Winter Wonderland, A Christmas Quartet

Touched by His Christmas Magic (novella)

The Firestorm Dragon Chronicles

Stroke of Fire

Dance of the Dragon

Storm of Flames

Spark of Fury

Talaenian Fae Novels

Forbidden Heart

Destined Desires

Cat's Paw Cove

A Fae's Wishmas: Felines and Festivities Anthology

Zombie Year 2099

Hellsbreath Sector

Short Stories/Novellas

The Gala Lover

Blood Born: The Beginning

Sinister Seas

AUTHOR'S NOTE

Author Note

Dear Readers,

If this is your first journey into the world of the Firestorm dragons and their lifemates, welcome! I hope you find their world and ways as fascinating as I have. If you wish to start from the beginning, be sure to read A Dragon Speaks Her Name and A Dragon Gambles for His Girl, both of which are part of Nocturne Falls Universe.

As always, I wish to warn you that this book does contain implied situations, darker content—perhaps not as dark as some previous books—and scenes of explicit violence and language that may be disturbing to some. These scenes can be skimmed without losing context of the story, though they do enrich the storyline.

The Firestorm dragons will do anything for their lifemates, brethren, and the civilians they protect. *Anything*. Blood will spill, enemies will die—sometimes extremely unpleasant deaths—but in the end, when it comes to protecting what is theirs, they will kill mercilessly for their mates, or die defending them.

Happy reading!

Kira Nyte

BRUSH OF EMBERS

Brush of Embers

Seraphina Allaze grew up in a small Colorado town knowing it was only a matter of time before the dragons returned to take her people back to their magical homeland, The Hollow. She also grew up knowing her own father hated her for killing his beloved wife with her birth. Fortunately, she has the love and support of her honorary uncle and aunt and their daughter, her best friend.

But when the dragons finally appear, they bring with them more heartache than she ever could have imagined. Secrets are revealed. Lives shattered.

Emery LaRouche has watched all his brethren find their lifemates and thinks he knows what to expect when it happens to him. Meet the woman. Bond with the woman. Be ecstatically happy.

No one told him what to do if she's the *wrong* woman.

Emery is known as the most easygoing dragon of the Firestorm clan but Sera rouses all his most primal instincts. He will do anything—*anything*—to convince her that no matter what she believes, they are fated to be together. He will accept nothing else.

ACKNOWLEDGEMENT

Acknowledgement

These last few years have thrown some difficult times at us all. I was no exception. What I found to be my most cherished outlet and hobby had become lost to me. Despite the blocks and obstacles, I finally made it back onto a path, a new path, a better path. In all honestly, at some of my darkest moments, my readers were the ones who kept me going. The emails, the messages, the words of encouragement.

The *interaction.*

I know I'm not the only one who's been through highs and lows, some small, some unimaginable, but together, with all of your continued support, I have reclaimed my path and found my way back to what I love the most: creating worlds, characters, and stories for your escape!

xoxo

CHAPTER ONE

"Are you insane? Absolutely not!"

"Sera, I lost my diamond bracel—"

Seraphina Allaze smacked her hand over Jeslyn Rogue's mouth and hushed her with a finger against her own pursed lips. Her best friend's brown eyes grew wider than she thought possible. Sera cast the route to the living room a sharp glance. After a few heart-thudding seconds with no indication that they'd been overheard, she straightened up and released Jes's mouth, burning her gaze deep into the pit of the woman's soul.

"Keep your voice down," Sera hissed, drawing closer to her friend. "I wouldn't be surprised if my father placed secret cameras around this house after our last escapade to hear and see everything that's going on."

"I wouldn't blame him for a moment." Jes prodded a finger against her shoulder. Sera responded with a sharp arch of a brow. Jes crossed her arms over her chest. "You got yourself caught. And *arrested*."

"*We* got caught. *I* got arrested to save your ass from further trouble trying to get your damn bracelet back, which was nowhere to be found in that bar, by the way. Breaking and entering after hours for nothing. Thank the Gods above *your* father saw fit to front my bail, because mine would've let me rot."

Uncle Slade always came to her rescue. Her own father chose to criticize her for everything she did, including breathe. Sad part was, Slade was "uncle" not by blood but by common ground, both men being Keepers to elusive Firestorm dragons—which none of the younger generation had ever seen. Whether they lived in some longstanding fantasy game or not remained to be seen, especially when one looked at Uncle Slade and his seemingly grounded character and successful business ventures. It was easier to picture her own father living in a dreamworld.

"Yeah, well…" Jes's cheeks burned red. She tried to rub the flush away as she always did, and managed to deepen the color more. With a sigh, she nodded. "Okay. You're right. As always. It's just a bracelet, after all. Do you think your dad will let you go to the bonfire tonight?"

"As long as Uncle Slade confirms there's going to *be* a bonfire, I don't see why not. Regardless, I'll climb out my window if I have to."

"There's no grounding you, is there?"

Sera scoffed, stealing another glance over her shoulder. She wondered where her father was, considering he had a knack for appearing at the most inopportune moments in conversations. It was one of the reasons she believed he had cameras throughout the house. He always knew when she was planning some frivolous adventure.

"I'm twenty-six, an adult with my own business. I've been adulting more than most people my age for a while now. I'm beyond the realm of grounding." She tucked a wave behind her ear and shed a smile on her friend. "Grounding never worked when he *could* ground me."

"You're the reason he has gray hair."

"He doesn't have a single gray hair, but if he did, that would be on him. Not me."

Her unspoken explanation hung in the air between them. Jes would understand exactly what she meant. It wasn't until Sera grew into her teen years that she began to comprehend the animosity her father held toward her. He tried to hide it beneath smiles and praise, but it forever lingered. A foul prickle that took up residence beneath her skin and refused to leave. By the time she reached early adulthood, her father didn't try to hide it as much. She found herself spending more and more time with Jes and her family than her own father, which most likely caused the solid wedge between them now.

All over something she had absolutely no control over.

Sera sidled past her friend and pulled open the fridge door. She removed a carton of orange juice and some mixed berries she had washed earlier that day, and placed them on the counter. "Want a glass?"

"Sure." Jes grabbed the glasses from the cabinet. Placing them close to the juice carton, she leaned in and added in a hushed tone, "So, you really think my bracelet is a lost cause?"

Sera glared at her friend. "Yes. Lost. Done. Case closed." She poured out two servings of juice. "Besides, there's something off about that joint that doesn't sit well with me. A foul vibe. It makes me think of those recent, unexplainable events—New Orleans, that psych ward in Alabama, the hospital breakout outside of Seattle. Things that point to a thread of truth behind all the stories Uncle Slade, my father, and their friends have told over the years." Because, deep down, she *knew* they weren't just stories. They were *facts* that gave her the strength to endure every day of her dismal existence. Handing Jes a glass, she added, "Maybe we can finally see if our parents are nuts or if we're really part of some mythological race, biding our time here in this hellhole until the dragons return and take us away."

When Jes accepted her drink, Sera blinked at her friend's dreamy expression. A new shade of pink touched her cheeks now, one that had nothing to do with embarrassment and frustration and everything to do with some heated daydream.

"I can't wait to meet my father's dragon. To see if the lore of lifemates is true. That instant attraction, the love-at-first-sight phenomena. I want all of it. Could you imagine?" She giggled like a teen with her first crush. "Being mated to a *dragon*. We'd have nothing to worry about for the rest of our lives."

Oh, she'd thought about it plenty. Finding Rayze would put an end to her father's sour moods and endless criticism. Uniting with Rayze would break her chains from a father who could care less about her and take her far away from this misery.

There were days she wondered how she and her father were even related.

"I don't doubt the minute Emery lays eyes on you, he'll be done for."

Jes gave her a friendly shove and giggled again. "Between the two of us, Rayze will win the lifemate lottery with you. And a lifetime of keeping you out of trouble."

Sera tapped her glass to Jes's. "I'll drink to that."

"Hey, girls."

Sera sipped her juice as she turned to face the doorway to the living room. Her father leaned against the archway, ankles crossed, thumbs tucked in the pockets of his jeans.

"Good afternoon, Uncle Nick." Jes waved a hand toward

his unusually nice choice of dress. Sera's brows pinched over her nose. "Don't you look handsome today. Date?"

"Business meeting."

"Spiffy, eh?" Sera inquired, holding the glass between both hands. Yeah, her father was dressed in his dark blue jeans, white button-down, and shiny shoes. Definitely not fit attire for a day under car hoods. "You own the shop. Who are you having a fancy meeting with?"

"Don't worry yourself about it. Slade called a bit ago and said he's having a bonfire at the house with some of the other families. I suppose you already planned to go," her father said, quirking a single brow over dark brown eyes. He'd even gone as far as to shave his signature five o'clock shadow. Definitely not giving off the meeting vibe. "I'll be swinging by after work."

"You mean you're actually going to join in the festivities for once?"

Sera smiled to lighten the tinge of bitterness that made its way into her comment. Her father was never one to partake in Keeper activities outside of an occasional birthday celebration or their quarterly meetings. He was more reclusive, choosing to be an associate more than a member of the Keeper family. It seemed that Keepers had been tight-knit until the attacks that drove the entire secret society out of their magical realm and into this world. A tidbit she couldn't quite picture of her father, being tight-knit with anyone.

He shrugged a shoulder, his eyes sharpening as his gaze picked away at her face. "Think it's time I started getting more involved, don't you?"

"Of course, Uncle Nick. I'm sure my dad would love to hear you're joining us." Jes clapped her hands together, a little too excitedly, and beamed a smile toward Sera's father. One that left Sera wrinkling a brow. Sure, she'd seen Jes and her father get along better than she got along with him, but that wasn't just a happy niece smile. That was more of a…

Okay, enough. That's just…eww.

Sera blinked. When her gaze landed on her friend again, her suspicions vanished. There was nothing but an overenthusiastic woman excited the loner uncle was joining in the festivities. Whatever she *thought* she'd seen was gone without a speck of evidence to suspect otherwise.

"Oh, it'll be so nice to have you there."

"Well, thank you, Jes. I'm looking forward to catching up with some of the guys." He stepped up to the island, grabbed himself an apple from the bowl in the center, and raised it in a salute toward Sera. "I'll speak with you later. I suspect you'll be heading into your shop." He turned to leave, but paused in the archway. Without looking back, he warned, "Keep yourself out of trouble, Seraphina."

Sera released an internal huff as her father disappeared. A moment later, she listened to the front door to their small home squeak open, then click shut. She sipped her juice, staring at the open space where her father had stood a few minutes before, contemplating the entire encounter. Just yesterday, she was still under the authoritative side-eye and firm-lipped punisher treatment. Today, her father presented himself as too chipper and eager.

"What's he up to?" she murmured against the rim of her glass.

"Maybe he's come to some self-resolution after twenty-six years and realizes life's too short to hide away beneath cars and behind doors?"

Sera cast Jes a side glance, finished off her juice, and placed the glass in the sink. "The man must've had some extensive epiphany for the complete one-eighty. He's trying to keep tabs on me like I'm an unruly teen. Meanwhile, I have my own business and life goals, no thanks to him." With a sigh, she shook her head, ignoring Jes's curious stare as she nibbled on a strawberry. "He does realize it's Saturday, right? My shop is open Monday through Friday. Then again, I don't know why I'd think he cares."

"His head did seem in the clouds. Maybe he *is* going on a date and doesn't feel it's the right time to disclose that information. He's a looker. Can have any girl he wants." Jes clapped her shoulder as she grimaced at Jes's open appreciation. "Cut him some slack. He's been through a lot these last two days."

Sera rolled her eyes. "I'd say Uncle Slade's been through more, handling my situation. And he's still cheery."

"Takes a lot to get Dad down."

"We both know your dad wasn't the most straight-line person in his youth."

"At least he doesn't try to hide it."

Jes glanced at her watch, a pretty top-end piece with diamonds that sparkled beneath the kitchen lights. Not that Sera was a materialistic person, but every once in a while she wondered what it would be like to have parents like Jes's, who doted on their daughter without batting an eyelash. Who provided not only material things, but love and support rather than disdain and criticism. Sure, the Rogues were generous toward her, but it didn't stop her from wondering what it would be like to be their daughter, too.

Well, whether or not the dragons were real, or even still alive, Sera was dead set on making something great of herself.

"I have to go," Jes said. "I promised Mom I'd help clean up the yard and set up for the night. Swing by later and give us a hand. We can start the fun early."

The subtle, unspoken implication that glimmered in Jes's

eyes couldn't be ignored. Jes expected Sera to be present to help set up. Sera flashed a smile and nodded.

"Give me a couple hours. How's that sound?"

Jes clapped her hands with a bounce on her toes and shot Sera a thumbs-up. "Perfect! See you soon."

After a quick hug and locking up the front door after her friend left, Sera slipped into the small guest room that doubled as an office for her father, foraged through the cabinets, and found the item she sought. If her father hid cameras in the room, he'd never once mentioned he'd seen her take this very box out on multiple occasions. It wasn't like he hid it well. She first found it sitting on the top shelf, the very same shelf it remained perched on for over a decade. The gold embossing had caught her curiosity when she was ten, and when she asked about it, her father shared its secret with her. It was one of the rare occasions she recalled him showing her genuine compassion and emotion. His face lit up when he spoke of Rayze's dragonstone and divulged some of the secrets of Keepers and dragons.

It was also the first and only time he gave any insight as to why she heard random thoughts and conversations in her head whenever she was around other people. Uncle Slade taught her how to gain control over what she heard and when, and she had perfected her ability to control her internal volume so that she heard voices only when she wanted, and silence the rest of the time. Uncle Slade had called her a rarity—not even his own daughter could completely shut the voices out—while her own father doubted her ability, saying it was impossible to achieve complete silence.

Box and key in hand, Sera slipped out of the office and retreated to her room, locking the door behind her. The motion offered her a sense of privacy and security she sought at times, even if she was alone in the house. But with the lock came a heaviness that sat on her shoulders, as it often did when the outside world wasn't distracting her from emotions she didn't necessarily care to indulge.

Loneliness. Her bane. Never having someone she could truly find comfort in. Watching Jes enjoy the company of her parents. Immerse herself in the bonds they all shared with the other Keepers and their families. A yearning Sera secreted away behind an upbeat and outgoing shell.

With a heavy sigh, she sat on her twin-size bed, fit the key into the lock, and popped open the lid. Nestled on a bed of black velvety cloth rested one of the most precious stones she'd ever laid eyes on. Rayze's dragonstone, forged of magic and the first shedding of his scales. A burnished red and black creation that shimmered with veins of mercurial gold, its surface smooth and cool to the touch. A doorway to her father's dragon, a window for communication.

Every time she opened the box, her heart stammered, her belly fluttered, and mixed emotions surfaced. Never the excitement she often imagined one day she'd feel. Instead, despite the wistful hope that fantasies existed, there was always a disconnect. Something was missing on the other end of this jewel. She couldn't quite put her finger on it, but the energy that flowed through the intricate web of colors and veins didn't align with her own.

"It was a massacre. We were lucky to escape. But how many civilians were lost remains unknown. How many dragons..."

Her father's words resounded in her mind, a repetitive reminder that no one in their small group of friends knew the true outcome of the attacks over thirty years ago in their magical home, The Hollow. No one knew who had survived outside their circle.

Sera lifted the stone from its bed and brought it to eye

level. The golden veins caught the light from her lamp, shimmering like liquid gold. When she tipped it at certain angles, she caught the faint lines of red deep within the stone. The entire creation presented itself as a living entity outside of its dragon. A magical and priceless possession.

"I can only hope to meet you one day soon, Rayze. To put speculation to rest and realize my silly, foolish dreams aren't silly and foolish after all." She traced a single vein, seeking to connect with the energy that teased her skin but never encompassed her soul. "Dad needs you. I truly believe that when you return, things will get better for him."

Her lips pulled tight. The weight of loneliness intensified, thickening the air, making the next breath she drew into her lungs difficult.

For the first time in a long time, the alien sting of tears burned across her eyes.

"And me."

CHAPTER TWO

Emery caught his brother's gaze across the table. The faint hum of energy that skated across his mind piqued his curiosity. He and Gabe had spent most of the day scouring this small forest-and-mountain town in Colorado, seeking a lead to Slade's whereabouts with no success. Gabe had attempted to coax one of the receptionists at the police department into sharing the address of their most recent arrestee—a twenty-six-year-old woman named Seraphina Allaze—and got them both kicked out of the station.

Allaze.

That came as a surprise, and it also came with an unease Emery couldn't quite shake. After all, Cade had said Slade used funds to bail the woman, presumably his daughter, out of jail. Not the descendant of another Keeper.

This new tingle didn't help matters. A vaguely familiar essence, but not one that hooked directly to him or Gabe.

"What are you thinking, brother?" Gabe asked, stirring his whiskey with a red plastic straw. His gaze pierced Emery, searching for an answer before Emery could muster up words. His brother's sharp-cut personality irritated him at times—he preferred a lighter, more carefree type of lifestyle—but right now, that razor edge reflected his own.

"You feel that." It wasn't a question. Gabe nodded once and sipped his drink. Emery leaned back in his chair and cast the quiet pub a meaningful glance. The essence wasn't from this place, but it was nearby. "A dragonstone, but not ours."

"Would make sense if Slade and Nick are in close proximity. Nick would have Rayze's dragonstone, just like all the Keepers have their dragon's stone. The quintessential means of communication." Gabe lowered his tumbler. "I'd say let's try to trace it, but something else is bothering you."

Indeed.

He hadn't lived through a major massacre of dragons before. None of them had except for Cade, perhaps, so the phenomena of lifemates wasn't entirely clear, other than that all their Keepers fathered daughters to preserve their dying race.

Would that extend to those Keepers who'd lost their dragons? Wouldn't nature be better served having male children born from those lines in anticipation of creating future dragon-Keeper bonds as he and his brethren brought younglings into the world?

"You're thinking too hard, Em. Your brain isn't used to such subjected torture." Gabe shoved his chair back and stood, tipping his head one way and then the other, his neck cracking. Emery followed suit, sans the cervical manipulation, and dug out a crisp hundred from his pocket. "This is the first lead since we've arrived. Let's not lose it."

Tucking the bill under his glass, Emery followed Gabe out of the pub and to their rented pickup truck. Despite his initial argument about who controlled the wheel, Emery climbed into the passenger seat and relinquished control while his mind stirred with disquiet.

"If the two are together, if they managed to stay close all these years, you know as well as I do we're going to be breaking terrible news to Nick."

Emery didn't need to look at his brother to know he held the same solemn expression that pulled his own lips tight. Nothing about relaying the death of a dragon to his Keeper was easy. Death itself haunted them daily. Gabe's own Keeper had been murdered by humans, his Keeper's wife murdered by Baroqueth while under Emery's protection.

A raw point to this day that he hadn't been able to save Ellie and that his failure caused his brother's lifemate heart-wrenching grief. Even though Skylar had assured him time and time again that she didn't blame him for her mother's death, *he* held himself responsible.

All of them held a degree of guilt and self-loathing when it came to each and every encounter with a new lifemate, the Baroqueth, and the subsequent injuries sustained. They were *dragons*, for Goddess's sake! They were supposed to protect and save. Prevent harm from touching lifemates, Keepers, and civilians.

And yet, the war sparked by the massacre over thiry years ago hadn't ended.

No one was safe.

Dragons were immortal—until they weren't. Baroqueth held powers and longevity, but not immortality. Hollow civilians possessed longevity as well, outlasting even the Baroqueth's lifespans of a hundred and fifty years, on average.

But death could hit at any moment. After the events over the last year, each and every one of them was keenly reminded that no one was invisible, despite all the magic in the worlds.

"Which way are you feeling, brother?" Gabe asked, guiding the truck along a winding mountain road. The sun sank out of sight for the night, leaving vivid rays of fire red and orange on the horizon. Streetlights had already switched on along the treacherous two-lane road, with its hairpin turns and steep drops. Emery punched the map on the touchscreen and scrutinized roads, directions, and that pull in the pit of his stomach. "Or have you lost it?"

"Have you?"

Gabe shrugged. "I felt it, but I'm connected too strongly with my own dragonstone and Sky to hone in on it. It comes and goes for me."

"I still feel it." Emery pointed on the map to what appeared to be a lookout or rest spot. "Head off here. I want to test something."

Gabe followed his instructions without hesitation, and about ten minutes later, Emery climbed out of the truck and walked up to the edge of the rest spot. A simple double-slat railing provided the only barrier should someone venture too close to the edge of the cliff while adoring the majestic scenery of twinkling lights dotting the towns below. A mountain breeze persisted, blowing his hair across his forehead, and cooling his otherwise hot skin. At the brink of winter, the air was crisp and clean, cold but not biting. Nothing like the mountains around The Hollow. Man, did he love those mountains, the snow and ice and refreshing air.

He closed his eyes and turned his focus inward, seeking the long-lost connection he'd shut down shortly after the massacre. The fact that he caught a vibe off another's dragonstone assured him they were close to Nick, which meant they were close to Slade, if his Keeper had bailed Nick's daughter out of jail. It was a risky move, but he couldn't delay any longer. If he was aware of the energy, he wouldn't put it past any potential Baroqueth who might stalk the area to latch onto it and locate Hollow residents.

Nothing was out of the realm of possibility. The hunt for Keepers and lifemates by both dragons and Baroqueth was piping hot.

"You trying to reestablish the telepathic line?"

Emery nodded once, keeping his eyes shut as he felt his brother's presence beside him. "He has never once opened the dragonstone box. I can't follow the stone, but he's near."

There!

Deep in slumber, the old energy line forged through a blood bond and vows began to spark and glow. It pulsed, stretched, yawned as it rose from sleep. His heart gave a hard thud in his chest.

"Slade, do your dragon a favor and open the box."

Slowly, Emery opened his eyes, seeing the world through an array of thermal colors, mostly blues and greens as the Colorado cold blanketed the area. A few dots and streaks of warmer hues pinpointed where wildlife resided beyond the tree line. He hadn't realized how tensely he stood until he heard the metal of the top rail creak beneath the pressure of his clenched fingers.

Gabe snorted, folding his arms over his chest like the conceited bastard he was, and shook his head. "Taxpayers are gonna love you."

"I don't think it's going to be a priority for the town."

"Not until some poor soul plunges to their death and the family sues the county because of faulty guardrails."

Emery grunted, waiting for any response from his Keeper. "You've quite an imagination." The bond brightened, but then did something he wasn't expecting. It began to unravel, a strange sensation of being molded into a different form, different shape, splitting yet staying the same. "So, Gabe. You never did tell me if a bond was instantaneous between you and Sky."

"It definitely was. I think each initial crossing and connection is a little different. With Syn and Briella, I think the lifemate connection overrode his dragon-Keeper bond with Gio. It's still there, but his bond with Briella takes precedence. Terrence was dead, so the bond was solely with Sky, and I recognized it before my eyes landed on her. If I'm not mistaken, something similar was the case with Alazar and Ariah, where Mark remains Al's Keeper, but the lifemate bond overrides the actual connection."

"They both bled into the dragonstones, though."

"Bro, a lifemate bond breaks all rules. Mindspeak usually happens only after your Keeper bleeds…"

"Emery?"

"…into the dragonstone, whereas lifemates automatically have that—"

"Wait," Emery hissed, waving a hand to silence his brother as his bond with Slade blazed to life. Meanwhile, the rebel flint peeling away from the parent bond began to pulse with its own glimmering gold light. The essence of a being connected at the other end of this newly birthed line shocked him with a bolt of liquid heat that stirred low in his groin and roused his dragon.

Well, I'll be damned.

"Unless you have another dragon you've been frolicking with over the last few decades who has telepathic superiority, it's me." A smile began to pull at this mouth. *"What do you say, old pal? Want to open the box and invite me over for dinner?"*

A flood of excitement hit him dead center in the chest, compliments of his Keeper. Air whooshed from his lungs, along with a few spurts of sparks and some smoke, but he quickly composed himself with a slight cough and chuckled. "Guess that's a yes."

"Pinged Slade?"

Keeping his mind open, he rolled out his shoulder and turned to Gabe. "Seems so." His smile turned feral, that wicked flint stoking dangerous desires alive. "And a little something more."

CHAPTER THREE

The bonfire crackled, popped, sending sparks into the wintry air. Laughter boomed around the fire and throughout the extensive yard as members of four Keeper families drank and danced and enjoyed the assortment of finger foods spread along a fold-out table. Strings of lights hung between strategically placed posts around the yard, providing light in areas the firelight didn't reach. The blinds at the back of Uncle Slade's house were all open, spilling more light onto the yard as adults fussed over drinks and games and more food.

Silas Jacobi, one of the few non-magical guests and Sera's longtime eye candy, returned to his seat beside her and handed her a plate loaded up with fruits and cheese, and a few chicken wings. He graced her temple with a playful kiss and leaned back, dangling his long-neck bottle between his thumb and forefinger, an amused smile on his pretty mouth as he watched Uncle Jax and Aunt Margo's three sons battle it out over a rowdy game of beer pong.

"Slade knows how to throw a party," Silas observed, adjusting his beer to take a healthy chug. Sera couldn't help but admire his profile. The man was utterly handsome and had a charm about him that lured everyone in. He'd become a favorite amongst the Keepers' kids at a young age, though the adults kept a distance between anyone outside their little clique until they were older. Only then did they allow outsiders in, after thorough vetting. Silas was one of three who'd made it through the rigorous initiation, and the poor guy hadn't a clue he was under a microscope the entire time. "Always a grand event."

"My dad had a bit of a wild side when he was younger, if what my mom says is true," Jes chimed in, picking a grape off Sera's plate.

Sera cleared her throat and flashed Silas a smile when he caught her staring at him. He winked, his dark eyes sparkling with the reflection of firelight as a playful dimple formed on the right side of his mouth. Sera lowered her gaze to her plate and chose a strawberry from her pickings to wet her dry mouth and keep her mind occupied with things that didn't necessarily involve Silas and forbidden games. Her father had already shared his two cents regarding any relationship that went outside their circle of half-mortal Keeper families. He'd told her to wait for Rayze, if she cared to oblige him.

Which she did, out of respect.

Yet the idea of her father's dragon—*my potential lifemate* —left her feeling that same unsettling disconnect that came anytime she admired the dragonstone. She felt a step behind, or a level below, simply not on the same plane as Rayze. Jes assured her that when he introduced himself to Sera, things would align. At least, that's what Aunt Claire had told Jes about the legends behind dragons and their lifemates.

"Speaking of, where the hell is my dad?" Jes twisted in her Adirondack chair, scanning the grounds. "He's not been out here for the last forty-five minutes."

"He said he was replenishing the beers and whatever that drink is in the dispenser on the table," Silas said, his attention wholly focused on Sera.

"He's a mean mixologist, isn't he?" she asked, her face warming under his unabashed gaze. He didn't try to hide his lust, or temper the intensity of his admiration. He simply picked away at the layers she held in place, caressing each newly discovered depth as he went.

Who was she to stop him? They'd played this game for years. She only wished he'd take the risk with her, overstep boundaries, allow her the smallest taste...

Sera offered Silas an item from the plate he'd gathered for her. His fingers hovered over a chicken wing until his gaze grazed hers and his smile darkened. He picked up the last strawberry, gathering it by the leaves, and lifted it to her mouth, pressing the blunt end against her lips.

The strangest sensation of warmth skated through her limbs, coiling through her muscles, following a singular path that led to a singular end. The rush of desire licked at her belly and teased areas further south. She faltered as she opened her mouth, her throat suddenly tickling with the essence of a hundred tiny moth wings fluttering around, choking her in the most pleasant of ways. Warmth increased to a boiling heat that surely darkened her cheeks and flushed her chest.

What on Earth is happening?

Never had she reacted to Silas in such a way. Never. It didn't make sense, and yet, she delighted in the force of its conquering.

Slowly, she accepted the strawberry with a small bite, holding his gaze steady as she chewed the piece and licked her lips clean of the juice. Silas's grin leveled, dissolved by a rare glimpse of carnality he hid so well behind his charming mask.

Jes groaned. "Good Goddess, you two. Will you take those sappy love eyes somewhere else?" She pushed to her feet, quickly followed by Silas, and waved a hand toward them. "You're as bad as Aunt Margo's son and his girlfriend."

Sera laughed, trying to disperse the sweltering air that had collapsed on top of her. She climbed to her feet, leaving the plate on the arm of her chair, and brushed her fingers off on her skinny jeans.

"I'm grabbing a glass of Uncle Slade's specialty cocktail. Be right back."

With her back to Jes and Silas, her smile fell as heat crept up the nape of her neck. Her skin tingled, prickled with an energy she couldn't quite place. All she knew was that it did not come from Silas. In fact, the origin was nowhere to be seen. Rubbing the back of her neck, she helped herself to a shot of the mixed drink from the dispenser, knocked it back in one swallow, then filled her cup with a pour she intended to sip and savor.

"Let me see if you follow me tonight. This game of cat and mouse needs to come to a head."

Sera's body stiffened as Silas's thoughts projected into her mind. Despite her uncle's warning not to divulge her gifts to him, she had confided in him her ability to hear thoughts. What harm would come of it, right? She wasn't the only one in the human world who had such a gift. There were numerous stories of people who could hear others. Didn't matter that most heard the dead speak, and that she'd told him she could pick up on thoughts only when they were projected to her. A tiny little white lie to make him comfortable around her, because who in their right mind wanted to be with someone who could hear *all* the thoughts of *all* people? Everyone was an open book to her, twenty-four-seven.

Right now, he used his knowledge to tease her. And it sure as hell worked.

She turned away from the table, taking care to appear as nonchalant as possible despite this new burn that threatened to consume her with unrivaled arousal. Indescribably wild and untamed, and fuck if she didn't want to tap into it, explore it, and allow it to devour her tonight. She'd gone far too long without a night of pleasure. She was way overdue.

Silas meandered beyond the ring of strung lights, leisurely sipping his beer as he made his way closer to the tree line leading into the few acres of forest that skirted Uncle Slade's property. His solid form—broad shoulders, narrow waist, lean physique—taunted her, beckoning her to follow, promising her something she didn't want to miss. The shadows reached for him, slowly swallowing him up as he entered the forest.

"I won't tell anyone if you follow," Jes whispered close to her ear from behind her. Her friend prodded her in the back with a gentle finger. "You two have been playing this game far too long, and the guy's mad about you."

Sera raised her cup to her lips and hummed a quiet, "Mmm."

Jes rolled against Sera's arm and flicked her cup. "At least you have some hot man-candy fawning over you while we wait for these dragons. Might as well make the best of the time until we're hitched to our forever men."

"*If* they ever come."

Sera swirled her drink, gazing out at the forest. Her own words acted as a harsh reminder that she could easily waste away her life in this realm waiting for a dragon who would never come. The massacre happened over thirty years ago and still not a sign, a sound, a whisper of dragons.

Meanwhile, she had the attention of a sought-after bachelor who doted on her every moment they were together while dancing this tedious waltz around what was right, what was expected, and what was forbidden.

She was sick of it.

Her body hummed with desire, burned for attention, yearned for the skilled touch of a man, and Silas fit the bill.

Before she could change her mind, she pushed her cup into Jes's hand and took off down the sloping yard, a bounce in her step and a lightness about her shoulders.

"Are you coming, kitten?"

She smirked at Silas's question, tossing a shaded glance toward the party behind her, noting that no one seemed to notice her disappearance, and rushed into the forest.

Oh, if you only realized how true your endearment is. You're my mouse. Wait until I find you.

She splayed a hand against the trunk of a thick aspen, a feral hunger coiling tight in her belly and leaving the apex of her thighs wet and sensitive. She loved adventure, thrived off adrenaline. It was both an aphrodisiac and a lifeline.

But this…

This was something altogether different. Intense. Unnatural, and yet, completely natural.

She listened for any indication as to which direction Silas had galivanted, but the forest was silent of snapping twigs and crunching leaves. Her smile grew, her skin hypersensitive beneath her heavy sweater and camisole. Despite the chill in the air, she'd shed her coat back at the fire due to the heat of the flames. She had always tolerated the cold better than Jes, and most people, for that matter. The coolness of winter's breath fed her life and excitement, just as these moments hunting Silas in the deep shadows of night through the forest did. Her blood ran hot, feverish, untouched by the chill. The deeper she drove into the forest, the more her body hummed and sang with the anticipation of this evening coming to an explosive head.

Where are you, Silas? Where do you try to hide?

A seductive giggle bubbled up in her throat, but she quickly swallowed it down when she spotted the shadow of a dark figure glide between the trees and disappear a dozen feet away. The erotic burn through her body intensified. She prowled toward the shadow, careful to keep her steps as silent as the forest floor would allow. A faint breeze unfurled through the trees, carrying with it a strange and intoxicating scent. She hadn't realized the fire smoke had reached this far until now, and it poured over her, through her, ingraining its scent into each fiber of her being until she craved it with every breath.

Another swift blur of shadows in the dark. This time, to her right. Closer, yet still too far.

Her heart thundered in her chest, legs growing weak. Her breaths came shallow and quick. She pressed her back to the closest tree, palms flat against the rough bark. The world around her tilted, her head dizzy, her body overheating, arousal so potent, consuming. Her nerves hummed from her head to her toes, and targeted her core.

I know you're near.

Every cell in her body confirmed it, too. Silas was so close. She blinked, staring straight ahead, honing her senses until she swore she could become one with the forest. She'd wandered deeper than she thought, barely able to make out the flickering lights from the house.

Somehow, the alluring scent of bonfire smoke caressed her nostrils and filled her lungs. Slightly different than the smoke from the yard, an underlying sultry scent, a delicacy on this wild hunt.

Closing her eyes, she listened for any telltale sign of Silas's approach. She battled for control over her body. Maybe there was something in the drinks that enhanced this arousal, or perhaps her libido was pissed at her for leaving herself unattended for so long. Her heart damn near punched through her sternum, and her lungs could barely fill with air before they expelled a breath for another.

These...sensations were beyond comprehension, but she clung to them in hopes of finding herself—

The definitive snap of a tree branch behind her cut through her thoughts. The brush was too dense to allow it to echo far, meaning her prey was close. Her fingers curled into her palms as a new rush of heat pummeled her, this time pouring down her spine, through every limb, leaving her skin warm and her muscles taut.

Her breath hitched.

The faintest sound, something deep, gravelly, and brimming with carnality, carried through the trees. Her skin lit with the electric essence of her prey and the excitement of what was about to transpire. She felt him near, so near, his breath a whisper across her bare shoulder where her sweater had slid off.

"Do you?"

Oh. Dear. Gods.

The deep, seductive timbre of his voice, a pitch she'd never before heard from Silas, almost drew a moan from her throat. She sucked her lower lip between her teeth.

And rolled against the tree to seek her target behind her.

The dark figure moved, following in her path, a proverbial tail she chased.

She spun. Reversed.

Caught Silas by the shoulders and pulled his head down for the starved kiss she so craved.

Wait.

The second her mouth hit the heat of pliant lips, a small warning went off in her mind. Strong arms encompassed her, holding her flush against a body far larger than Silas's, far taller, and by the Gods, too solid and hard to be the Silas she knew.

Oh, Gods, who is this?

When his tongue slipped past her lips and his possessive kiss filled her mouth, all she could do was moan, arch into his chest, wrap an arm around his neck and rake her fingers upward through warm, thick hair. Logic abandoned her as she danced with a stranger who ignited something so delicious and taboo from the pit of her soul. He tasted of heat and warm whiskey. Smelled of delicious campfire and that taunting sultry scent she couldn't place. When she tried to pull away, his hand caught the base of her skull and held her still, devouring her mouth in an impossibly tender way. She'd never felt so full and complete while realizing just how vulnerable she'd made herself. No one knew where she was in this forest.

"My sneaky little kitten, have you given up?"

Silas's tease lanced her with the sense she'd abandoned, but as she drew back from the stranger's kiss, her chest ached and her heart burned as a chill settled in her throbbing muscle. The man's hand at the back of her neck kept their foreheads together while she fought for composure and to steady her breath. She couldn't bring herself to open her eyes, to face the reality that she'd been foolish enough to treat this game of cat and mouse as carelessly as she had.

She'd become prey to a bigger cat than she. A king.

His hand slid along the side of her neck, his calloused thumb brushing her rapid pulse before tracing her jawline and lingering on her lower lip.

"I hope you don't make a habit of kissing strangers in dark forests." The man's voice poured over her, barely more than a whisper, but it filled her soul. A rustic baritone, a pitch that hummed through her nerves and set her on fire. A knot formed at the base of her throat, stopping each breath before it could reach her lungs. His lips brushed against her cheek, leaving a burning path to her ear. "*Kitten.*"

The hand gripping her hip slipped beneath her sweater and came to rest on her waist, just above the top of her jeans. The flesh of his palm was feverish, his fingers iron strong. She let him angle her until his large form caged her against the tree.

And Gods help her, she didn't give a fuck.

His teeth scraped the tender flesh beneath her ear. Another bolt of pleasure squeezed a gasp of delight from her lips as she tipped her head to the side, giving him access to the column of her throat. She needed to get control of herself, but...

I don't want to.

"There are more dangerous creatures lurking in the dark than kittens and mice," he murmured against her skin just before his tongue flicked out and swirled over the sensitive area. Her fingers curled against his scalp, enticing a growl from his chest while she fisted a supple leather jacket at his shoulder. "Creatures who would stop at nothing to ravage your exquisite self."

Ravage me. I'll simmer in regret later.

Because she'd long since lost any sense when it came to this rendezvous. Whatever magic played between her and this shadow-cloaked stranger, she never wanted it to end.

Until the strange sensation of…fangs scraped along her throat.

Her eyes shot open. She dropped her hand from his hair

and shoved at both his shoulders. In the deep forest night, she could barely make out his features, but a strange spark in his eyes that quickly snuffed out tinkered with a warning bell at the back of her mind while her damn traitorous soul yearned to coil herself around him and never let him go.

"Kitten?"

Silas called from nearby, his voice hitched with concern, having lost interest in their game.

"Coming!"

For a long moment, she held the stranger's gaze, one she felt more than saw, then wriggled out of the cage of his body. He didn't stop her, which left her foolishly disappointed. She stumbled away in the direction of Silas's voice and his muffled footsteps cracking twigs and crunching leaves. The stranger's gaze scorched her back as she hurried off in the direction of the man who'd landed her in this forest to start with.

Stolen moments with her longtime crush, obliviated by a taboo encounter with a shadow creature who—*damn him*—ripped her world to shreds and stoked an untamed beast within she'd never realized she possessed.

All with one powerful kiss.

The rich rumble of a languid chuckle infiltrated her mind in a way very unlike the random thoughts she could easily tune out as she spotted Silas and closed the gap between them. That sound pitched lower, vibrated down to her core, stirred at the pleasure he'd stoked. She had the nagging feeling that it was more than a signal she'd picked up. More like a direct connection between another's mind and her own.

Silas caught her by one shoulder and flung his phone's light up to her face, looking her over, his actions a notch shy of frantic. The only thing he'd see was a flushed and bewildered woman who'd taken a turn around a tree with a stranger, tasted the most delicious sin and temptation, and wanted to run back for more against any and all common sense.

"Are you okay? I was worried you'd gotten lost." Silas drew a knuckle over her cheek, tucking a tendril of hair that had escaped her ponytail behind her ear. "I didn't realize how dark it would be tonight. Should've thought this through a bit more."

Sera tucked her chin to hide the conflict battering her head and churning her gut.

Silas didn't feel *right*. Not now. Not anymore. No, she wanted the forbidden. The dangerous. She wanted the consuming heat that stole thought and reason. She wanted sultry campfire scents, steely muscle and unforgiving possession.

She forced a quiet laugh and nodded, avoiding his assessing gaze until the light dropped from her face and lit the ground at their feet. "I'm fine. Let's get back to the party."

He slung an arm around her shoulders and guided her toward Uncle Slade's yard, the whitewash glow of the light forging a path along the leaf-covered ground. A prickle along the nape of her neck unsettled her, as did an uncharacteristic discomfort she felt at Silas's touch. Gods, what the hell was happening to her?

The feral growl of a possessive beast curled through her mind, washing clean the heady chuckle from moments earlier.

"Catch you later, little flame."

Every muscle stiffened. That was *not* a stray thought she'd tuned in to. That was most certainly a promise *spoken* inside her mind. Sera cast the forest a glance over her shoulder, more specifically the direction she recalled having her tryst with a phantom.

Her heart stuttered.

Silas squeezed her shoulder, bringing her back to him. "Are you sure you're okay? You're tense."

Sera nodded again, pasting another smile on her face for his sake. "Course." Hugging her midsection, she hid the unease behind a fake shiver. "Getting cold is all."

"Now that's worrisome coming from you, the walking, talking furnace."

She had nothing to say, because her thoughts were stuck on someone else. Some*thing* else. Her phantom fling had a set of blunt fangs and the potential to communicate through telepathy.

She closed her eyes, recalling the image of what she beheld with her quick glance. She would bet a pretty penny her sight hadn't deceived her.

Fire.

Two orbs of molten flames suspended in the darkness before disappearing into blackness.

CHAPTER FOUR

"Where'd you disappear to?"

Emery rounded the truck, staving off the fervor that had consumed him from the moment he'd located *her*. The pull had been indescribable and immediate upon parking in front of the two-story monstrosity that belonged to Slade. He'd hopped out of the truck before Gabe braked completely and took off, tracing the bond into the dense forest that surrounded the property.

He hadn't expected to walk into a game of hide and seek between *his* woman and another man. Nor was he thrilled that she had taken her safety so lightly, trekking into a deep, dark forest without so much as a flashlight. Maybe she wasn't aware of the dangers stalking the dragons and lifemates, but that didn't make her carelessness any easier to digest.

When she outright took him and kissed him the way she had, realizing that kiss had been intended for another man…

His cock gave a tormenting jerk while the beast within rumbled with jealousy. Before he could stop himself, he swiped his tongue over his bottom lip, tasting her all over again and craving more. Further reason to reunite with his Keeper and officially meet the little flame.

His brother's shoulders straightened, and one brow lifted slowly. Emery waved him away and brushed past him, heading toward the house, which blazed like a bright beacon in the night with all the lights aglow in the dozens of windows. Cars crowded the circular driveway and flowed onto the street while music broadcast from the backyard. Laughter filtered to the street, hoots and cheers, most likely over games and challenges. Thankfully, it seemed Slade had chosen a remote place to lay some roots and build this mini mecca of a homestead.

"Ah, my brother's silence speaks more than words." Gabe chuckled as he fell in step beside Emery and playfully decked him in the arm. Emery bared his teeth. "You went on a hunt, didn't you." His chin dipped sharply before he inhaled. "I smell a woman on you."

"Not sure which is more disconcerting—your nose sniffing a man or your nose sniffing your own brother." Emery gave him a playful shove then hopped up the steps to the front door. He knocked loudly, ignoring the bell, and cast a devious smile at his brother. "Don't go making Sky jealous. I don't want to end up on her shit list. She scares me almost as much as Briella."

Gabe settled on the expansive stoop and hooked his thumbs in his jeans. A menacing gleam lit his eyes, one that Emery would entertain any other time but now. "'Fraid my woman will kick your ass?"

"Any woman could kick my ass, brother. I'll never lift a finger to a woman."

"Oh, the chivalry hasn't left us dragons yet."

"Gotta give myth-lovers some hope to hold onto, right?" A distorted figure moved beyond the cut-glass windows, rushing to the door. Emery winked and tipped his head toward the commotion. "Showtime."

Gabe's grin darkened an instant before the door swung open.

Emery gazed down on the familiar face of a woman who'd barely aged in the thirty years since he last saw her. Claire Rogue. The same rich golden hair, only half the length it used to be. Same brilliant chocolate eyes that sparked with specks of amber. Same olive skin that hinted at fine lines at the very corners of her eyes and mouth, but nothing more. Her curves had filled out more since their last encounter. Then again, she'd had a child since the attacks rained down chaos on The Hollow.

As realization of who he was sank in, her eyes widened and her smile grew until it could grow no more. The petite woman threw herself into him, wrapping her thin arms around his neck with a shriek.

"Emery!"

He laughed, catching her up in his embrace, feet swept right off the stoop as he spun her around. "Look at you, sweetness." He placed her gently on her feet again and graced her forehead with a kiss before holding her at arm's length. "You look marvelous. I'm sure I can't say the same for your old man."

Claire smacked his arm and giggled. "Slade hasn't changed much, either." Her glittering gaze turned to Gabe before she embraced him as well. "Gabriel. You two are the same as you were when we last saw you. Thank the Goddess you two made it out." As she leaned back, her smile faded, her excitement melting into hesitation. "What of the others? How many survived?"

Emery took her gently by her narrow shoulders and offered a grin, followed by a jut of his chin toward the grand foyer. "Why don't we go inside? Slade should be expecting me, since I *did* reach out to him. Unless he's too busy wrangling partygoers in the back. Still following his old ways?"

Claire folded her hand over his and led Emery and Gabe into the house.

"He's settled down a bit, but still enjoys the wild side of things."

Gabe pushed the door closed behind them. They both took in the opulence of the room with muted emotions. Gabe flicked the fringe of a pencil lamp and snorted under his breath. Emery cast him a curious glance as he veered off to the right, peeking into what appeared to be an oversized study at the base of a curving marble staircase. A dazzling three-tier chandelier hung from a dome ceiling of ivory and gold.

"Apparently so," Emery said with a considering hum.

This place was so much more than Slade had ever expressed he wanted in The Hollow. A small part of his heart tweaked. Would his Keeper even want to return? What would he be leaving here, other than magicless days and Baroqueth threats?

"He's in the kitchen with some of the guys. They were about to restock the tables and drinks." Claire squeezed his hand, her excitement barely contained behind tense muscles and hurried steps. "The sly bastard didn't mention a word about you coming. I'll throttle him for it, too, keeping a secret such as this from me."

"Wait until I have my hello with him before you go snuffing the life from my Keeper, please."

Claire's laugh filled the air and echoed through the hall as she dragged them into a ginormous kitchen—why the hell did Slade need *two* kitchens?—in pristine white marble and soft gray accents. Food, drinks, bottles, containers, everything that raged "party" littered the numerous counters and double islands.

The group of four men who chortled and roared with laughter around said mess mere seconds before he and Gabe entered the kitchen grew unnervingly silent as their gazes focused on them. A heaviness settled in the room, one strewn with a mixture of disbelief and cautionary excitement building until, at last, the elation tore through the seams and erupted.

"Emery!" Slade greeted, rushing him like a kid who hadn't seen his best friend in decades, which, in all honesty, was the case. Emery met him a few steps from Claire and hugged him with a few hard claps on his back. "*By Gods*, at long last!"

Emery straightened back, hands gripping Slade's biceps, and looked his Keeper over. "What a sight, old man. What have you done to yourself?" He flicked a lock of deep brown hair that held no evidence of gray and snickered. "Ugly as ever."

Slade knocked him lightly in the jaw. "Since when do you wear scruff?"

"About the same time you started, I'd assume." He stroked the short scruff that lined his jaw and chin with a wink. "At least I keep mine trimmed and neat."

Emery shoved down the urge to ask about a daughter despite the pulsing ache demanding he do so. These moments were for his Keeper, and with this reunion, the solemn reality that the other three Keepers eagerly greeting him and Gabe with handshakes and shoulder claps and a glimmer of hope in their eyes would be dealt the devastating news about their dragons. A responsibility Emery didn't care to broach this very minute.

"You'd love to think so." Slade rounded Emery and

greeted Gabe with another hug and clap on his arm. "Damn dragons never change. Though I'd bet a coin your menacing nature hasn't improved any."

"Not a bit," Gabe confirmed with a dark half-grin. "No fun in walking the straight and narrow."

"Don't we know it." Slade cast the yard, and his guests, a glance through the oversized windows before he motioned toward the hallway they'd just come from. "Why don't we take this in the front office." When his gaze leveled on Emery once more, his smile faded a fraction. *"I'm sure not all news is good news this evening."*

"Unfortunately, no." Thirty-plus years of separation hadn't dulled their ability to read each other. "As long as your whiskey is stocked in your sideboard, we can move the party."

With a hand clasping Emery's shoulder, Slade guided him toward the foyer. Gabe entertained the three other Keepers—Jax, Lauro, and a reserved Nick, who nursed a beer bottle while observing the reunion with a cautious gaze—who followed at their heels while Claire gathered a serving tray of food items and took up the rear.

"How long have you been back?" Slade asked. Harmless banter to catch up on times, Emery supposed. The air between them stirred, rife with tension and not for the better.

"We got here yesterday."

"You've been holed up in The Hollow these last few decades, despite the action that had us speculating your return?"

Emery snickered. "And what action are you referring to? We've been pretty well-behaved."

Slade laughed, the sound overexaggerated. Emery gave his Keeper credit for trying to keep the air light, but as they rounded the double pocket doors into the lavish office, no degree of laughter could cut away the heaviness that finally took hold. Gabe waited for everyone to come into the large space before taking the tray from Claire and closing the doors behind her when she left.

"Lauro, want to serve up a few shots of whiskey?" Slade asked. Lauro nodded and went straight to the sideboard that was tucked in a generous alcove at the back of the office area. A long sofa and a few upholstered chairs were strategically placed around a wood-burning fireplace, currently lit with a calm flame swaying over the logs. As Slade motioned for Emery to sit—he chose one of the chairs to better see his audience—Lauro approached with a tumbler half-filled with amber liquid. Emery sniffed the beverage and smiled at the warm, spiced scent of a good whiskey. He helped himself to a sip before he settled back in the chair and caught his Keeper's cautious gaze. "Heard good ol' NOLA was up in arms over some interesting activity a while back. Dragons and sorcerers?" He shook his head. "Way to be stealth, Em."

"In our defense, they attacked first. We simply defended ourselves the best way we could in this realm."

"How about the Washington State incident? The hotel?" Jax said, humor curling his mouth while hesitation clouded his eyes.

The more Emery observed this group of Keepers, the more he realized the hope they clung to was fragile at best. Jax and Lauro both appeared to wait with bated breath for a blow. When Emery caught sight of Nick perched on the far arm of the sofa, he saw the first hint of certainty. Emery kicked up his ankle onto his knee and swirled the whiskey in the glass as firelight glinted off the liquid through the cut facets of the crystal, making it glow.

"Well, there were two different hotel incidents, but again, one was because the Baroqueth attacked first. The second, we left before they caught up to us. The hospital?" Emery waved his hand in the air. "What the hell happened to HIPAA?"

"No patient information was released, but staff leaked stories about monsters with fire in their eyes and red scales," Lauro said with a shrug. He chuckled at the lip of his glass. "Not hard for people paying attention to the trends that started in New Orleans to catch on pretty quick."

"I suppose not."

"So, you've all been trekking the human realm for at least half a year and just now decided to come to the mountains."

Emery flashed Nick a dark smile. "You make it sound so negative when you put it like that."

"We've been waiting for your return. This place is definitely not The Hollow."

With a leisurely look about the alcove, Emery nodded slowly. "No, but it does have pretty nice accents."

"Maybe Slade's does."

Emery brought his attention back to Nick and watched the man take a hearty drink from his beer as he cast a glance around. The corner of his mouth twitched, and a cloaked satisfaction gleamed in his eyes. He wasn't very familiar with the Keeper, not to the extent Slade and his friends must be. Before the attacks, the dragons interacted with other Keepers, but the bonds and friendships didn't necessarily go to the extent of those shared between bonded partners. Being two of the youngest dragons, Emery and his brother were often taken by the older ones for training. Their relationships with outside Keepers never had time to flourish like those Syn and his older brethren shared with them. However, there was an unspoken respect for all Keepers.

"Now, now, Nick. Green doesn't jive with your hair color," Emery retorted, smoothing the bite with a wink when

Nick's attention cut back to him. "I'm sure you've been well cared for, too."

"Seems you've been far more generous with allowances," Jax said, tipping his glass toward Slade. At least he didn't house jealousy behind his words.

"Actually, none of us were able to flood the banking systems in this realm. Cade had some sophisticated networks set up to keep the source of funding secret." Emery snickered. "He's a wise old bat, that one."

"Old, for sure," Slade added.

"Emery, Gabe, we've been in this world for decades, left in the dark about what happened," Lauro began, the edge to his voice preceding the unease that swept through the room again. Jax groaned, elbowing Lauro in the arm. Lauro held up his unoccupied hand defensively. "What? We're gonna find out one way or another. Why push it off? You and I both had boys, Jax. The only two who had girls after the attack were Slade and Nick. That says enough in my mind, but"—Lauro's arm lowered and his shoulders collapsed forward. His expression melted from the carefully held hope to solemn acceptance—"it'll be helpful for Emery to confirm what I've already suspected. I know you've suspected it, too."

Jax stared at Lauro for a long moment. The air suffocated Emery as he processed the loud silence filling each second. Two girls. Slade's and Nick's, which raised his curiosity, since Rayze was dead. He cast Gabe a shaded glance and watched his brother scrutinize Nick from a seemingly casual mask. If he read his brother right, and he'd bet both his wings he did, Gabe's thoughts were aligned with his.

How was it possible for a Keeper to father a daughter when his dragon perished before the babe was a thought in his mind?

Gabe tilted his head, bringing his gaze to Emery's with a

faint nod. The flicker of skepticism was enough to prod Emery's dragon to dive into the unpleasantness of this conversation.

Placing his glass on the small side table, he leaned forward, rested his elbows on his knees, and clasped his hands together.

"The attack on The Hollow decimated the majority of our people. And dragons. Dozens of civilians perished, and most of us were wiped out. The Baroqueth shed so much blood during their genocide that it took our land years to absorb all of it to the point where rain wouldn't leak red into the rivers and pools. Only eight dragons survived." Out of the periphery of his vision, he saw Gabe push off his perch on Slade's desk and quietly approach the back of the sofa, hands tucked in the pockets of his leather jacket. The Keepers cast each other disbelieving glances. "We've been searching for survivors here in the human realm ever since the Baroqueth made the first renewed attack against Zareh and his lifemate in Georgia. We have very few leads to go off of, since we don't know how many Keepers and civilians survived."

Lauro's eyes widened and he straightened up. "Talius survived?" He laughed and smacked a hand against his knee. "That old bugger embodied stealth!"

"Actually, he was killed by Baroqueth in order to save his daughter," Gabe cut in. Lauro's smile dropped like a weight as he shifted to look back at Gabe. His brother's solemn expression, a rarity, touched a desolate place Emery kept buried deep inside his chest. Failure always brought that darkness back, compiling the layers of guilt and regret more and more each time. Logically, he knew none of them could have saved Talius, Zareh's Keeper, but finding out their enemies had targeted him in their first attack after thirty years of silence touched a raw nerve. It reminded the surviving dragons daily they could *never* let their guard down. "Kaylae was the first surviving descendant we learned about. Since her, we went into full search for Hollow members in order to rescue them and bring them home as Baroqueth attacks turned more brazen."

"New Orleans," Jax murmured.

Emery nodded. "Syn. And Taryn. Taryn had a house in the French Quarter. Syn met up with Gio and Saralyn's daughter there."

"Please tell me Gio and Saralyn survived. Those two deserve life," Lauro said, his voice strained with pain. His brows furrowed as he placed his drink on the coffee table.

"They're alive and thriving back at The Hollow."

Slade pressed a hand to his chest with a relieved sigh. "Thank the Goddess. They have always been admired and impeccable role models for the rest of us misfits. Saralyn, even though a year younger than myself, knew how to put us rowdy boys in our places when we got out of line."

"She hasn't lost her spark, so when you get back home, you'd better be on your best behavior," Emery teased, though his smile barely curled his lips. As he surveyed the other three Keepers, he knew they were mentally tallying the dragons. He had two to go, and the smugness in Nick's gaze when he looked at the man didn't sit well with him. He didn't understand it, but the Keeper gave off a strange vibe, one that didn't fit with all the other Keepers he knew, dead or alive. "But her gardens are flourishing again."

"Oh, good! She has a knack for growing some delicious fruits." Jax threw back the rest of his whiskey and dropped his glass beside Lauro's. "You know, Corvin gave the back of Kearn to those two in hopes they escaped. That sacrifice cost Corvin his life." The man shook his head, his gaze growing distant as the weight of that confession added to the pressure in the room. "He was on the next dragon out. Behind Coal, who managed to get us all out. That's how we stayed together. We watched the strike that took them down. Does Taryn know?"

"Taryn knew Corvin died saving those in The Hollow. What he didn't know was he laid with a tramp who bore a baby girl."

"Don't tell me he fucked Janice," Nick groaned. "Anything out of that woman is a curse."

"Nick, knock it off," Gabe growled. At least the man had the decency to bite his tongue behind a swig of his beer as his cheeks flushed. "Gabby is the spitting image of Corvin from her looks to her heart. Trust me when I say Janice didn't deserve a daughter like her, but Taryn deserves the lifemate Corvin left him. She's a wonderful woman."

"And you? Is Terrence at The Hollow? I heard rumors about some martial arts place in Alabama following a psych facility incident," Lauro said, a valiant attempt to cut the tension Gabe's glower at Nick had produced.

Gabe snorted after a few more seconds of burning his gaze into Nick. "Yeah, that would have been me trying to get Ellie out of that prison. Sadly, Terrence was murdered about a year ago and Ellie was killed by Baroqueth while we were planning our return home." When the men continued to stare at him expectantly, he caved, which made Emery snicker behind his folded hands. "Yes, they had a daughter. And yes, she's my lifemate. And yes, Terrence taught her well, so she's very capable of putting each of you in your place." He shrugged. "You've been warned."

"She'll be kicking your ass for being gone more than a day," Emery chimed in.

"She might try." His grin grew wicked, as did the gleam in his green eyes. "But she knows I'll always win."

"Heard that last round, she gave you a run for your money."

"I think this is about to take an inappropriate turn," Lauro interrupted, throwing a hand up with a laugh. "You two haven't changed."

"Maybe a little," Emery said, the truth of his statement woven behind his smile.

"Who are the last two lucky beasts? And Keepers?" Jax asked.

Emery motioned to Slade with a jut of his chin. "Mark reminds me very much of you, old man. Your tastes in the extravagant are very similar, with these big houses and the expensive décor. One would think the two of you have kept in touch over the years. Or are trying to compensate for lacking in other departments."

Slade roared a laugh that did wonders to lighten the air. His friends joined in, the laughter contagious. Lauro made a quick trip to the sidebar and grabbed the entire decanter of whiskey to refill the glasses on the tables as the laughter settled.

"Actually, as much as it gives the appearance of overindulgence and luxuries, Claire and I both long to return to our cottage back home." His smile dimmed. "I'm sure it didn't survive the attacks, though."

"We've been rebuilding. Progress is being made daily. I'll help you and Claire rebuild your cottage. It'll be a testament to everything you survived."

"*We*." Slade took a somber sip of whiskey. "What happened to us should have never happened. We've always been a peaceful civilization."

"Where there's power, there will always be conflict. People wanting power, wanting wealth, wanting domination. That has not changed in thousands of years, and it will still exist thousands of years from now. There is no avoiding the conflict between us and the Baroqueth. And if not the Baroqueth, another power-hungry group of magic-wielding crazies will come about. It's a vicious cycle that spans history. All we can do is make sure we're more prepared for the next attack and hope it doesn't happen."

Silence hung in the room, one of quiet agreement and understanding. Firestorm dragons were peacekeepers, in a sense. They didn't start wars or battles or fights, but often found themselves on the receiving end of such.

"I'm going to assume Alazar and Rayze are the last two surviving dragons," Jax said, breaking the silence after a full minute.

Gabe cleared his throat, slowly circling the sofa to come to stand at the back of Emery's chair at the same moment a sizzle of heat coasted down Emery's body. That rogue thread, the one that connected him with his lifemate, flared to life as much as he tried to smother it at this very moment. He wasn't ready to face one battle when he was about to lay a blow to the hopeful man at the opposite end of the sofa and stir more questions than he had answers for over the fact that two daughters had been born of two Keepers with only one surviving dragon between the two of them. Cade was out of the equation.

Yet...

Dear Goddess. What I'd do to embrace this hunger right about now.

It was certainly a more appetizing thought to entertain. In response, his body taunted him with a hot wave through his belly that rushed his cock like a witch-sprung storm in the middle of the sea. He swallowed back the growl that scraped up his throat and shifted in the chair to hide his sudden discomfort. At least he heard no thoughts from his little flame, which meant one of two things: she had none or she knew how to hide them.

"Alazar, yes. Unfortunately, Rayze was shot down before he could fly out. We lost him, and the half-dozen civilians he tried to save with him," Gabe said, resting a reassuring hand on Emery's shoulder.

His brother knew he'd wanted to be the one to deliver this news tonight. It wasn't Gabe's responsibility, yet his brother took it upon himself to deal the blow neither of them ever wanted to deal. As Nick's expression melted into a dozen different emotions, the heaviness that threatened to suffocate them all earlier returned. Nick stared, unblinking, at Emery and Gabe, stared as if he saw through them, saw something none of them could see or fathom, creating an eerie energy that chilled his scales. Only the heat his mysterious lifemate fed through their bond kept the chill at bay. Held his dragon in check as he prepared for a reaction from Nick, because Nick wasn't like Jax and Lauro. He wasn't accepting from the beginning.

No.

Nick had a daughter, which would make any of them believe that his dragon had survived.

"Who is the last?" Slade asked, his brow creased as he cast Nick a concerned glance.

"Tajan."

Nick shut down. Like an iron door slamming shut on the world. His eyes dimmed and his expression flattened, unreadable. At last, he blinked, but it didn't clear the thickening haze in his eyes. He pushed off the arm of the sofa and turned his back to everyone, shuffling to the window, where he remained. Emery tried to listen to the man's thoughts, tried to grasp what was going on inside his head, see if there was any way he could soothe the news of

Rayze's demise, but all he received was silence. Not so much as a whisper—

"Daddy! There you are! We've been waiting for you out...side..."

Emery pulled his attention away from Nick to the young woman who had just joined them in the office. He hadn't heard the pocket doors open, let alone footsteps to announce this new visitor. Dark brown eyes, golden brown hair, curvy and petite with a pretty face, she was a perfect blend of Slade and Claire. No confirmation needed for who this was, and to whom she belonged.

He couldn't keep his brow from pinching.

This was *not* the woman he'd kissed in the woods.

Where are you?

Because his head was about to spin and his dragon reel.

Slade rose to his feet, rounded the sofa's arm, and slung an arm around the woman's slender shoulders. Her attention bounced between Gabe and Emery, her cheeks flushing and her eyes growing brighter. She knew who they were, *what* they were, but the glowing thread was *not* reaching for her. No. It was going in a completely different direction.

"Jeslyn, you made perfect time. I'd like to introduce you to a couple people."

Jeslyn. Slade's daughter. The woman who should be his lifemate. The woman who should elicit every Gods-forsaken hunger and desire from the deepest corners of his soul. The woman who should make the world disappear and the need to protect blossom.

"If I didn't know you better, I'd say you look a bit ashen," Gabe whispered against his ear. Emery shuttered his expression and cast his brother a deadpan glance as Slade drew up to the side of the chair. Slowly, Emery rose to his feet, fighting back the confusion and sickening roll of his gut as the woman beamed up at him.

Fuck me.

How the hell would he explain this to Slade?

Who the fuck was the woman in the forest?

His mouth felt stiff as scales as he forced a small smile and tried, fucking *tried*, to appear normal. Happy, even.

His eyes drifted briefly to Nick. Back to Slade. Down to the woman who gazed up at him, glowing.

"Jes, this is Emery"—Slade held a hand toward him, then cut it to Gabe—"and his brother, Gabriel. They arrived a short time ago."

Emery didn't think the woman's mouth could stretch any further, but she proved him wrong as her grin widened. He hesitated before holding out a hand to Jeslyn. "Pleasure to meet you."

"You're my father's dragon," she breathed, taking his hand in a timid grip. If Emery were honest, the woman was a head-turner, had his interests not been caught by another. Right now, though, he needed to focus on some positives. Until he learned of the mystery woman whose mouth he still tasted and whose body had impressed itself against his and stamped his mind. Whose sultry voice whispered in his head over and over. "A real dragon."

"I'm sure Slade wouldn't mind putting a collar around my neck and taking me for walks every now and again," Emery said, trying a shot at his usual humor. He lowered his hand and lifted his gaze to his Keeper, whose cheeks flushed slightly as his fingers tightened on Jeslyn's shoulder. "Not sure how the neighbors would take a beast far larger than them trapsing through the streets." He leaned toward his Keeper and Jeslyn, and added in a quiet voice, "I might scare them."

Jeslyn's breath hitched, but not out of fear. Her pupils dilated and her nostrils flared. Emery slowly straightened up, catching the quickened pace of her heartbeat.

Damn me.

"We've shared our histories with our kids. All of them."

Emery winced inwardly. The only thing he had going for him was that none of these men had witnessed the instantaneous bond his brethren had experienced when they first crossed paths with their lifemates. Slade wouldn't realize Emery's cool reaction toward his daughter wasn't normal.

Gabe, on the other hand, knew immediately. As his brother crossed the room to return to his perch on the desk to observe the spectacle, his eyes glowed with unasked questions. He folded his arms over his chest and leaned on the edge of the desk, his attention honed on Emery as he stumbled through this mess.

"When we finish here, we'll head out back. I'm sure everyone would be thrilled to see you two, even with somber news to share. Knowing we may be returning to our old home is cause for—"

"Jes, your mom said you're in here."

Emery's entire body stiffened as he fought back the unfurling of his dragon and the sudden wash of desire.

That *voice*.

Low, sexy, purring words like a spell she had no idea she cast. His heart did the strangest dance, making it hard for him to breathe as he narrowed his eyes and slowly turned his attention to the incoming clap of sneakers on the hardwood floor. Gabe's brow lifted toward him before he turned his head to the newest addition to their little office party.

This woman…

This woman.

Emery swallowed back the smoke brewing deep in his

throat when the woman came to a screeching halt the moment her eyes fell on him. A hand shot up to her chest, her pillowy lips parting on a sharp exhale, like someone gut-punched her. Waves of jet-black hair fell over her cheeks, a few strands catching at the corner of her mouth from her abrupt stop. Clear gray eyes stared, unblinking, her creamy skin paling as her body failed to take in air. Her loose-knit sweater hung off one narrow shoulder so low on her arm her camisole peeked over the collar, which teased the swell of her breast, but couldn't hide what he knew lay beneath. A slender waist, hips encased in tight jeans, long, lithe legs.

"Sera! Guess who…"

Jeslyn's excited words faded as the name struck him straight through the chest. He caught Gabe's carefully controlled gaze, his brother's unspoken confusion etched into fine lines around his tightly drawn mouth. Subtle signs only he could read on his blood brother. Together, they slowly looked across the room at Nick, who had angled away from the window enough to catch Sera from the corner of his eye.

Sera.

Seraphina Allaze.

His eyes narrowed further as he tipped his head back to the very creature who demanded all his attention, and more.

Her ankle appeared to give out, but she caught her balance and cleared her throat. "I, uh, I…" She struggled with more than words as her attention tried to stay off him. Such a foolish battle, one he refused to wage because he *wanted* to drink this woman in for as long as he could. An unsteady smile touched her mouth—*Goddess, why must she do that… now?*—and she shuffled back. "Sorry. I'll catch up with you later, Jes."

Before he could try to stop her—another foolish thought, considering how complicated his situation had just become—

she disappeared. Only this time, he held tight to the glowing thread attached to her and mentally noted where she sought refuge.

He had no idea how long he stared at the empty space where Sera had stood, but when he finally returned his focus to Slade, his Keeper's expression had morphed into something unreadable. A shaded side-glance toward Nick exposed a man who'd suddenly turned his focus on Emery.

Clearing his throat, Slade chuckled. "Why don't we move this outside where the party is? Seems to be getting a little stuffy in this old office." With his daughter still tucked under his arm, he waved his arm to the other men. "Let's not keep the surprise to ourselves."

Emery waited for everyone to file out of the room before taking up the tail, a few feet behind the rest. Gabe fell in step beside him, remaining silent until they had reached the foyer.

"Seems this expedition brings a few twists, huh?" Gabe murmured.

Emery glanced up the elegant staircase leading to a split second floor. His dragon rumbled, a quiet demand for him to seek out the treasure he had discovered this evening. As much as he wanted to break from the procession and follow his beacon thread to the source of all his turmoil, he held steady and strong against the pull.

"Doesn't make sense, brother."

"No, it doesn't. But it is what the Goddess deems. Honestly, it suits you, too."

Bastard.

CHAPTER FIVE

*E*mery LaRouche.

Every time she repeated that name in her head, her body unleashed relentless waves of butterfly wings and heat, and encouraged an ache between her legs she couldn't tame. Every time she blinked, the image of a forbidden man filled her mind. An utterly gorgeous man who could easily create dreams she would never want to wake from. The second her eyes landed on Emery, she *knew*. Her body recognized him before her eyes could process every Gods-forsaken cut and edge of his sharp face, the warm whiskey eyes with those alluring amber flecks, the height and build of a formidable man beneath a fitted thermal sweater under a leather jacket she had fisted less than a half-hour earlier, and dark jeans that hugged powerful legs.

She shook her head for the umpteenth time, trying to dispel the images, however futile her attempts proved. He'd flood her mind in a hot minute and she'd go through the same suffering all over again. The cycle had proven unforgiving for the last hour as she holed up in a dark second-floor study and watched the festivities continue in the yard from the window.

On a few occasions, she opened her mind to the thoughts of those enjoying themselves, celebrating the return of Slade's dragon and his brother, drinks flowing more freely than before. Silas and Jes wondered where she had gone, but Jes's thoughts immediately returned to Emery as she followed him about the yard, speaking to him whenever he wasn't being bombarded by the other families. Gabe entertained those who left Emery alone with Jes.

His lifemate.

Emery and Jeslyn.

Whatever this is, forget it. Fight it. Ignore it. It'll pass.

When she tried to turn her focus on Silas, what she felt a couple of hours earlier no longer manifested for him now. As hard as she tried to imagine kissing him simply to turn the focus away from a particular dragon, it caused a rebound effect and all she could think about was said dragon. The way he smelled so warm and perfect and like everything she never realized she craved. The way he possessed her, not only with his kiss, but in the position of his body when he held her against him, pinned her to the tree, a mixture of tenderness and dominance. She had felt safe, protected, and at the mercy of his prowess.

Liquid fire poured through her once more.

With a groan, she dropped her head against the back of the chair she had pulled up to the window and closed her eyes. She was doomed. One single kiss in a dark forest wrecked her.

"Somehow, I don't picture you to be the type of woman to hide away in a dark room."

Sera gasped, springing to the edge of her chair as she twisted.

And instantly regretted it.

The shock of laying eyes on her forbidden desire lanced through her heart with the precision of a sharpshooter.

Gods, had her mind carried her so far away she hadn't heard a man his size approach?

Emery leaned against the back of the chair, his hands dangling over the top, mere inches from where her head had been. So at ease, so confident, but then again, he was a dragon with a lifemate and a Keeper. He was *complete*.

All she had was a father who'd learned his dragon died, and no hope for herself of a happy life with a dragon mate. Any hope of her father accepting her now went straight out the window. After all, she'd taken the last thing from him that held any worth. This all came from the little bits and pieces she'd picked out of casual thoughts from those in full celebration below, including her own father.

Twenty-six years of tenuous hopes and dreams shattered in a single evening.

"Mind if I join you?"

The sound of his voice alone constricted her throat. The same baritone that held a gravelly undertone along the edges of his words. A voice made to seduce the mind and body.

Without waiting for her to answer, Emery drew up a chair and turned it around, aligning the right arm of her chair with his. He settled in the seat and kicked an ankle onto his knee. He had shed his leather jacket at some point, but the fire smoke scent she vividly remembered from the forest filled her lungs and somehow relaxed her. She soon sank back into her chair and drew a knee up to her chest. His whiskey eyes watched her closely, her every minuscule motion most certainly being analyzed and committed to memory. His acute survey didn't do a damn thing to douse the fire burning up her insides when it should have made her wary.

"You've abandoned quite a party," she said. "Seems you've given everyone something to celebrate."

His head rested back on the chair, tipping enough for him to continue his intimate perusal, because the way those eyes slid over her face ignited the potent memory of the way his lips moved about a similar path. Her gaze lowered to his hands, folded over his belt. Strong, capable hands that had touched her in ways that elicited raw hunger…

She cleared her throat, again, and turned back to the window, but his reflection held her attention more than the happenings at the party.

"Celebrations are fun in moderation. Gabe and I don't care for all the pomp and circumstance, especially when it wasn't planned or expected." His chuckle teased her nerves as much as his mouth had earlier. She shifted in the chair, then stilled and looked at Emery. The devilish beast's lips curled in the sexiest half-grin she'd ever seen on a man. The shadow of a beard intensified the strong cut of his jaw, the hollows of his cheeks, and showcased his wicked lips that had teased her more ways to the moon in a matter of minutes than any man before him. The shadows created a masterpiece of hues and angles that dried her mouth and messed with her head. "I digress to my original assumption. I don't take you as a woman to sit in a dark room while a party's going on. Somehow, I take you for a woman who indulges in adventure rather than solitude."

Thank the Gods for the darkness as her cheeks flushed. She folded her hands over her knee and rested her chin on her knuckles. His double entendre wasn't lost on her, nor was the confirming glint in his eyes. She hated that he'd stolen her backbone. Stolen her strength and confidence and ability to toss some comeback at him.

All because she starved for an unobtainable man, and felt like the biggest scumbag for it.

Pretend it never happened. Maybe he doesn't know I'm the one he kissed...

His brow lifted and she shut her mind away. She hadn't realized she'd left a few blinds open to her thoughts. She sighed, trying to look anywhere except him, but he demanded her attention, all unforgiving rugged beauty and enigmatic essence. He called to her, and not superficially like some passerby. His call was deep, soul deep, entwining with her organs, her vessels, her cells until his presence elicited a visceral reaction to his nearness. The desire to climb over the chair arms and sink into his lap. Allow him to tease her more with that dangerous mouth and those taunting hands.

She gave up the fight and met his gaze once more. Her eyes widened at the sight of flames—dark red and orange *flames*—that flickered and swirled in his eyes, painting over the familiar whiskey color. His nostrils flared a little, and she swore she caught deeper shadows sweep over his face before disappearing.

He blinked, a languid motion that snuffed the flames from his irises.

"I had a bit to drink. Needed some time to regain my composure before I made a complete fool of myself," Sera finally said.

"Ah." Emery snickered. He finally turned his head away, tipping his chin skyward. "Slade had a heavy pour back in the day. Though alcohol metabolizes differently in us Hollow folk. Takes a bit more than a normal human to start feeling the effects."

He dug. She refused to take his bait.

"I started early."

"Mm-hmm. The gems in your mind I've caught so far

seem very clear." The blasted beast rolled that handsome head to her and his roguish mouth curled into a grin she could only describe as feral. The flames flashed in his eyes again but didn't remain. "Should we blame the events from earlier on your consumption as well? I tasted a little alcohol, but mostly the sweetness of berries. Strawberries, to be precise."

Sera coughed, dropping her foot to the floor and shoving herself off the chair. "Think I'm sober enough to return to the party. You shouldn't keep Jeslyn waiting." Shifting the sagging sleeve of her sweater back onto her shoulder, she added, "She's waited a long time for this day."

She rounded the back of Emery's chair, giving it a wide berth, and came up short when the man of her dreams, nightmares, and conflictions rolled off his seat to stand in front of her, blocking her only exit with his overwhelming form and intense essence. She could maneuver around him, but the thought of coming so close left her dizzy. She had to keep her wits about her. Jeslyn deserved better.

"This-this isn't right," she stammered, her tongue heavy in her mouth, words thick in her throat. Gods, how she wanted to close the distance between them, wrap her arms around his neck, and give in to this insatiable need. "What happened earlier"—she rubbed the back of her neck, fidgeting on her feet as she forced her lips to form words that tore at her heart—"should never have happened. I-I have a boyfriend and…and—"

"Why lie?" He tipped his head, his narrowed eyes piercing her own. "What are you afraid of, Seraphina?"

This!

The fleeting strength to walk away as her name rolled off his tongue for the very first time. The persistent ache in her chest at the thought of abandoning him while something tethered them together. The conflict brewing inside her conscience over the thought of throwing herself at a man who was off the market to her. A man belonging to her closest friend.

What kind of person does this make me?

After a few seconds, Emery lifted his chin and slowly stepped to the side, opening her escape.

He's letting me go.

A piece of her shattered at the understanding. He was letting her go. Without an argument. Without trying to convince her to stay. He abided by her unspoken wishes, and she hated him for it.

Hated the battle it waged inside her soul.

In this simple motion, he acknowledged she was right. Their meeting in the forest was nothing more than an accident that could not happen again, and therefore, must be forgotten.

Jeslyn could never find out.

Swallowing down any opportunity to remain, she rushed past him, avoiding eye contact at all costs.

He grabbed her wrist as she stepped by, drawing her to a halt and swiveling her toward him. He stood, unmoving, staring straight ahead for a few heartbeats. The contact with his fingers against her skin fueled the maddening chaos driving her crazy, questioning her morals, her loyalty, the goodness of her very character.

Like a man built from grace beneath a shell of muscle, Emery angled himself toward her, closing the small gap between them. She could feel the heat of his body. Smell the unique scent that belonged to him, fire and fresh air. Gods, did he smell divine. Though his grip was firm, it wasn't in any way threatening. His stance was wide enough to straddle her own, encompassing in his posture but not a bit hostile.

"You're perfect," he whispered, lifting his fingers to tuck

a rebel wave behind her ear. "Don't ever think less of yourself."

His fingers trailed along her cheek to the corner of her mouth. Her eyelids grew heavy beneath the magic of his touch, her body weak as she leaned into his fingertips cresting along the curve of her upper lip. Those slow-trekking fingers slid over her lower lip, chin, caressed her throat as they skimmed down to the hollow of her neck before his hand curved to her nape and drew her closer.

"Do you feel that?" His eyes had grown dark, his forehead hovering over hers. Her lips tingled with the nearness of his, a few breaths away but close enough to muddle her thoughts. She wanted to get closer, complete a circuit that sparked with anticipation of being closed. She barely remembered reaching for his waist, but her fingers curled in the sweatshirt, a vicious mental tug of war between pulling him closer and pushing him away. He adjusted his grip from her forearm to close over her hand, the sensation of his warm skin against hers electric. Her entire being hummed with more energy than ever. She was *alive.* "It's not going away. There is no running from it. No hiding. It will burn until it consumes everything in its path to reach its endpoint, and when it does, there will be no stopping it from devouring you. Fight it, Seraphina, and when it finally claims you, you'll be powerless to stop it."

"Why?" she breathed.

She swore she heard a primitive growl thrum in his chest. It hitched her breath.

"No questions need to be asked when the obvious presents so clearly."

The ends of his hair tickled her cheeks. The tip of his nose brushed hers. Gods, she could taste his lips again and it damn near broke her resolve.

Jeslyn.

With a sharp huff of breath, she flattened her palms against his solid stomach and pressed away.

"You need to forget me, Emery. We need to forget any of this. All of this. Somehow, the wires got crossed. The dragon who was supposed to be my lifemate is dead and the woman destined to be yours is searching for you this very minute. And that woman is the closest person to a sister I'll ever have. She's my closest friend and I will *not* betray her."

Those last words gave her the strength she needed to break free of the rapture that came with Emery, if only long enough to escape. With a deep breath, she twisted away from him, out of his grip, and hurried to the door.

"The only one you're betraying is yourself, sweet flame."

His voice permeated her mind, causing her to stumble in her escape. Her pace slowed as his words sank in, deep into her marrow. She felt the truth in the statement as if he'd forged something tangible with those words and punched it straight into the core of her heart. They *hurt*. Physically *hurt*.

Dad said telepathy only occurred between lifemates unless a dragon-Keeper bond was created. He shouldn't be able to speak to me like this, unless Dad was wrong.

He had to be wrong. That was the only reasonable answer.

"Before you leave, tell me something, Seraphina. What were you doing the night you were arrested for trespassing?"

She'd made it to the door, hand reaching for the doorknob. She was so close to escaping when he delivered the low-blow question that it caught her completely off guard. A flutter of unease wove into the thought-fettering ride of emotions that came with his presence. She shot him a stiff-shouldered look. He was looking down at his hand, turning it over as he scrutinized something she couldn't see. His profile was bone-melting, and with the dim glow from the lights outside, there was no room for doubt when it came to the subtle curls of smoke rising from his nostrils and mouth. Thin ribbons that coiled and danced and added another layer of perfection to an already perfect creature.

She fisted a hand at her side to fight back the scream of yearning her soul bellowed.

"I don't know what you're talking about," she whispered.

"Don't you?"

Emery rolled out his shoulders and faced her once more. This time, his expression held more shadows than the small light could cut away. She saw the predator in the man, and it invoked too many emotions inside her to bear.

"At first, I was under the impression that my Keeper bailed his daughter out of jail, moving money after a long stretch of silence that drew Cade's attention. What a surprise to learn that the arrestee hadn't been Jeslyn, but you." The very corner of his mouth curled as he took a step toward her. "I'm very aware Slade has done well for himself over the last few decades, using little of my funding to help him along the way." Another prowling step. Sera grasped for the doorknob blindly, unable to take her eyes off Emery as he approached. She missed her first two tries. "I can also determine with pretty good accuracy without confirming with Cade that Nick's accounts were filled with much of Rayze's wealth after he was killed in order to help him here. If that's so, why was it that Slade posted your bail and with a dragon's money when he obviously doesn't need it?"

"Are you interested in my criminal record or my family finances?" Sera flexed and fisted her hand again, using the motion for grounding. But really, what was Emery after other than setting her ablaze? "Because the first I'm not interested in discussing, since it bears no weight on you. The latter I couldn't answer even if I wanted to."

The bite in her response seemed to either please him or entertain him. She wasn't sure which, but his eyes held her, stronger, darker, taunting her further than he had up until now. The curl at the corner of his mouth stretched across his delicious lips, but the smile was far from humored. In fact, her skin itched with a new level of heat.

"I'm interested, Seraphina, in you and what would make you break laws."

"Well, you can keep stewing in your interest, because I'm off-limits and your lifemate is spick-n-span clean when it comes to crime."

Before he could take another step closer, she wrenched open the door and stormed out of the room with one goal amid her flusters. She ignored the persistent burn of a dragon's gaze hooked onto her back and the laughter and fun that poured into the house from the yard. She cut her path quickly to the front door, scooping her keys off the foyer table, and left the house, slamming the door behind her. She hopped off the stoop, ignoring the stairs, and didn't glance back as she wove between parked cars to reach her own.

When she was behind the wheel, engine purring, she finally looked up at the house again. She clutched the steering wheel between her two hands, unable to temper the way they shook. She tried to take a deep breath, only to realize how tight her chest had become and how much she hurt from walking away.

She had no idea what she was going to do, but she had to stay the hell away from Emery. Far, far away from the dragon predestined to be Jeslyn's lifemate. Distance *had* to be the solution, but distancing herself from Emery would inevitably include Jeslyn, too. What would she say to her best friend when she asked why she'd been put out of Sera's life?

"One thing at a time, Sera. Start with the dragon." The wrench inside her chest twisted. She winced at the twinge of pain as she backed up around the cars and pulled onto the lonely, open road. "Must keep him away. Far, far away."

The Gods knew she was strong, but she only possessed so much strength before she'd break.

EMERY SENSED HIS BROTHER BUT DIDN'T BOTHER PINPOINTING his exact location. His attention homed in on Seraphina as the beautiful woman bolted down the stairs and out the front door, barely slowing to grab her car keys from the table in the foyer. Now, a few minutes later, he remained standing in the doorway of the study at the top of the stairs, staring at the closed front door. She may be gone but his dragon objected to her leaving. His arms, crossed over his chest, tensed in an attempt to keep his riled beast at bay. Where the dragon fed off the bones of a situation, his brain dealt with the flesh of logic and consequences.

Except for the throb that scorched his cock and burned straight up his spine. A fucking hinderance, considering it aligned with the desires of the dragon to go after his woman.

Gabe rounded the banister at the base of the stairs a short time later. He lifted his gaze from the door to his brother as the man casually climbed the curved marble stairs, thumbs hooked in the pockets of his jeans, lips pursed as the bastard whistled a haunting tune.

Whistled.

Emery scowled.

Gabe withheld words, taunting him with the slow, desolate melody until he leaned against the wall beside Emery, kicking his booted foot back on the wood paneling. Emery rested his shoulder against the doorframe and lowered his arms, tucking his hands into his jeans pockets. At the very least, the thread between himself and Seraphina remained bright, a lead to her whereabouts if he chose to track her.

"You know, brother, we've witnessed some pretty fucked up things over this last year or so. A crazy scavenger hunt left for Kaylae. Ariah's father's spiral into madness after Mark married his Baroqueth mixed-blood lady friend. Gabby's mother—need I say more? The dynamics between Dorian, Kean, and James and where that landed Caryssa." He tipped his head toward the front door, his brows raised. "Coming here tonight, realizing that for once, Keepers didn't withhold the truth from their kids, I held hope for a pretty cut-and-dry lifemate introduction for you. At least one of us deserved an easy ride."

"Not in the cards."

Gabe snickered. "No fucking kidding."

Emery clenched his teeth, willing away the relentless hard-on for a woman who'd abandoned him. A woman strong enough to resist the craze-inducing bond and leave him without so much as a glance over her shoulder.

Despite his frustration, he found her stubbornness and willpower impressive. If he wanted to be honest with himself, Sera's strength drew his adoration more than he cared to admit. Like the game of cat and mouse in the forest, her resistance could be rather fun to challenge. Foreplay until he conquered and claimed. Where his brethren took him as the fun and easygoing dragon, he held a ruthlessness as dark and dangerous as the rest.

"What are you going to do?"

As he turned Gabe's question over in his mind, several

answers presented themselves. None sat well with his conscience, except one. One that irritated him more than the rest, because it meant waiting.

He did *not* want to wait to be with his lifemate, but he couldn't rush into this recklessly, either.

"What am I going to do?" Pushing off the doorframe, Emery rolled out the ache in his shoulders from the tension riding his muscles. "Easy." Turning to his brother, his lips pulled tight in a feral grin. "She wants to forget what happened between us?" He chuckled. "Who am I to refuse her wishes? I'll give her *anything* she wants just to see how long it takes for her to concede."

You like playing games, little flame? Careful you don't get burned.

THE FRONT DOOR SQUEAKED OPEN, FOLLOWED BY A ROUGH slam as the early morning hour closed in on two o'clock. Sera lifted her focus from the dragonstone resting in her palm to the archway that opened to the hallway between the living room and the kitchen. A fury-infused bark preceded a vicious thump that made her jump where she sat on the sofa. A loud screech followed, then a cacophony of thuds and crashes that made her cringe. She cradled the stone between her hands and brought it to her chest, closing her eyes to reinforce her nerves as she listened to glass shatter and more thumps and thuds and barks and roars.

Her father losing control. The control he'd held carefully at the party fled him as he raged in the entryway. Each reaction tightened her muscles a little more, apprehension trying to win over bravery. She'd seen her father like this a handful of times, usually after something went wrong in his life, and after many drinks into his misery. Every time he'd get to this point, Sera learned to leave him alone. It was best to let him calm down, but she couldn't tonight.

She needed answers. She hoped he would give them to her.

As the destruction settled and her father's outbursts tapered off, she slowly pressed to her feet and made her way to the hall. His labored breaths greeted her, followed by the tickling dust as she breathed. As she approached the archway, she beheld the destruction caused by the hands of her father. Holes, half a dozen, punched through the wall. The entry table lying on its side, everything on top, including pictures of her mother, a glass bowl and vase and the lamp, strewn over the floor, most broken and shattered.

She paused in the archway, staring at her father's back, shoulders heaving with each heavy breath he took. He leaned against the wall, head against his arms, knuckles bleeding, fingers fisting and stretching, making those cuts ooze more crimson. The air around him pulsed with anger and grief, as electric as a live wire slithering over pavement after a storm. For the first time in a long time, Sera experienced a swell of sympathy for her father. Losing a dragon must be like losing a close family member. One whose bond couldn't ever be matched or replaced.

"Dad."

The weight of the dragonstone in her hands seemed more than ever before. A dead weight, now that she understood the reason for the disconnect. The dragon had been dead all along. There was no connection to be made.

Her father's breath hitched. The corded muscles along his forearms became more pronounced beneath his tension. For a long moment, he didn't move, breathe, make any indication that he'd heard her. Just when she was opening her mouth to address him again, he pushed off the wall and turned to her.

The glow in his eyes infused a chill that reached straight to her marrow. The tick along his jaw as he ground his teeth made the hairs rise on her arms. She swallowed down the ridiculous fear that choked her and held out the stone. Her father didn't so much as glance toward the object, choosing to bore all his manic emotions between her eyes. In that instant, she saw a stranger in her father's body. A man crazed and fueled by rage, not necessarily grief. Gods, was this how he was when her mother died?

Without warning, he bridged the gap between them, snatched the stone from her hands, and pitched it into the living room. A deafening crack-crash-crackle made her gasp and spin to see the dragonstone come to a rolling stop amidst the mess of more picture frames, figurines, and the chipped mantel over the fireplace.

"Worthless," her father hissed close to her ear. She jerked back, startled by his nearness. The stench of alcohol poured from his mouth, reddened his eyes, and flushed his face. She'd only seen him this drunk a few times, his temper unleashed each time, but tonight was different. Tonight, he carried an air of danger that said he'd make good on it if provoked. Sera shuffled back, wishing to be out of her father's line of sight, hating the way he glowered at her like she was poison he wanted to destroy. Every ounce of his disdain lanced her through, front to back, over and over. "Stay out of my way, girl. *Far* away."

Without waiting for her to respond, Nick Allaze stormed toward his bedroom. Another door slammed, shaking the walls. A breath rushed from her lungs, a breath she hadn't realized she'd been holding. She staggered, muscles weak. Her head spun. The man who was her father appeared to be a complete stranger. She'd known the news of Rayze's demise would paint her in an even more displeasing light, but she couldn't shake the feeling that her father's last words to her came as a warning.

She was no good to him now. Her last hope had been to make her father proud by being mated to his dragon. Ultimately, she was nothing more than an object to give away to please a beast while making her father beam with self-gratitude and satisfaction while loathing her. Had her mother survived her birth, maybe things would have been different, but the more time passed, the more Sera wondered if there was any pleasing the man.

The door to her father's bedroom crashed open. Heavy steps tore down the hallway. Sera scurried to the safety of the wall and pressed her back to it, listening to him huff and puff to the front door without casting her a glance. A few minutes later, he disappeared into the night, the rumble of his Mustang's engine fading as he drove off.

Navigating the shattered glass in the hallway, she hurried to her room and packed herself a large weekender bag with basic necessities, all the while her heart pounding, arms shaking, and her knees threatening to give out beneath her. There was no telling if or when Nick would return, but she'd be damned if she was here when he did. She pulled on her sneakers and coat, slung the heavy bag over her shoulder, and made her escape from the desolate prison of this foul-essence home to the freedom of the night.

CHAPTER SIX

*E*mery browsed the shelves of books blankly as he listened to Slade speak on the phone. It had been over twenty-four hours since Nick was seen leaving the party, and longer since anyone had heard a word from Seraphina. The man who believed himself someone significant in his lifemate's existence had come by and taken Jeslyn out to hunt Sera down. Meanwhile, Slade placed calls to every business, bar, and shop he knew Nick to frequent, whether it be daily or once a month.

So far, no luck.

The only thing keeping Emery from full-blown panic was the bright beacon that filtered along their lifemate bond. A bond that disappeared in a cloud, obscuring a direct location to her whereabouts. That thread assured him Sera was alive and well, at least physically. He'd have to find her to determine how she was holding up emotionally, and even then, knowing she could shut him out completely, he would have to rely on her honesty.

"Yes, if he does, I'd appreciate it."

Emery twisted, pinpointing Slade tapping a finger on

random objects lining the front of his desk. He'd long since unfastened the collar of his shirt, and his neatly combed-back hair had fallen over his forehead after multiple rakes and tugs.

"No. It's not that serious. No reason to get the police involved at this point, but it's important that I speak with him. Thank you again." Slade ended the call and groaned, tossing the phone on his desk. "Well, that was the last place I knew of. No one's seen him. The two guys he employs said he didn't show up today."

"It's Sunday."

"Ever since Dina's death, the man works seven days a week. He seldom takes a day off." The hesitation Emery caught in Slade's tone brought him away from the bookshelves to where his Keeper perched a hip on the corner of his desk.

"What *aren't* you saying that you want to?"

Slade pressed his lips together, lowering his gaze. "Nick and Sera don't share a very close relationship. He's always held some ridiculous resentment toward her over Dina's death."

"Deflection much?"

Slade shrugged and rubbed a hand over his beard. "Logic tends to escape many during the grieving process."

"It's been twenty-six years, yes?" Emery quirked a brow when Slade turned away and folded his arms over his chest. Something about the man's stance was off, but Emery couldn't quite put a finger on why. "I understand that everyone grieves differently, but I'd think that Nick would spoil his daughter—the last link to his dead wife—and treat her like a priceless treasure."

After a few seconds, Slade turned furrowed brows and a curious gaze on him. "You're awfully defensive on her behalf."

"Why shouldn't I be when someone who you obviously care deeply for is missing, and now you tell me her father doesn't care for her?" Ah, yes. Slade was hiding something. "Is that why you bailed her out of jail? What else have you done for Nick's daughter that Nick hasn't done?"

"Why would it matter? Aren't you happy with Jes?"

Emery tipped his chin and hooked his thumbs on his jeans. "And why would you ask me that?"

Slade dropped his arms and faced Emery. "Why won't you answer? Thirty years doesn't erase my memory of your body language or erase how well I can read you. That's ingrained here"—he pointed at his head—"and is part of our bond. I didn't miss the way you reacted to Sera when she came into the office, nor did I miss the confusion you felt when you saw Jes. You didn't close yourself off completely to me." Slade took a single step closer, shrinking the gap between them. "Is there something you'd like to share with me?"

"There's a lot I'd like to share with you, but you need to take the initial step. Who knows? Maybe things will make a bit more sense. That connection you speak of goes both ways, Slade." Emery pointed to his watch. "But while we play guessing games, we're wasting time that could be better utilized locating Nick, Sera, or both. I think we need to ask whether or not Nick is capable of hurting his own daughter."

"Absolutely not. Nick might hold some resentment, but he would never hurt her. He's not capable of hurting others. He'd abandon her before laying a finger on her." Slade's narrowed glower held his for a few more moments before his Keeper deflated and turned away from the desk. "I've run out of options."

"Maybe." Emery toyed with possibilities they may have

missed until one sparked alive. A confident grin threatened to creep across his mouth. "Or maybe not."

EMERY'S FIRST IDEA FELL FLAT WHEN SLADE ASSURED HIM that Nick and his deceased wife had no special places they shared before her death.

Thirty-minutes later, he stood beneath a sprawling oak that shattered the moonlight into a million pieces across the ground, highlighting the high-polished faces of the nearest headstones before illuminating the rest of the cemetery in silvery light and midnight shadows. Among the rows, he found his quarry, crushed beer cans littering the pristine grounds around the drunk man who slouched against a black marble headstone, muttering incoherently. For a long while, Emery observed the broken man, cringing inwardly as he spilled beer down his sweater when he missed his mouth. The aimless motions of his hands and arms. The waxing and waning of his alertness between chugs of beer.

When Nick tried to adjust his position against the headstone and failed—three times—ending up splayed over the frozen ground, Emery shook his head and decided to approach. Not that Nick could lift a finger against him in his inebriated state. He tucked his hands in his coat pockets and took his time weaving through headstones, waiting for Nick to realize he wasn't alone. It took him toeing two cans out of his path before the man lifted a heavy head and glassy eyes to him, his face flushed while his fingers took on a waxy white appearance, lacking the blood supply his face demanded. A pungent odor teased Emery's nostrils when the breeze changed direction. He craned around the back of the headstone and found the source of the odor—a sludgy puddle of vomit splattered over the marble base.

As he relaxed back on his heels and turned his attention to Nick, he said quietly, "You're worse for the wear, my friend. How long have you been at this?"

Nick mumbled something Emery couldn't make out, as hard as he tried. He gave the man a few minutes to try and gain a smidgen of composure, diverting his attention to the face of the stone. *Dina Allaze. Beloved wife, taken too soon.* No mention of a daughter. No mention of being a mother. To Nick, it was solely himself and his wife. The obsession made Emery wonder whether the man held any room in his heart to grieve Rayze.

As the minutes ticked by, Nick's clarity failed to return. The stench of beer, sweat—despite the frigid temperature—piss, and vomit began to take a toll on Emery's senses. He lowered to his haunches and easily took the can from Nick's weak grip when the man tried to raise it to his mouth for another drink, tossing it aside.

"Hey!"

"I think you're over your limit." Emery removed the case of remaining beers from Nick's fumbling reach and tsked. "That's saying a lot, considering alcohol doesn't have the effect on us that it has on humans, unless you drink a substantial amount." His eyes skimmed over the littered cans and he sighed. "And by the looks of it, you've taken to cheap beer over the last twenty-four hours at an impressive rate."

Nick attempted to push off the headstone, immediately falling back against it. He stretched out a hand toward the case of beer, but couldn't keep his arm up. It dropped to the ground beside him. "Gimme dat!"

"Nick, it's time to go. You've had everyone worried about you." He tilted his head, the battle to hold Nick's quivering gaze painful. "Sera's missing, too. No one has been able to reach her."

"Good," he slurred. Emery swore a scowl made an appearance, but couldn't be entirely sure, since the slackened muscles of Nick's face formed random expressions that didn't make sense. However, his lack of concern over his daughter sparked a dangerous light inside Emery, one he had to snuff before he made matters worse. Right now, Nick was his closest means of finding Sera. "She's mine."

Emery's brows furrowed. "Who? Sera?"

With a sigh, Nick reached over his shoulder. It took him several tries before his fingers managed to find Dina's name etched in the marble face. He stroked the engraving, and for the first time, Emery witnessed a mask of contentment fall over the man.

"Dey 'adit all. Buh not-her."

Goddess, was this man wasted.

Emery moved closer. "Okay, Nick. Time to go."

He hooked an arm around the man's chest and tucked his hand beneath his arm. Nick twisted violently, the strength behind his resistance shocking. Emery readjusted his grip and hoisted them both from the ground. Nick's legs gave out beneath his weight, body sagging against Emery's side. Emery closed his eyes and took a slow breath, one that he used to filter out the foulness with a tinge of smoke and flame. Slinging Nick's arm around his shoulder and holding his wrist for leverage, he began the arduous journey back to his truck, dragging the man's dead weight along the way.

"Notter. Notter. He'd ever have'er. Dina's mine. I did-don't dezzz-erver, 'ut she'd mine."

"Yes, Nick. Dina was your wife. She loved you, I'm sure, but it's time to go." He hoisted Nick's slack body once more, catching the man securely around the waist. "I don't think

Dina would want to see you like this. It's unbecoming of a Keeper."

To his surprise, Nick managed to hiss and spit in response. "Ne'er cared. Just me."

Emery gave up trying to make sense of the continual babble that spilled from Nick's mouth. Most of what escaped him was nothing more than a slew of sounds. Every few feet, the man would twist and resist moving forward with another endless stream of incomprehensible nonsense, but relent and allow Emery to continue to the car path he'd parked along. It took far longer than necessary— in part, Emery didn't want to carry the grown man covered in his own body fluids and then some—and once they reached the truck, Emery laid his jacket on the passenger seat to protect the leather. He'd pick up a new one tomorrow.

"Up you go." Emery boosted Nick into the seat, fastened the seatbelt and closed the door, releasing a sharp breath as he rounded the front of the truck. By the time he got behind the wheel, Nick had slumped against the door, snoring loudly. He chuckled and shook his head, starting the engine. "Damn, I don't know if Rayze would be pissed or proud as fuck. You both were a danger to each other when you were together."

Emery cracked the windows to air out the cabin on their fifteen-minute drive back to Nick's house. The entire ride, Nick slumbered, his snores deep and rattling. The dragon in Emery growled in frustration at the delay while he simply endured the ruckus with some music from the radio and a gentle hold on his lifemate's thread, which glowed but remained disconnected from the woman's location. How she managed to work that magic, he could only surmise. Right now, it irritated him more than piqued his curiosity. He'd find her soon enough. With Nick in his care, he'd have an excuse to peruse the house and possibly find some clues as to her whereabouts.

The small two-story house was dark when he pulled up, as it had been earlier in the evening when he swung by on the off-chance of catching someone home. He cut the engine and hopped from the cab, taking a deep, clean breath. Sure, none of the dragons or Keepers were saints when it came to overindulgences and poor decisions when lives weren't on the line. It had just been a long while since his nostrils burned because of something other than the heat of his own flames. He pulled open the passenger door and released the belt only to have Nick pour out of the seat into his unprepared arms. He shifted beneath the awkward position and made quick adjustments when Nick gave no indication he would wake up.

"What a sight this would be," he grumbled, the man's dead weight on his back as he held his arms over his shoulders. Thankfully, Emery had a half a foot on Nick, otherwise he'd wake up to scuffed boot toes. He didn't bother trying to find a key—he'd already tried the door earlier, and it was locked—and snapped the knob until the door drifted inward. He made it two steps before he switched to his thermal vision and saw the mess that greeted him underfoot. "What the hell?"

His momentary panic subsided when he noted the destruction didn't go beyond the entryway. A quick glance at Nick's torn knuckles told him what had likely caused the holes in the walls. The rest, then, made sense, considering Nick's current state. Emery's boots crunched over shattered glass as he moved deeper into the house, locating the master bedroom toward the back. He lowered Nick onto the bed and rolled out his shoulders.

"I sure hope you wake up feeling better than you look, friend." He pushed the man toward the center of the bed and brushed his hands on his jeans. "I'm going to check your place and make sure it's secure before I head out."

Speaking to a passed-out Keeper made him feel a little better about his true motive for bringing Nick home—the chance to snoop around Sera's room. Hers was on the second floor, at the opposite side of the house from Nick's room. He wasn't sure what he expected when he opened her door. He'd tasted adventure in his lifemate's mind, mischief, a dash of recklessness.

So when he laid eyes on Sera's choice of dark tones and ominous décor, he paused, wondering if there wasn't another room somewhere that belonged to her and he'd happened by this room by accident. It reminded him of something out of New Orleans, right up Amelia's alley. Witchy things on her black dresser. A few brown boxes stacked in corners. One was open, displaying an array of crystals.

"Not quite what I had in mind."

Shaking the confusion, he crossed the room to the closest stack of boxes and checked the shipping label taped to the top. A smile slowly crossed his mouth.

"Think I found you, little flame."

Broomsticks and Baubles was a tiny shop with a glass door and two windows on either side, blinds closed tight. The thread burned bright inside him, detecting Sera's immediate presence, her nearness. The low-pitch hum of her energy. The gentle lap of heat ignited from a bond she had yet to accept. Jeslyn hadn't been forthcoming about Sera's employment—that she was a shop owner, no less—though his Keeper's daughter said she had tried to locate her friend here, with no success.

Seraphina *was* here, of that much he was certain.

Through a gap in the blinds, he surveyed the interior, draped in near-pitch. Without using his dragon's sight, he could make out a handful of rows of shadowy shelves and a counter that ran the depth of the store to the right. His attention settled toward the rear of the storefront, where a faint, flickering light was obscured by something he couldn't make out. A back room, he was sure, and most likely where he'd find his missing lifemate.

With a glance along the sidewalk—the hour crept in on two, and this small swath of downtown had shut down long ago—he extended a talon and manipulated the flimsy lock. The door opened with ease, no dinging bell to announce his presence, and he took care to close it silently, engaging the lock once more.

Here, in the seclusion of the store, he switched to his dragon's sight and perused the surroundings more thoroughly. The knickknacks he'd found in Seraphina's room made more sense now, seeing as how similar merchandise filled the aisles and shelves of the small, quaint store. The counter to the right was glass, housing crystals and jewelry and other odds and ends. Ironically, not a piece of what he saw fit his flame's persona. Her energy might be wild, but she certainly wasn't engrossed in witchcraft or the occult. He didn't quite understand her, but he would, eventually.

Keeping his steps quiet, he made his way to the back room, separated from the front of the shop by two thick pieces of fabric tacked to the doorframe. For a long while, he stood mere inches from the cloth, staring through the tiny split in the fabric, absorbing the heat from Sera's nearness, and fought down the urge to growl. His dragon grew restless, coiling within his body, choking his spirit, wanting release and craving a claim.

Simmer down. Not yet.

Lips pressed together, he slowly inched the fabric curtain aside as he laid eyes on his sleeping woman curled up on an old sofa, threadbare blankets tucked around her body. Safe, yes, but her circumstances were not the best. There was an oversized weekender bag tucked in the corner, open to show enough packed clothing and toiletries to last for days. The flickering light came from an iPad on the small side table, streaming a quiet series. To his left, there was a tiny bathroom with a pedestal sink and a rickety toilet. Nothing about this space provided accommodation for permanent residency. The stacks of unopened boxes strewn throughout left little room to live. It was nothing more than an oversized storage area where the cold bite of winter seeped through the poorly insulated walls and left a chill in the air that touched Sera in sleep. She shivered beneath the shabby blanket but didn't wake.

Dammit, flame. Why must you be so stubborn?

He wanted to scoop her up and whisk her away from this drab place. Bring her back to his cabin and tuck her into the warm bed beside him. He'd melt away the chill with his own body heat and chase away the misery that haunted the edges of her mind like ghostly creatures lapping along the surface of a storm-churned sea. He had no idea what the last twenty-four hours had entailed for his lifemate, but he'd learn the details soon enough. Somehow.

Conceding to the reality that he could not take his woman out of this place tonight, he found a single chair and silently positioned it to face Sera in the only empty corner, beside the bathroom door, and settled in to wait for the next few hours while, Goddess willing, the woman slept. He opened to his dragon, allowing the inferno within his soul to warm the room until the twitches and shivers subsided from his sleeping wonder and she relaxed into deeper sleep.

He'd keep watch over her through the remainder of this night. Should she insist on repeating this tomorrow, he'd watch over her again. He'd not leave her in such desolation if he could do something about it, regardless of their unbonded circumstances. He'd keep his hands to himself, as much as his fingers burned to touch her, trace the arch of her brow, feel the beat of her pulse along her neck, elicit those shallow breaths that whispered of her desires.

And while she slept, he'd torment her in her dreams.

She wanted to shut him out during the day. Push him away with all her might.

Very well. At night, he'd plant seeds in her subconscious mind. Seeds that would unfurl and allow her a taste of what she refused otherwise. A taste of what would eventually consume her, because no one was immune to the Goddess-given gift of the lifemate bond.

CHAPTER SEVEN

Sera blew out a sharp breath as she finished unpacking the last of the merchandise and laying it out on the table in the back room. Her store, her pride and joy, found itself in a slump with the current economic downturn, but she still had loyal customers who came in and helped support her small business. Since hers was one of the only shops in town to boast an array of occult things—herbs, crystals, spell-casting equipment—those who practiced their craft came to her when in a pinch.

However, today felt different. Her usual motivation had been eclipsed by the haunting dreams that stuck with her, even hours after waking. Dreams of caves and fires and dark desires. A shadow figure that never touched her, never approached her, but whose presence thickened the air with feral hunger that tingled through her nerves and had her waking up with a throb between her legs and a need she couldn't dispel. Even now, her core felt thick, heavy, and her clit hummed with residual arousal.

His scent lingered in her nostrils, a tattoo needled into her mind. She blamed the dreams for waking to the memory of that sultry perfume. It made sense, because nothing was out of place in her tiny room to suggest she'd had a secret visitor during the night.

Wishful thinking. He has no reason to bother with you.

The metal of the front door creaked as a customer entered. She brushed her hands against her leggings and headed toward the thick curtains separating her back room from the main storefront.

She barely made it a full step into the front of the store before Jes slung her arms around her in a severe hug that could have cracked a few vertebrae along her back and huffed the breath from her lungs.

"Why the hell have you been hiding these last couple of days?" her friend demanded. "Silas and I have called you more times than we can count. We came here and stopped by your house. Uncle Nick never answered calls from Dad, nor opened the door when we stopped by. Dad's been worried about him since the bonfire, after—"

"My father's been out. He's been grieving Rayze in his own way," Sera cut in before Jes had the chance to reopen wounds and realities in her mindless rambling. She leaned away from her friend's embrace. Jes meant well, but sometimes her closest friend didn't take heed of how her words affected others. Right now, as Sera worked through her dilemmas and disappointments, she didn't need needles flung at her. "I haven't seen him much since the party. He hasn't made himself available to me, either."

One truth, at least. Ever since her father's ominous warning to her at the house, she'd made good on her intention to stay far away. She spent yesterday trying to settle into her temporary home in the back room, keeping her doors locked and her store dark. She mulled over calling Uncle Slade for help but decided it was best to shut herself up in her shop and let things simmer down and smooth out. Her last thread of a relationship with her father had snapped. There would be no repairing it. What little had survived years of stress, staying strong on expectations, shattered with the delivery of the news of Rayze's death.

Her father blamed her completely for the death of her mother, the only woman he'd ever loved. With his dragon dead, he had no reason to keep up the paternal front when his only daughter had no prestigious future as a dragon's lifemate.

She was *worthless* to him.

With a forced smile, Sera waved Jes into the back room so she could gather her newest merch and put it out on display while they talked. The battle she fought in the presence of Jes after her encounter with Emery left her stomach in knots and her chest tight with anxiety. She had no right to entertain any connection to the dragon meant to be her friend's lifemate. She didn't need to suffer the relentless burn and merciless desire she did in his presence. It was misplaced. She had no business pining after him.

The faster she accepted that, the better the situation would be.

Right now, as licks of heat teased her lower belly, she silently cursed her libido for misbehaving.

Those damn dreams…

"Ser, what the hell is this?"

At Jes's concerned tone, she tossed her friend a glance over her shoulder. Her cheeks warmed as she followed Jes's stare to the pitiful makeshift bed she'd converted from a run-down sofa squeezed into the tight space of her storeroom. Jes panned her shocked gaze back to Sera, a faint crease deepening between her brows. Sera waved her concern away and brushed her thumb over the crease marring Jes's perfect skin. Jes swatted her hand away.

"You're not staying here, are you?" She shook her head. "No, you're not. You're coming home with me. I'm not letting you stay here. It's not safe. You don't even have a decent alarm system on this place!"

"It's okay. I just needed to get out of the house for a few days. The energy there is…bad." Sera's attempt to lighten the situation failed as her smile flatlined. "It's only temporary."

Jes continued to shake her head. "Ser, absolutely *not*. And if you refuse to stay in your room at my house, then I'll call Silas and have him drag you out of here and you'll stay at his apartment."

Sera gasped at the same moment she swore she *felt* the rumble of a growl along her nerves. "What? No! You wouldn't." When Jes folded her arms over her chest and cocked her head with her signature determined glare, Sera groaned and threw up her arms, turning her back to Jes. "Fine. I'll go home tonight. I'm sure my dad isn't going to be there anyhow."

"I'll make sure you get home. Meaning, you're stuck with me for the next two hours until you close up shop. We'll grab dinner before heading back home."

Sera stewed in the vicious turmoil twisting her gut as she carefully collected a few figurines and faced Jes. Her friend's unyielding expression fractured, exposing the one thing Sera couldn't handle, next to the confusion she felt about Emery.

Pity.

She didn't *want* pity.

"Can you grab some of those crystals for me?" Sera asked, shouldering through the curtain into the main store. Precariously balancing her new wares, she rounded the last aisle, where she kept all the figurines and worship objects.

She came up short a few steps down the aisle, the strap around her chest cinching tight. She gasped, stumbled, one of the pentagram-engraved onyx skulls tumbling from her fingertips as a fierce tremor wracked her muscles. The entire store trembled, or maybe it was her vision and the shock of laying eyes on the very creature she'd sworn she'd keep far away from.

Emery's reflexes were startling as he easily caught the skull before it hit the floor. His captivating gaze held hers ruthlessly, pouring liquid fire straight down to her toes. All the torturous desire that had teased the outskirts of her mind exploded, the intensity of his nearness as he straightened up to his full, enticing height strangling the very last notion of sense from her. Her mouth went dry, her lips separated foolishly as she stared up into those warm whiskey eyes that tore away every barrier she'd put in place and saw straight down to the raw configuration of her soul.

The fire that spread through her burned up her neck and into her face.

Pooled between her legs until her clit throbbed and the ache made her shift on her feet.

She swore his nostrils flared a hairsbreadth. His pupils certainly stretched, widening and reforming into blunt vertical slits as he lifted the onyx skull between them.

"Careful," he said, his voice a hushed coo that held more than a face-value meaning. *"Don't want to cause undue strife between you and Jeslyn."*

His telepathic reminder snapped her out of her momentary rapture. She cut her head down, breaking the intense stare, and cleared her throat, shuffling back a few steps. Her fucking gaze had to coast over his jeans, and the very evident hard-on he possessed.

Of course he'd be hard. Jes is here. They probably had a toss in the sack before checking in on poor Sera.

With an inward grimace, she juggled her merch and relieved Emery of the skull, careful to avoid touching his fingertips. Fingertips that had grown the onyx points of talons from lightly scaled skin. She held back her surprise—and delight—at her second glimpse of his true dragon self. A grin twitched at the corner of her mouth as she sidled past him, trying her damnedest to ignore the delicious scent of fire smoke and fresh air that she hadn't been able to escape since their forbidden kiss in the forest.

The same scent that haunted her upon waking.

"Ser, where do you want these?"

"First aisle by the register. I've had kids try and pocket them in the past, so I keep a close eye on them." Sera located a spot on the shelf for the skull, casting Emery a short side glance. The dragon lounged against the shelves, arms and ankles crossed, watching her every move like she was an interesting specimen under a microscope. "Your dragon scared the shit out of me, but saved my skull from shattering on the floor."

Emery's sinful mouth curled in an amused grin, a single brow lifting over his slanted eye.

"Cute, little flame."

She scowled, his voice in her head bringing foreplay to an unimaginable level.

Jes appeared behind Emery, her eyes wide, arms loaded up with crystals. "I should've said he was here. I was more concerned about you, relieved I had finally found you."

"Let me help you there," Emery said, having refocused on the correct woman in the store. He relieved Jes of half the crystals and disappeared from the aisle without a glance back. Jes approached, her mischievous smile piquing Sera's curiosity, as much as it drew a foulness from her depths. She hated the darkness. It was unwarranted.

She was truly happy for Jeslyn.

Truly.

Really happy. I am.

Then why this viscous jealousy?

Ugh.

"How're things going?" Sera asked, keeping her voice down as she busied herself organizing the new inventory on the shelves. "He seems like a good guy, uh, dragon."

The glow in her friend's eyes finalized her determination to keep the fortress up between her and the dragon. These strange feelings would subside. They merely lingered after the adventure and risk of what happened in the forest. They'd fade.

Hopefully.

"He is *ahh-mazing*, Ser. The guys here hold nothing to him. He possesses this Old World respect and mannerisms that are so refreshing. Walking proof chivalry still lives. He's got this incredible sense of humor that puts even the most uptight person at ease."

Jes sighed, fanning her flushed face as she recounted the excellent points of Emery's character. Sera plastered a smile to her mouth for her friend as something withered inside. The violent twist of her stomach gave her pause. That was when she noticed how her hands shook. Jes didn't miss it, either, her joy dissipating instantly as she grasped one of Sera's hands.

"What's wrong? Are you sick?" She pressed the back of her hand to Sera's forehead before she could duck away. Jes's brows furrowed, her lips taut with worry. "You're pale as snow and your hands are like ice. You're *never* cold. Hey,

Em? Think you could run down the street and grab some tea for us? Maybe something sweet?"

Emery reappeared, his face tight with concern as his gaze roved over Sera. "Sit her down."

"What's wrong, flame?"

She lifted her eyes from Jes to Emery. The dragon edged between them, causing Sera to stumble back. He moved with her, a hand cupping the side of her neck, his thumb aligned with her pulse point, his eyes penetrating as they roved over her face.

Jes hung on his every move, her worry deepening while Sera's mind spun viciously at his touch. She struggled to catch more than shallow gasps, the inner battle her conscience waged with her body threatening to rip her to shreds.

"...a little too concerned for her..."

Sera blinked as the vile thought whispered through her mind. A thought steeped in prickly disdain that sounded awfully like Jes. She caught her friend's expression for a split second before Emery blocked her view.

Had to have misheard. Panicking.

"Sit," Emery said quietly, his voice a delivery of soothing calm that did not reflect in his piercing assessment. He guided her to the floor and positioned her back to the shelves, crouched on his haunches beside her.

"What's wrong, Seraphina? Tell me. Here. Along our line."

Sera stared at him, speechless, then shut him out behind closed lids and willed this foolishness away. She didn't understand it. She couldn't make sense of it.

"You. You're the problem. And you need to stop."

She sensed him tense, the stillness in his fingers along her neck causing instant regret. Those words spilled into his head out of desperation, because *he* was the reason for this, as much as she wished he wasn't.

"Me. I don't think that's the case."

"It is. I'm fine when you're not around."

She swore he snorted in her head. *"Are you, little flame?"*

He pulled back and she opened her eyes, her gaze following him as he straightened up on his feet. His eyes held hers, narrowed slightly, sending a faint chill through her blood. That was not the look he'd graced her with on all their previous encounters. She dared to assume the dragon masked a degree of frustration behind a carefully constructed expression of concern.

"I'll be right back," Emery said, abruptly taking his leave. His sudden absence ripped into her chest but lightened the air enough for her to breathe easier. Jes slid beside her, taking Emery's place, and grasped her hands.

"Ser, I've been so worried about you. I didn't want to bring this up, but you've been off since you came back from the forest with Silas."

Sera stiffened as she shifted her attention to Jes. Her friend's gaze gleamed, hesitation and apprehension softening the usual edge in her chocolate eyes.

But…something was off. A faint tingling tension settled between them. The way Jes held her hands was…distant.

"Did something happen between you and Silas? Did he… do something you didn't want? Because you avoided him shortly after you two returned. I sensed the difference in the air between the two of you immediately. He said nothing happened, but"—she squeezed Sera's hands—"I want to hear it from you."

A few heartbeats passed before Sera released a sigh of relief. Thank the Gods Jes didn't suspect anything more than that.

As for the discord, she blamed her panic attack. Her imagination was playing tricks on her vulnerable mind.

"Oh, no. Nothing happened between us. Nothing. *At all.* I had gotten lost too deep in the forest, so the chase ended before the fun could even begin." Sera managed a laugh and shook her head before she rested it back against the shelf. "I think the events of these last few days have driven me to the brink. Maybe I need a nice hike or something to clear my head and regain my sense of self."

Jes eyed her skeptically, her manicured brows furrowed. "If you say so."

Sera gave her friend's hand a reassuring pat and released a constricted breath.

Gods, she very much needed that to be so.

CHAPTER EIGHT

"Brother, you need to calm down."

Emery hissed, a plume of smoke erupting from his mouth as he turned on Gabe, hands clenched into fists. His body was wound so tight he trembled beneath the tension in his muscles. His dragon stirred, restless. Ripples of scales coasted over his skin beneath his clothing. The razor-sharp points of his talons pierced the heels of his palms, drawing blood before his dragon healed the wounds and protected the consequences of his mild tantrum with more scales.

This was insanity!

Gabe clasped either side of his face with his hands and held him steady, forcing Emery's gaze to lock with his brother's hard green eyes. "Stop, Em. You're causing this as much as she is, so take a deep fucking breath and *calm down*."

Emery concentrated on his brother's steadfast gaze as he regained control over his body and his frustration. He fisted and flexed his hands at his sides, expelling tension with each flick of his fingers. The muscles along his back began to loosen and his thermal vision faded to normal.

A few minutes later, Emery trusted himself to lift his head from Gabe's hands and turn his eyes up to the sky. "What a fucking mess."

"Not the first time we've stated the obvious over these last couple days."

"I don't know if she doesn't realize it, if she's in denial, or honest to Goddess despises me that much that she wants nothing to do with me."

"I don't think it's any of the above. Not with her reactions. The more you fight the bond, the more it wears you down. It's unnatural to fight the inevitable. The problem lies in the fact your lifemate is Sera and not Jeslyn. How Nick's daughter is your Goddess-chosen and not your own Keeper's daughter."

"Yeah, no fucking shit."

Emery dropped back against the truck. He'd called Gabe the minute he'd stepped out of Sera's shop, his blood burning hot and irritation at a dangerous level, raging into fury territory. Gabe met him in an overgrown and abandoned parking lot a few blocks away in record time, where traffic tapered to only a car here and there. Not that it mattered. They were pretty well hidden.

Gabe leaned against the truck beside him, kicking a foot against the door and crossing his arms over his chest. He followed Emery's gaze to the cloud-swollen sky, the scent of snow lingering in the air. The storm had brewed steadily throughout the day, waiting for the right moment to fall upon the land. Despite the chilly temperatures, Emery's skin burned. He'd considered shedding his jacket and shirt just to feel the cold against his body in hopes of taming the beast that roiled beneath this skin.

"You still haven't put a call out to Cade, have you." Gabe's words were a statement without need for an answer.

Emery ground his teeth, trying to dispel some of the lingering tension that thrummed in his head. He'd never suffered a headache before, but sweet Goddess, he swore he was on the brink of one of those pesky aches now.

Gabe continued, "Maybe you should. See if he can give you insight. He'll have to be informed of the Keepers' presence here sooner rather than later. You know our time is limited."

"For the moment, the Baroqueth don't seem to know they're here, but I'm aware of the time constraints." Emery scuffed the toe of his boot against the pebbled ground. "I'm beginning to wish Slade and the others never opened their mouths about our history. Seems to me that as much of a shock as it was for all the other lifemates to find out about us, they came around pretty quickly. Here I am, trying to dance around two women, four Keepers, and a fucking web I'm bound to get trapped in. There's no way around it." He growled. "I'd almost choose to battle it out with those fucking slayers than continue this delicate waltz."

Gabe grunted. "Careful what you wish for, brother."

For a short time, they stood in silence, staring skyward. Wistful visions of launching into the sky and releasing his frustrations in flight taunted him, but soon morphed into images of Seraphina strapped to his back as he spiraled up and dove through the clouds. He swore he could hear her laughter and exhilaration, feel her excitement as an extension of his own. Experience her thrill, her joy, the moment she understood who she truly was.

Mine.

He filled his lungs with the fresh mountain air and rubbed a hand down his face, releasing the last tension on a controlled exhale. "I'm supposed to return with tea."

"Hope there was a long line at the café."

"It'll be as long as I need it to be." Resolving himself to return to face a stubborn Sera and a preening Jeslyn, Emery pushed off the truck. "Jes has assigned herself as Sera's personal caretaker for the remainder of the day. Seems Sera's been sleeping in her shop."

Gabe quirked a brow. "Why?"

"It wasn't hard to pick up on the unsettled vibe between Nick and his daughter. I'm not privy to the details around it, since Sera can't bear to be around me long enough to strike up friendly conversation, but I intend to dig around and figure it out." Emery grumbled, "I don't necessarily like the idea of her working. Rooted too deep in a single place. Easy to find."

"Nick has his own body shop the next town over. They live simply, from my investigation. Nothing like Slade. Wonder if Nick blew through Rayze's hoard or if he's not cared to touch it." Gabe glanced down at his watch and tapped the face. "You've been gone at least a half-hour, and you're still tea-less. I'll head over to Sera's shop for a surprise visit and hang around for the duration of your torture to help keep your head on straight."

Emery peeled his lips back from his partially extended fangs. Gabe chuckled, knocking him in the shoulder with a solid fist.

"Hey, you're the one who wants to play the game. I didn't suggest it, nor do I find any reason for it."

"I'm doing this for her. It's what she wants."

Gabe snorted and shook his head. "It's a moot point, Em. The outcome will be the same. Someone will get hurt. *How* hurt will be measured by how long you continue this ridiculous ruse." He pulled the door open and climbed behind the wheel. "Just be prepared when you both finally stop fucking around for the impact of fighting the bond so long. Make sure when that time comes, she doesn't regret losing control."

"I've a feeling this one won't lose control that easily." *Goddess, don't I wish she would, though.* "Woman has a backbone of fucking diamond plates and a will of scales stronger than our own."

"Now that's pushing it, brother. But why not put your theory to the test?" Gabe reached around the cab and shoved Emery off the back door. "Get your ass moving."

Emery waited for Gabe to disappear around the block, the rumble of the truck fading as the distance grew. He pulled his phone from his pocket and dialed up Cade as he started his hike back to the comely street and the café he'd neglected to go to.

"I was beginning to wonder if you were going to call or if I had to hunt you two down."

Cade's growly voice reverberated along the phone line, a man who was never fully a man, nor completely a beast, but a mixture of the two at all times. As the oldest surviving Firestorm dragon, and the *tatsu* leader for centuries before Emery's birth, he was the epitome of a true dragon-man. Right now, the sound of his voice gave him a bit of strength he'd lost in his current state of vicious turmoil.

"No need for the hunt. Been caught up dealing with some intricate situations." Emery kept his head down, but his eyes and ears alert to his surroundings. He wasn't one to dismiss the absence of Baroqueth activity. They'd all been fooled one too many times to think they were safe in this world. "We located Slade, along with Nick, Jax, and Lauro, and their respective families."

"In one place that hasn't been targeted by Baroqueth. Interesting."

"They've been together since escaping The Hollow."

"I assume you have also been in contact with your Keeper's daughter?"

Emery snickered, the bitterness bleeding into the sound. He swore he felt Cade's brows lift, having seen the dragon's expression more times than not when he wanted an explanation and was willing to give the dragons the opportunity to fill him in before prodding. He'd spent way too much time at the table with Cade prior to the attack, he and Gabe being the youngest of the clan. He had become very familiar with the tiny nuances of their leader.

"And therein lies the problem. My Keeper bailed Nick's daughter out of jail, not his own."

A sound left Cade, but words didn't follow. Instead, he remained silent, but the implication to continue to explain weighed heavily over the line.

Emery swore he was going mad, and the burst of laughter that escaped him may have been a clue, because he sure as hell didn't feel happy.

"The funny thing, Cade? Someone up there in the heavens is fucking with my head, and frankly, I don't appreciate being the butt of the joke."

"Emery, what's going on?"

His smile brittle, he rounded the street that led to the main road. He slammed his fist into the brick of the building beside him as he turned, leaving a plume of dust and debris sprinkling over the sidewalk.

Didn't make him feel any better.

"So, Nick and Slade both had daughters, but guess who *isn't* my lifemate."

A low-pitched, *"Hmmm,"* was his answer, followed by another stretch of electric silence.

"Oh! It gets so much better, boss man. The woman who is my lifemate refuses to accept that very blessing for the sake of self-preservation, friendship, and loyalty to her best friend. I've found myself in a twisted reality show just waiting for the shit to hit the fan."

"Emery." Cade drew out his name like a father on the brink of scolding an unruly child. The warning woven through the rumble of his voice brought Emery to pause in the alleyway. Somehow, in those few seconds of silence, hearing his name roll from his leader's mouth infused clarity he hadn't had since his first encounter with Sera in the forest. "Step cautiously. There is more to this than you're aware."

"Do you know something?"

"I don't, no. But in the history of lifemates, this would be a first."

Emery snorted. "Great. Give me the trial run for future dragons."

"I stated 'would be,' which, in my opinion, *won't* be a first. There's more to this situation. I'd suggest you sit down with Slade and discuss this sooner rather than later."

"I'd love to, if I could shake his daughter from my arm long enough to do so without causing a perpetual meltdown from the woman who believes she's my lifemate, and logically so. All we need is internal conflict while we're trying to gauge the Baroqueth's next move."

"And speaking of Baroqueth, I'll be coming out to speak with the Keepers about bringing them back to The Hollow. Let's not gamble our luck this time."

Taking in a deep, controlled breath and releasing it with as much control, Emery nodded. "Agreed." He resumed his café trip. "This can be resolved in the safety of our world."

And maybe he could finally convince his true lifemate just where she belonged in this fucked up mess.

By his side, in his arms, beneath his body, in his bed.

If she wanted to play hard, he'd turn the tables.

He'd play dirty with a few cards he'd stashed up his sleeve.

CHAPTER NINE

They couldn't have made it any more obvious if they flat out announced it. In fact, she might respect them a little more had they spewed their plan to play babysitter to a grown woman like she might be a threat to herself and others. Cornered in a booth, Silas beside her, Jes across from her, and the wickedly devious, and utterly handsome dragon-brother duo guarding the end of the table. Granted, Emery sat beside Jes, though an awkward couple of feet stayed between them as Emery and Gabe hovered close to each other, exchanging some private conversation.

She was caged, with no way out while forced to endure the nearness of Silas and the proximity of Emery with all the visceral effects he triggered. Her mind spun while trying to figure out how the hell she'd gotten herself into this situation and how she'd get out of it. No amount of trivia games they engaged in dismantled the utterly disparaging reality that every person at the table held her prisoner to their good intentions.

She was grateful for her friends. But this was taking it to a whole other level that was demoralizing. After all, she could hold her own. Her father's neglect instilled in her a backbone and a thriving sense of independence most women her age would struggle to understand. She had her small business, a roof over her head—even if it wasn't inside a house—and food in her belly. Her mental health might be fragile, but she would never consider taking her turmoil to an extreme.

She just needed...time. Time to sort through everything and plan how to move forward.

"You've got to know this answer, Ser," Silas groused, finishing his beer as he tapped the table in front of the game screen. The televisions around the bar displayed a mix of trivia and sports games. Music pumped through the joint. Billiards clacked across the way and four teams at the two dart stations cheered or cussed. Cigarette smoke created a haze throughout the bar. The energy in the place was wild.

Trivia at Jake's was a tradition on Mondays. Competition ignited.

Right now, their table was in second place.

"It's C," Sera offered, shoving a fry into her mouth. She dropped her cheek against her palm, focusing on her barely touched burger and cheese-smothered fries while Silas punched in the answer. The timer quickly completed its rotation. The ticking hand on the timer's circle mocked her internal battle, the sensation of the world closing in on her. The burn of a particular dragon's gaze complicated things, commanding her attention. She glanced away from the greasy food on her plate to the magnificent creature who hovered close to his brother, chin tipped but head angled to cast her an inconspicuous look. His expression was shrouded in shadows that melted her more than ever, those whiskey warm eyes darker in the dim bar lighting. Strands of hair that didn't quite keep with the rest in a band at his crown caressed his jawline and cheek, an irresistible temptation that made her fingers burn to tuck them behind his ear or sink deep to his scalp and fist.

Gods, to be back in the forest...

Sera cut their gaze and swallowed the lump in her throat down with a few chugs of beer.

"Yes!" Silas cheered with a sharp clap. Jes shrieked and bounced in her seat, then fist-bumped Silas over the table. It took Sera a few seconds and a quick hug from Silas to realize what the excitement was about. There was no mistaking the growl that reverberated inside her head. Emery couldn't hide his sneer at Silas quickly enough from her half-second glance. "We're only a few points behind the first-place team now! We'll kick them out of the top spot soon enough."

"That's because our girl here knows her trivia," Jes crooned, scooting closer to Emery. She stroked his arm, her eyes turning up to him in that seductive manner Sera had seen many times before. Jes knew exactly how to get a man to turn to mush in her hand with minimal effort, and Emery proved no different than the rest. "Would you mind grabbing a round of shots and another round of beers for us?"

Emery's smile stretched as he rested his hand over hers, countering her with his own alluring gaze and charm. He lifted her hand to his mouth and pressed a flirtatious kiss to her knuckles. "Of course."

Sera's stomach twisted into a knot that threatened to squeeze the little she'd eaten up her throat. She tried her hardest to swallow it back and shifted uncomfortably on the bench, rubbing a hand gingerly over her flushed cheek. Emery climbed out of the booth and headed to the bar. Jes and Silas shared words drowned by the thrum of her blood rushing against her eardrums as her gaze followed Emery to the bar. When she finally reeled back her control, her attention glanced off Jes, who narrowed her eyes on Sera.

"You hit the lottery, Jes. Not me," Sera said, trying to dispel the unease of Jes catching her ogle her dragon. Jes's mouth tipped in a tight smile, her eyes glinting. Silas draped an arm around Sera's shoulder and tugged her close.

"I think we both did." Jes's smile loosened and she shook her head, like she was coming out of a trance.

Sera shifted in the seat, making the mistake of lifting her gaze to Gabe. The dragon-man who held a dangerous edge in every facet of his person hooked her gaze with minimal effort and maximum impact. He lazily swirled his drink in the tumbler, his posture exuding a casualness that belied acute intention. A viper waiting to strike when the time was right. It didn't help her nerves that he'd barely spoken a handful of words in any of their encounters yet had plenty to say in private to his brother. He was Emery's shadow. A potential devil whispering in his brother's ear. A sinfully gorgeous devil whose half-smirk curled his mouth with devious effect that whispered of mischief. His eyes reminded her of smoky emeralds, intricate and deep, filled with decades of wisdom as he picked her apart.

"Ah, mythology. You and Jes should get this one without a thought," Silas said, shattering the intense staring contest she had been holding with Gabe. "This one comes with bonus points. Who was the titan of prophetic radiance?"

Good question.

"Phoebe."

Sera cast Emery a sharp glance. He simply smiled from the bar and turned away to speak with the bartender.

"Ass," she whispered under her breath as she punched in the corresponding letter to the answer, locking them in first. Jes's brows furrowed, her eyes flickering up to Sera's.

"How did you know that? *I* don't even know that."

Sera waved her hand. "Remember reading a book with Phoebe as a supporting character. Happenstance, really."

"Good save, flame."

"You're not helping."

"Quite the contrary. I helped you close the gap."

"You should be in Jes's head, not mine."

From his place at the bar, Emery dropped his arm to his side and made a tsking motion with one finger beside his leg.

"But yours is so much more…interesting."

Fuck the dragon for purring that last word into her mind like hot silk. She slammed the walls up around her mind and hunkered down behind her steel barriers.

Silas's arm tightened around her shoulders. She shifted in the seat, trying to inch away from him, or at least put more than two shirts of space between them. Somehow. The last thing she needed to complicate matters was Silas thinking her befuddlement was caused by a nonexistent attraction to him when it was Emery's presence that sent her all askew.

She froze.

When did Silas lose all *attraction for me?*

Sure, things had changed after her encounter in the forest with Emery, but she didn't think it hit to the degree where Silas's arm around her made her severely uncomfortable and his nearness made her itch to run away. An alien sensation stirred in her belly and wove through her chest. A feeling of…guilt? Gods help her, what the hell did she have to feel guilty over, except for her infatuation with Jes's lifemate?

Sera squeezed her eyes shut and fisted her hands beneath the table. *Stop it, stop it, stop it.*

She needed to leave. She was suffocating in the corner of this booth, in the presence of her two closest friends. Her thoughts were wrecking balls punching holes through her head and her body was a failing shell short-circuiting over the most minuscule things. She needed to get out. Get away. Time to think things through and maybe, just maybe, the distance would help settle things down. Problem was, she'd tried to escape and been caught. Now, she'd always have eyes on her like a criminal who'd failed to escape her cell the first time.

In all honesty, her last escape didn't help much. It simply allowed her to wallow in thoughts of Emery. Thoughts of things she wanted him to do, things she craved, things forbidden. He infiltrated her barriers, suffused her every waking moment, and last night—*Gods, last night*—he consumed her dreams.

He was her promise, her poison, her strength and her demise.

She loved it. She hated it.

A clink of glasses drew her attention from her thoughts. *Speak of the devil and the devil appears.*

Emery slid the beer mugs across the table, the bartender following suit with the shots. The trivia screen flashed, and the answer highlighted.

Shouts and cheers boomed throughout the bar, along with cusses and groans. An announcement was made through the karaoke mic, listing the current standings for the top prizes. Their team was still in second place but trailing by a mere point. With two more questions left in the game, it could go either way, but the energy at her table was electric and humming with anticipation, an energy she couldn't connect with.

Silas finally released her shoulders and rubbed his palms together. "Okay, crew. We've got this one in the bag. Two questions, and a three-hundred-dollar prize."

He stole a huge bite of his burger and wiped his fingers on his crumpled paper napkin. Jes sidled closer to Emery, thanking him for the beers and shots while Emery placated her with a doting gaze that roiled Sera's insides. She cleared her throat and gulped down a portion of her cold beer, choosing to hide her disgruntlement behind a few fries in hopes her stomach wouldn't revolt. It wasn't Emery who caught her when she cast the brother duo a shaded sideglance, but the shadow. His eyes gleamed with understanding as he smirked at the rim of his tumbler and tossed the remaining alcohol back, never once breaking eye contact.

"Are you sure you want to play this game, Sera? It's a brutal road to endure when, in the end, you'll concede to the whims of the Goddess anyhow. Everything circles back. Fate's a fickle bitch from whom there is no escape."

Sera's shoulders stiffened as her spine straightened. Slowly, she looked completely at Gabe as one of his brows lifted over his eye and he casually shrugged a shoulder. The motion attracted Emery's attention, who cast a look between them before landing on his brother. Sera tried to shake the impression of Gabe's thought from her mind—because they *were* thoughts, not telepathically spoken—but the inquiry left a new turmoil rising inside her chest.

"Here we go. Which years were Queen Victoria alive?" Silas's brows pinched as he turned to her. Sera cast a questioning glance across the table to Jes, who chewed her lower lip as she contemplated the answers quickly coming onto the screen.

"It's B," Gabe answered. "1819 to 1901."

Silas and Sera jabbed at the touchscreen simultaneously, locking in their answer. Silas graced her with a small smile that reinforced the flicker of adoration in his eyes. It soured her belly and she turned away.

"We'll be splitting our earnings five ways," Jes joked, holding out a fry to Emery. He politely declined, clinking his mug to hers instead. Her friend's cheeks darkened as she sipped her beer, her eyes latched onto Emery's every move. It was borderline overkill, the way she hung on Emery's every breath. It didn't take a genius to recognize the mild disconnect that offset the energy between them.

No, that's your warped mind hoping what they have isn't real.

"No need. We're the support crew." Gabe contemplated his empty tumbler, his lips quirked. "You three enjoy the fruits of your labor."

"If you'll excuse me. As much as I appreciate being trapped in the corner for my own good, I do need to use the restroom," Sera said, nudging Silas's arm. Silas made haste to move out of the booth and helped her off the bench. His hand low on her waist didn't sit right with her, nor someone else, if she interpreted the deep-pitched rumble in her head correctly. With an awkward grin, she eased his hand away.

"I'll come with you." Jes scooted out of the booth after Emery and hooked her arm in Sera's. "I'm two beers in with no relief. We've got a few minutes, so let's make haste." To Emery, she flashed an adoring smile and wiggled her fingers. "Be right back."

Jes pulled her through the crowd to the quiet hallway of restrooms, all the while chatting about trivia and the dragons being their secret weapon. Well, there were benefits to living over a hundred years or more. Firsthand accounts of history came in handy for trivia.

"I think Silas is hoping to pursue what didn't happen at the party. He's had his eyes glued to you, but"—Jes finished reapplying her lipstick and pursed her lips in the mirror as her gaze caught Sera's reflection—"you seem aloof."

"I've got a lot on my mind right now. Seems much has

changed in a couple days, and I'm trying to figure everything out."

"If it's Uncle Nick, your dad will come around. I asked mine how a Keeper grieves the loss of their dragon, and he told me it's like losing one of your closest friends and family members, but magnified because of the blood bond. It's hard, and Uncle Nick's never been good with coping." Jes twisted, perching her hip on the sink counter as she dropped her lipstick into her brand-name crossover bag. "That doesn't mean you have to suffer, Sera. Now that we know who all the surviving dragons are, things can move ahead accordingly, right?"

The corner of Sera's mouth twitched into some semblance of a half-smile, but she avoided Jes's pitying gaze to fix her ponytail. Whether or not Jes realized it, Sera caught the hidden message between her words. *My dragon is alive but your dragon is dead, so you don't have anything holding you back from Silas.* Suppressing the urge to scowl, Sera blew out a sharp breath, adjusted the wisps of hair that framed her face—a face that appeared pale, sallow, and hinted at the ghosts of circles under her tired eyes. The weight of recent events, the war waged inside her own mind, was wearing her to the quick.

"I think right now I need to turn my focus to other things. Everything has changed, Jes."

"Well, yeah. To a degree." Jes's brows furrowed. She tilted her head, scrutinizing Sera. "What else is going on, Ser? Does it have to do with you sleeping in your shop?"

Sera dropped her hands to the counter and finally faced her friend. "I can't go home. Not while my father is in one of his states." *Not ever.* "So I'm staying at my shop. You and Emery deserve your time to get acquainted without me around. As much as I appreciate your insistence that I stay at your house, it's not the best solution."

"Sera, you can't—"

"Yes"—Sera interjected, raising her hand—"I can. I will. I'm fine there. It's rather cozy."

Jes's mouth hung agape. She blinked a few times before shaking her head, pushing off the counter. "It's freezing in that back room and it's not safe! Not to mention you can barely move in that place. How are you showering? In that tiny sink? Can you even *clean* yourself?"

Okay, that was a low blow. Sera clenched her teeth and turned away, heading for the door. Jes grabbed her arm as she stepped into the hallway, wedging her smaller frame in front of Sera, forcing her to stop. Sera folded her arms over her chest, barely containing a frustrated huff. Jes frowned, the pull of her brows almost painful to witness. The pity in her eyes struck a sensitive nerve under Sera's skin. She wasn't helpless. She may not have all the lavish comforts of wealth at her fingertips like Jes did, but she had her will and determination. What her friend saw as subpar and unlivable, Sera saw as a private refuge away from all this torment.

"Sera, what else is going on? This is not like you. At all. You've been utterly preoccupied and almost...*depressed* lately, and it's worrying me. You've never refused offers to stay at the house. You have your own room and everything, so it's not like you'll be in the way of Emery and me if you choose not to be. I just want to know my closest friend, my sister in heart, is safe and well. You *are not* safe and well in the back room of your shop. Even you can't deny that." She shifted closer, her voice lowering. "And Silas? You may not realize what you're doing, but I've been watching you since we got here and you're keeping your distance every time he tries to get close to you. You appear *uncomfortable* with him.

It has me suspecting you weren't entirely truthful when it came to the forest."

Sera groaned and rubbed a hand down her face. "Listen. There was nothing that happened with Silas that night. Nothing, not even a kiss. We'd gotten lost and by the time we found each other, I was too flustered to even think of why we went into the forest to begin with. We came straight back out. My father, on the other hand, is in a toxic state that I refuse to be around. My priorities have shifted a little, focusing more on my steps moving forward. I can't keep scrounging off you and Uncle Slade and Aunt Claire. It's not right. I'm twenty-six, an adult, and I'm capable of acting like one." As the bar erupted in a cacophony of cheers and groans, Sera jutted her chin toward the table. "Let's get back. One more trivia question, then I think it'll be time to head out. I'm getting tired."

Sera insisted on staying out of the corner of the booth despite Silas waiting for her upon her arrival with a meager motion to usher her back in. Thankfully, he obliged her wishes, preoccupied with his excitement.

"We moved into first, ladies! All we need to do is get this last one and we're claiming the prize tonight!"

Jes released a squeak as she slid into the booth, clapping her hands, smile glowing across her face. Her eyes glittered with anticipation, lacking any evidence of her worry moments earlier. Sera dropped onto the bench, keeping her attention averted from the brothers.

"Get those shots ready for the celebratory toast," Silas said.

He slid one glass closer to Sera, who accepted it with a small, "Thanks." She rolled the shot glass between her fingertips, trying to ignore the storm in her stomach, the heat of eyes on her, and the new desire to flee, now that she could.

The crescent shape of an onyx claw inched into her view,

pushing another shot glass close to hers. She looked up at Gabe, who nodded toward the glass.

"Looks like it'll do you more good than me."

"I'm not into shots when I have to drive."

Gabe straightened up in his chair and tossed a casual glance over his shoulder toward the front door. "If I recall, you left your car at your shop." Those piercing eyes fell back on her. "Ease that tension a bit."

"You're not helping matters," Sera grumbled under her breath.

"He comes off pretty intense, but he's mush beneath the scales," Emery assured her, proving he was paying attention to their exchange.

Gabe knocked him in the shoulder. "Don't minimize my intensity."

Emery laughed, and Gods help her if the sound didn't stroke every erotic cord throughout the fabric of her being. She pressed her lips together and focused on one of the television screens over the bar.

"You do have an edge, Gabe," Jes said.

"I'm a dragon. I have plenty of edges."

"He's got a point." Silas chuckled. "I'm sure the scales aren't soft. Oh! Buckle up, we're a go."

Sera blinked as the question typed across the screen. *What in this universe thinks I've done something wrong?*

"These sisters are responsible for predetermined paths and destinies—"

"The Fates," Sera answered before the answers began to pop up. She hadn't realized she'd been clenching her teeth until she spoke, and the tension released in her jaw.

Her first mistake was cutting her attention to Emery. He watched her, his attention hot, like she'd imagine the sun's fire, as he took a pull from his beer mug.

Her second mistake was breaking that gaze and turning desperately to Jes, only to find her friend sliding up to Emery's side and whispering something in his ear. The sight of them together lanced straight through her chest, leaving her breathless with an achy jaw and an unwarranted prickle across her eyes.

"Locked in." Silas dropped back in the booth and drummed his fingers on the tabletop, staring at the screen. "This next minute is going to be long."

Sera hid her frustrating unease—*jealousy, girl, call it what it is*—behind the shot Gabe had slid her way. Whatever it was burned a track down her throat to her gut. She felt it move, the heat of the alcohol coating the inside of her stomach and spreading warmth through her limbs. Enough warmth to fracture the tension Gabe had mentioned. Something had to give, and fast. The last forty-eight hours proved grueling. Ever since the dragons came waltzing into Uncle Slade's party and making her question her own loyalty to her best friend.

"How about another round of shots, since you couldn't wait until after this last question?" Emery asked, already climbing out of the booth. He gently unlatched Jes's arm from his with a smile before his piercing gaze cut to Sera for the briefest of moments, smile waning to something she couldn't decipher. "Let's see if I can do this in forty-five seconds or less."

Sera glanced over the table. She and Jes were the only two who'd downed a shot, and Sera still had one left. Silas hadn't touched his, too preoccupied with the clock on the screen to notice. He cast her a short look, then relaxed and took her hand in his. A chill poured down her body from his touch, a touch he'd performed so many times before and had always left her warm with anticipation. Now, she wanted to pull her hand away.

"If we get this, you should take her out to celebrate, Silas," Jes said. "I don't need the cut. Spoil our girl instead."

"That sounds like a perfect idea," Silas agreed, his gaze lowering to her mouth. She turned away and withdrew her hand, cupping her beer mug. His assessing gaze never left her. "I think we owe it to ourselves, don't you?"

She forced a semblance of a smile. Lifting the mug to her lips, she muffled her despondent, "Sure."

"Uh, ah!" Jes clapped her hands. "We got it!"

Silas whooped. "That should put us... Hell, yes!"

Sera had no time to react. She barely processed her head being wrenched around and cool dampness crushing against her mouth. Vile darkness unleashed through her, the resonant guttural growl that filled her head as her stomach revolted at Silas's spontaneous celebratory kiss leaving her entire body stiff with tension. Her fingers balled into painful fists against her legs. Silas pulled back, his cheeks flushed, his eyes dark with desire. His hands stayed on either side of her face, but his grip had loosened to something gentler. A sense of wonder crept over his expression while she fought down a sudden swell of panic entwined with something foul. The beat of her heart pounded in her head as a more powerful emotion blended into the essences that churned and knotted behind her sternum.

He kissed me.

Oh, Gods. Silas kissed her.

And as his gaze lowered back to her mouth, every warning bell she had screamed inside her soul.

Too dumbstruck to speak, Sera tore away from his grip, clambered out of the booth, and made haste to escape this newest level of hell.

CHAPTER TEN

"What the fuck just happened in there? How could she... How could that..."

Gabe grabbed Emery's shoulders, claws digging deep through his jacket but not breaking skin.

The dragon within Emery unleashed his fury, his jealous rage, battering his mind and soul after witnessing *his* woman, his *lifemate*, engaging in that kiss. The very second that bastard had his mouth on Sera, he'd taken off, worried he'd not be able to control his fury and frustration over everything he was forced to witness. The wrong woman on his arm while the right woman was kissing another fucking man. No man had a claim to his woman's mouth. No man should know what he knew after their stolen kisses in the forest.

Mine!

He didn't see his brother taking chase after him until Gabe caught his fist before it hit the brick wall of the building and dragged him away from the bar's entrance.

"You're going to cause more issues letting your dragon get out of hand. These people don't need to see their fairytale dreams and nightmares become reality while they're fighting their own demons with shots and beers. You losing control isn't going to help the situation. Calm the *fuck down*."

"Easy for you to say."

His biggest nightmare had just manifested in front of his very eyes. He should have been able to swallow it down and deal with it, since he was supposed to be with Jeslyn, but fighting this bond was proving impossible. He'd seen and heard of subtle resistance, watched the sparks and misery between Taj and Caryssa during their early days. But this? Sera wanted nothing—*nothing*—to do with him! How was she able to repel him so easily?

What is wrong with me*?*

"This is out of hand, Gabe. This has gone too far. She wants me to entertain her friend while she plays martyr, but *that*"—Emery jabbed a clawed finger toward the bar, his teeth clenched while scales rippled to the surface beneath his clothing, and his vision flickered between thermal and human—"crosses the fucking line. I'm not *kissing* Jeslyn or implying anything romantic with her, yet she has the audacity to let that guy *kiss* her...*in front of me*!"

"Brother, I know it doesn't make the sight any less disturbing, but she didn't instigate it. It was all the man. And honestly, I don't think I've ever seen a woman go so stiff so quick as I witnessed back there."

"She didn't *stop* him!"

Emery dropped his arm, his entire body trembling with a potent mix of emotions. Part of him wanted to rip that man to shreds. Part wanted to roar at Sera for playing this game. Part wanted to snatch her away and set her right. And the part with a heart that beat for a woman who'd rejected him over and over in a mere couple of days wanted to do whatever it took to *please* her, even if it meant enduring the unbearable.

"Goddess, watching this pain you suffer is agonizing,

Emery. I'm not going to lie. If this is what fighting a bond creates, I'd never wish it on anyone, especially you. But the truth is, it's not just Sera. It's you as well. I didn't play games with Sky, brother. Her denial was impressive, but I kept hitting her with truths and facts because I wasn't messing around." Gabe sighed and shook his head. "Sit down with Slade. Talk to your Keeper. Let him know the truth. Somehow, you ended up fated to Nick's daughter, not his. It'll be hard for him to accept, but he *will* accept it. He knows as much as all of them that when that lifemate bond exists, it's out of everyone's control. It's a Goddess-set match, and not a single one of us can persuade Her to choose otherwise—"

Emery felt the surge of wild energy and the intense heat of emotions running high before the door flew open to the entrance. Sera rushed down the steps in the opposite direction from the two dragons. Gabe turned, but Emery's focus hung solely on one person. One creation. Her presence, a powerful, pulsing ball of knotted energy, pierced him straight to his core and demanded his full attention. The bright beaming thread that connected them glowed a blinding white, its light searing him from the inside out.

On the outside, though, the woman herself was in a frazzle. She walk-jogged toward the street, stopped, fisted her hands in her hair, turned toward the parking lot, spun back to the building. She hadn't noticed him or Gabe, but after the split-second glance he saw of her face—skin pale, eyes wide, mouth tight, an expression of sheer horror stamped into lines of confusion and absolute defeat—nothing could hold him back.

Gabe grabbed his hand as he started past him. Metal and plastic pressed to his palm.

"I'll take care of the mess inside. Use this opportunity, Em. *Wisely.*"

"Thanks."

Stuffing the keys into his pocket, he hurried down the sidewalk after Sera, who'd decided the main road was her best route. He caught up to her as she sniffled, a rough arm crossing her face to swipe at tears. Her hair had small tuffs loose from where she'd torn into the ponytail. She hugged her belly with her other arm like she'd be sick. The glimpse of her she hadn't shut out of his mind confirmed the roil of her belly and the tenuous control on the brink of shattering.

"...can't...can't...can't do it..."

In her mindless state, her foot slipped off the edge of the curb. Emery caught her before she fell, setting her aright on her feet.

Time ceased to exist. He held her wrapped in his arms, her smaller frame tucked like a precious gift against his chest. She clung to him in return, fingers fisted in his jacket, face to his chest, muscles slowly relaxing. The echo of her heart beating as her walls crumbled from her mind. At long last, he could see the pure essence of the woman who owned every molecule of his being and claimed his existence for her own. The depth of her inner battles to keep him away while struggling with the natural pull toward him. The unyielding war of loyalty. And yet, in these moments as she relaxed into him, she never wanted to leave. This was where she belonged. This was *right*.

And he'd make sure she understood that tonight.

"Careful," he murmured, smoothing a hand up her back until his fingertips crested her neck and cupped the base of her skull. He absorbed the small tremors that persisted through her body, and filled her with warmth and calm from where his palm rested against her bare nape. She didn't fight him, a small blessing. He dipped his head and inhaled the scent of her hair, the floral essence not familiar from their last encounter. It didn't matter. It clung to his woman, and anything that represented her, he indulged.

At last, a long breath escaped her, and the tremors faded. The chaos he'd witnessed in her mind subsided, but her thoughts remained tangled and brimming with concern.

Guilt.

A heavy, despondent sense of guilt and hopelessness.

He hated what he did next, but knew if he didn't, she'd do it, and her reaction would be worse. He stepped back, enough to break their connection, and shifted his hold to her elbows. Her head dipped but she couldn't hide the way she worried her lower lip or the taut confliction in her face. She held his forearms, consciously or unconsciously, he wasn't sure.

When she finally lifted her gaze to his, his heart twisted but his dragon crooned. He saw her battle, her war. Felt the fight in the pit of his soul and hated everything it stood for. Behind that veil of struggle and pain, he found exactly what he knew he would.

Contentment. Longing. Desire.

"Gabe went back inside. I'll bring you home." Her brow began to furrow, but he quickly smoothed it out with a gentle brush of his thumb. "Youv'e had enough excitement for one night, I must say."

"I-I—"

Emery dipped his head a little to level their gazes. "Seraphina, you're safe with me. I'll bring you home."

She nodded, a mere twitch of her head, and allowed him to lead her across the parking lot to the pickup truck. She stayed close to his side, not withdrawing her arm from his light grasp. He wondered how much his proximity truly calmed her, since she'd blamed him more than once for causing her angst. He could only understand the lifemate bond as far as his brethren explained it, or as much as he'd witnessed it himself, but one thing he knew was that a certain level of ease always accompanied lifemates and dragons. It was part of the package.

No words were spoken on their walk. He listened to her quiet steps, soaked in the warmth of her nearness, cherished the fact that she didn't resist but fell into a comfortable place beside him. Their bond threads pulsed bright, no discord or inconsistencies. Just a pure, bright glow that wove deeper and deeper into the fabric of their intertwined souls. It was perfection on the inside, despite the imperfections that had brought them to this point.

He disarmed the alarm as they approached the hulking black truck tucked in shadows. He opened the door, guided her into the passenger seat, and waited for her to settle in, belt secured. She didn't look at him as he closed the door or when he hopped in behind the wheel and started the engine. As content as she may have been walking to the truck, as he backed out of the spot and left the parking lot, unease slithered through the bond between them. Her hands knotted between her knees, her muscles grew stiffer with each passing minute, and she kept close to the door. He kept his right hand on the steering wheel and rested his temple on his left, which he propped on the window ledge.

"My shop is the other way," she finally murmured as he took a turn away from downtown toward Nick's house.

"Your shop isn't home."

He cast her a side glance when he felt the heat of her gaze land on him. She watched him from narrowed eyes that lacked a fight.

"I can't go to the house."

"And you can't go to the shop. It's not safe."

"Now you sound like Jes."

He snickered. "Maybe she sounds like me."

He had been the one to voice his concerns over the minimal security at Sera's shop and Jeslyn clung to it like he found her often clinging to him.

"I *can't* go to the house, Emery."

Emery hesitated, the corner of his mouth dropping from the minuscule grin he kept hidden. As quietly as she spoke, the desperation behind her declaration raised a single question in his mind. It hung there, on the edge of their bond, waiting for him to press it forward. He resisted, noting the way she fidgeted in her seat before turning to stare out the window. Her discomfort—he slowed enough to observe her fully for a few seconds, because it wasn't only discomfort he sensed, but something far more potent that made absolutely no sense—settled like a thick cape over her, dimming her light and smothering the spark of life he adored.

A wave of protectiveness coasted through him, washing over the dragon as he recalled the destruction in the entryway of Nick's house. Had he harmed Emery's woman in his rage? Was that what he sensed deep in the murky darkness she refused to share?

"Would you be willing to trust yourself with me, Sera? Trust in my suggestion?"

"Depends. What are you going to suggest?"

Emery cut a U-turn in the middle of the road and took a side street away from everything. Sera shot straight up in her seat, hand gripping the door handle as she faced him. He dropped his hand to the console and caught her wrist, pouring another dose of calm into her body.

"What are you doing?" She looked down at the connection, brows pinched. "You did this to me earlier. In the shop. What is it?"

"Helping you relax, because you're not allowing yourself to do so. You're no good to yourself worked up the way you've been. I may not *know* you, but I can read you incredibly well. And before you go on the offense, think about it." He slid his pointer over her pulse point and felt her pulse slow as she calmed. He hit a straight stretch of dark mountain road and offered her a small smile. "Okay?"

"You work magic on everyone who panics?"

Goddess, he wanted to slip his fingers between hers and pull her a little closer. The way she looked up at him—her eyes hung on hope while he knew her conscience tried to fill her with doubt—weakened his resolve enough to leave him contemplating temptation and risking the night over a simple move.

"It's a rare gift that works on a select few."

"And I've been selected."

In more ways than you're willing to accept.

Emery released a short breath and nodded once. She danced the sharp edge of implication and being forthcoming about what she wanted, but he understood her statement more than perhaps she did. She wanted him to tell her the truth, to confirm what she already knew, but she wasn't sure if she'd accept it or rebuff it.

Slowly, she twisted her wrist from his encircling fingers and leaned against the door, watching the shadow-cast scenery fly by.

"I don't bite, you know," he offered quietly, trying to lighten the tension.

"You do. I know."

He opened his mouth to argue, but quickly closed it when he realized she had a point about their encounter in the forest. "Actually, I didn't bite. I teased."

"With teeth."

"You didn't protest."

He stole a thermal glance at her then and smiled to

himself as he watched the heat swell up through her neck and face. She recalled all too well, and her silence assured him she was reliving those moments in the forest with utter clarity.

The remaining fifteen-minute ride lacked tension and discomfort. A soothing energy ebbed and flowed between them as he turned the radio on and filled the truck with some gentle background noise. He stole several glances of her as she sat, caught up in her thoughts while staring out the window. Several times, she stroked her wrist where he had held her, or gingerly touched her neck before realizing what she was doing and tucking her hand into her side. Those few motions led her heart into a flutter that sang to him more than the radio.

Emery turned onto a narrow dirt road flanked by thick forest and decorative boulders and followed it up the steep drive until it widened and opened to the rented lakeside cabin. He pulled the truck up to the stairs that led to the front porch and the entrance to the modest two-story house and cut the engine. While Sera took in the sight, he got out of the truck, circled to her side and opened the door, holding a hand out for her.

"Come on. I think you'll appreciate the view." His mouth curled. "And the escape."

To his delight, she accepted his hand, and his help, climbing out of the truck. Just as quickly, though, she pulled back and tucked her arms around herself with a shiver. Her coat was thin and didn't provide much insulation. The tip of her nose had taken on a cute blush and the cold of the night made her eyes glitter brightly, like warm steel in moonlight. He could stare at her for hours and not tire of her beauty. He could spend a lifetime learning how each emotion played in her eyes. Discover what created the fine creases in her brows or made her lips pull tight.

Heat rose along his skin as his dragon slinked through his mind, pushing him to claim what was inevitable. His body burned to do more than hold her close and keep her warm. His cock throbbed in his jeans when he scented the first hint of her arousal and watched her pupils widen the longer he held her gaze. Her cheeks darkened and she dropped her head, rubbing the side of her face against her shoulder.

"It'll be warmer inside." Hesitating for a few seconds more, Emery finally led her up the stairs and unlocked the front door, allowing her in. She thanked him quietly as she passed him in the doorway and stopped as he closed the door behind them. Settling beside her, he followed her awe-stricken gaze to the wall of floor-to-ceiling windows and the sliding door that opened to the back deck and an unobstructed view of the enormous lake a few hundred feet away. Her arms slowly dropped to her sides and her lips parted as she looked up at him. Wonder flooded his soul, her potent reaction pouring through their connection with no filtration. "I'm glad you like it."

She blinked, slow, seductive. It left him fighting to keep his hands to himself. The way her long, thick lashes fanned over her cheeks, and the sultry glow of her eyes when they revealed themselves again choked his thoughts.

"You read my mind?" she whispered.

"No." He lifted a hand and brushed a small wave that had caught at the corner of her mouth behind her ear. Her eyelids lowered and he swore she leaned into his touch when his fingers caressed the shell of her ear before falling away. "Whether you want to believe it or not, Seraphina, our connection goes far deeper than a dragon-civilian connection." He leaned close, bringing his mouth to her ear and whispered, "Ours is a gift, flame. Yours and mine. Goddess-given."

He straightened up, refusing to release her gaze.

"...can't breathe...my heart...but Jes..."

Jeslyn. An eager young lady, but she was quickly becoming a thorn in his fucking sjde. He stepped back to lighten the air thickening between them. If he had any hope of not tucking her under him, he had to step away. Always stepping away.

Sliding out of his jacket and tossing it over the back of a tall chair at the counter, he pushed up his sleeves and rounded the counter to the kitchen. He caught her pressing her hand flat to her chest as breath filled her lungs.

"What would you like to drink?" He pulled open the fridge door. "Beer, wine, liquor, water, soda, coffee, or tea?"

"Umm..."

Thank the Goddess for small things. With the fridge door open, she couldn't see how the husky purr of that single sound struck him straight to the core. The contents of the fridge went from clear-cut objects to silhouettes of blues and greens as his dragon pushed to the surface. His cock gave a throb that nearly drew a growl from his chest. Maybe this wasn't such a great idea, at least until she accepted their bond.

"I should probably stick with non-alcoholic beverages. Tea, if it's not too much trouble."

Reinforcing his resolve, he closed the fridge door and couldn't help the grin that pushed through when Sera quickly averted her gaze and her cheeks flushed. The pink spread to the tips of her ears, which he found absolutely endearing.

"I wouldn't offer if it's too much trouble. Alas, sweet flame, I find so few of your requests to be troublesome." He unhooked two mugs from a countertop mug tree, filled the electric kettle with water and switched it on. "Why don't we go onto the deck?"

He rounded the counter and crossed the living room to the sliding door, motioning for her to follow. He pulled it open as she approached and spread his arm in invitation toward the extensive deck with its sofa set and firepit table, several seats across the platform, and wrought-iron railing. Strings of Edison lights hung from the rafters and draped each thick square beam that acted as sectioned posts along the edge of the deck.

The way the moon dappled over the mirror surface of the lake topped the entire atmosphere. A stunning scene that promoted tranquility.

He could only hope she'd find it peaceful enough to keep from pushing him further away.

CHAPTER ELEVEN

Sera stepped onto the deck and into an enchanted dream. The night was quiet except for the faint scraping of barren tree branches and the fall of pinecones from the evergreens in the lakeside breeze. Swells of snow gave the night a soft glow beneath the moonlight. The lake provided a stunning backdrop to the nightscape, eerie and magical at the same time, framed by thick copses of trees and an occasional lake house far off in the distance with a light or two that reflected on the glassy surface like fairy lights. A picturesque vision that made her forget all her problems and worries.

It was the company that really helped put her mind at ease.

"Make yourself comfortable. I'll be right back with your tea."

The dragon-man who'd gifted her with these moments of peace returned to the house without asking how she liked her tea. He demanded her attention despite her fight to keep her eyes off him and had won every time so far this evening. She wished he'd put the jacket back on. At least then she wouldn't be so enthralled by the way his fitted shirt clung to his body like a second skin and highlighted every curve of muscle and tempted her to trace said muscles. He erased her promise to herself of loyalty to Jes with his chivalry and generosity.

Oh, and the magic he'd performed to calm her down. Whether he understood how much she needed it or not, she was thankful for his selfless offering and grateful for the emotional escape from the last couple of days, even if the root of some of her anxiety was because of him. His presence created so many internal conflictions, but his nearness provided her comfort and security, something she craved when he wasn't around. It wasn't just the intense desires, but the sensation of wholeness she'd never been given a chance to experience. Completion. Emery somehow filled every gap and break within her fractured self and made her strong and solid.

Which was absurd, since he didn't belong to her.

Stop fooling yourself. Nothing you've done has made this situation any easier or better. Everything has only made it worse, and the rebound effect will be excruciating.

Swallowing down that hard truth, she crossed the deck to the railing and leaned her forearms against the wood cap, tucking her hands into her sleeves to stay warm. Even if the cold didn't bother her nearly as much as it did most people, the air tonight presented a needling chill she couldn't quite shake. The only time she realized it didn't cut through to her marrow—when it didn't touch her at all—was when a certain someone hovered close by.

She angled her head until she pinpointed Emery in the kitchen through the windows, moving about as he fixed their teas. The hard cords of muscles along his forearms flexed and smoothed as he worked, drying her mouth and leaving all moisture to pool elsewhere. His dark hair gleamed under the warm kitchen lights while the sharp cuts of his face hosted delicious shades of shadows.

He cast every last ounce of coldness away. Every single time. As she turned back to the lake, she knew the moment he returned to her side, the wintry air would no longer touch her. *He* would shatter the ice and disperse it with his ever-present warmth.

Thoughts wrapped around the enigma of a man, she didn't hear him return until he presented her with a stoneware mug between a set of onyx talons. They weren't long enough to create crescent moons like Gabe's, but extended enough to show off a bit of dragon that transitioned seamlessly back into his fingers. She took the mug between both her hands, warming her palms against the stone while Emery struck the cold from all else. She swore heat radiated from his skin in waves.

"Firestorm dragons are essentially walking, talking furnaces," he supplied, the corner of his mouth quirking into a half-grin. "Before you ask in I'm invading your mind, I don't think you realize you project your thoughts without barriers."

Warmth crept up her neck and spread over her face. "How much have you heard?"

Those sultry, mercurial irises watched her closely as he took a sip of his tea. The rebel waves that escaped their tie at the back of his head teased the hollows of his cheeks as he drank. Gods, she remembered just how silky his hair felt, and the memory of sinking her fingers into it unleashed a rush of wings from the base of her throat to the apex of her thighs.

She recalled so much more than just his hair, and the very thought of their encounter shook her vision and tested her strength to remain standing on weakened legs.

So as not to embarrass herself, she turned back to the lake, rested her elbows on the rail, and held her mug to her lips. The spiced scent of herbs helped to clear her mind as she sipped the hot liquid. To her surprise, he had prepared her drink to perfection. Minimal honey—the distinct flavor of honey over sugar would be one she'd never mistake—and a hint of lemon provided a harmonic flavor that danced over her tongue and lulled calm to the surface.

Seduction.

Nothing about these moments was calm. Everything was a dance with ruthless enticement, making her bow more and more to his seduction.

"Did you buy this cabin when you came to Colorado?" she asked, diverting her focus from the physical effect he had on her to something as mundane as real estate. "You got yourself a pretty nice place."

"Nah. Gabe and I aren't setting down roots. This was one of those rental homes that we found and bartered for with the owners."

"Bartered." Sera snickered as she took another sip of tea. "Why do I get the feeling there's more to that term when it comes to dragons?"

"Because dragons don't barter like normal humans?" Emery mimicked her position, only he was far more relaxed, holding his mug with one hand and draping his arm over the railing. "I provided a nice bonus for the month. Deal was that the owners left us to our own devices for the duration of our stay. In turn, they made out very well, monetarily."

As much as she wanted to look at him, she kept her gaze

out on the lake. Barely. "Are you sure you haven't confused barter with bribe?"

"Now, now, darling. I have a little experience with the two. I assure you, there was nothing to bribe. To be frank, I don't think we'll occupy this place past a week."

Why did that make her stomach roll with the prospect of saying goodbye? The anticipation of separation crept up and dealt an irrational blow she hadn't expected. As much as she tried to do everything to keep him away, she didn't want him to truly leave.

"Plan's to return to The Hollow as soon as possible. Gabe and I've already started talks with Slade and the others to begin preparations."

"The Hollow. Your home. Another realm from this, yes?"

"Not just *my* home. It's *our* home. Yours as much as mine. A world for Firestorms and Keepers, and the civilians that belong within the protected confines of the veil. Far away from the chaos of the mortal realm. It's a world that exists of magic and has for as long as it's existed."

"Uncle Slade used to tell Jes and I stories about The Hollow, and how beautiful it was. The world provided magic and protection. He used to try and draw pictures for us to visualize a world he pulled from memories." Sera's lips turned up as her mind wandered to those sweet images of her and Jes sitting at Uncle Slade's kitchen table as he penciled sketches of mountains and forests, fields and lakes. Her fingertips curled against the mug, nostalgia lending bittersweet warmth to her cheeks. "I remember daydreaming of the time when I would finally see it for myself. My father never divulged much to me, but my imagination took flight when Uncle Slade shared stories about how things were in the dragon world. Food was all homegrown and raised, or fresh from a hunt. Civilians specialized in all manner of trade to create a world that needed for nothing from the human realm. I imagined the day Rayze would return..." She shrugged as her face burned under the sharp scrutiny of Emery's sudden attention. "Jes and I spent many of our younger years imagining our futures with dragons."

"Women and their fantasies. Always so *fascinating*."

"I'm sure you've had your fair share to know." It was a low blow in response to his sarcasm, she knew. But his snort of disbelief made her smile. "You're a dragon, after all. Practically immortal, which makes me wonder—how old are you?"

It was a weak attempt to turn this ship into other seas before she got caught up in the brewing storm of grief over lost childhood dreams.

His chuckle stroked along her spine and stirred that sweet sensation humming through her belly. Every bit of effort went into keeping steady on her feet and not shifting to alleviate the growing ache between her legs.

"Are you trying to come up with a rational excuse to run away?"

"I figured it would be a good thing to get to know you." She lowered her mug and shot him a quick look. "You know, for Jes's sake."

"Mm." Why did that small sound hold such dissatisfaction. "Seraphina, I enjoy messing around and keeping things light, for the most part. However, there are times when my age does catch up to me, and there are certain things I no longer find appealing. With that said, I'm two-hundred and fifty-seven. My brother is younger than me by a few years, making him the youngest surviving Firestorm dragon. Cade, our leader, is the oldest, nearing a millennia, if not more." His body tilted toward her, but he remained forward facing, his attention on the lake. "Ask your questions for yourself. Don't hide behind your friend to mask your curiosity. I know the root of your inquiry and it's *not* for Jes."

He sipped his tea once more before he shifted his focus to her, bracing over his now folded arms on the railing. The intensity of his gaze struck her speechless. Her hands trembled, spilling some of her tea over the lip of the mug, but he didn't seem to notice.

"You entertain me," Sera finally said. When one brow slowly lifted over his eye, she scoffed and shook her head. "Jes said you're a perfect gentleman, keeping chivalry alive with mannerisms and humor. I watch how you are with her, and she deserves the happiness you provide."

She swore his lips began to peel back into a scowl, but the motion was so quick, she doubted herself.

"Is that what you think?" The cuts of his face sharpened for a brief moment. His face twisted in frustration before flattening as his gaze pinned her ruthlessly. "Tell me, Sera. When you see me with your friend, what do you *truly* see?"

"I'm not sure I understand."

"Don't understand or don't want to answer?"

He angled his body to her, setting his mug on one of the small deck tables closest to them. He'd shifted closer and would have crowded her had he been any other man, but he was Emery LaRouche, the dragon-man who stirred her innermost hunger to life and called to her soul with compelling ferocity.

"Not sure? How about this." He took a step toward her, into her, forcing her to back up even if her soul screamed for her to hold steady and not let him overcome her space. Overcome *her*. "You know what I see when I watch *you*? I see a woman struggling in a battle that she will not win, and she knows it. I see a woman who hurts exponentially for the sake of a friend when, in the end, her friend would not endure the suffering if their roles were reversed. I see a woman so distraught and brutalized by her own conscience that in two days of first meeting her, brimming with fire and life and independence, she is nothing but a shell of herself. And what's more than observing this?" Emery pressed two fingers to his temple, eyes narrowing as if the motion pained him. "I experience it when the barriers she tries so hard to erect around her mind fracture and fail." His fingers lowered to his chest, over his heart. Sera's own heart twisted as the unabashed truth of his words sank in. "I *feel* it as much as I'm sure she's experienced these same reflections from me." His eyes shadowed and his expression tightened. "Most certainly this evening after her *win*."

Sera opened her mouth to say something, anything, but her words tripped on her tongue. Never in her life had a man dumbfounded her as much as he. Never before would she have allowed someone to get the upper hand in a situation that put her dignity in jeopardy. And yet, here she was, speechless, allowing this man to cage her against one of the posts after plucking her mug from her hands and leaving it on the railing.

Bracing one hand beside her head, he leaned in close. He posed no threat, unless she counted how easily he crushed her resolve. The way he hovered over her, encompassed her not so unlike the way he had in the forest, left her reeling for ground to stand on. A way to keep her mind her own and not at the mercy of the inferno spreading from her very core to every limb, nerve and cell.

"What I'm finding *troublesome*, Seraphina, is this game I've been playing to appease you and your misguided idea that what you feel for me is going to disappear if you stay away. It will *not*, and I fancy you know that damn well."

The hand beside her head stretched up, bringing him

closer as he braced against both forearms, his hands tenting above her head against the post. His feverish breath caressed her lips, sending a low-grade tingle along her skin. She pressed her back as hard as she could into the post—fighting the natural pull to arch into him—but he surrounded her, filled her with every essence of himself. His scent poured through her, wove into the fabric of her being, deconstructing the old version of herself while building up a new woman in its stead. A woman who would never be the old Sera without this man to keep her whole.

The heat of his leg as he rested his knee against the post burned through her pants, further caging her in his seductive embrace. One without physical connection that did far more damage to her resolve through this tenuous dance.

His eyes flashed before molten fire consumed the warm whiskey color. That fire felt like it burned straight down her body, squeezing a gasp from her throat that she tried to capture by biting her lower lip. His gaze dropped, the potent heat directed on her mouth until she swore she could feel his kiss as she had a few nights ago.

Gods help her, she wanted him again. More than she had that night.

"You've had me walking a fucking tightrope, Seraphina, and I don't walk ropes of any kind. I fly *over* them. The only thing that keeps me going is seeing you on the platform at the end. Hoping that when I reach that platform, you'll pull me out of this fucking circus performance and finally *accept* me. Accept *us*."

"It's not right. It's not supposed to be like this," she whispered. "I don't understand this."

"Oh, flame." He tilted his head slightly, nostrils flared and lips parted a hairsbreadth as he inhaled deeply. *"But you do."*

He hovered close. So utterly close and yet still so far

away. Mere inches, at most, stood between them, perhaps centimeters at their closest proximity. His nearness cloaked her, caressed her, teased her without physical connection. Her skin flushed. Something buried deep inside her pulsed and glowed, imagining his touch, his kiss, his claim on her body. It cinched her chest, trying to contain a heart that beat wildly and unhindered by the complexities of her situation, treasuring what only a heart could understand.

Does it hurt you as much as me?

"You're holding your breath."

"I'm savoring the scent of your sweet arousal that you'd deny to my face otherwise."

Oh, Gods, he did not *just say that.*

His molten eyes flared as his slitted pupils widened.

"Does the truth bother you, Sera? Do you prefer lies to coddle your conscience?" The way he burned his gaze into her reached the deepest parts of her soul, even if his words held a tinge of condescension. He melted her from the inside out. Caused her heart to malfunction and her lungs to spasm in the best possible ways. Made her wet between her legs to the point she'd need to change her panties when she got out of this mess. Her hips craved to tip, connect with his, discover if he was just as turned on.

She should hate him for mocking her. But it wasn't mockery. Emery spoke an unfiltered truth she struggled to accept.

He leaned closer, if that was even possible, and still managed to keep their bodies from touching. His head dipped, his gaze not breaking from hers until the only way she could maintain it was to follow his movement, which would surely bring them skin to skin. Instead, she closed her eyes, every muscle stiff with anticipation, her mind hyper-focused on one thing, one person, as his feverish hot breath danced over her earlobe, tickled the sensitive area beneath her ear, caused the rebel strands of hair to tease her frenzied nerves along her skin.

"While we're *entertaining* each other, it's your turn to humor me."

Gods, it was not fair for him to possess a voice that defined liquid sex. A voice she experienced pouring over her skin and filling her mouth with the essence of pleasure. It threatened to draw a moan from her throat as her fingers fisted tighter against her palms. A low, gravelly orchestra of sounds that hummed through the foundational fibers of her soul, played the taut nerves between her legs, and threatened to bring her to her knees. She gasped, a slight sound right before she clamped her teeth down on her lower lip again. She swore she felt the air shift as his lips curled into a smug grin.

This challenge would shred her to pieces.

"I'm willing to bet you're as wet for me as I am hard for you. As wet as I make you every day you insist on playing this self-righteous game when the ending is predestined. The longer it goes on, the more you'll fray until you lose complete and utter control." A shiver of raw pleasure rippled down to her toes. A fierce throb pulsed from her clit straight through her lower belly. His voice rasped on those last few words, their truth like teeth teasing down her spine. Forbidden foreplay, and he had yet to *touch* her. "You know what this is, Sera, and you know there is no changing the will of the Goddess."

Against the last standing brick of her resolve, she tipped her head. It was enough to brush her cheek against his, feather light, but the shock of the contact unleashed a trail of explosives throughout her nerves. She needed no confirmation where his mouth rested in proximity to hers. The corner of her lips tingled being so close to his. She could practically taste his mouth again, and it took every ounce of willpower she had left not to turn just a little bit more.

"But of course"—slowly, he straightened up, the separation indescribably painful, drawing a quiet hiss from her lips. He may as well have skinned her alive—"it seems you'd prefer to put wasted efforts into a man who sees you as a challenge and a trophy, sharing meaningless kisses and caresses to prolong your self-imposed suffering for us both."

The wintry air slammed into her full force when Emery took a long step back, his eyes having returned to their fluid whiskey despite his hardened expression. She blinked several times, her whiplashed mind trying to make sense of what had happened in the last few seconds. One moment, he melted her with his erotic claims and unspoken promises. The next, he backed away from her like she'd contaminate him with some devastating disease. The crushing pressure inside her chest made it difficult to breathe.

It wasn't until he turned back to the house that anger prickled along her skin and a wave of frustration crashed down on her.

"Fuck you, Emery." She lunged after him. "For a dragon, you're blind as a fucking mole! *I* didn't kiss *him*. *He* kissed *me*!" She grabbed his arm, fingers biting into his hard biceps, but he didn't slow, pulling her along. "It caught me by complete surprise, but I didn't instigate it. What difference does it make, anyhow? I'm sure you've had your mouth all over my best friend's—"

"Enough," he growled inside her head in the same second he whipped around, grabbed her face and crushed his mouth over hers. She grappled for his arms, finding purchase against his forearms as the strangest sensation slid along her palms and disappeared. The initial shock of his advance melted away as he consumed her mouth, mind, soul with his starved

kiss. He claimed her with each sweep of his tongue, the soft rumble of a possessive growl resonating through her bones.

This.

This was what she craved. This was what she needed.

Emery ended the kiss as suddenly as he'd initiated it. His eyes glowed once more, the fire a mere thin frame of color around yawning pupils. His lips glistened. Thin ribbons of smoke escaped his flared nostrils as he searched her face for something. His thumbs brushed over her cheeks as she fought for air. How could he feed her life and suffocate her in the same instant? Her own lips burned from the roughness of his kisses, but she wanted more. The taste of him wasn't enough. She needed to explore, learn, understand everything about him, starting with the smoke-and-spice flavor that lingered on her tongue.

"Does that answer your question if it hurts me as much as it does you? This ridiculous fucking game? This *torture*? Lifemates, Seraphina, are not meant to repel each other, and that's what we've been doing. Upon your request, not mine. I go along to oblige *you* and your self-martyring ways. This goes against everything natural"—he brought his forehead to hers and said from between clenched teeth—"and it's *destroying* me inside."

With a strained groan, he stepped back, releasing her face and leaving her to reel in the piercing honesty of his confession while one single word haunted her.

Lifemates.

Yes, it made sense, the intensity of these feelings, but in the same breath, it didn't. Her father's dragon was dead. Rayze should have been her lifemate, had he survived the attack. Not Emery. Not her uncle's dragon. Uncle Slade *had* a daughter, her closest friend.

"That was the last time I'll come to you until you either

accept or reject what is. You're trying to do well by your friend, but she would not return the favor to you. Hollow civilians or not, emotions run rampant in all living creatures, and jealousy affects us no differently than mortals. In fact, it's magnified. Keepers and dragons have been betrayed before by those closest to them over the desire for power. It's the reason we have enemies, Sera. The reason the Baroqueth exist and hunt us down. No matter what, this will cause problems. Problems you're trying to avoid." Emery waved his hand, his face twisted with frustration and hurt and annoyance as he continued to back away. "Between you and Jeslyn. Between me and Slade. Between Slade and Nick. Between *everyone* involved. It's going to shake the foundation you've been standing on for the last twenty-six years, but how you approach it will determine how you land. You're a brilliant woman. You've got fire and independence and strength. Are you willing to face the truth? Or are you going to continue this path of...of..."

His gaze raked over her, from head to toe and back again. When his eyes met hers once more, they'd taken on a sharpness that may as well have speared her heart with ice. Her body jerked from the visceral effect of his piercing glower.

He spun away and stormed into the house, calling back, "I'm bringing you home."

The flip of his temper froze her where she stood, watching the cruelly gorgeous man. He reached for his jacket, gave it a violent shake as burnished red scales rippled over his bare forearms, and tugged it on. Her palms burned at the reminder of the strange smoothness she'd experienced during their kiss, her fingers curling into the fleshy heels of her palms as she released a sharp breath and shook her head.

No.

She wouldn't—*couldn't*—keep this up. If he only knew how much it destroyed her, too.

No.

Shattering her paralysis, she rushed into the house as he yanked his arm through the last sleeve, twisting toward her.

Fool or not, it was her turn to act irrational and desperate. She wrapped both arms around his neck and lifted to her toes, stealing the words from his lips as he opened his mouth in a kiss that matched his previous ferocious hunger. Only this time, she wouldn't end it. She drank in everything he offered. Each pull and push of breath as they battled for control. The heat of his mouth. The rumble of the beast that drew her closer. His fingers dove upward into her hair and fisted, the sharp pinch against her ponytail unleashing a rush of pleasure and a delighted whimper. She lifted higher, climbing up Emery's solid body, gasping when he lifted her with his free hand on her thigh, spun and pressed her back hard to the wall. Oh, sweet Gods, how her body hummed at the feel of his cock pressed firmly right where she wanted him. She locked her ankles around his waist, tightening her arms, hands tangling in his hair as she deepened the kiss. Teeth scraped, moans and growls lost between their desperately seeking tongues and fervent lips.

"There's no going back," he warned, voice breathless in her head as she'd imagine it would be had he spoken those words out loud.

"I don't want to go back."

His hand untangled from her hair, his fingers slipping around her throat and applying a delightful pressure. She whimpered as he drew back enough to break their kiss. Barely.

"You tore the wall down, flame. There's no rebuilding it

and I wouldn't allow you to try if you could. Tell me again you don't want to go back."

Sera struggled to catch her breath, her mind racing, hunger overwhelming her thoughts to the point she tried to kiss him again, only to have his hand about her throat press a little tighter as he leaned back another inch. Her lips separated on a desperate sound, tongue tracing the plump flesh, drawing his feral attention back to her mouth.

"I don't want to go back, Emery. Gods help me, Gods forgive me for betraying my best friend, but I can't keep fighting."

"You've only betrayed yourself, sweetness." He leaned closer, his lips so close her own they tingled. She flicked her tongue in hopes of catching his lip and missed. His eyes darkened, a faint wave of scales flittering over the delicious edges of his cheeks. "This is just the beginning. I'll lead you through these fires ahead and protect you from the blaze. We'll come out stronger, you and I. Forged in flames."

She nodded, not trusting her voice as she fought back the urge to rip his hand off her throat and devour his mouth again. His thumb slid up to her jaw, tilting her head and lengthening the plane of her neck before that sinful mouth slid beneath her ear and nipped the sensitive flesh. Her fingers clenched his hair and a sharp rush of air left her lungs. Her body moved of its own accord, hips rolling tight against the bulge between her legs. Her body was on fire, the nerves taut, coiled, plucked with every strategic nip, lick, kiss of Emery's sinful mouth as he worked his way to the crux of her shoulder.

Without warning, he spun her away from the wall, his mouth on hers again. Each kiss deepened, each stroke possessive and claiming. He held far more control than she cared for, leading her in a restrained dance when all she wanted was to let go. It didn't help the fever building beneath her skin, the relentless throb between her legs, as she burned for a ruthless, consuming union. She tugged at his jacket until he shook it off and tore hers from her arms. He cradled her as she tipped backwards until he laid her on an unyielding surface, caught her wrists and pinned them over her head with one strong hand.

The bastard had to lift his head, rip his kiss away from her, land her back into reality as a breathless, writhing, blistering, wanton mess. She lifted her head off the table, followed his mouth, groaning when he taunted her, keeping just out of reach. His eyes smoldered in a pool of ever-changing colors that matched different hues of lava. Smoke curled up from his nostrils and his kiss-swollen lips.

Sera tightened her legs around his waist, drawing a carnal grin to his wicked mouth.

"You forced my patience to the brink, sweet Seraphina. Don't think I'm going to cave now." His chuckle was sin, a tease of heady temptation that trickled over her skin and caused the aching knot of pleasure in her lower belly to clench. He trailed his fingers over her chin, along her throat, between her breasts, heavy and sensitive to the way her sweater scraped over her hard nipples. She instinctively arched into his touch. Lower still, his gaze following as his light caress tickled her stomach and made her hiss, over the waistline of her leggings, lower, lower...

He wedged his hand between her legs, cupping her in his palm, the heel of his strong hand rubbing deliciously over her clit. The feral growl that resonated from his chest, one that intensified the vibrations already driving her insane, choked a gasp from her throat as she rolled her hips into his working palm.

There was no room for shame in the way he played her

closer and closer toward this pent-up climax she'd deprived herself of since she'd kissed him at the party.

"Goddess, you're *wet*."

"Are you surprised?" she breathed. When she opened her eyes, he was hovering over her, everything about his face predatorial and wild. "And you're hard. As hard for me as I am wet for you."

His lips stretched in a knowing smile as she echoed his taunt, the hint of two fangs extended. The simple fact that she *knew* how those fangs could send her to a different level of arousal had her tipping her head slightly, extending her neck. Gods, if he would only free her hands and let her to torment him in return. He laid her out on display for his hungry gaze to consume, and she loved every second of it.

His hand slid over her center once more, and he dragged his fingers against her clit through her leggings with deliberate pressure that sent her reeling.

"Don't stop." She could barely get the words out. Her throat constricted as she felt the beginning of her climax boil up from the pit of her soul like a cresting storm-capped wave building strength before it crashed. Emery's chuckle filled the space around her head before he scraped those blunt fangs along her neck as he pulled his hand completely away to slide beneath her sweater and find her breast. "No-no-no. Please."

His mouth lifted to her ear, and he whispered, "There's no fun in instant satisfaction. I want to see my flame become an inferno before I make that fire explode."

He licked the shell of her ear, making her shiver and moan while his rough palm shoved her bra upward and he captured her nipple between his fingers. Pinch. Roll. Tug. Each change in pressure and sensation made her legs shake. She would all but melt into the damn table if he kept this leisurely pace.

She didn't doubt the rebound effect now. Two days of stamping down the desire she'd believed misplaced, trying to convince herself this could never be.

All she wanted right now, this instant, was Emery. Every inch of him. Every incredible muscle and cord and hair and growl. She craved to be as close to him as she could physically get, and prayed there was a way to get closer still.

He looked upon her, his satisfied grin having turned to something more primitive and possessive. "You have no idea how I plan to feast on you, laid out on this table like a banquet solely for my enjoyment. Mine, Seraphina. You are mine as much as I'm yours."

His ministrations to her nipple and breast ceased as he pulled his hand from beneath her sweater and brushed the backs of his knuckles over her cheek. Something burned in the embers of his eyes, something deeper and intangible. It curled through her chest and bloomed throughout her soul. The tenderness in his caress, the gentle trace of her brow with the edge of a talon, all infused her with lost control. Her breathing was unsteady at best, her mind a whirlwind of incoherent thoughts as he drew her in with his gaze.

When she realized what he was doing, how he'd let her run until he was ready to pull her back in, a torturous game of foreplay she didn't think she'd withstand in her state, it allowed her to remember just how ill-prepared she was for any sexual activities.

Clearing her throat, heat burning up through her cheeks that had nothing to do with the sensual hum he'd created throughout her nervous system, she gave a small tug on her arms.

"I think we need to take this slow."

Emery blinked. Slow, lazy, seductive as hell. The fire

extinguished. His brow began to furrow as he tilted his head to consider her with confusion.

Sera dropped her legs from his waist. "I should really take a shower."

"A...shower?"

She nodded once, finally breaking their intense gaze. A swell of embarrassment rose, cutting through her previous confidence. "Yeah. You can only bathe yourself so much in an old, tiny pedestal sink."

She felt his gaze move over her, tracing her body inch by inch with his eyes like he had with his skilled fingers. His hand loosened around her wrists, and he pushed off the table, catching the back of her neck and pulling her upright with him. She took in a sharp breath at the surprising motion, catching him by the shoulders as he pressed a lingering kiss to her forehead. Despite the simmering desire that was still thick in the air, this kiss spoke of adoration and protection. With this single kiss, he impressed upon her just how precious she was to him.

"You have to go and tease me so, flame." Emery's hand slipped from the back of her neck to the side of her face, cupping her cheek when he leaned back and looked at her. "Go ahead, if it'll make you feel better. While you're doing that, how about I make us something to eat, since you barely touched your burger tonight?"

Sera reached up and traced his jaw. Solid, angular, the short hairs that created deeper shadows along his cheeks tickling the pads of her fingertips. She caught the locks of rebel waves and tucked them behind his ear, allowing the strands to slide through her fingers like cool silk. Pressing up from her perch on the edge of the table, she caught his bottom lip between hers, lingering for a few seconds, not wanting to break away from these special moments.

"How about you wait until I'm done and I help you make something?"

His lips curled against hers. She was helpless to do anything but mirror his smile.

"Now, now. That can be taken two very different ways, and I rather like my interpretation better than the original, shower or not."

"Then I'd better get my ass in the shower before dinner is served, sans the food."

CHAPTER TWELVE

*A*fter taking her time in Emery's shower and sifting through the small collection of his clothes to find something clean to wear, she headed out of the bedroom. Emery had already started preparing food, which seemed to have taken a back seat to his hyper-focused attention on her as she closed the bedroom door and crossed the living room to join him. The carefree smile he wore melted into something wicked and carnal. His eyes flickered with firelight as shadows deepened the sharp angles of his face.

"What's your ETA?"

Sera's brows furrowed. Her gaze dropped to the counter, and pinpointed Emery's phone beside a produce bag of bell peppers.

"Whenever I've cleared her mind," Emery said, lowering the knife beside the board of half-chopped vegetables. He cleared his throat and shook his head slightly as she pulled back one of the counter stools and settled into the seat. She leaned forward on her forearms, grin stretching, cheeks warming.

"We know how clearing of the head—"

"You're on speaker, brother."

"Good. No need to sugar-coat things. Sera, make sure he earns his time with you. He's had it too easy most of his life."

"Something tells me you've had it easy, too," she responded, earning a wink from her dragon. "Don't worry. I think I've tortured him long enough."

"You've no idea," Gabe grumbled. "I've been dealing with him."

"Go back to distracting. I'll call you when we're leaving." Emery disconnected the call, cutting off his brother's words without a care. He shoved the phone away and braced himself on his arms, mirroring Sera, and flicked a finger up and down. "If I'd known you'd be raiding my meager stores of clothing, I'd have been sure to hide everything and make you walk out naked."

Her face simmered, but her smile grew. "If I'd been unsuccessful finding something in your meager stores, I'd have climbed back into my own dirty clothes and been just fine. Figured you wouldn't mind me borrowing a shirt." She pinched the V-neck collar and let it snap back against her chest. "I'll wash it and return it when I'm done."

He tsked. "I don't take things back from a woman they look better on."

That set her stomach in a knot. A dark, jealous-tinged knot. She leaned closer, pushing the bag of peppers aside with the back of her fingers. "How many women own your clothing now?"

"As many as men who own yours."

Sera stared at him, confused. He chuckled and pushed off his arms, picking up the knife and resuming his preparations. The crease between her brows deepened. When he glanced at her, he paused, one brow lifting.

"Don't tell me I'll be collecting your clothing from a bunch of men over the next day or two."

"I don't leave things behind." When he scowled and started chopping cucumbers with lethal force, she laughed. "Those veggies didn't do anything to earn such punishment."

"It's called a rough chop."

"It's called I got under your skin. I'm not a whore, Emery, but let's face it—neither of us are virgins. I would be delusional to expect you, over two centuries old, to have never been with a woman." The words tasted bitter on her tongue. She couldn't stop the scrunch of her nose or smooth it out before Emery caught the expression. His scowl pulled into a shaded grin. "I don't have to like the idea, but that's reality. At least I'm only twenty-six and haven't had the years to build up a rap sheet that you have."

The blade screeched as it deflected off diamond scales that protected his fingers before he could cut off a digit. With a groan, he dropped the knife, lifted a hand, curled his finger in a motion for her to come closer, then pointed to the empty spot by his side. Sera brought her folded hands up beneath her chin and rested it on her knuckles, brows lifting.

"Come here." As playful as his grin appeared, she sensed the predator slinking beneath the surface. The hunger of a beast waiting for the right second to strike. The flickering flames in his eyes hadn't grown to full-blown fire, but she'd become utterly familiar with their meaning, especially as they smoldered more the longer he stared at her. "Or are you reconsidering your words from earlier? Reconsidering everything while sitting in my shirt with nothing on beneath it?"

If her body could heat any more, she'd melt right off the seat. It wouldn't take a genius to conclude she wore no bra, but how he knew she wore nothing…

She pressed her lips together, trying to swallow against a

faint flutter that built at the back of her throat. Her heart did a funny dance in her chest, locking up her lungs.

"I dare you, little flame. Come a little closer." His finger flicked to the empty space again. "You *did* say you wanted to help cook."

"And if I'm no longer hungry?"

But her body had already begun to move, sliding off the stool. Emery's feral gaze followed her as she rounded the counter and stopped just out of reach. His attention hung on her face, his silence weighted with unspent energy. Slowly, he burned his gaze along every inch of her, shamelessly feasting on her form as her legs weakened and her head became light.

Like a serpent, he struck, grabbing her around the waist and pulling her flush against him. A small breath fled her lips. When she tried to look away, he caught her chin, holding her steady, eyes burning deep into her soul with promises to do more than torment. Oh, he'd destroy her from the inside out, and she'd love every second of it.

He dipped his head, hovering close to her ear. Her eyelids grew heavy as she listened to the sound of him taking a deep breath, inhaling her scent, a faint rumble deep in his chest reverberating against her sternum.

"I'm a dragon, love. I don't leave things for others unless for good reason. What's mine stays with me." His lips teased the edges of her ear, his breath a caress that she felt in the pit of her belly, stirring desire alive. His hard cock dug into her hip, and it took more effort than she cared to keep from jumping into his arms and locking her ankles around his waist again, just to feel him between her legs. The hand he'd had on the small of her back crested the top of her ass. His fingers pressed firmly against the globe of her flesh. She sucked in a sharp breath when a blunt fang scraped her earlobe. Gods, she wasn't going to make it to dinner. "Mine, flame. And in turn, what's mine is yours."

She hadn't realized she'd grabbed his waist until he lifted his head away and leaned back enough to look down at her. The thermal material fisted in her hands, against the hard muscles of his obliques. She swayed on her feet. He turned her into a sack of mush held together by weakened bones, tendons, and skin. She didn't care how pathetic she appeared. She'd fought this long enough. Fought Emery.

His thumb brushed across her cheek, a tender gesture, considering the primitive edge of his expression. "Why don't you show me the proper way to cut cucumbers, since apparently my technique isn't up to your standards."

A strangled sound escaped her, and she dropped her forehead against his shoulder, soaking in the soothing scent she'd become all too familiar with. His chest moved with a quiet laugh, his fingers sinking into her damp hair and holding her tight. Shameless as she'd become, she released his shirt and slipped her hands beneath the fabric, wrapping her arms around his waist, splaying her hands over the hard contours of his back, relishing the smooth heat of his skin.

"You're torture."

"I'm only what trials I've been through."

Torture we've both endured.

Seconds ticked by, and she couldn't bring herself to move. Instead, she basked in the gentle rise and fall of his chest with each breath, the strong beat of his heart beneath her ear, the possessive yet tender way he held her in his arms. Gods, why had she fought this? Why had she put them both through the agony of separation when this was the very thing she wanted most?

With a sigh, she finally gained enough strength to peel away from the comfort of his embrace and turn her face up to him with a faint smile. "You really want a lesson in how to handle a cucumber?"

Emery's wicked smile returned, and she earned a playful pinch of her chin. "Entertain me, sweet Seraphina."

"Oh, I'm sure it'll be entertaining," she murmured, twisting in the tight confines of his body and the counter. Taking up the knife and positioning the remaining cucumber, she began cutting. "But not the entertainment you're hoping for. While I'm demonstrating how *not* to mutilate innocent vegetables during food preparation, tell me about you. The Hollow. The dragons. I know I'm fortunate to have been told the truth of who I am, but I'd like to hear more about everything from you."

"Pretty easy, actually. The Hollow you'll see soon enough. Us dragons are a notorious bunch. Me, well, what you see is what you get."

Sera paused and cast an exasperated look over her shoulder. Emery reached around her, snatched a cucumber slice, and snapped a bite off with his front teeth. He leaned back against the counter and held the remainder of the slice to her lips. She took it from his fingers with her teeth, earning his heated gaze on her mouth.

"The Hollow is magic. Spirits, Gods, the Goddess. They provide for the world and feed it life. Our magic is alive when we're home. Other than our dragons' characteristics, we lack power here in this world. You do as well. Gabe's lifemate, Skylar, has been tapping into the world's energy sources and learning to hone her skills with magic. She's been teaching the other lifemates, and they're all picking up on these dormant characteristics they could never access here. The Hollow is complex in that aspect, but it's simple otherwise. None of this technology. None of the pollution or destruction. The village is being rebuilt, but with natural materials given to us by the land. Food is fresh, delicious, and in abundance. Dragons and civilians work together to make our home thrive. We're not segregated from those we protect. We are part of them. Before the attack on The Hollow, only a few dragons ever held their position over the heads of the civilians, but when it came down to it, they sacrificed everything to protect those who couldn't protect themselves."

Emery scooped up the cucumber pieces and dropped them into a bowl that held chopped lettuce and tomatoes. Sera pulled out one of the peppers and rinsed it quickly, then returned to the counter and began cutting it up.

"When you get there, you'll feel the energy in everything. You'll behold sights so beautiful they'll take your breath away. Nothing in this world can compare to what The Hollow has. It overflows with life. Everything is vibrant and stunning. You'll love it."

She hadn't realized her smile had changed until he traced her bottom lip with a single finger. When she looked up at him, the starved beast she'd encountered only minutes ago had been pushed aside by adoration.

"I can't wait to see the look on your face when you first come through the veil and see the world your roots come from. We may not have cars and television and gadgets like here, but the serenity is priceless."

"I appreciate serenity more than material objects."

His fingers curled and drew lightly across her cheek. "I know." After a moment, he nudged her aside, relieved her of the knife, and took over the task of slicing the pepper. "As far as the dragons go, there are only eight of us left. Firestorms are myths within the lore. We are the myths of dragons. Other races exist, and they thrive within their clans and colonies, but we value the seclusion of The Hollow and prefer to keep to our world."

"I would, too, if it's all I've been told it is. Uncle Slade has described it as a dreamlike oasis."

"It is."

"Magic runs deep in the land. He once said there are springs that can heal."

"He's correct. We rely on the spring's water for its healing properties. It helped heal Caryssa's father after he was beaten to Death's doorstep a little over a week ago." When she arched an inquiring brow, he explained, "The incident at the hospital in Washington. Long story short, he was framed for the murder of his wife, spent a decade behind bars, his brother had inmates watching him, and they decided to try to kill him when he contacted his daughter."

She gasped. "You're kidding!"

"I told you, being dragons, Keepers, or Hollow civilians doesn't make us infallible. At times, it creates more jealousy and tension than not. A lot comes with being the Keeper to a dragon. Station, power, privilege, security. Most of us keep low-key rather than flaunting our advantages, but not everyone. Caryssa's uncle was the eldest and should have been next in line to be Keeper, but Tajan's dragonstone rejected him and chose Dorian instead."

"Ouch."

"There's little we have control over when it comes to who the Goddess chooses for us, but we all trust in her judgment. Trust that we are graced with those who will help us grow as dragons and men, and allow us to protect the people who depend on us."

He put the knife down and turned to face her. "Whether or not you believe this, I know deep in my soul that we are a perfect balance, and therefore, a perfect match. The dragon inside me recognized you that night in the forest, and wanted nothing more than to keep you by my side. It's driven me insane holding my tongue and playing the game until you came around to accepting this. I don't have answers as to why you and not Jeslyn but"—he cupped the side of her face, keeping her head from dropping to avoid his gaze—"I would never ask for anyone else."

"You barely know me."

"I know you more than you think I do. Sometimes, Sera, it's not about the trivial things. What color is your favorite. What season you prefer. Those are learned things over time, yes. But sometimes familiarity goes deeper. Soul deep. Recognition is woven into the fabric of our souls, grows within our hearts, and creates the bond that tethers us together. The intuition to make a cup of tea without asking how you like it. The understanding of why one chooses to suffer in silence for the sake of a friend, even if I hated every second of it. When you finally open yourself up to everything this bond offers, you'll understand you don't need to hear things to learn your mate. Your soul already knows me. There will never be anything more intimate than the bond between a dragon and his lifemate. A dragon will gladly surrender himself to a finite life as long as he knows his woman will be by his side."

Sera covered his hand with hers, lost in the soft glow of his eyes as he spoke words that filled her with warmth and consumed her heart. He was right. She might not know his favorite color—though, judging by the closet of clothes, she'd bet his was black—or know some of his preferences, but if she were to guess, she believed she'd guess correctly. The answers to Emery lay within her own mind, her heart, and the throbbing golden bond.

"You give up immortality when your lifemate bleeds into your dragonstone."

Emery nodded. "But my life would be meaningless if you

weren't in it. Now that I've found you, convinced you to stop resisting me, I never want to live a day without you."

"You seem far more sentimental than your brother."

Emery blinked once, then laughed, lowering his hand from her cheek. "Gabe thrives off being rough and tough. I prefer the laidback approach to life. Sky is a perfect balance for him, too. She can parry him in a match that'll make you wonder who the better fighter is." He wagged a finger. "Sky's really good, but my brother will always best her. He's a dragon. He has a bit of an advantage, not to mention he taught Sky's father the fighting skills Terrence taught her."

"She's a fighter and a magician." Sera nodded with a thoughtful purse of her lips. "I like her already. Think she'd teach me a few things?"

"I'm sure she'd be more than happy to teach you anything you'd like to learn, especially if she could bear witness to you knocking me flat on my ass." He stepped into her, trapping her against the counter. The tip of a talon scraped along her jaw. Her entire body trembled, goosebumps rising over her arms. Her core gave a pulse as a powerful ache built between her legs. That pointed nail trailed down the front of her throat until it hooked on the V of the collar. "I may let you win just to see you on top of me. Or I may not. But despite all fun and games, we *will* spill blood ruthlessly to protect our women, and our people."

The hiss of fabric ripping at the V emphasized his words, and his intentions. His claw tore down the shirt with little resistance, stopping only when he reached the spot between her breasts. Sera licked her lips, drawing his attention to her mouth.

Just when she thought he'd take her mouth with his, he gently turned her around, guided her in front of the cutting board again, and caged her against the counter. "Back to preparations."

Sera pressed her lips together tight, splaying her fingers over the counter. She glanced down at the ruined shirt, the torn flaps exposing her chest, the swells of her breasts, and if she leaned forward a bit more, straight through to her toes. His fingers gathered her hair at her temple, an airy caress against her skin, smoothed behind her ear and draped the damp locks over her shoulder.

"What's wrong, Seraphina? You're trembling."

His mouth against her ear again sent her mind roiling and set her body ablaze. The very tips of his fingers trailed down the side of her throat, tickling her skin. He teased her willpower. Broke down the little resistance she'd managed to piece back together to make it through dinner. Her meager defenses were nothing more than splintered matchsticks against the force of a fire dragon.

His lips brushed against her neck, below her ear. The feverish breaths that spread across her skin sent a delightful tremor through her. He may as well have licked her seam with that small breath, the way her core simmered in response. She squeezed her thighs together, as tightly as her eyelids, her thoughts far from dinner preparations.

He continued to trace the pulsing vein in her neck with his lips. Gentle kisses. Light flicks of his tongue. "No dinner"— he hiked the hem of the shirt up her thigh and slipped his hand against her hip, dipping along the contour toward the very place she wanted those fingers—"no dessert."

"For some reason, I'm no longer hungry."

His head tilted, his teeth capturing her earlobe and giving it a gentle tug. "Pity."

She tipped her chin to try and meet his mouth, but he slid

a hand roughly up between her breasts to catch her by the throat, lifting her head and keeping her away.

"For food," she clarified on a sharp exhale. His deep, rumbling chuckle weakened her at the knees as she whimpered. He nuzzled her nape, stealing erotic nips along each vertebra until he met the collar of the shirt. His fingers held fast at the crease of her hip, hinting at pleasure to be administered later, but promised torture now.

"Emery," she whispered, seeking his hand beneath the shirt. She tried to guide him between her legs, hoped he'd relieve the intense pressure his antics had masterfully created to wreak havoc with her control. Instead, he bit the crux of her shoulder. She hissed, a sinful blend of pain and pleasure shocking her body. She bowed against him, gasping in shallow breaths as his teeth bruised her skin. The hand at her throat continued to hold her steady, relinquishing her freedom. She squeezed his hand, grappled for the edge of the counter, fought for a sense of reality as he finally, finally slipped those wicked fingers between her legs, through the wet folds of her seam. He played her clit mercilessly, pace and pressure maddening. "Gods."

He released her shoulder from his bite. Her throat from his grip. That hand dropped to the tear in the shirt, fisted the destroyed flap.

Tore it wide open.

"*Now* you can say I bite," he growled. The tip of a finger found her entrance, hesitated as she counted her heartbeats. One. Two. Three—

He pressed into her, two fingers knuckle deep. She cried out, folding forward as tremors claimed her beneath the sweep of intense pleasure. His sharp breath feathered her shoulder blades as he tore the remaining scraps of shirt off and licked her from the base of her spine to the nape of her neck.

"Tight." His voice, a few octaves deeper and thick with a hint of danger, poured over her nerves and set her entire being humming. Each thrust of his fingers drove her closer to the release she'd been desperate for since their tryst in the forest. She'd never once been able to cast the arousal aside completely, but now, oh, Gods, now, arousal filled her entirely. "*Wet.*"

"I told you I was wet for you. I've no reason to lie," she breathed, barely able to speak above a whisper.

"I can have you screaming in no time. I know your body without having to explore you. I can sense your climax building."

He cupped her breast and rolled her pebbled nipple between his finger and thumb. She sucked in a breath between clenched teeth, dropping her forehead to her hand on the counter. If only his fingers were something else. If only it was his cock driving her to the moon.

Emery pulled her off the counter. She looped her arms back, finding purchase on his neck, fingers tangling in the ends of his thick hair. His knee hooked beneath hers and spread her wide, filling her with a third finger on his next thorough invasion. Her head dropped against his shoulder, her eyes squeezed shut and forehead creased. She rolled her hips in time with each of his thrusts, riding his fingers, his palm, shameless in his embrace.

Between his fingers playing her nipple and his hand between her legs, her muscles began to tense, coil, build at the tip of the peak—

"Mm," he sighed, his fingers pulling out of her body as he released her nipple, "I've suddenly become hungry."

It took Sera's foggy mind more than a few rapid heartbeats to comprehend what was happening. She blinked her eyes open, staring blankly at the room ahead of her without seeing much beyond a resounding pulse in her vision that matched the hard pulse in her clit. Slowly, her arms released him and fell, weak and heavy, to her sides.

"No. You didn't," she whispered.

"I didn't what, flame?" His voice brimmed with a taunting edge. She found the strength to roll her head against his shoulder and find his eyes, that fiery blaze that watched her with acute keenness. He *knew*, damn him. Knew exactly what he was doing. A dark grin curled the edges of his mouth as he lifted his fingers, glistening with her juice, to his lips. The earthy scent of her arousal teased her nostrils as he licked his fingers. "Mmm, mmm, mmm."

Her breath ceased as his pupils smothered the flames in his eyes. His nostrils flared and a feral shadow coasted across his face. He pulled those fingers from his mouth and pressed them to her lower lip.

"I can't *wait* for dessert." He pressed the tips of his fingers between her lips, along her tongue. The residual flavor of her arousal on his strong fingers left her mind whirling. "Seems you can't, either." He withdrew his fingers, trailing the wet digits down her chin. "Remember, I've become the king of patience these last few days."

Sera stared at the man as he stepped back, a walking, breathing embodiment of sexual prowess. She held fast to the edge of the counter, fighting to bring her breathing and her pulse rate under control before her lungs burst and her heart ripped out of her chest. Her body hurt with the need for release, ached to the point she wanted to relieve herself, but refused to let Emery work her up, only to step away with an animalist smirk. He stripped her of everything, including control. Took the scraps of cloth and shed them to the floor around her feet. She stood before his starved gaze, naked, exposed, and yet the idea that she was the one who drove that hunger in his eyes, that she brought the fierce beast to the surface in the faint rippling of scales and fire in his piercing gaze, empowered her.

"Even the strongest of kings fall."

Sera twisted, grabbed his shirt by the shoulders and shoved him back until he slammed into the fridge. She didn't give him time to recover from the surprise before bunching his shirt and pushing it up his body until he leaned forward for her to rip it from his body and toss it aside.

For a long moment, she admired the man beneath the clothes. The fine-honed muscles that made up a rippled stomach, deep-cut pecs, and broad shoulders. She traced the intricate dragon tattoo that draped over his shoulder and curled around his left arm, the colors utterly similar to the scales coasting across his skin. The fiery pupil and the vertical slit. An impression of the Firestorm dragon living within Emery.

"Beautiful," she said quietly, tracing the highly detailed maw.

"Just the art?" His hands came down on her hips. "Because I find *everything* about the sight before me breathtaking."

In response to his question, Sera leaned forward and pressed her lips to his left pec, above his dark nipple. She opened her mouth slightly, inhaling the campfire and wilderness scent of his skin through her nostrils while tasting it across her tongue. Slowly, she bridged a series of kisses and licks to his other pec, then trekked upward, to his shoulder, his neck, soaking in the way his fingers tightened on her waist. How his heart sped up in his chest.

"You, dragon. You are beautiful."

Her fingers trailed down his abs and hooked on his belt.

Her thumbs faintly shaped the bulge in his jeans before she unfastened his belt, the button and zipper on his jeans, and tugged the denim down. His cock sprang forth from the suffocating confines, a thick, large delight she immediately took in her hands. The wide crown glistened with arousal she slid her thumb through, spreading it over the smooth skin.

A low-pitched rumble began in Emery's chest as she played with his cock, exploring the velvety skin and the veins molded down his long shaft. Gods, he was a masterpiece, from head to toe, and everything in between.

"Keep that up, flame. I'll bend you over the table and claim you. Very improperly."

"Seems you're proper in public." She snickered, lifting her gaze to the embers brushing his eyes and burning into her soul. "But a wicked beast behind closed doors."

"Wicked." He chuckled and looked away. Without warning, he shackled her wrists and yanked her hands from his cock, folding her arms behind her and crushing her flush against him. When he caught her gaze again, it shattered her mind and melted her bones. "I'll show you just how *wicked* I can be, love."

CHAPTER THIRTEEN

Nothing about this night had turned out the way he'd planned. Nothing, and he was as fucking grateful as a boy who'd started to build his very own hoard.

Except…

Emery sank his fingers into the thick, damp locks of Sera's hair, pulled her up to him, and crushed his mouth to hers. She would be his everlasting fountain, an ever-flowing means of life. He'd broken the walls around her, destroyed the fortress she'd erected, desecrated the last obstacle to bring them here. To this very moment.

To her, naked in his arms, her soft skin pressed to his. The taste of her arousal on his tongue. The scent of her skin and her body as she reacted to him filling his lungs. The hunger behind each desperate sweep of her tongue as she tried to overcome his control in their shared kiss. The hard swells of her nipples pressed to his chest, teasing his dragon. He wanted to suck those small pearls into his mouth, nip and tug at them with his teeth and watch her writhe beneath him, because he knew her breasts were especially erogenous for her.

He wanted to make her squirm.

Scream.

Explode.

He'd hoped to claim her in his bed, in The Hollow. But tonight brought a different story, a different path, and he wasn't going to let her go without making her his. Not after she'd taunted him with those soft hands, played with a cock that had suffered days and nights of endless agony his own fist couldn't relieve. Not after she'd haunted his mind, tortured his soul for just as long.

Not as she arched her lithe body into his, shameless.

His fingers curled against her scalp, fisted in her hair. Her kiss stalled on a gasp, and he took advantage of the moment to seize her lower lip between his teeth and tug. He pushed away from the fridge and hoisted her over his shoulder, shoving the jeans off his legs and leaving them on the kitchen floor.

"Emery!"

"As tempting as the table sounded"—he rounded the counter, the dining room table, and nuzzled his nose against her hip as he crossed the living room—"I can do so much more to you in the bed."

She tried to push up against his lower back. A quick glance over his shoulder brought a chuckle to his throat. Oh, Goddess, the mask of desire that smoothed over her beautiful face, those gray eyes trading the wary edge for a soft hue of lust instead. The red of her lips from the brash kiss and his possessive nip. The long cape of jet hair that poured over her shoulder, exposing the fine lines of delicate muscle along her back.

He switched the arms that looped around her legs and slid his fingers between her legs, seeking and finding the wetness he craved in his mouth. She slackened over his shoulder as he stroked her clit, but his little nymph had her own plan that nearly caused him to stumble into the bedroom door. Her fingers closed tightly around his cock and began to stroke him, from the base to his tip.

"Two can play dirty, your majesty."

Fuck him, because he wanted to play with her until she begged for release. He wanted to feast on her body, taste her before she came, learn every tiny sound that she made leading up to her shattering. He wanted to torture her in the most pleasurable ways.

He kicked the door open—to hell with closing it—and ate up the distance to the bed. He hoisted her off his shoulder, catching her back in his arm to lower her to the mattress carefully. She scrambled backwards, cheeks flushed, those dark, damp waves of hair obstructing his view of her perfect breasts. He climbed onto the mattress after her, grabbing her ankle only when she was centered on the bed, and yanked her beneath him. He caught her wrists and pinned them to the mattress on either side of her head, and stared down at her, reeling back the desire to ravage his woman. The dragon craved her on every level, every aspect, craved the taste of her skin, her arousal, her mouth. He stood at the brink of losing control to his primitive nature.

He enjoyed life, living it with ease. The bedroom was a different story, as the red and welted mark on her shoulder proved.

And he wasn't one bit sorry for it.

Her mind glowed, their bond thrumming with energy. She gazed up at him, eyes heavy lidded, with not a glint of fear or apprehension.

"I can sense your hunger. Feel your desire. You're burning up and need only a breath of air to lose control." His fucking cock responded with an achy jerk, and a dribble of precum dripped onto her belly. She smirked, strained against his grip to lift her head from the bed, and whispered, "You're about to lose it, aren't you, dragon?"

The corner of his mouth twitched. "You don't want me to lose it, siren."

His nostrils flared as he scented her heady aroma. Dropping his head, he adjusted himself between her legs, releasing her wrists only when he couldn't hold her any longer. He relinquished control of her hands for the heaven between her legs, spreading her thighs and taking his first drink from her wet center.

Damn if his cock didn't harden further when she cried out, knees drawing up, hands fisting in his hair. He feasted heartily, groaning as her arousal filled his mouth, the possessive beast inside him bursting with pride. *This* was what he did to Sera. The breathy whimpers when he clamped down on her clit and sucked gently, drawing her closer and closer to climax.

"Emery, Emery—oh, Gods!"

"Don't worry, my sweet." At the first sign she was about to crest, he turned his face away and trailed kisses and nips on her inner thigh. *"I won't let you come yet."*

A flood of disbelief hit him in the chest. Sera's disbelief, which she launched through their bond. He laughed quietly against her leg, laughed harder when she released a muffled shriek.

"You Godsforsaken beast of a fucking—"

He spread himself over her body and caught the last of her words in a deep, penetrating kiss that stole her breath and melted her beneath him. Her arms snaked around him, shaky but strong. He hooked her leg around his waist, teasing her slick folds with his cock, sliding back and forth until he swore he'd pour himself over the blanket before he experienced the heat of her body around him.

"Please, please, please. It's too much. Too much."

"I've barely done a thing."

As he lifted away from her delicious mouth, she traced his brow with the tips of her fingers.

"You've done more than you'll ever know, Emery. You've ruined me without claiming me. I'm not as patient as you, nor as strong."

"I beg to differ, my bright, burning flame." He fit the tip of his cock at her entrance. The way she bit down on her lower lip. The way her pupils consumed the soft gray of her eyes. He brushed aside a rebel wave that caught at the corner of her mouth and traced the delicate angle of her jaw. "You are one of the strongest people I know, to endure these last few days alone and still have the willpower to resist me."

"Right now, I want you to make me yours."

Emery fulfilled her request with one slow thrust. She gasped, her nails digging into his shoulders, hips rolling to meet his as he stretched her, filled her, claimed her at last. He shifted between her legs, gathered one of her hands, and folded his fingers between hers as he pinned it to the bed.

"Seraphina, you were mine in the forest."

He drew out to his crown and pushed back in, loving the moan that fled her swollen lips. Her legs locked around his waist as he quickened his pace, driving into her, watching the pleasure ripple across her face, darken her cheeks to rose, make her writhe against the mattress beneath him.

He dipped his head and lavished her neck with kisses.

"The same night you claimed me as yours."

His lovely flame grew tense, the grip of her fingers tightening between his, her arm clinging to his shoulders as those short nails bit into his skin and broke his flesh. Her legs squeezed his waist, guiding his pistoning hips, providing leverage as she lifted to meet each thrust, bringing him deeper into the heat of her body. Deep, so deep, so tight, so…so…

He tipped his hips and drove into her, time and time again, until the rapid beat of her heart and the choked breaths from her lungs were all he could hear.

She arched off the bed, her beautiful face taut, brow creased, and screamed. "Emery!"

The silken heat of her body clenched down on his cock, wave after wave of delightful orgasm milking him until he could hold back no more, and roared his release right behind her. She shattered along their bond and pulverized him in tandem, until he was nothing more than the raw, untainted essence of pleasure in the arms of his lifemate.

He dropped beside Sera, gathered her up with heavy arms, her smaller frame beset with tremors as her shallow breaths caressed his chest. They lay together, a tangle of arms and legs, wild hearts and recovering breaths. He traced his fingers along her spine, up and down, the dampness of her skin warm despite the cool air of the room. She played her fingers over his shoulder, tracing the dragon tattoo despite how her hand shook.

"I don't ever want to leave," she whispered as her breaths slowed. She lifted her head against his arm and caught his gaze. He cupped the side of her face and stroked her soft cheek with his thumb. "No more fighting."

"If that's what it takes for you to stop fighting, then wage a war every morning as the sun rises and I'll deliver you to the heavens every night as it sets." He mirrored the content grin that crossed her mouth. A mouth he stole in a chaste kiss on the lips, followed by a kiss to her forehead. "There's no going back, remember? Not that I'd let you now."

"Don't ever let me go."

Emery wrapped her in a tight embrace and took a deep breath. "You're mine, Seraphina Allaze. Us dragons don't know how to let our women go. You've nothing to worry about there."

"Good." She lifted her leg higher on his hip to dangle over him as she returned the strength in his embrace. "I still can't believe this is real."

"You, my dear, have a pretty enviable sense of loyalty and an infuriatingly stubborn flare." He lifted her chin until he peered down into her soulful eyes again. His smile faded, his heart surrendering to the woman beside him. "It's been real all along. You've only finally decided to embrace us at last."

CHAPTER FOURTEEN

"Ready?"

Sera hadn't realized her fingers had tied into tight knots until Emery lay his hand over hers, drawing her attention away from the enormous house that was lit up inside and out. The snow across the property made the house glow brighter, like a blazing beacon in the dead of night. For the first time in her life, the house loomed, intimidating her in its immensity.

She knew what was about to happen, or at least she'd spent the last half-hour forming every worst-case scenario in her head. Breaking her best friend's heart had never been her intention, but killing herself slowly wasn't, either. Betrayal would be inevitable. Emery said the only person she had betrayed was herself, until tonight. He didn't understand how this would affect Jes. She could only hope that, over time, Jes would learn to forgive her. Learn to understand.

She felt the familiar warmth and calm Emery sent through their bond suffuse her muscles and relax the tension that had mounted over the thirty-minute drive back to Uncle Slade's house. There was no easy way to do this, but it had to be done.

Licking her dry lips, she settled into the seat and met Emery's warm gaze. The strength he exuded reinforced her worn-down resistance for the first time in a few days. She was finally beginning to feel more herself, more empowered.

"There's no going back, right?"

The corner of his mouth quirked in a sexy half-grin, his gaze lifting past her to the house.

"We can always go back to the cabin for a little while longer." He lowered his attention back to her, his expression shadowed with the true meaning behind his suggestion. Her face flushed beneath his intense eyes. "But we'd be putting off the inevitable. Best to get this out in the open now and we'll figure things out from there." He jutted his chin toward Uncle Slade's house. "Gabe's here, too, if we need reinforcements. Which we won't."

"Two-man army."

Emery chuckled, reaching up to pinch her chin gently between the tips of his talons. He drew her close, meeting her over the wide console, and teased her with a feathery kiss across her lips. His mouth trailed up her cheek until he reached her temple, and there he pressed an endearing kiss.

"I don't need another man to be an army, sweet flame. I'm a dragon who's finally found the source of life in the woman sitting beside me."

"Romantic dragon."

He tilted his head and shrugged nonchalantly. "Guess I can be."

"When not spitting flames."

"You've not seen me spit flames. And"—he dragged his thumb across her bottom lip—"for the record, I don't spit flames. I breathe an inferno."

That wicked mouth of his brushed its way to her ear. His teeth scraped her lobe. She shivered with delight, a submissive sigh fleeing her throat.

"That sound, right there. I'll have you singing that sigh again soon enough."

His unforgiving promise caught up in the sexy rumble of his blended man-beast voice quickly sent her blood into a fever. She drew her fingers over his shoulder, trekking down between his pecs as he teased her neck with kisses and nips. Down over his hard abdomen, his belt—

"Flame, careful."

She chuckled, a sound thick with desire as her fingers slid over the hard mound of his cock and rubbed her palm over his hard shaft. His mouth faltered against her skin, a dangerous growl filling the cab.

"You started this."

Emery leaned back enough to catch her eyes, fierce and feral. "Would you like me to finish it? Here?" His lips curled in a sinful grin when he dropped his hand between her legs and stroked her clit through her pants. "I'll be more than happy to oblige, but you may not be willing to walk into that house looking like a pleasured woman."

He stroked her again, her body thirsting for his touch. Somehow, she gathered her control, pulled her hand off his cock, and scowled. "Let's get this done so I can reap the blast from Jes and earn the hate from my uncle after ripping a family apart."

Emery stared at her, the hunger draining into something she would only call puzzlement. She lifted his hand from between her legs, eased him back into his seat, and left the truck. *"I'll go ahead of you."*

"Slade would not hate you."

She snorted under her breath as she hiked up the drive to

the door. She wasn't surprised to find it unlocked and let herself in as she heard the truck door close when Emery left the vehicle. Her stomach tightened as she stepped beneath the exuberant brightness of the chandelier in the domed foyer. Her mouth went dry as her nerves ratcheted up a notch. She listened for a few heartbeats, finally hearing the sound of voices coming from the back of the house. Laughter? Closing her eyes, she opened her mind to try and determine the mood of her friends, but received nothing more than bits and pieces of thoughts while unintelligible conversation passed in the distance.

To her right, Uncle Slade's office doors were pulled closed, a crack between them offering her a distorted view of her uncle moving deeper into the study. Must be working late, although that would come to a halt once Emery reached the house.

Sucking in a reaffirming breath, she followed the voices, the knot in her stomach making her sick. She'd never been one to stand down from confrontation, but she certainly didn't like it any more than the next person. Knowing this particular confrontation would break off the only remaining supports she had in her life created an overwhelming sense of doom.

She'd barely turned the corner of the hallway leading to the kitchen when a resounding bellow echoed through the front of the house. She hadn't even caught sight of the group before she spun around and ran back the way she had come. She burst into the foyer as the hollering continued from behind those ajar pocket doors and bolted straight to Uncle Slade's study. The wild bellow that shook the doors hit her hard in the chest when she realized who the enraged voice belonged to, causing her to pause with her hands on the handles. She hadn't seen her father's car anywhere around the driveway, or saw any indication her father was in the house. He had no reason to come, but the volatile air swirling and thickening around him told another story.

She pushed the doors open.

And froze.

There, across the room, her father rocked on his feet, adrenaline stiffening every muscle in his body. The sight of a revolver aimed straight between Uncle Slade's eyes stilled her heart and snatched her breath.

"All these years, Slade. All. These. Years! *You*!" Her father rocked like an agitated man on the brink of losing control. Completely unhinged. His veins bulged in his reddened neck. Sera didn't doubt that with each second ticking by, an unfavorable resolution drew closer. Her father leaned into her uncle and barked, "Does Claire know? Does she know?!"

Uncle Slade barely spared Sera a glance, but he flicked his hand, which rested calmly at his side. A small motion instructing her, she didn't doubt, to leave. Sera shook her head, her brows pinching deep.

"Leave, Sera. Now." The impression of her uncle's demand, a hollow insinuation of thought he focused directly to her.

How could she? How could she walk away when her own father shook a gun in her uncle's face? The man who had helped her through so much in her life when her father couldn't be bothered?

"Yes. She's knows. She's known from the beginning."

Her father roared, a sound that strangled her while sending her stumbling back a few steps in fear of his wrath. The power of his storm weighed heavy in the room, making the air hard to pull into her lungs while sizzling with unspent energy. He spun around, raking a hand through his hair, playing the gun without awareness, just like his apparent inattention to who else entered the room. The split-second sight of her father's expression chilled her to the marrow. He was a man completely and utterly consumed by rage.

What the hell had happened?

When Nick swung around, he leveled his revolver with frightening accuracy back at Uncle Slade's head. This time, not a single muscle twitched, shook, or wavered his aim. A blanket of dark energy dropped over the room, bringing the hairs on her arms to stand on end.

Oh, my Gods. He's going to shoot.

"Emery!" Sera rushed into the room. "Dad!"

Nick spun, gun steadily held in his outstretched arm.

A streak of black blurred her vision.

A shot rang throughout the office.

Drywall rained down over her head, the dust tickling her throat, causing her to cough as she tried to wave away the cloud while covering her head from falling debris.

"Are you *crazy*?" The sound of a smack echoed in the room, followed closely by the sound of something scraping across the wooden floor.

As the dust cleared, Sera opened her eyes. Gabe had arrived at some point and stood beside his brother. Jes stumbled around the doorframe, coming up short just inside the door, her eyes wide and round as her jaw slackened and her skin paled. Aunt Claire and Silas came to a halt beside Jes, fear exploding in Aunt Claire's expression. She smacked her hands over her mouth. Her eyes brimmed with fresh tears.

When she made to rush to Uncle Slade's side, Emery threw up a hand and impaled his silent command with a burst of flames from his fingertips and a flood of scales over his face that just as soon disappeared. She froze.

This was the lethal dragon she sensed below the surface, always out of sight but never out of reach.

"Seraphina, get out of here. Take them with you."

"No. I'm not leaving."

Emery's mouth twitched, but he didn't look at her. He separated the two Keepers enough for Gabe to slide in and act as an additional barrier between Nick and Emery while Emery protected Slade. Both men's eyes glowed with dragon's fire. So different from the desire-fueled flames she'd come to recognize with Emery. When Emery's lips curled in a scowl, the beginnings of fangs appeared where human eye teeth would be, and smoke rose in curls from the corners of his mouth. He cast a hard glance at Uncle Slade, then back to her father while Gabe remained an unmovable force holding steady where he stood.

"What the fuck is going on here?" Gone was the deep, sultry voice she'd heard over the last couple of hours, replaced by the gravelly growl of a beast.

"Why don't you ask your Keeper? Why don't you ask him about loyalty and betrayal for the whole fucking audience to hear." Nick stalked closer to Uncle Slade, ignoring Gabe until the dragon's hand lashed out and smacked against Nick's chest, forcing a huff of breath from his lungs.

"Back. Up. I won't warn you again," Gabe rumbled.

Nick scoffed, a sound so cold it left a chill along Sera's arms. Her father scowled down at Gabe's hand, but slowly took a step back. Tension hummed in the air, making her heart race and her stomach tilt precariously. Her father stared at the two dragons and Uncle Slade, his burning gaze calculating and precise.

"Em, it's okay," Uncle Slade said, his voice quiet.

The moment he rounded Emery's side, her father attacked, succeeding in landing a fierce right hook to her uncle's face before Gabe kicked his legs out from beneath him. Both men hit the floor, her father on his side, Uncle Slade on one hand and a knee as he cupped the side of his face with his other hand. Aunt Claire screamed. Silas tried to comfort her, holding her as he slowly pulled her out of the room. Sera grabbed Jes's arm when her friend made to run to her father and stopped her from interfering. Her own worry marred her forehead as she shook her head at Jes.

"What happened?" Jes whimpered.

Sera lifted a shaky hand in a confused shrug. "I-I don't know."

Emery had grabbed her father by the collar and lifted him off the floor as Uncle Slade regained his composure and rose to his feet. Blood poured from his nose and lip, but the gleam in his eyes remained sharp. He used a handkerchief he'd pulled from his pocket to dab at the wounds.

Emery cut Sera a sharp look. "Get out of here. All of you. *Now.*"

Sera was about to protest when her father released a maniacal laugh. "Let her stay. It has to do with her, after all."

Ice poured down her body from some unseen fissure in her soul. Her stomach gave a threatening jerk. A faintness began to spread through her chest.

"Nick, I'm warning you—"

"Shut up, Emery! Let your perfect fucking Keeper tell you what he did. Let him tell you why I *don't have my wife!*" Her father jabbed a finger toward Uncle Slade, the creases in his face deepening as the color darkened. His eyes shone with animalist hunger. She'd never seen her father like this. Never. Never thought it possible for the man to lose control to this extent. Gabe cast Uncle Slade a cautious glance. "You're protecting a bastard who fucks another Keeper's wife, sows his seed, and plays his face of friendship all these years!

Plays himself as the savior Keeper, responsible for holding this little community together. The fucking piece of shit who kept his mouth sealed while I suffered twenty-six fucking years because he couldn't keep his dick in his pants!"

Sera blinked. The ground beneath her feet shuddered. Her entire world quaked.

No.

Her head shook in denial. Shook and shook, slow, disbelieving.

Oh, Gods, no.

The air thickened and the periphery of her vision dimmed slightly before returning. Jes turned, her eyes filled with as much confusion as Sera felt. It damn near burned through her skin, her friend's hesitancy. Her friend's slow realization.

She blinked again, her focus on her father fading as she panned to Uncle Slade, dabbing delicately at his nose with his handkerchief. Those sharp eyes held hers, unmoving, unyielding of secrets, but somehow silently implying the very thread of truth behind her father's accusations in his unwavering gaze.

At last, she lifted her attention to Emery, who observed her through narrowed eyes. Eyes that seemed to pick away at a puzzle he'd been trying to figure out that only now revealed the missing pieces. A gaze that flickered with understanding mixed with familiar heat while Sera's mind tried to make sense of what she was hearing. She tried to latch onto the warmth she'd always connected with Emery, the lifeline she so desperately needed right now, but his thoughts were hushed, closed behind gated walls.

Everything is about to change.

The ominous realization teased her anxious consciousness.

He hasn't denied the accusations.

She'd already figured it out.

"You took everything from me, Slade!" Her father's bellowing accusation drew her attention, though now she felt like she was swimming in a slow-motion wave pool that would either deliver her gently to the shore or pull her under. "My dragon's dead. My wife is dead."

Emery's grip slipped on Nick's collar. Her father shook free and took several steps back, looking for an opening to reach Uncle Slade. The dragon parried Nick's every move, maintaining the barrier between the two men. Gabe had abandoned the men for Aunt Claire, Silas, and Jes, ushering them out of the room. Jes broke away and remained, despite Gabe's command to leave. In the fray, Sera barely noticed that Jes had already moved away from her, her expression drawn, confused, closed.

The entire room felt like it was caving in on her, making each breath more difficult to draw than the last. Creating pressure around her chest that slowly spread up to her neck and down to her waist. This had to be a dream. A nightmare. Any moment, she'd wake up on the sofa in her shop, none of this day having happened. Her father would remain estranged, her focus still on building a future to support herself after Emery and Gabe told him Rayze was dead.

The last twenty-four hours never would have happened.

But, that would mean she and Emery...

Any moment, she'd wake up. Any moment...

"Emery, move out of my way," her father said, his voice lethal and low. "Stop defending a coward."

"Over my—"

"Em, it's okay. I deserve every bit of his wrath," Uncle Slade finally said, stepping out from behind Emery. Emery lifted an arm, a last-ditch effort to keep some barrier between him and the enraged man. Uncle Slade lifted his chin, his dark hair mussed and strands hanging over his forehead. Blood splatters stained his white button-down shirt. The skin beneath his eyes had begun to turn purple. Sera's father puffed out his chest, his teeth bared and clenched, his fingers curling and uncurling by his sides. "He's right. There's no reason for me to deny it now. But Nick, you were also to blame. Do you not remember what drove her away?"

"You will *not* turn this around on me! *I* didn't fuck *your* wife!"

A gasp fled Jes, her eyes so round and wide. Sera released a breath, and with it, the strength escaped her legs. She dropped to the floor, too stunned to lower herself with any semblance of grace. Dull pain shot up through her hip, her leg, as the world around her shuddered, darkened.

Gabe was at her side a second later, supporting her as she swayed. "Sera, you should leave. Let them handle this. I'll help you."

"No," she whispered.

"Enough! The both of you! Your daughters are in the room," Emery roared. *"Sera, go with my brother. Please. I'll find you when this is settled."*

Sera met Emery's gaze. Held it. *"It's too late, Emery. The damage is done."*

Gabe's arm around her shoulder tightened, a hand on her biceps, one beneath her hand, an attempt to bring her to her feet. She had no strength to get her legs beneath her, her mind rocking from the discovery. Her father paced like a caged tiger, raking his hands through his hair over and over, pieces flittering from between his fingers as he tore strands from his scalp. His gaze leveled on her, cut to both dragons, Uncle Slade, then he paced again.

In that fraction of a second beneath his wild attention, she saw a man she didn't recognize. A man who had remained detached from her for twenty-six years, dealing with her antics while Uncle Slade supported her in everything she did. Now, it made sense. If everything she had just witnessed and heard was true, it all made crystal clear sense.

Something burned across her eyes. She sought grounding. Understanding. Clarity and assurance while her father started his tirade once more. His words were faded, muffled, her blood rushing too hard and fast through her body to allow her to hear anything of worth.

Slowly, she lifted her gaze away from her father.

And came to the only person in the room who made her body burn and her heart swell. The only person who could fill her with waves of comfort and warmth despite how broken and cold she remained. Despite the conflict, his magic infiltrated her mind enough to give her a little strength as Gabe stood her on her feet.

Forbidden dragon.

Emery's whiskey eyes blazed with frustration as he grabbed her father's shoulder, spun him around, and shoved him toward the open office doors.

"Wait!"

Sera twisted from Gabe's hold, stumbling, nearly pitching forward on her face. Somehow, she caught herself and ran after the two men. She caught up with them in the foyer as her father wrenched his arm from Emery's grasp and stormed from the house. Ignoring Emery's half-hearted attempt to block her, she pushed past him, her attention hooked on her father's retreating figure.

"Dad, wait! What...what just—"

"I am *not* your father, girl!" he bellowed as he spun to face her, those wild eyes chilling her to the marrow. Her breath choked her, spreading with painful iciness along her chest where it lodged like a blade in her heart. He swung his arm to the house, pointing viciously toward the looming structure behind her. "I knew it all along! I knew you weren't mine, but I could never say for certain my gut was right. Never!"

He prowled up to her, his anger palpable, making her skin burn from the hatred and cold he concentrated on her. He stopped a few feet away, his teeth bared in an expression filled with such loathing she recoiled as that burn in her eyes blurred her vision and wetness leaked down her cheeks.

"You have been nothing but a thorn in my side since the day you came into this world. Nothing but the epitome of my bane. You have caused me nothing but strife and pain."

A vein pulsed in his forehead, saliva spraying from between his clenched teeth as he spoke in a low, hateful tone. Each word stabbed the blade deeper into her heart and tore her open more and more with every retrieval. Her head spun, her legs shook, but she couldn't say anything. Her words were lost in her disbelief. In this silent agony and dread.

"I should've known earlier. I should've dug earlier. You are dead to me, girl. *Dead*. Just like the only woman I ever loved."

"Seraphina."

Her heart thundered in her chest and echoed in her head, those words from her single most troublesome dilemma piercing the fog. She never heard Emery until he placed himself between her and her father, a hand on his shoulder to force him away. He reached back at the same time without a glance and gently gripped her trembling hand.

"Stop, Nick. *Now*." Emery lowered his hand from her father's shoulder, but his stance widened, a silent warning to keep away. "Your problem is with Slade, not Sera. Watch your tongue before you say something you regret. She's the innocent party in this."

"Regret?" He laughed, the sound so chilling a shiver wracked her body before she could suppress it, earning her a shaded side-glance from the dragon-man acting as her shield. "*Innocent?*"

"Yes, Nick. Innocent. Whatever happened is your problem with Slade. Not her. Mind your words. Carefully."

If there was ever a threat woven into words, Sera believed she'd just witnessed the power of a curse in that last sentence. Emery's fingers tightened slightly around hers when she stepped out from behind him. He didn't look at her, his eyes burning with live fire as he glowered at her father.

"I don't need to watch my words any longer, because the only things I have left to say are the honest to Goddess truths."

Her father's rage-infused gaze cut to her, his finger jabbing the air a few inches from her face, causing her to flinch and shuffle back. Emery grabbed his hand, tilted his head, and narrowed his eyes, but Nick snapped his hand back and bared his teeth. He rounded Emery, his sights pinned to her. He didn't make it past the dragon's shoulder before Emery caught him by the throat, lifted him to his toes, and leaned into him. Sera heard the gravelly voice of a man overcome by a beast, whose words were indecipherable to the human ear, but resounded loud and clear in her mind.

"And the honest to Goddess truth I leave with you as your last warning, Nick, is this: Whether you like it or not, she's my woman, my lifemate, and I'll be damned if I let you rip her heart to shreds with words you can't take back. Your behavior has done damage enough."

Sera's knees threatened to buckle again. The harder she tried to breathe, the harder it became to pull in a breath. Dear Gods, the world was fading around her and she had nothing to ground her.

Except that Emery shoved her father back, rolled out his shoulders and took two long steps without a glance until he stood beside her, his arm creeping around her waist, fingers tight to keep her from falling. Her face went from hot to cold, her stomach twisted like a web of knots. His solid form fed her strength and support, but the revelations of this evening were simply too much.

Nick glowered at him. "Sure, dragon. Have it your way."

That icy gaze turned on her, his grin melting into a sneer.

"The only woman who held my heart is dead, six feet in the ground and rotted. The one woman who you killed to take your first breath in this world. The creation of another man's fucking betrayal, to whom I relinquish all responsibility of you to."

Sera watched in haunted silence as Nicholas Allaze drilled that last statement into her head before he twisted and disappeared down the sidewalk. A couple minutes later, his old Mustang roared to life from down the road and sped past the house, leaving twin trails of smoke to rise from the pavement where he'd burned out.

Sera stared out at the dark street, unable to put her thoughts together. She smacked a hand to her chest as her lungs opened to allow air into her deprived organs. The sluggish waves of emotions warned of the storm about to hit her, and yet, the chill slithering through her blood, her bones, her muscles, kept them in check.

"Sera."

Instantly, she threw the walls up around her mind. She couldn't. She simply couldn't deal with the effects of Emery in her head, cooing, coaxing, providing the heavy pillar of support she knew she needed as the weight of these last few minutes came crashing down.

This went deeper than a crossing of lifemate lines. This went oh so much deeper.

We're lifemates. True lifemates not *by accident.*

There would be no escaping the tsunami.

There would be no escaping the destruction it would inevitably cause.

She couldn't see through the fog of her pulsing vision. Beyond that empty spot on the street, the fading roar of the engine far in the distance.

"Emery?"

Jes's timid voice cut through her horrified state. Her head turned on a stilted spine until she caught sight of her best friend—*my* half-*sister?*—looping an arm through Emery's while his gaze roved over Sera's face, wracked with concern and an underlying anger. He had not relinquished his hold on her, nor did he seem to want to, despite Jes's gaze lowering to where they were connected. The air thickened more than Sera thought possible. Emery's touch burned her skin, not in a bad way but in a way that fueled every other tingling nerve and desire she'd done so well to push aside until tonight. All for Jes's sake.

Oh, Gods.

Emery's attention was solely for her, not Jeslyn, who hung on him like a wanton woman trying to lure her man away from some tempting treat. A woman to whom Sera had planned to deliver the news of betrayal...

Gods help me, it runs in the family.

Jes tugged at Emery's arm, which ignited both a flare of jealousy and a spark of realization to life. The turmoil had only just begun.

A switch flicked on inside Sera's mind. She twisted from Emery's hold. She needed to leave. Get as far away from here as possible. Escape the madness, the storm pressing down on her shoulders, the guilt, the hunger, the horror of this night. Uncle Slade—her *father*—emerged to stand on the front stoop as she shuffled away with turbulent emotions.

"Sera—"

"No." She flung up a hand to stop Emery from proceeding, her gaze dropping to Jes. Her closest friend hung on Emery's arm, the look she sent Sera one of pure malice. She spun and rushed down the driveway.

"Sera!" Emery called after her, both telepathically and verbally. She shut her mind to everything and everyone, ignoring the sound of boots on the pavement behind her as she picked up speed and sprinted away.

CHAPTER FIFTEEN

"I'll follow," Gabe said, stopping Emery at the end of the driveway. "I'll make sure she's safe until you're through here."

Emery fought back the urge to scowl, but the emptiness in his mind and the agony in his heart cut away any edges and fierceness he might have had. Right now, Sera needed support, and for whatever reason, she'd chosen to run away from him instead of find comfort in him. Gabe's gaze dropped to the side, silently reminding Emery of another woman who *did* seek his company, making her way toward him at a hasty pace after he'd shaken her off to chase after his lifemate.

"I won't be long," Emery promised. Gabe nodded once and hurried off in Sera's footsteps. Emery turned back to the house as Jeslyn caught up with him and reached for his arm. This time, he didn't have Sera's tangled thoughts and the hurricane of emotions ripping through him to distract him from this woman's intention. He brushed past her, keeping his arm from her grip as he headed back up the driveway, his sights anchored on one person. The man who remained on the front stoop. "Jeslyn, I need to speak with my Keeper."

"But Emery, what about us? I'm so confused." She managed to catch his wrist and pull herself closer as he stormed up the drive. He tried to gently pry her fingers away, but she clung hard and fast, her attention shifting between the darkness where Gabe had disappeared after Sera and himself. His blood boiled with frustration as he groaned and looked down at her. To his absolute disgust, she turned a besotted face up to him, wearing a smile that contradicted her claimed confusion. He'd formed an opinion of her from the start, voiced his opinion to Sera earlier this evening, and now witnessed the truth behind it all. The woman he'd entertained on his arm for the last few days while he tried to figure out the puzzle surrounding Sera didn't appear in the least bit worried that her best friend had stormed off into the night, devastated and broken. Not an ounce of sympathy was to be seen. "I-I don't see how this is happening to me. Us. How this is—"

"Jeslyn."

He sent a pointed look at her hands on his wrist, the childish antics to hold him back when *nothing* would be able to hold him back. Even if Sera shut him out completely. He had hit a solid, unyielding wall when he tried to calm her mind. The degree of turmoil in her eyes when she looked up at him before she took off tore him apart. He ground his teeth, smoke seeping out from his nostrils. Deep down, he knew Nick failed to heed his warning. The stabbing pain he felt through Sera was enough for him to know Nick's attack was on her mind. And now...

He freed his arm from Jeslyn's grip and threw up a hand to stop her when she reached for him again. Her expression twisted into something dark and disturbing, all her false distress struck through to reveal unhindered annoyance.

"Em, she'll be fine. Silas will go after her. A few drinks at Jake's and she'll be back to her normal self—"

Emery narrowed his eyes on Jes. "There's no coming back from this, Jeslyn. And your lack of concern for her well-being is rather disheartening. Not something I care to witness." He returned to the house, Jes at his heels, mumbling nonsense. Slade lifted his chin as Emery approached and flicked a talon-curved nail toward the study before he crested the stairs. "*Now.*"

Slade obliged, leading Emery back to the study. He ignored the weighted stares of Claire and the human man at the base of the grand staircase, crossing into the study as Slade started to pull the doors closed. Jeslyn hurried into the room on his heels. Goddess help him, he couldn't stop from rolling his eyes to the ceiling. The only thing keeping him from snapping at the woman was her connection to Slade.

"This is between your father and I."

"But—"

"Jes, honey. Leave us be," Slade said, his voice hard with authority despite his endearment. Jes's shoulders slumped, and she nodded once, trudging out of the room. Her attitude scraped Emery the wrong way, disgust rising in his soul like the taste of smoke lingering at the back of his throat. Slade closed the doors and locked them, then led Emery to the alcove where a fire burned in the large fireplace. He poured two tumblers of whiskey, handed one to Emery and fell into a chair, defeated. "This was never how I anticipated them learning the truth."

"No, I couldn't imagine so." Emery placed the tumbler on a table and took the seat cattycorner to his Keeper. "What the absolute *fuck* did you do? Sleeping with a fellow Keeper's wife is low, Slade."

"It wasn't just a rut, Em. It's a little more complicated." Slade rubbed a hand down his face, wincing as he pressed against the bruising flesh beneath his eye, and released a long sigh as his fingers smoothed over his beard. "It was never a rut."

"Well"—Emery spread his arms wide, dropping back in the chair—"I'm waiting, because if things weren't complicated enough, you throw in paternal rights at the most *opportune* time. Do you know the *complications* this has unleashed? With Jeslyn?"

Slade blinked, then studied him. Emery arched a brow, lowering his arms to cross over his chest and kicking an ankle onto his knee.

"What problems would it cause? You and Jeslyn have been growing tight."

"Oh, for fuck's sake, Slade. Are you that dense? In denial? Or just completely disconnected from your surroundings and delusional? Coming from my sharp Keeper known for his keen attention to detail, I'd hate to see that thirty-plus years in the human realm has dumbed you down."

"That's hitting—"

Emery flicked up a finger, silencing him immediately. "I'm done playing games. No, Slade. Jeslyn is *not* my lifemate. And you damn well *know it*." He leaned toward Slade, whose eyes widened and cheeks turned rose. "Seraphina is. Now it all makes sense. And you've known since she came running in here looking for Jes the night I arrived."

"But Jes is older—"

"Apparently it doesn't really matter, being as they're from two different women. And since you have two daughters, the Goddess made the decision that Sera is mine, not Jes. Do you have any idea the fucking *torture* I've been through fighting a predestined bond because Sera didn't want to betray her best friend? Three days of the worst possible suffering to please my lifemate for the sake of Jes. Such a selfless sacrifice on her behalf when it's been just as tormenting for her. Three days of banging my head against a proverbial wall, trying to figure out how the hell Rayze's Keeper produced *my* lifemate and not you. Yet tonight, she finally accepted the truth. We came here to discuss it with you and Jeslyn, but you had a bigger surprise to share. You realize the complications that'll come from this, right? So, what the hell happened? Because as far as I knew, you and Claire were the perfect couple."

"Things aren't always what they seem on the outside, Em." The mental walls of resistance around his Keeper began to falter. "There had always been a disconnect between Nick and the rest of us. Even before the attacks, but it grew worse after. Rayze was a young dragon, frivolous with his hoard. He didn't have much for Nick, so it really wasn't a surprise when his funds tapered off years ago. None of us knew until you delivered the news about the dead dragons that Rayze didn't survive the attacks, so we thought that he went through his hoard and Cade could no longer pull funds for Nick. Every one of us knew how Rayze was, and how aloof Nick had always been. The two were a dangerous pair, because neither one kept the other in a line they desperately needed. They were like two toddlers without parental supervision, and the messes we cleaned up to keep them under the radar were asinine at times."

Slade's brows creased, the pull deepening over the bridge of his nose. A haunted mask settled over his face, darkening his expression while a weight appeared to press down on his shoulders. He sipped at his whiskey, his gaze unfocused, his thoughts churning like the sky before a storm. Emery pulled back from his Keeper's mind, the electric hiss of untampered emotions reacting to his own heightened feelings, primarily focused on one woman who needed him more than she realized. The only reason he hadn't abandoned his Keeper was because he trusted his brother to ensure her safety, and momentary solitude, in his absence. He'd go to her as soon as he understood every damn nuance of what had happened between his Keeper and Nick's dead wife. He wasn't leaving without every obstacle between him and Sera being dissolved.

"Back to Sera," Emery redirected.

Slade cleared his throat and blinked several times. He rubbed his temple, the faintest of grimaces ghosting his mouth before disappearing.

"Nick had been philandering, and his wife found out. She came here to talk to Claire, but Claire had gone away for the weekend with Margo. Lauro and Jax were here. We were playing cards and drinking. Guys' weekend type of thing. I had invited Nick, but as usual, he stood us up to seek his entertainment elsewhere." Slade swirled his whiskey, lifting his gaze to Emery's. "You know, Em, not everyone has happy relationships in the Keeper world. We're not all like Saralyn and Gio or Dorian and Larissa. We have our problems just like all couples do. In the Hollow, everything was perfect on the outside, but many Keepers had their faults and they came to light when we came to the human realm. These last thirty years amplified our faults. Reminded us that, although, we're not completely human, we may be more human than we think."

"I never fooled myself into believing any of us were perfect, but having morals and an understanding of right and wrong I *do* expect." Emery cut him off with a flick of a finger when Slade opened his mouth to rebut that statement. "And accepting of consequences when wrong, Slade. That's what I'm most disappointed about right now."

"In what meaning?"

A caustic laugh scraped up his throat and escaped his lips on a plume of smoke. "What meaning?" He cast the locked doors a hard look, catching the spread of a shadow along the floor that could only be Jeslyn eavesdropping. Lowering his voice, he leveled his full attention on Slade. "You left your biological daughter with a man who treated her terribly because he always blamed her for his wife's death. You never owned up to what you did before tonight to anyone other than Claire. You left the most important person in this entire equation high and dry while creating more waves with your other daughter, leading her to believe she and I are lifemates. *That* meaning."

"Goddess, Em. I thought I was doing the *right* thing. I didn't want to hurt Nick more than he was already hurting when he lost his wife hours after Sera was born. I always thought she would provide some peace to the broken man, but I was wrong. It wasn't until about ten or so years ago that I noticed the change in his demeanor toward her, and that's when I really stepped in and tried to fill the gaps of fatherhood he left wide open without causing rifts. Our girls grew up together like sisters—"

"Which they are," Emery cut in.

"Yes."

Slade worried his lip as he swirled his whiskey, his thoughts nothing more than hushed impressions that Emery picked up through their bond. He waited, albeit impatiently, for his Keeper to put the last piece of this fucked-up puzzle in place for him to completely understand how Sera, the younger daughter, was his chosen lifemate. He thanked the

Goddess for choosing her for him over Jeslyn, especially after tonight.

He waited a silent eternity, taking his level gaze from Slade only to toss a glance toward the closed pocket doors. Jeslyn hadn't moved from her post, and the idea that the woman was so obsessed irked him more than anything.

"You know, Dina and I dated back in The Hollow. In secret. Her parents had their hearts set on Nick because they had been friends with his parents, but she and I"—Slade threw back his whiskey and opted for a second—"there was always a connection between us. She came to me often in the beginning of their marriage with concerns about Nick and Rayze. She wasn't happy, but she knew how to put on a good face for all to see. She hid her misery well, but I always knew. She chose Nick over me to appease her parents. It had been the hardest truth for me to swallow back then. Then Claire came around and I slowly shifted my attention away from the woman I had loved with all my heart, and still love to this day, to the woman I grew to love with the remnants of a heart that had been broken."

After a few more moments of silence, Slade finally met his gaze. Only then did Emery see the depth of his Keeper's love for Nick's dead wife, the mother of his lifemate. The sorrow and grief that shadowed the usual clarity startled him enough that he kept quiet.

"Everyone wears a mask, Em. Everyone. Look at you, what you've been doing these last few days for Jes's sake. I can only imagine how difficult it's been, if I understand the lifemate bond as I believe I do. For that, I'm sorry. For making you suffer." He shook his head. "You're right about me sensing it Saturday night. My mind saw the connection instantly, but my expectations refused the truth."

"That's the past now." With a slow, deep breath, Emery

nodded. "You didn't end your relationship with Dina, even after her marriage, did you."

Shame painted his cheeks, but Slade kept his chin up. "We kept a relationship, yes, but it was a friendly one. Claire and I were expecting Jeslyn when Dina came over that night. It's like all those years apart vanished and I wanted to take away her pain. Take it all away and show her that there was happiness. There was goodness. She still had me, and I showed her she still *had me*."

His voice broke at the end, his declaration a hoarse proclamation emphasized with a fist to his chest. His eyes misted and his jaw set as his teeth clenched.

"We both had more to drink than we should have, being alone after the boys left. We knew the dangers but still indulged, and things … happened." Slade shook his head, tossed down his second whiskey, and dropped the tumbler on the table beside Emery's untouched glass. With his elbows on his knees and his shoulders hunched, Slade sighed. "She told me a few weeks later she was pregnant. She didn't have to tell me the baby was mine. My gut confirmed it, and Goddess help me, the absolute elation I felt was overwhelming. I'd never felt that joy with Claire, but Dina had been my first true love, and she'd remained the love I could never have completely."

"How did Nick not suspect something?"

"She and Nick had been trying for a baby since their marriage, but it never happened. She told me that they still tried several times a month, when he wasn't out messing around with other women, so it wasn't hard for him to believe the baby was his. Over the months, we spoke often about our dilemma, our wishes for the baby, and how we would raise our child. We'd agreed to designate me as Uncle and Claire as Aunt, and Dina started to push Nick to join me and the boys for more outings and such to build a bond with the guy."

"I don't understand why Nick would seek other women if he loved Dina as much as he proclaimed tonight."

Slade twisted his hands, palms to the ceiling, in a motion of uncertainty. "I wish I knew the answer to that. I don't doubt he loved her, but I don't think Nick ever knew what true love was and chalked up his feeling of victory over having Dina as his wife as love. I'd venture to say the guy may believe love and possession to be the same. He possessed power with Rayze, which he no longer has. He possessed a beautiful woman as his wife, who died after birthing Sera."

Emery turned this new information over in his head. Seraphina was Slade's biological daughter, which answered how it was possible for her to be his lifemate. He was hung up on the order of his Keeper's children, being that Sera was the younger of the two.

Until now. Listening to Slade quietly divulge a secret side of himself to Emery, the love he shared with another man's wife for years before she became forbidden, he understood why Sera had been chosen as his lifemate.

She was a creation out of wholesome, untainted love. She possessed the purity of heart and soul and spirit because of the priceless relationship her parents had shared.

She was *perfect*.

He ached to find her, but he had more questions that needed to be answered so he could approach this turn of events in the most effective way.

"You said Claire knew. When did you tell Claire?"

"Shortly after Dina told me the news. Dina and I talked at great length about it and we both agreed Claire deserved to know the truth."

"I can't imagine she took it well, being pregnant and all."

Slade's lips pulled tight. "It was a rocky time for us. The rest of her pregnancy was rough because of the stress our relationship was under."

"But you came out of that storm pretty well."

His Keeper tented his fingers and rested his chin on the tips. His eyes slid toward Emery, pain etched in the dark irises. *"She'll never admit it to me, Em, but the reason we are still together and happy is because she didn't have to compete with Dina. She accepted Sera as a part of our family, never held contempt toward the child I created with a woman whom she knew still held a big piece of my heart, but when she learned Dina had died, her relief was evident. Things changed after that."*

The switch to mindspeak piqued his curiosity, but Slade didn't make him ask why.

"I was thinking of leaving Claire, Em. As Dina's due date approached, I considered it more and more. I was making plans to set Claire and Jeslyn up so they didn't have to want for anything. Jeslyn was thriving as an infant. We had a full-time nanny, someone I vetted thoroughly, and the boys' wives were over doting on the baby more than I was home to enjoy the time.

"We found out Dina hemorrhaged after giving birth. Against all advice, Nick had taken her to the hospital when she went into labor. Jax's mother-in-law had delivered many babies back at The Hollow. His wife learned the trade and was the midwife for all our children once we came here. She was prepared to help with the delivery, but Nick refused her help and took Dina to the hospital, knowing the complications that could arise because of our inhuman genetics and their human medications and procedures. I don't know what transpired at the hospital, but Dina had made sure I was

updated on her progress without Nick's knowledge. I received a call in the middle of the night from the doctor who was overseeing her care. She told me Dina had gone into cardiac arrest and didn't survive. Claire and I rushed to the hospital immediately. We all did."

Slade looked away, his brows pinched, fingers having threaded together tightly. Emery sat in silence, a weight on his shoulders. The air had thickened during Slade's revelation, and it did little to ease the tension riding his muscles. Seemed his dragon didn't know what to make of this, either, coiled up tight and attentive, with not a single rumble of reaction.

"Think of me as you will after this, but as I said before, we're not all happy in the Keeper world. Some of us pine for a bond like Gio and Saralyn have. Some of us aren't lucky enough to obtain it, for whatever reason."

"I won't lie, I'm shocked," Emery admitted. After all, Slade had always had a wild side, but he'd been morally sound. Or so he'd thought. Then again, matters of the heart were often out of their control. Despite his faults, his Keeper's heart and soul were good. That hadn't changed. "But it all makes perfect sense now." Cracking a small grin when Slade glanced his way, he shook a finger at him. "I didn't want to believe it that first night, but I see her in you. Quite a bit. At least her looks come from her mother's side."

Despite the evident grief Slade relived, he chuckled and sat up. "You never met Dina."

"No. You obviously hid her from me, which will be a discussion for another day."

"Come here."

The man waved for him to follow as they stood up and crossed the room to the desk. Slade removed a key from a secret compartment on the inside of one of the bookshelves and unlocked the bottom drawer of his desk.

"I keep confidential documents in here, so the lock isn't suspicious," he said in answer to Emery's quirked brow. When he pulled the drawer open, it was filled with neatly organized files. Slade fingered through a few toward the back before he opened one. He withdrew a single photo of a stunning woman with waist-length black hair, thick and wavy like her daughter's, a face that tapered to a gently pointed chin, full lips, sloping brows, narrow nose and pronounced cheeks that played perfectly with light and shadow. She held a large bouquet of wildflowers, her crystal blue eyes gleaming with joy. "I took this picture of her the day after she told me she was carrying Sera."

Pain twinged Emery's heart. For his Keeper. For his lifemate. For the tragic love story. Things made more sense. The opulence of the house. The immersion into wealth and materialistic possessions. Slade *was* compensating for something, but that something was love lost that could never be replaced. What should have been a happy family died with the woman who brought his lifemate into this world against all odds.

Emery handed the photo back to Slade, who gazed upon it like a man whose heart had been ripped open again. He rested a hand on Slade's shoulder, pulling his attention from the photo, the memories. Tears moistened his Keeper's eyes.

"You haven't lost everything, Slade," Emery said quietly.

"I know, but the losses I've had aren't easy at times."

With a sigh, Emery pulled Slade into a tight embrace. His Keeper's body was stiff, clearly staving off the tears that desperately fought for freedom. The swell of emotions pummeled Emery through their bond, a dark, heavy, agonizing pain Slade held to tightly. He'd never been one to show weakness except in privacy, and only with Emery, but this? This suffering was ruthless.

"You know I'll take care of her. You know she's safe with me. She'll have everything in the world I could give her to make her the happiest woman alive. I'll earn her heart, her love, and cherish her until I take my last breath."

"I know you will, Em." Slade released a trembling breath. "She's so precious to me. That I've had to hide my adoration all her life hurts, but she deserves you and what you'll provide for her."

Emery squeezed Slade before leaning back. "It won't be me alone, old man. Dragon's out of the lair, so to speak. Time to step up to the dad plate and make up for lost time."

"I just hope she'll forgive me." Slade attempted to smile, but it fell flat. "I've one more thing for you, because I know you're itching to go. Surprised you hung around this long." He replaced the photo in the folder and reached to the back of the drawer. When he straightened up this time, he held a familiar engraved wooden box out to Emery. "Think it's time you passed it to the one who truly deserves it."

A faint grin touched the corners of Emery's mouth as he took the ornate box, feeling the weight of his dragonstone for the first time in decades. A sense of fullness settled in his chest. He hefted the box a few times in his hand, then held it back out to Slade. His Keeper's brows lifted.

"You're still my Keeper, Slade. Until she's ready to bleed. I've entrusted it to your care all these years, to use as you need." When Slade took the box from his palm, Emery rolled out his shoulders and released a pent-up breath of relief. "I'll reach out to you later. I suggest you deal with the family here." He ticked a finger. "I have one more question before I go. Why did you tap into the account for Sera's bail? You have plenty of funds without having to dig into mine."

"Call it wishful thinking. Reaching for straws. A hunch. With all the events happening that pointed to Firestorm dragons and Baroqueth, I was willing to give it a try and see if it triggered you to find me." Slade grinned and shrugged. "It worked. You're here, at long last."

"I always appreciated your subtle tactics, old man."

He wasn't surprised to find Jeslyn hovering outside the doors when he slid them open. She made to reach for his waist in a hug, but he sidestepped, held up a hand, and shook his head once. "Your father needs to speak with you." As her cheeks flushed and those persistently doting eyes turned cold, he pointed to the office. He leveled his gaze on Claire and the human sap—any semblance of civility for the man went out the door when he'd dared to put his mouth on Sera—and added, "You as well, Claire."

"It's Sera, isn't it?" Claire asked as he spun on a heel toward the front door and made haste to leave. "I know the truth about her. I know Slade fathered her with Dina."

"Mom!" Jeslyn shrieked.

Emery slowed long enough to glance over his shoulder and study the flood of emotions that twisted and darkened Claire's pretty face. The woman pushed off her perch on the stair, shrugging Silas away, and lifted her chin. Despite the pride she clung to, a crushing pain cut through her eyes.

"His heart was never mine. He'd given it to Dina long before I came into the picture." Her lips tightened, staving off the faint quiver of her chin. "I-I know Sera's your true lifemate."

Emery held her gaze for a few heartbeats longer, ignoring Jeslyn's aghast reaction before he left the house without a word.

CHAPTER SIXTEEN

*E*mery clung to the rippling threads of the lifemate bond while following the potent dragon scent of his brother along the quiet mountain road. Half a mile down from Slade's house, he caught his first whiff of Sera, followed by the taste of her anguish across his tongue. The metallic flavor brought a scowl to his lips as he hastened his chase, drawing on his dragon vision to pinpoint Sera and Gabe's exact location. The frayed ends of the pulsating lifemate bond pointed him in several directions, but all centered in one general direction. He sensed the fracture in her walls, received pulses of torment through those cracks before they sealed up as she regained her strength.

After several minutes of running between trees beside the road, following the strengthening scents and tenuous air of energy, he reached for his cell—

A scream tore through the night, peeling across the mountainscape, pummeling through the trees. It ripped deep into his chest and shredded his soul. The tethering thread of his bond burst with energy, flooded his senses with agony and grief, bringing him to a sudden halt and a few backpedals from its force.

That scream. A scream of raw pain.

"Fuck."

He bolted forward, unleashing his dragon form and pulling upward with spread wings. He grazed the canopy of the trees, his mind engulfed in desperation as he sought his woman, the source of that pain, that torture, that *scream*.

The ache throbbed along his bones, into his head, a drum beat that strengthened with every hit. The tightening of a chest that echoed his lifemate's strain. The whirling thoughts and memories infusing his mind while he scanned the grounds below. How the hell did she make it this far? Why had Gabe not stopped her?

Goddess!

Twin flashes of heat in the cold forest kicked his heartbeat upward as he pulled in his wings, his dragon, to drop through the trees and land on booted feet, walking out of the contact without a thud a few steps in front of Gabe. The leaves swirled around him from the force of his descent, and the sudden halt he came to when he spotted Sera a dozen or so yards ahead. She clutched tight fists to her chest, curled over as she cried shamelessly, and dropped to her knees.

Cries with no restraint, nothing to temper the anguish behind each emotionally charged sound that stabbed over and over into her heart. *His* heart.

Gabe skidded to a stop when Emery threw up his arm.

"I'll grab the truck," Gabe said quietly.

Emery barely heard him turn and leave. The woman breaking on the outside while shattering inside, fracturing the shell that protected her fragile emotions from the world, had his full attention. She fell onto her side, curled into a fetal position as he slowly approached, his steps silent, his dragon restless, his soul trying to draw this pain away from her to protect her, soothe her. He'd give anything to take it all away from her, protect her from the hurt, the betrayal. To turn back time. Turn it back to the beginning and let the truth be known before it got to this.

He circled around, approaching her head as she rolled onto her back, body heaving with the power of her sobs, her face flushed, strained, her lips peeled back from clenched teeth, hands fisted so tight her fingers had turned white as she punched at the ground and drew her knees up, feet flat against the rocks and brush.

The sight of her in such distress crushed him. Goddess, it tore him to pieces to witness the degree of hurt she suffered.

He'd take it all away. He would.

He swore to the Goddess, *he would.*

She gave no indication she heard him as he silently lowered to his knees and settled on the ground, resting his head beside hers, his body opposite her own. He stared up into the black sky through the swaying branches and pines, a haze of clouds obscuring the crystalline stars and dimming the moonlight.

He curved his arm around her head, his hand above her shoulder, fingers outstretched.

"Give me your hand."

He waited, counting the seconds, her quieting sobs, each beat of her heart as it began to slow, until he believed she'd refuse him a modicum of trust as she reverted to their previous estrangement. As he began to curl his fingers into his palm, her trembling hand sought and found his, clinging desperately. Slowly, he began to siphon her pain, her agony into himself while filling her with warmth and calm. He closed his eyes, drawing on the root of her distress, pulling at the dark, foul essences coiling through her mind.

Memories. Potent and poisonous.

Nick.

Emery clenched his teeth to keep a growl suppressed as he listened to the bastard's gut-wrenching last words to Sera before he left. The man never heeded his warning, and by unleashing his thoughts while high on emotions, laid a lethal punch to Sera's soul, leaving her vulnerable, injured, and aching like no living creature should. He caught glimpses of her as a child, experiencing the coldness of a man who didn't care for his daughter at an age when she couldn't comprehend his lack of love toward her. She witnessed the warmth between Slade and Jes, a bond she secretly wished she had, but would never verbalize. She suffered a pain she could never identify, emptiness with an unknown root.

Now, she knew the truth and it hurt as much as the phantom aches and loneliness she'd come to terms with over the course of her life. The understanding that came with learning the truth created more turmoil within her mind, her heart. Her guilt at betraying Jeslyn, only to realize the betrayal went so much deeper. Secrets cast deep canyons between family members and families. Her tumultuous thoughts spared moments for her closest friend and the bereft ache when she saw through the mask of kindness and loyalty this evening before she'd taken off.

He witnessed it all.

Through Sera.

Lost.

"Through all tribulations, you find where you're meant to be, my sweet," he whispered. Leaves crinkled beneath her head as she turned it to look at him. When she didn't look away, he eased his face to hers. Her eyes glowed from tears, red-rimmed and swollen. Her lashes clumped, tears both damp and dry streaking her rosy cheeks. "Let me take you away from here."

"Where?" She barely spoke above a whisper, her voice raw and thick.

"Home." He reached over and drew his thumb beneath a single eye, drying the tears hanging on her lower lashes. "*Our* home."

Her eyes closed, lips growing taut. He remained on the outskirts of her mind, her walls destroyed and her emotions rampant beneath the cape of calm he provided. Fractional thoughts of abandoning her shop. Trying to filter through her new reality.

She nodded. "Yes."

Emery withheld the small smile that wanted so badly to break across his mouth. He dug his phone from his jacket pocket, pulled Gabe up on his list, and pressed the phone to his ear.

"Everything okay?" Gabe answered. The purr of the truck's engine turning over in the background pinned his location.

"Go home. I'll meet you there when we land."

"Best news yet."

Disconnecting the call, he sat up and came around Sera's right side, holding fast to her hand until he scooped her into the cradle of his arms and stood. She tucked her head against his shoulder, a hand loosely on his shoulder.

"Do you trust me, sweet flame?"

"You have been the only one who's shown me no deception."

That tweaked at his heart. He tightened his arms on her and pressed a lingering kiss to the top of her head, whispering, "I'll never deceive you."

"I trust you."

"Two things. Don't forget to breathe."

She turned her face up to his, those beautiful eyes of hers sparkling. "And the second?"

Emery grinned. "I will *never* let you fall."

He rocketed into the sky, body twisting and transforming as his wings pulled them into the clouds. He adjusted his taloned grip on Sera to tuck her close to his dragon's chest and keep her warm against the frigid drop of temperature at their increasing altitude. Once above the hazy clouds, he extended his wings and leveled out, gliding along the current toward The Hollow. In his grip, Sera clung to his scale-covered fingers. Her fear was overridden by wonder. He angled his head to catch a glimpse of her, wide-eyed and drinking in the view.

"How're you doing?"

"This is wild."

He chuckled, allowing the sound to roll through his precious woman as he banked north. *"Wait until you're on my back and we're spiraling through the clouds."*

"One step at a time."

He smiled to himself, despite the exhaustion that filtered into his consciousness. Sera's emotional wells had practically dried up. The mental toll of the evening landed a blow to her that even the excitement of flight couldn't quite wash away.

Halfway home, Gabe caught up with them, flipping onto his back beneath Emery to observe Sera. Smoke curved along the sides of his snout on a snort as he rolled out from beneath his brother and righted himself at his left wing. His eye closed and he folded his claws in a motion of sleep. Emery's heart thumped, filling with a sense of satisfaction and a surge of protectiveness. She trusted him enough to fall asleep in the claws of a dragon thousands of feet in the air.

Hers was a trust he would never betray.

Emery and his brother arrived at The Hollow quietly, catching only the attention of those civilians who'd stayed out late over mead and music. Despite the attack less than a week ago, the village appeared to have resumed normal activity as if nothing had happened, although there was a sense of vigilance that hadn't been there before. Their world may be safe, but the attack was a stark reminder that even the safest of havens wasn't impenetrable to evil.

Gabe followed Emery onto his landing shelf, both reining in their dragons as their hind feet hit the mountain stone. Dirt stirred around their boots and the breeze from their wings rustled the leaves of cliffside brush.

Emery adjusted his sleeping lifemate in the cradle of his arms and faced his brother. "Go to Sky. I'm going to tuck her in before heading to Cade. Regardless of what happened tonight, we need to return the Keepers to where they belong. It would be nice to have an eventless mission for once."

"Better knock on some wood before you jinx it. Besides" —Gabe stretched his arms over his head, his spine cracking —"we've had enough drama these last few days to take the place of Baroqueth ambushes."

Emery snorted in agreement and headed toward the entrance to his mountain home.

"I'll be back with Sky shortly. This way, we can go dig the caveman out of hiding together and Sera will have someone here if she wakes up while we're gone."

Gabe dove off the shelf, releasing the dragon and banking toward his home.

Emery followed the winding tunnels deep into the mountain until he reached the main living quarters. His home sat in quiet darkness, the air cool from the stone walls and everlasting breeze filtering through the slitted cuts in the rock fashioned to be windows. He hadn't readied his home for his lifemate like his brethren had. His place lacked the warmth of a home and was more a lair with minimal furniture and no lavish decorations. He only hoped she'd be comfortable enough until he could create a palace worthy of her appreciation.

The dark bedroom came to life beneath the magic of his fire as he set the oversized fireplace ablaze, the flames lending warmth to the otherwise chilly room. He carried his precious woman to the bed and rested her in the center of the furs, unfolding one of the thick fur throws and tucking it around her curled figure. She barely moved during the transfer, her mind a soothing ripple of dreamless sleep fed magical calm through his touch. He smoothed back a few of the thick waves that had cascaded over her face and tucked them behind her ear.

"You're home, sweet flame. Where you're meant to be. Rest easy. I'll return soon."

With a light kiss to her temple, Emery walked out to the living area and waited for Gabe to return with Sky. To his surprise, he didn't have to wait long, which brought a crease to his brow and a devious grin to his mouth. Gabe burned a warning glance at him when Sky broke away from his arm and greeted Emery with a hug.

"Glad you two made it back without much action," Sky said, her voice hushed. She stepped back and smiled, reaching up to pat his cheek like a youngling. Emery groaned. "Lifemate looks good on you, Em. You've got a different glow to your eyes."

"And how the fuck would you know the difference in my brother's eyes?" Gabe growled. Sky huffed an exasperated groan and turned to Gabe as he approached her, his arms crossed over his chest and his mouth tight. Only a gleam in his eyes gave away his humor.

"Would you rather me look at other parts of his anatomy when I talk to him?"

"Okay, before this goes further, I'm the innocent party in this." Emery threw up his hands and took a step back, the corners of his mouth lifting as he earned the couple's attention. "I think you should've released some of this energy before coming here."

"I wasn't going to hold you both up. Besides, I can't wait to meet my brother-in-law's woman."

Emery lowered his arms, his smile warming from Sky's genuine excitement. Despite her hard-edged exterior, the woman had a heart as big and soft as all his brethren's lifemates. She simply hid it well beneath thickets and thorns, except from those she chose to let into her guarded life. His dragon settled, content with knowing Sky would take to Sera like a sister, one who would cherish the bond rather than destroy it.

"She's sleeping right now. I don't know if she'll wake up before we return. She's had a rough night," Emery said.

Sky nodded once, casting Gabe a lingering glance as her expression softened. It wasn't so long ago that he'd failed to save her mother from a Baroqueth attack, and that guilt had burrowed itself deep in his conscience. Sky never held it against him, forgave him selflessly, even if he hadn't been able to forgive himself, and loved Emery wholeheartedly as the brother he'd come to be.

"Gabe told me a bit of what happened. Sounds like a sticky little web."

"In essence, but nothing I can't cut through." Emery motioned to the corridor that led to the launch shelf. "Ready, brother?"

"Waiting on you two," Gabe taunted, his smile melting into something feral when Sky turned to him. He cupped her face between his hands and brought her to her toes.

Emery brushed by the two before he was forced to witness the same raw desire that simmered within his own body. The pull to return to Sera threatened his plan to speak with Cade and put the final details on returning the rest of the Keepers and their families to The Hollow. Fortunately, luck was on their side, but none of them knew when that luck would run out. One final trip to the human realm and back. They would continue seeking out straggler Hollow members over time, but these last couple of years spent seeking out missing Keepers, discovering lifemates, and cutting down Baroqueth would end.

They all needed the respite. Time to build lives anew, start a new generation of dragons and Keepers and rebuild their world, their lives, bigger, better, and stronger. Impenetrable.

Gabe caught up to him halfway to the shelf, clapping his shoulder as he fell in step beside him. "When I told Sky you brought Sera home, the woman practically burst at the seams. She's already taken her on as her sister."

Emery's heart gave a funny thump. "I think they'll have more in common than most. They both have a similar fire inside them, a fiercely independent streak, and a Godsawful pretentious shell that hides a beautiful soul. Though they may not be blood, I have a feeling our women will be as close as blood-born siblings." He pressed his lips together thoughtfully. "It'll be nice for Sera to have someone she could call her sister whose loyalty she won't have to second-guess."

"You didn't tell me about the end result with Jeslyn."

"Need I say anything? I'm sure you can guess how it went."

Gabe snickered. "She's not at all like Slade. What is that

term humans use? Shallow?" He shook his head. "At least the Goddess had the insight as to which daughter would be better suited as your lifemate."

"Look at all of us, brother. Our small clan of survivors is a formidable group."

"That's no lie."

When they reached the shelf, Emery came to a sudden halt. Gabe stepped up alongside Emery and shook his head. Cade leaned casually against the curved opening to Emery's home, playing with fire that danced about his taloned fingers. Flames reflected in his deep red eyes, eyes that glowed with the inner light of his ever-present beast.

"Always skulking about caves and tunnels, Cade. Doesn't look good on you, old man," Gabe taunted. "One might believe you're becoming a hermit."

"Tongue, youngling," Cade growled, flicking the flames from his onyx talons. The small flickers of light shot toward Emery and his brother, but before they could reach either of them, they pulled up a fiery wall that absorbed the playful attack. Emery smiled at his brother, who winked as an unspoken plan blossomed between them.

Until a sharp pain erupted from his neck.

Gabe barked as Emery spun around, their fire wall vanishing in smoke at their backs. Emery swung his arm to fend off whatever had bitten him, only to find himself face to face with the flaming essence of a small serpentine dragon. An illusion, a magical creation. Twin serpents, bobbing heads on long airy necks outlined in fire. The one in front of Emery yawned, grumbled, and melted into the ground at his feet.

"I'm not sure if I should be elated by your rare playful antics, or worried you've lost your Goddess-damned mind," Emery finally muttered, turning back to Cade while Gabe entertained Cade's illusionary dragon as the image taunted his brother with nips. "Gabe, it's not real."

"Fucking thing *bit* me like it *is* real."

"Because something may not be real in essence doesn't mean it can't lay a lethal blow. If you two didn't learn that from the last attack on our own soil, you're ill-prepared for the next attack. Which means you'll be meeting up with the other dragons at the first sign of dawn to resume your long overdue training sessions."

"We just got back—"

"I don't care, Gabe. We'll meet on the summit at dawn. I'm making my rounds to let everyone know, since you *are* back." Cade pressed off the mountain, folding his arms over his chest. The wind blew his dark red hair, left untied and wild, about his face while his eyes burned like embers between the rogue strands. Those soul-piercing eyes, eyes that held too many centuries of wisdom and knowledge, shifted to Emery. "Afterwards, we'll make a trip back to collect the remaining Keepers and their families. I'm going to reset the wards and spells around the veil once we're all through. It can't keep the Baroqueth out indefinitely, but it'll cause strife if they try to break through the veil." His gaze narrowed slightly. "Did you figure things out with Slade?"

Emery chuckled, the sound lacking the usual carefree humor. "Oh, did I ever. Down to his secret love child with Nick's wife."

Cade blinked slowly. The corner of his mouth twitched. "So, Sera is Slade's biological daughter, which makes more sense."

"Nick lost his ever-loving fucking mind tonight because he found out Sera wasn't his," Gabe said. "Put a bullet in the ceiling that may have hit Slade or Sera, had Em not knocked his arm askew."

A deep red brow lifted over one of Cade's eyes. Emery shrugged a shoulder.

"I think he would've been happy had that bullet hit either of them. Nick has no love for Sera, blamed her for Dina's death, and relinquished any further connection to her tonight. The only reason he's still walking on two legs and intact is because I respect him as a Keeper to one of our fallen brethren. Should he dare threaten Sera again, I'll be flossing my fangs with his innards," Emery promised, his voice losing all hint of playfulness and melting into a vicious rumble.

"Should he pose a threat to anyone, I'll be sure justice is served." Cade lifted his chin and glanced over his shoulder. That was a promise everyone in The Hollow knew Cade would keep, and then some. His private dungeon was proof of how Cade's justice system prevailed. "I'll have a long discussion with him when he returns. As for the rest of the night"—he brought his attention back to Emery—"is there anything you need to help settle Sera in?"

He shook his head. "Nah. She's sleeping comfortably in my bed. I'll work on getting my place in order once you free us from our punishment."

Cade's chuckle resonated in the entryway, a deep, feral sound that the rock of the mountain absorbed and redispersed in Emery's bones. "It'll only be punishment should you allow it to be."

Without another word, his transformed into his ginormous beast and took flight from the edge of the shelf. Emery rolled out the tension from his shoulders and tilted his neck both ways, delighting in the crack of his spine. It had been years since they had formally gathered for training, choosing to keep up their skills alone or in small groups. As much as the idea of spending hours away from Sera to recondition irked him, he knew he lacked the discipline he once held when training had been consistent and every other day.

It didn't take a seer or prophet to know that coming home with the last remaining lifemate did not bring closure against the threat that was always on their heels. Oh, no. It was only a matter of time before another battle rained down on their heads.

Only this time, they'd be ready. Each and every one of them. They'd be ready to fight at the blink of an eye, to protect the world that swore allegiance to the dragons and their people. If blood spilled, it would be that of their enemies.

For tonight, though, Emery planned to cast every ounce of impending threats aside for a night of holding his beloved lifemate in his arms.

Tonight, all that existed was Sera.

CHAPTER SEVENTEEN

The distant chirping of birds greeted her ears as her mind shed the last of hazy dreams with no clarity. She stretched her arms over her head and moaned behind clenched teeth as her spine popped in several places and her muscles loosened from hours of sleep. Good, solid sleep. When she opened her eyes, she blinked at the sight of brilliant streaks of golden sunlight stretching through several narrow slits in a wall of dark brown rock. She lolled her head from one side to the other, mentally measuring the enormous bed piled with soft furs and a silk blanket. Silk. The material smoothed like cool water beneath her hand as she stretched her arm toward the ruffled pillow beside her. It held a slight indentation, as did the blankets. Rolling onto her side, she pressed her face into the pillow and inhaled deeply. The warm, rich scent of Emery's fire and fresh air essence, hinting at a bit of pine, filled her lungs and brought a timid smile to her mouth, only for realization to set in.

He may have been beside her during the night, but she woke alone, in a bed far larger than anything she'd ever seen, in a room that held no definitive shape. It appeared to have been careved out of rock. The ceilings were rough and angular, forming arches and domes. Alcoves filled spaces between close quarters, but one thing struck her—despite the natural elegance of the room, Emery had furnished and decorated it with an Old World air that filled her with a new level of appreciation for her absent dragon-man.

Across the way from the foot of the bed, an oversized fireplace burned bright with healthy flames, lending a comfortable warmth to the room. Shelves had been carved into the rock, and books lined the expansive walls on either side of the fireplace. Chairs had been strategically placed to the side of the fireplace, a table tucked between them. A small, cozy sitting area had been created from the open space immediately to her left, and to the right of the bed, an open doorway led somewhere she couldn't see.

Despite the events of the night before, her heart felt lighter this morning. Tension no longer rode her like a punishing weight. The truth was finally out, all of it, and whatever came in the next few days because of it, she'd handle. She was exactly where she belonged, with the man who claimed her in every facet of the meaning.

For now, curiosity bubbled inside her as she dropped her feet to the stone floor and pushed off the bed.

"Emery?"

The golden beacon of warmth she'd fought so hard to keep out of her mind and away from her heart pulsed with vibrant energy. Her hands folded over her chest before she realized what she was doing, holding tight to the intangible bond. She never wanted to dim its magnificent glow. She never wanted to be without the low-frequency hum that assured her Emery remained close, even if he didn't respond to her call.

She took a few more minutes to explore the sizable quarters, which included a dining area, nooks fashioned into wardrobes, and a bathroom that exceeded anything her imagination might have put together. Rustic and gorgeous, created with marble and stone, gold fixtures and an open shower against the far wall that trickled water from several burrowed holes in the ceiling. Nature's raining showerhead. An oversized tub fashioned from marble sat at an angle opposite the shower.

"Emery, can you hear me?"

The bond thrummed in response, but Emery remained quiet. She wasn't exactly sure how far their mindspeak would work, or where he had gone that would take him out of reach. Regardless, she took to the sink to wash her face and brush her teeth with a set of new toiletries Emery must've gotten for her. She fingered through some of his clothes, hoping to find something to change into until he returned and she could ask about getting clothes of her own. The problem came with the stark memory of her last attempt to wear something of his, only to have him destroy the shirt along with any residual barrier between them.

Her body gave a fierce shiver as heat stirred alive in her face and slithered down to her core. She had to brace a hand on the wall to keep from stumbling, her legs hot and watery as her belly hummed and an unforgiving ache settled between her thighs.

"Gods help me," she whispered, rubbing a trembling hand over her face despite the elated grin that continued to stretch across her mouth. "I'm completely hopeless."

Forfeiting a change of clothes, she giggled at the scribbled semblance of a map drawn on a piece of paper Emery had stabbed onto a pointy edge of rock by the door as she prepared to find her way through his home.

"Cute, dragon."

The lines reminded her of a toddler's drawing, only these lines were accompanied by arrows that pointed her through a few tunnels and corridors until she came to an enormous open space.

And a beautiful woman sitting in the center of a sofa in the sparsely decorated area, engrossed in a book while playing with a grape between her fingers. Clear turquoise eyes lifted from the book and hung on her for a long moment. Sera sized up the woman in the heavy silence while they regarded each other. The woman's hair was the color of snow, dappled with a few hues of sunlight. Even seated, she was smaller in stature, but her crop top showed off a ridiculously toned stomach and the small sleeves revealed femininely muscled arms.

The woman dropped the book on the simple wooden table, the grape on the plate beside it, and straightened to her feet. Sera's assessment of her height wasn't far off. She had a few inches on the stranger, but the way the other woman carried herself exuded more confidence than Sera could ever muster.

"Seraphina, right?" The woman's voice reminded her of a cat purring. Silky and sultry. As she approached, she held out her hand. "I'm Skylar. Or Sky. Gabe brought me over so you wouldn't be alone when you woke up." Her pink lips widened in a smile. "When he told me about you last night, I couldn't wait to meet you. Seeing as our dragons are the only blood brothers of the eight."

Sera shook Sky's hand, muscles she hadn't realized grown taut relaxing on her next breath. Her mouth curled. "Nice to finally meet you. Heard a lot about you from the guys." She glanced around the open room as she lowered her hand. "Are they here?"

Sky snickered, brushing one of her braids behind her

shoulder. "They're getting their asses beat on the summit. Cade called for a spontaneous training session because, from my understanding, the dragons haven't had a formal lesson in quite some time." She motioned toward another doorway, or what should be a doorway, but the arch was unevenly carved and Sera couldn't see beyond it. "We'll work on getting your place more fit for living, but for now, I brought over some food and a thermos of coffee and one of tea."

She rounded the sofa and led Sera into the adjoining room. It was wide and spacious, but simply furnished, like the main room. A table, a pair of chairs, sparse dishware, and mugs. A pit that looked like it hadn't been used in ages, with old, charred wood and a pile of ash beneath a cauldron on an iron hook.

Despite the simplicity of it all, Sera's heart swelled with comfort. Emery might have the means to live an extravagant lifestyle, but chose modesty over riches. Although she'd not mind having an actual stove to cook on, or a few cabinets to organize some of the dishware.

Sera took a seat at the table, Sky across from her. She watched the woman unwrap the dishes spread out between them, revealing patties of meat, chunks of potatoes, a dish filled with fruits, another with several rolls and slices of seeded bread. The last dish had a layout of fish and what looked like chicken.

"Help yourself. I hope it's to your liking." She tapped one of the thermoses. "Coffee or tea?"

"Coffee, please." Sera picked several different items from the plates and smiled at Sky. "It all looks wonderful. I'm sure I'll enjoy it. Thank you."

"Much of the food here is like what we have back in the human realm. The meats tend to be a bit gamier, but with the right seasonings, they're fabulous until your tastes adjust. The produce is far better than anything I had in Alabama, including the farmers markets and farm stands I'd go to."

She glanced up at Gabe's lifemate as the woman handed her a mug of steaming coffee, already lightened with milk. Sky grabbed a small bowl and removed the lid, offering sugar.

"Em said you like a little milk in your coffee."

Her brow cinched. "And how would he know that? He's only made me tea, and that he got lucky."

Sky laughed and shook her head. The woman's ease was refreshing and connected with something beneath the surface of Sera's mind. This woman was essentially her sister-in-law, and her acceptance of a stranger was welcoming. She'd come from a small, tightly knit group of families who kept a little distance between themselves and the world, except for those few that the elders deemed worthy of allowing into their circle. Instant acceptance wasn't something she was used to, but she was thoroughly grateful for it.

"If I'm to guess, Emery knew or he pried. I'm sure he asked the right questions of Slade's daughter to learn everything he could of you while you kept him at arm's length. He's charming enough to make anyone comfortable enough to pour out their secrets without realizing it. And yet"—she pointed the prongs of her fork in Sera's direction—"you managed to keep your wits about you, despite how easy it is to like him *and* the pull of the lifemate bond."

"Oh, my wits got pushed to the brink many times." Sera fixed her coffee with sugar and took a sip, relishing that first burst of caffeine with a sigh. It managed to dull the sourness that hit over the mention of Jes and Uncle Slade. She winced inwardly. "He's relentless."

"He's a dragon, and he's a LaRouche. Those bastard brothers have a way of getting everyone to let their guards down and striking at the right time. Em set me up good when I was trying to slip out of the hotel we'd been holed up in for a short time. Thought I was smart, but he's way too cunning. All his laidback and fun character hides the predator. They're *all* predators, but they love fiercely and bleed with loyalty." Her eyes took on a seriousness that impressed upon Sera's soul. "Giving yourself to a dragon will provide you with no safer home than within their embrace. Holding their heart is no greater gift. It's yin-yang. The balance we share with our lifemates is the epitome of perfection, a balance you'll never find elsewhere. Doesn't mean there won't be bumps in the road, but we are our dragons, and they are us. I can't imagine a world or a life without Gabe."

The corner of Sera's mouth had curled up as Sky expressed a sincerity that resounded viscerally within her body. She was new to this, only having accepted the inevitable less than twenty-four hours earlier, but the truth of Sky's words burned bright in Sera's chest. She'd fought against herself in fighting against Emery. The end result would have always been the same. She could've found the contentment and wholeness within his arms earlier had she not been so damn stubborn.

Now that she had it, she'd die before she let it go. It would kill her otherwise.

Sera tried some of the meats, surprised by the flavor and tenderness. The juices flowed over her tongue and made her stomach grumble in response to the deliciousness. Covering her mouth with the back of her hand, she murmured, "Wow. Incredible."

Sky nodded, her smile returning. The woman reminded Sera of herself, with a muted show of emotions she chose to temper rather than let run wild. "Right? Something to be said about all-natural food."

"No kidding." Sera indulged in a few more bites, savoring each piece, committing the flavors to memory. She'd be craving some of this again.

"Gabe told me that you were raised with full knowledge of The Hollow and the dragons. Had a small group of Keepers and their families living near Slade?"

Sera tried to hold back her grimace. She had yet to digest the full weight of her discovery last night. Her breakdown in the forest had left her numb. She barely remembered falling asleep in Emery's claws. She recalled how beautiful he had been in dragon form, but her mind, utterly worn out from the entire night, simply couldn't process anything beyond shallow observation and minimal understanding.

After a moment, she nodded, washing down a few potatoes with her coffee. "Yeah. Reared on all the stories and histories. Not so much the Baroqueth other than quick mentions, but my understanding is that they're our enemy and they've made a resurgence, hence the urgency to get everyone back here?"

Sky nodded. "You know, you're the only lifemate with prior understanding of who you are. The others and I learned of the dragons when they found us. It was an adjustment for some more than others, and still is, but we're all settling in well. As far as the Baroqueth go, I'm not sure how much Emery's told you, but they've been a nuisance, to say the least. We had an attack here less than a week ago, right before Em and Gabe went off to find you. Managed to get through it unscathed, but after the boys left, Briella confided in us that something bad was about to happen and we need to be prepared."

Her stomach rolled at the ominous statement. Slowly, she

finished the bite in her mouth and set her fork to the edge of her plate. Sky played with the food on her own dish, her gaze averted.

"Briella. She's another lifemate?"

"She's Syn's lifemate, and has prophetic visions." With a heavy sigh, Sky abandoned her food and leaned back in the chair, lifting her gaze. "They're hunting us, the lifemates, primarily. To create broodmares to replenish their numbers. When all of this started, when Zareh's Keeper had been found and killed and his lifemate sent on the run, the belief was that they resurged for the sake of obtaining power through the dragons. Being sorcerers of dark magic, they learned to override the Keeper bonds with the dragonstones and force the dragons into compliance. The dragons would be nothing more than puppets to their whims. Far too much power for anyone of evil intent. However, things changed when a Baroqueth woman, Malla, came into the picture. She tried to capture Briella in New Orleans but released her without a fight. Briella hasn't confided why, but the more things develop, the more we're speculating about the reasons. She saved Gabby during another attack outside the veil, and Cade let her escape without repercussions. I personally haven't had an encounter with her, but about a week ago, she appeared again at the bedside of Caryssa's father, Dorian, while he was in the ICU and stabilized him for the return trip for further healing. Gabe also mentioned Taj detected she wasn't entirely forthcoming when she appeared at Caryssa's uncle's strip club and killed him before Taj had the opportunity to do so himself. Her role in all of this has been unsettling, because she continues to help the dragons, but she's Baroqueth. And an enviable one at that."

"Enviable," Sera murmured as she mentally ticked off the

events she recalled hearing about that aligned with everything Sky said. "What do you mean?"

The corner of Sky's mouth twitched. "She's a female who once led Baroqueth to pursue us but suddenly turned on her own people. She possesses more power than most Baroqueth, and she's elusive, like a shadow. We don't know what her plan is, what her strategy is. She's giving us reasons to trust her, but I've been taught to keep your enemies close. It begs the question of whether she's trying to whittle her way into our lives to destroy us from within or did she really turn traitor. And who the hell is she? Baroqueth don't have female leaders or commanders. At least that's what the dragons believed until she came along. They're male-dominated."

Sera mulled over this information as she sipped her coffee, trying to figure out a mystery she'd only just been thrown into. It helped keep her mind off last night's discoveries while she waited for Emery to return. Sky's account intrigued her, quite honestly. She wanted to learn everything, immerse herself in this life and those who would be part of it, danger or not. This was who she was, the life she'd be building moving forward. And she'd take the good with the bad, as long as Emery was by her side.

"They'd be upset to learn I won't be a broodmare." Sera snorted and placed her mug on the table. "If my history is correct, didn't the Baroqueth evolve from a rogue Keeper who turned on his dragon?"

Sky showed no outward discomfort, but the air around her shifted. A resistant energy hummed, a discord Sera couldn't nail down.

"So the story goes. The Keeper was greedy and wanted more power than he already had by being blood-bound to his dragon. He used his power to manipulate his dragon and managed to siphon the dragon's power through the dragonstone. Ultimately, he killed his dragon by depleting him, and when he tried to obtain more power, he was shut down by the other dragons and Keepers, fleeing with a small group of his devoted followers. From there, the Baroqueth race was born, and over time, they became a force to be reckoned with. Their blood was infused with the magic of this world, thanks to his dragon, which allows them the ability to reach The Hollow and connect with the land, despite the resistance that they meet at the veil and pushback from the spirits of The Hollow trying to protect what is theirs." Sky shrugged. "I got the Cliffs Notes version of what started this war."

"Bottom line is that the Baroqueth are nothing more than descendants of rogue Keepers, which make them like us, or our parents. A darker version of us."

Sky contemplated this, watching Sera curiously. Sera pushed her plate aside as her thoughts continued to form ideas and scenarios.

"And that being said, if our parents had a generation of girls because the dragons were near extinction, who is to say something similar wouldn't happen with the Baroqueth? That they might start producing females as well?"

"You just arrived here and you're putting more together than we've been able to. That's impressive." Sky pressed her lips together and rubbed the back of her neck. "It's unnerving."

Sera's brow furrowed. What did she say wrong? "I-I don't—"

"No, I didn't mean it in a bad way. But what you're alluding to is really giving weight to our speculation surrounding the female Baroqueth. *That's* unnerving."

The crease in her brows deepened. "Why?"

"Because we're all beginning to believe that Malla isn't simply some Baroqueth commander or leader or something like that, but somehow connected to The Hollow. Connected to Cade."

"Our dragon leader." Sera narrowed her eyes, then gasped as a heavy weight seemed to slam down, fitting itself perfectly into an open hole in this entire scenario. "His *lifemate*."

Sky stiffened the moment the words were out of Sera's mouth. She blinked several times, then leaned forward, elbows perched on the table, a conspiratorial gleam in her eyes. "Goddess, it would make sense! I've heard that Cade becomes overly defensive when anyone brings up his actions, or lack of, toward Malla, especially after the woman healed Gabby. He had the perfect opportunity to capture her, but instead let her go. Gabe caught wind that she'd given something to Taj to deliver to Cade after the encounter at the strip club. Briella had forewarned us of an impending war, and that she's going to somehow be the main source of contention between the Baroqueth and the Firestorms." She smacked her hands on the table, startling Sera as the dishes rattled. Her chair scraped on the floor as she shot up, grabbed Sera's wrist, and urged her out of her seat. "Come on! We've got to talk to the others."

Sera stumbled off her chair, trying to keep up with Sky's urgent tugs. She nearly tripped over her own feet as the smaller woman led them down a tunnel she'd yet to explore. Their sneakers smacked the rock, echoing through the endless passage as the firelight grew more distant between sconces and left patches of the tunnel dim.

"Wait, where are we going?"

"We'll head to Briella's first. I'll put out an impression to the others to meet us over there."

"But—"

"Ready to meet the crew?" Sky flashed her a mischievous grin. "We're storming in like a wrecking ball."

Sera found herself the center of attention, squeezed tightly between Sky and a woman named Ariah on Briella's sofa, surrounded by five additional women, one trying to keep a baby from climbing out of her arms and growing frustrated with her child's behavior. She tried to keep the names straight, tried to keep their dragon mates in order, and felt like her head was on a swivel doing so.

Despite the strangeness of this gathering, Sera felt right at home.

"Give him to me," another woman said—Gabby, maybe?—reaching over to relieve an exhausted-looking Kaylae of her squirming infant. She cooed to the baby, who instantly became enthralled by the new face, pressing a small fist to his mouth as he suckled and babbled.

"You have a knack with that boy," Kaylae said on a long breath as she slumped in her chair and brushed mussed strands of dark hair from her rosy face. "He's a terror."

"Takes after his father," Saralyn, Briella's mother, said as she finished pouring tall glasses of fuscia-colored tea for everyone. She took up her seat beside her daughter, a gentle smile on her mouth as she rested her attention on Sera. "I think we got ahead of ourselves. Welcome to The Hollow. We're glad to have you here. Should you need anything at all, know that we'll help any way we can."

"Thanks. I appreciate that." Sera grinned. The woman displayed a mother's warmth without fault, tugging at faint threads Sera had long ago tucked away once she understood she had no living mother. The disconnect from a mother figure, yet the yearning to know a mother's kindness and love, swelled in the presence of this woman.

"Saralyn adopted us all," Caryssa said, her face beaming as she cast the older woman a warm glance. "And we love her for putting up with us."

"Aw, honey. None of you should be without a mother figure."

Her soft eyes turned to Sky, where her sympathetic gaze lingered. Sky shifted, taking up one of the glasses from the table. Sera caught the faint flush that touched the fierce woman's cheeks. Though Sky came off as strong and independent, she'd suffered the loss of her mother not long ago, and still suffered grief Sera couldn't understand completely. Her grief lay in not knowing her mother and craving a connection she never had a chance to establish. It was an emptiness that Aunt Claire had tried to fill but could never complete.

She'll probably despise me now.

A sad reality, but one she had to accept sooner rather than later.

Briella crossed her legs and leaned forward, elbows on her knees, blue-gray eyes honed on Sera. A faint smudge of gray paint dotted her forehead above her brow and stained her T-shirt and fingers, while the rogue strands of auburn hair that had escaped the messy bun tied high up on her head held their own streaks of paint.

"I think we're all settled now. Sorry for my poor manners when you first arrived." Briella set a glowering glance on Sky, then snickered. "I'm usually not so aloof."

"It's fine. I wasn't expecting to meet everyone under such pressing terms. Or what seems to be pressing. I'm still a bit confused," Sera admitted.

"If I caught Sky's impression correctly, you seem to

have figured out the big mystery surrounding Malla," Caryssa said. "You weren't sheltered from your true lineage, like the rest of us, so you have more understanding of the connections between Firestorms and Baroqueth, I suppose."

"Not entirely, but I've not had to exert the extra energy to try and adapt to a fantasy life that shouldn't exist, as you all have had to do." Sera glanced at Saralyn, who had lowered her head, then panned to Briella, lifting a brow. Briella simply smiled, a silent understanding of Sera's curiosity, and answered with a shrug of a shoulder. "You have visions, right?"

"I do."

"And you've had a vision that implies an upcoming war that involves Malla?"

"I have, in a sense."

"Why? What happens with her?"

Oh, the weight of everyone's gaze turned suffocating as these women gauged the new person in their group with a mix of emotions. Heat began to suffuse Sera's face, creeping up from her neck. Her stomach tilted. She placed her glass back on the table, uncertain whether she could drink it without it coming back up. She was never one to be the center of attention. She preferred privacy and small gatherings. Though this was small, the scrutiny was that of a hundred people.

After all, she'd come to The Hollow less than a day before and here she was, suggesting something crazy.

Briella finally blinked and cleared her throat. She took a drink from her glass and rested it on her knee. "I'm not sure. All I know is that she's going to play a major role in the upcoming conflict. I've not seen which side she's on, if that's what you're asking."

Sera shook her head. "No. I'm just trying to see if I can figure out more of this."

"The reason I wanted everyone here is because Sera said something that makes perfect sense. And"—Sky pointed to Briella—"if you've seen something in the past regarding Malla, I think you need to come clean. The more we know, the better prepared we'll be."

"She's got a valid point, Briella."

Sera twisted to face the new voice. Another woman, this one dressed in eclectic clothing, crossed the room and took an empty seat beside Gabby. Gabby smiled at the woman, then returned her attention to the baby as she rocked him in her arms. The precious boy's eyelids had begun to droop, his thumb having found purchase between his lips.

Violet eyes found her across the table. The woman was beautiful and demure, the air around her soothing and warm. She appeared not much older than the rest of them, but held herself more like Saralyn, with a maternal edge and knowledge etched deep into her gaze.

"You must be Seraphina. I'm Amelia, the one responsible for all things witchy, as Taryn likes to say."

"Nice to meet you," Sera said with a small nod, shifting her focus back to Briella.

"It's not my place to disclose another's personal information, Amelia," Briella murmured.

"Who is it you're trying to protect?" Ariah asked. No hostility wove through her voice, her question one of genuine curiosity.

Briella huffed a breath and leaned back.

"My thought, based on what I know of the history between Baroqueth and Firestorms, is that Malla may be Cade's lifemate," Sera said matter-of-factly. Gabby stiffened, her head slowly rising from the baby to stare at her in shock.

Ariah whispered something unintelligible under her breath. Kaylae's gaze narrowed. Saralyn exchanged a silent glance with her daughter, then Sky.

It was Amelia who set Sera on edge. Her expression hadn't changed in the least, still calm and soft but watchful, nonetheless.

"Briella?" Those violet eyes finally turned away to rest on Briella. Syn's lifemate's expression tightened as if she fought an inner battle, avoiding everyone who had turned away from Sera to focus on her. Sera hated the attention on the woman, and silently prayed it wouldn't cause a rift between them. This certainly wasn't the way she wanted her first introduction to go.

"Visions can be fickle things, can't they? At least I've heard such," Sera interrupted. Briella looked up at her, a flicker of thanks lighting her eyes. Sera offered a small smile. "Maybe nothing's been said because there's no certainty to the vision. I came to this on my own. It simply makes sense. *If*, and I emphasize *if*, Malla and Cade are lifemates, that means her father could very possibly be a blood relative to a Keeper or *the* Keeper who went rogue. It might explain a lot, including the strength of her magic and why a female Baroqueth is acting in a commanding position, right? Look at us here. A full generation of females born of surviving Keepers. What if she falls into this with us? Does Cade have a Keeper? Does his Keeper have a daughter? If my guess is correct"—Sera panned the entire group of women before returning to Briella—"and she and Cade are lifemates, I think it's safe to say that would certainly cause a war that centers around her."

The dark silence that consumed the large living room could have blocked out the sunlight filtering through the glassless windows and smothered them alive. Sera's muscles tensed as the silence stretched. She tried not to shrink beneath the numerous sets of eyes that touched on her before casting their quiet suspicions elsewhere.

"I wasn't aware someone died."

The deep, accented baritone cut through the impeding silence like a knife. Briella jumped up and ran over to a man who greeted her with an embrace that pulled her off her feet, and a kiss that made Sera squirm in her skin. This must be Syn, and he sure as hell looked the part.

Behind him, several other men poured out of the corridor, the last two being Gabe and Emery. Her heart did a strange flutter that tickled the back of her throat and made her head light. His presence alone set her at ease, melting away the tension and awkwardness that this meeting had caused. He cast her a tender smile when his gaze landed on her, and it took every ounce of her strength not to follow Briella's actions and launch herself into his arms.

Gods knew, he was all she craved at this very moment.

"Got word Syn was hosting a party and the invitations didn't reach us in time," a man with shoulder-length sandy hair announced as he rounded the circle of women and fell into the sofa beside Ariah. He leaned forward and held out his hand to Sera. "Alazar. Emery couldn't stop talking about you at training. Pleasure to meet you."

She accepted his hand. "Nice to meet you, too."

"Last time I put you in charge of a welcoming committee, sister," Emery interrupted, shooting Sky a playful glare as he sidled around the group to come up behind the sofa at Sera's back. The lightness in her chest grew as she twisted to soak in his handsome face and drown in those warm whiskey eyes that held her like nothing else in the universe existed. He squatted on his haunches, bringing himself to her level, and drew his knuckles over her cheek. *"Is everything okay?*

Briella managed to reach Syn during one of the breaks and told him you had all gathered here."

She folded her hand over his. *"I thought too hard on something, and it was cause for an immediate gathering, I guess. I'm fine."* She brought the tips of his fingers to her lips. *"Wish you hadn't left me alone this morning."*

"Sweet flame, how you fill me with such guilt." His mouth curled in a sexy half-grin. He craned over the back of the sofa and pressed a lingering kiss to her forehead. She let her eyelids close and leaned into his affectionate kiss, lost in their small piece of the world as it continued to spin around them. *"You'll have me all night and all morning to do with as you will to make up for my lack of consideration."*

"Oh, the temptation. I recall you saying you preferred the bed because you could do so much more to me there than on the table, and yet, I have a suspicion you held back."

The heat of his breath played across her forehead as he leaned back, the faint tinge of a smoky scent filling her nostrils. He slipped his palm against her cheek and stroked his thumb beneath her eye. "You've no idea."

Emery leaned back right before Gabe clapped his shoulder.

"When these ladies get together, it's dangerous." Gabe winked at Sera. "Don't follow in their footsteps. Having one woman who doesn't conspire against the rest of us would be greatly appreciated."

"There's no conspiracy," Sky groaned.

Gabe chuckled, lifting Sky's chin with the tip of a partially extended talon. The heated look she shared with him belied the edge in her voice from seconds ago.

Sera pushed off the sofa and made her way through the suddenly overly crowded area to the back of it to stand beside Emery. As much as she appreciated the group, she needed time to adjust to this new life and not be overwhelmed. As it stood, she had other things to work through first.

Surely sensing her uncertainty, Emery drew her into the side of his body. Gentle waves of calm pulsed through her, soothing those wrinkles until she wanted nothing more than to melt into him. The natural heat that poured off his body wrapped her in a blanket of comfort, the delicious scent that followed him everywhere infusing her soul. She hated that she'd fought this for as long as she had, especially understanding the bond more than any of these women had when they first encountered their lifemates. If there was one thing she could thank Nick Allaze for it was not hiding the truth of who she was. He'd given her little else, but having given her the truth of her heritage, she owed a small modicum of thanks to the man who otherwise deserved nothing more than contempt.

Another figure emerged from the tunnel. A large man with eyes that blazed red with fire. Deep red hair pulled back and tied behind his crown. A matching beard. An air that demanded attention and warned of danger. He eclipsed the room and all these massive men, his presence swallowing up everything in its path. Sera tilted her head, observing this latest arrival with more curiosity than concern.

Cade. Had to be Cade. A force more beast than man, more dragon than human. He'd often been described by Uncle Slade as an oversized Viking, and certainly fit the description. His cheeks angled sharply over the top of his beard, his eyes slanted to add a cruelness to the slope of dark red brows. Though he had his hands tucked in the pockets of dark blue jeans that hugged his muscled thighs, she doubted any way he presented himself would soften the fierceness of his appearance.

He was the oldest Firestorm dragon, after all, and the leader of this hidden world.

"Sorry to break up the party, folks. We should make our way beyond the veil to collect those remaining in the human realm before the day wears on."

His gaze hit every person in the room, and came to land on Sera. The corner of his mouth lifted, though his eyes narrowed ever so slightly. She watched his face transform a tiny bit, the sharp edges appearing smoother than they had a moment ago. The blaze in his eyes dimmed to a smoldering fire. He skated the outer circle of those gathered in the large room until he stood beside her, that half-grin spreading.

"Seraphina," he said, his voice a perfect blend of man and monster. Deep, rough, like the rest of him. He had a handful of inches on Emery, and Emery stood a head taller than her. He held out a hand to her. She accepted his greeting, his fingers swallowing her hand. "It's a pleasure to have finally found you and have you here. Heard Emery worked hard to earn you by his side."

Emery growled. Cade chuckled, and the sound eased the severity in the air. Sera glanced back at Emery, who wore a smirk despite the exasperated twist in his handsome features.

"I think it was mutual." She rested a hand against Emery's stomach, the hard ripple of muscle beneath his T-shirt teasing her libido enough to make her want to escape this gathering and spend time with him alone. "He took it like a champ."

"You didn't leave me much choice," he grumbled. His gaze burned into her and his fingers tightened on her waist. "I'm just glad I didn't have to suffer longer." To Cade, he added, "Fighting the lifemate bond is the worst kind of torture."

Sera observed Cade's reaction to Emery's comment, whether her dragon realized it or not. Cade's grin slowly fell flat, and his eyes smoldered a little darker. A shadow crossed his face, but quickly vanished, leaving her to wonder if it was a trick of the light. He rolled out his shoulders and nodded once.

"I would imagine so." He turned away from them to address the room. "Let's take flight so you can get back to your women."

CHAPTER EIGHTEEN

*E*mery strode up the driveway, sunglasses over his eyes to shield them from the glare of the afternoon sun. A few cars, including the pickup truck he and Gabe had rented, littered the drive, but couldn't obscure a flash memory of what had occurred out here the night before. A thin layer of fresh snow coated the grass of the yard. Most of the windows at the front of the house were fogged or frosted. Curtains were pulled over many of the panes, but a few remained open, allowing glimpses within of an empty living room and a brightly lit foyer.

"Hope you're home, Slade."

He led his brethren to the sweeping front stoop, all except for Zareh and Tajan, who remained at The Hollow for protective purposes, but he and Cade alone climbed the stairs while the rest hung around on the drive.

He'd barely started to lift his fist to knock when the front door pulled open. Faint shadows circled his Keeper's eyes and his face appeared haggard, a bruise having formed over his left cheek, but his delight when he saw his guests managed to lighten his features. Emery angled away from the door, allowing Slade to look upon the dragons who accompanied him. Slade's smile widened and that familiar, lighthearted gleam touched his eyes.

"I told you it wouldn't be long," Emery said, referring to their previous discussion about the need to prepare to return to The Hollow. "I hope you and the others figured out everything here."

"Even if we haven't, it wouldn't matter. I think we're all in agreement." He stepped aside, motioning for them to come in. "It's time to go home. Cade, it's wonderful to see you again."

"As well as you." Cade clapped his arm. "Anyone here with you?"

Slade cast Emery a solemn glance. "Claire is keeping company with Jax and Lauro's wives. The boys were planning to swing by in a bit. Jes went out after the tiff last night and she's been avoiding me in the brief moments she comes home." His head dropped a fraction. "Seems to be my latest achievement when it comes to my daughters."

"Mm. Heard about what happened last night."

Slade closed the door after Taryn and Syn brought up the rear and filled the foyer behind the rest of the group. He stepped up to Emery and hung his thumbs on his beltloops.

"How's Sera? Is she doing well?"

Emery offered a smile. "She'll be fine. Skylar's taken to her like a sister, and she's already been introduced to the other women. She doesn't have as much to adjust to as the others, which is good." He tipped his head slightly, boring his gaze into Slade. *"You need to speak with her when you get back. This can't go on long. She needs you."*

"I know, Em. I hope she's willing to listen."

"She will." Straightening his shoulders, he nodded toward the house's interior. "Why don't you gather the ladies

and put a call out for the guys? Has anyone heard from Nick?"

Slade snorted, combing a hand through his hair. "Don't think he'd be making any effort to come here, unless it's to burn the house to the ground. The man's a loose hinge."

"Well." Gabe drew the word out, long and slow and laden with meaning. Emery shot him a warning glance, pulling his upper lip from his teeth. Gabe snickered. Taryn, who'd been quiet up to this point, raised his brows at Slade, a mischievous curl hanging on the edge of his mouth. Syn knocked him in the arm with his elbow before Taryn had a chance to entertain his curiosity.

"Damn, you all act like you follow the straight and narrow." Alazar wedged between Emery and Cade, slung an arm around Slade's shoulders and surveyed the entryway. "Forgive your dragon for bringing up a sore subject. Why don't you show me around the place? You know, you and Mark have pretty similar tastes when it comes to the extravagant." He flicked away a lock of hair that had fallen over Slade's forehead. "And style. Think you were brothers from other mothers?"

Emery blinked at his Keeper's back as Alazar led him away. He looked at Cade, then his brethren.

"What the fuck just happened?" he asked.

Gabe chuckled and shook his head. "That's Alazar for you. Let's get the ball rolling here. I'd like to get back to my woman and stay put for more than a few hours."

As the dragons split up, Emery remained in the foyer with Cade. "I think I should try and find Nick, even if we separated on bad terms. He's a Keeper, after all."

"Why don't you bring your brother and I'll remain here to help with packing?" Cade's keen gaze took in every inch of the house from this position, his mouth tight. After a few moments of tense silence, the beast cleared his throat and faced Emery. "Go ahead. I'll make sure we're set to leave when you return. If you can't find Nick, I'll return on my own and try to locate him. Right now, we need to gather the other Keepers and find Slade's daughter."

"Everything good, old man?" Emery asked quietly.

Cade nodded once, unconvincingly. His eyes narrowed. "Let's get moving."

Emery gestured for Gabe to follow and they headed out of the house.

Once in the truck—thankfully, Gabe had had the mind to keep the keys on him—Gabe tapped the window with the curved back of his talon. "Cade seemed uneasy."

"You noticed that, too, huh?" Emery followed the back roads toward Nick's house. "Hate when he keeps shit to himself, especially if it involves us." After some hesitation, he asked, "Any Baroqueth vibes I may have missed?"

"I didn't get anything, but that's not to say there wasn't. Not like we did anything to draw attention."

"We haven't really drawn attention in the past. They happened to cross our paths by happenstance."

"Or tracking."

Emery's thoughts reverted to the day the Baroqueth attacked Syn and Taryn as they were leaving The Hollow with their women. The day Gabby nearly died, and Malla had saved her life with no residual magic that could be detected as a threat. The veil was no secret to the Baroqueth, however, their ability to cross through could be harrowing with the spells and wards in place. Unless they had someone leading them through, or they possessed an alternate means of crossing through the portal with stronger magic.

After the most recent attack in the village, where the Baroqueth bypassed the veil altogether, he was beginning to think the bastards were playing with them, waiting for the perfect time to strike.

Emery shook the thoughts from his head. Too convoluted for the time being. He'd bring it up when they returned home and had a meeting with Cade. Much needed to be discussed.

"Think we've got spies watching us come and go from The Hollow. Would make sense if they're planning an attack. Outposts at our only point of entry would give them the advantage of knowing how many of us were in The Hollow, and how many were here in this realm. They could easily take out those of us who leave alone." Emery turned down Nick's street, slowing down as he spotted the house toward the end of the road. A slithering curiosity wove through his muscles, one that Gabe echoed with the shift in his seat to lean forward. "What is she doing here?"

As Emery pulled the truck in behind Jeslyn's parked car along the curb, he met his brother's sharp gaze.

"Well, I've never been one to believe in coincidences," Gabe said, throwing open the door and hopping out of the truck. "Might as well find out. If they're both here, it'll make this trip much easier. If she's here snooping about, at least Slade will have his daughter back."

Emery followed his brother up the walkway, brushing his fingertips over the trunk of Jeslyn's car as he rounded the front of the truck. The metal was cold, but a faint spark of energy he couldn't quite place teased his fingers before they fell away. Folding his fingers into his palm, he climbed the two steps to the front door as Gabe knocked. They both heard the rush of footsteps within the house and exchanged glances.

Gabe spun off the stoop and disappeared around the side of the house. Emery waited a few more seconds before he twisted the doorknob, still broken from when he'd returned an inebriated Nick to the house a few days before, and let himself in.

The entryway remained littered with broken shards of glass and ceramic, as it had been the last time he'd stepped into this place. The holes in the walls hadn't been patched. At least the table had been righted. A dim light lit the living room, but the kitchen lay in darkness. A shriek pierced the otherwise heavy silence of the house, followed by his brother's hushed voice and dual sets of footsteps coming back into the house. Emery cut into the kitchen to the right and opened the adjoining door to the garage. His brows furrowed when he saw Nick's Mustang sitting pretty in the dark.

Closing the door, he turned as Gabe appeared in the kitchen archway, an infuriated Jeslyn caught in his grip. Her eyes sparked with frustration and anger, faltering only for a moment when they landed on Emery. He offered a small smile, one more for the sake of peace than true pleasure of seeing her again. When she came down from her outrage and apologized the Seraphina for her behavior, he'd consider repairing a bit of friendship, solely for his lifemate and Keeper, no other reason.

Jeslyn folded her arms over her chest and huffed like a spoiled brat. "Why are you here? Breaking and entering?"

Emery lifted his chin and regarded her through narrowed eyes down the slope of his nose. She wore an A-line skirt and a button-down satin blouse beneath a parka, and a pair of thigh-high boots. He tilted his head, contemplating her choice of attire when it was barely ten degrees outside. The little nuances he'd picked up from her over the last few days told him she picked her outfits carefully. Not once had she dressed like this for him, not that he cared, but it piqued his curiosity. Especially with the mildly disheveled shirt and a few strands of hair out of place of her usually perfect hair styles.

"You're not cold, are you?" he asked.

Her lips grew taut, her gaze anywhere but him. "What would you care after how you made a fool out of me?"

"I accept fault for playing into the game, yes, but how one is perceived often falls back on the shoulders of one's self. We're adults and make conscious decisions. Regardless, I do apologize for my behavior"—he ticked a finger—"until last night. This attitude is rather unbecoming of you, Jeslyn, and in poor taste."

She unfolded her arms on a sharp downward punch, fists tight by her sides, and marched up to him. Her cheeks burned red and her eyes flared with rage. "You have no business critiquing me on my behavior when yours wasn't anything to write home about. You led me on the entire fucking time and have no remorse for doing so! You are a piss-poor example of the dragons my father used to describe, and I thank the Gods for sparing me a life with the likes of *you*. You and Sera deserve each other."

The corner of his mouth curled in a dark grin. He chuckled, a sound that stirred low in his throat, and stepped up to Jeslyn. Into her. The woman had the intelligence to shuffle back a few inches, the fury draining from her eyes and a flicker of fear sparking in its stead.

"See, that's the attitude I was talking about. The envy turning you green. Let me explain something to you, and only because you are my Keeper's daughter. It was Sera who tried to keep away from me for *your* sake. She maintained her distance because of the loyalty she felt for you and your relationship. If she had any choice in this, she would have lived in torment just to see you happy, and yet you blame her for something that is completely out of her control. I own my guilt in the part I played to appease her, paying attention when I knew how things would end up. I have apologized.

Now, be an adult, Jeslyn, and see this for what it is. Fate formed by the Goddess, and the Goddess alone. Hate me all you want. Sera, your *half-sister*, does *not* deserve your animosity."

Seconds stretched as they battled wills in an unwavering locked gaze. He witnessed the knowledge of her defeat, but her persistence to maintain her dignity refused to allow her to admit it.

The creak of the back door tore him from the silent battle. Gabe bolted down the hallway. Emery grabbed Jeslyn's forearm and pulled her behind him as he followed his brother at a fast pace, bursting through the door only a few moments after Gabe.

The dark thrum of magic hit him square in the chest, knocking him back a step. Jeslyn whimpered behind him, pressed into his back as he used his body to shield her from a potential attack. Fire poured from Gabe's partially transformed maw into a whorl of black smoke that vanished a moment later. Sparks settled on the bone-dry bushes, making them smolder as Gabe pulled his dragon back.

Emery cast the now empty space of the backyard a hard glance, then slowly met his brother's bloodthirsty gaze.

"They grabbed Nick."

Emery cussed under his breath. He herded Jeslyn into the house and rushed down the hallway toward the front door, Gabe at his heels.

"W-what happened? What's going on?"

The genuine fear in her voice softened him, if only a fraction. He had to remind himself that neither Sera nor Jeslyn had been exposed to the Baroqueth threat. They'd been safe all these years. Until now.

"We've outstayed our welcome in Colorado," Gabe said, taking the lead into the front yard. His eyes blazed with fire as he scanned the area, searching for any Baroqueth. "Don't know why they took him and left us, but not going to question it."

"It's best to fly," Emery said. Gabe nodded once, then fully transformed into his dragon. Jeslyn gasped behind Emery as he brought her forward. Her eyes, wide as she took in the sight of her first real-life dragon, darted between Gabe and himself. "He'll carry you. I'm taking up the rear. Go."

Gabe didn't give her a chance to shuffle closer. He snatched her up in his front claw and launched into the sky, her brief scream echoing through the day. He followed on his brother's tail, spiraling into the clouds at his six, keeping his senses attuned to his surroundings as they made the quick trip to Slade's.

Cade was standing outside as they landed, Gabe steadying Jeslyn enough for her to stumble out of his grasp. Emery reined in his dragon as his back claws hit the pavement and walked out of the landing straight up to Cade.

"Baroqueth at Nick's. Time to leave," he said curtly. Hurrying up to the house, he reached out to Slade. *"Buddy, hope you're ready to go. Now. This instant."*

"My daughter—"

"Is here. We can't wait. They've found us. Tell me Jax and Lauro made it over."

He stormed into the foyer as Slade rushed down the circular staircase. Urgency flared in his eyes and colored his cheeks pink. The sight of his Keeper falling into his old role filled Emery with nostalgia. "What about Nick?"

Emery shook his head. "One of the Baroqueth grabbed him. We need to leave."

Slade faltered for only a moment at the news, then ran into the office, his face a sheet of hard, intense angles. He unlocked his private drawer and pulled out the box with the dragonstone, tucking it into his jacket pocket. The sound of footsteps clamored from different areas of the house, voices pitched with urgency and a low-grade panic. Emery made a quick sweep of the office as Slade hastily folded the single picture of Dina he'd shown Emery and tucked it into his back pocket, his eyes glancing off Emery.

The house rocked beneath an ear-piercing explosion. Glass imploded from every window at the front of the house, casting a brilliant, shimmering shower of shards over everyone. Screams filled the air. Emery threw up his scales and covered Slade's hunched form with his own body. The metallic scent of blood touched his nostrils, rolled over his slightly parted lips. The taste of blood...and spent energy.

"Out! Now!" Cade roared, unleashing his monstrous beast as he gathered the three people closest to him and shot skyward, bursting through the immaculate domed ceiling of Slade's mansion. A cape of fire ignited over the gaping hole as Cade created an escape for the rest of them while warding off their enemies. Taryn snatched up another three of the remaining group and rocketed up in Cade's path as debris from the ceiling rained down over the foyer, forcing the remaining group to scurry away from chunks of wood, stone, and metal. Syn torched the front entryway, fire pouring from his massive maw. Flames consumed the doorway, but not before Emery caught sight of his brother disappearing into the sky with Jeslyn between his claws.

Magic hummed throughout the house, vibrating through the floors at their feet. The air pulsed with unseen waves, that ominous underwater feeling preceding an imminent blow.

Emery caught Alazar and Syn's hardened glances.

Both dragons grabbed the members of the remaining group and hurtled through the opening in the ceiling.

Another explosion rocked the house, down to the foundation. Cracks webbed up the sides of the walls that soon began to crumble around Emery and Slade. He grabbed his Keeper by the wrist, his body changing as he picked his point of escape—

Indigo flames erupted along the open windows.

White fire poured through the ceiling, the cracks, rolling like lava toward the center of the room.

"Basement! I have an escape there."

"You serious?" Emery snapped, preparing to shield his Keeper through the intensity of this magical inferno. Slade twisted his hand, grabbed Emery's half-transformed claw, and pulled him out of the office. They dodged falling debris and puddles of tarry magic that would melt them the instant it touched their skin. There was no sign of Cade in the hole, no sign of fire. Goddess, Emery hoped the old dragon had the sense to leave and not wait for him.

Emery kept half an eye behind them as the front of the house continued to collapse in slow motion, blocking any escape from that direction.

"We're surrounded. Got the impression from Syn."

"And the basement will lead us to freedom."

"Slade, I think you've forgotten who we're dealing with here, and that our best chance of escape is up."

"Not if they're waiting for us."

As restless as his dragon was to take to the sky, Emery trusted Slade enough to follow at his heels, swatting aside chunks of the house before they had a chance to hit his Keeper. Slade knew the dangers that came with the Baroqueth. He wouldn't be so foolish as to place them both in a compromising position.

Slade brought him to a door beneath the stairs, pulled it open, and hurried through. Emery slammed the door shut behind them and took to his dragon's vision in the pitch-dark surroundings.

The ground trembled beneath another attack.

Drywall and cinderblock dust plinked around them. He grabbed Slade by the waist and jumped down the remaining stairs, landing lightly on his feet at the opening of a large, finished room now thick with dust. Rafter beams had fallen from their places in the ceiling, creating more obstacles around furniture and entertainment tables.

"This is not the time for poker or billiards, Slade."

Slade coughed. Emery shed his jacket and tore off his T-shirt, shredding a large piece off the bottom.

"Use it to protect your airway."

Slade took the fabric and pressed it to his nose and mouth. *"Straight ahead. There's an adjoining room. Another short set of stairs through the metal door at the back of the room. And a tunnel that'll lead out into the forest at the base of the backyard."*

"You're kidding me." He spared his Keeper a half-second glance of disbelief before a roguish grin pulled at his mouth and he chuckled. *"Smart son of a bitch."*

"I didn't make it this long in this world without a brain, dragon. Priority was always making sure we'd be able to escape. What better way than through tunnels?"

Without delay, Emery followed Slade's directions, knocking the door across the room down, leading his blind Keeper to the second door, which had a host of locks and padlocks. Emery's body filled out with some of the mass from his dragon as he barreled into the door, tearing it off its hinges. Metal clinked to the floor from broken locks as the door slammed into the cement wall beyond. Emery leaped over the stairs with Slade tucked at his side, and they landed on a packed-dirt floor.

Another quake of the house and ground. A deafening rumble followed by the insistent shaking of the world around them. Dust plumed from the trembling ground, the tunnel's walls stressed.

"The house is collapsing," Emery warned. He allowed his dragon to come forth, enough to utilize his beast's strength and agility and still fit the dimensions of the tunnel. He pulled Slade in front of him, wrapped his arms around his Keeper to secure him, back to front against his chest, and bolted down the tunnel. *"How long is this? I need to know how much time before the dust plume hits the tunnel and gives our exit away."*

"Roughly nine hundred feet. Long enough to get it into the forest."

Scales spread over his skin. Talons pierced through his boots, finding purchase in the ground to catapult them ahead at a faster clip. He swallowed up the tunnel, his partially emerged wings scraping along the wooden bracers that supported the walls.

At his back, he felt the first change in the air, the heaviness building, the pressure increasing.

That inevitable plume was about to hit.

He growled, pushing himself harder, faster, seeing the end of the tunnel coming up quick. One hundred feet. Seventy-five. Fifty.

The pressure behind him swelled, pressed on his eardrums, slid over his scales.

Dipping his right shoulder, he braced himself for the impact of the metal door, bursting through the barrier into the cold afternoon.

His dragon consumed his body and he shot up through the trees. A thick plume of dark gray smoke billowed at his tail. He ascended into the sky, wings pulling upward, the wind hitting him at mach force. He absorbed the ache in Slade's body, rusty from thirty-plus years of not experiencing the power of launch.

As he burst through the clouds, he shot his wings out completely, halting their brutal ascent. He didn't bother to try and see what they'd escaped. He could only imagine the devastation that remained of Slade's mansion.

"That was a little too close for comfort," Slade finally said as Emery glided through the sky for a few minutes, letting his Keeper recover. The man's muscles relaxed in his claw, followed by faint tremors he tried to sooth, just as he had tried to cover the tremor in his voice. Emery grunted in agreement, his attention on his surroundings. He wouldn't feel better until they were back at The Hollow. *"I'm not getting impressions from the others."*

"They had a bit of a head start."

Emery angled his body and banked to the left, then to the right, keeping his route obscured. No straight-line flying today. Thank the Goddess for the clouds.

Silence filled their telepathic connection, though worry simmered along the line. Slade's mind toiled with concerns, none of which Emery indulged. His focus was on everything in the vast world around them. He didn't trust the Baroqueth not to have figured out some magical means of flight to lay a surprise attack on them in the only place they were safe in this world: the sky.

He twisted and spiraled higher, heading west, then north, then coming back around toward The Hollow.

A short distance from the veil, Slade finally broke the silence. *"Do you think there is any chance of finding Nick?"*

As much as the topic of the Keeper soured his mood, Emery felt a small ounce of responsibility toward him. After all, a Keeper was a Keeper, living dragon or not.

"We'll discuss it with Cade once everyone is settled. We don't abandon our own, Slade. You know that. But it'll be tricky. He was caught and taken by the Baroqueth before we could stop it from happening."

A spoken truth that needled him more than his resentment toward the man who'd callously stabbed a proverbial knife through his lifemate's heart.

"You hanging in there?"

A dry laugh met his mind. *"Quite literally, you may say. But yes. I'm fine. Wish I had the harness to strap you up and ride you right."*

"Goddess, you know I don't swing like that. Nice to hear my old Keeper hasn't lost his spunk."

They shared a roaring laughter through mindspeak as Emery approached the mountains that hid the portal to The Hollow. His nerves settled as he increased his speed, preparing to break through the portal and bring them both back to their homeland safely—

An agonizing force crashed into his belly. Slade barked, pain shooting through Emery from his Keeper's mind. Emery roared, rolling onto his back to escape a second sphere of magic. He dove groundward, then curved back to the sky, managing to weave between blasts that exploded along the mountainside.

"You're hit."

Slade snorted. *"A graze. Nothing spring water can't heal."*

"How many slayers? Can you tell?"

Emery navigated the peaks and breaks in the mountains, banking through narrow formations. The attack ceased as he put distance between them and the veil. With keen sight, he scanned the area, picking up no unusual thermal areas.

"I saw shots coming from three different areas. I can't pick up on their thoughts."

Emery found a narrow shelf tucked into the mountain and landed as quietly as possible on the snowy platform. He instantly pulled his dragon in, leading Slade into the shallow divot, out of the open. Holding Slade by the shoulders, he looked over his Keeper's body, attention dropping to his favored left leg, where the fabric of his pants flapped above his knee. He tore open the split and growled.

"Graze my fucking ass."

Emery snatched the torn shirt from Slade's hands and made quick work to tie it around the hand-length gash that struck deep through skin and tissue. Slade ground his teeth together, his fingers digging into Emery's shoulder as Emery tightened the shirt and knotted the fabric to staunch the bleeding. Slinging an arm around Slade's waist to support his weight, he turned back to the great expanse of snow-capped mountains.

"What now?"

Emery cocked his head and listened for any residual explosions or an impending approach from their enemies. The small areas where he had pulled back his scales from his skin didn't tingle with the electric hum of magic. A single relief in this disaster.

"Your mind is silent?" When Slade nodded, Emery snickered, lacking all humor. "Wonder if the others encountered this welcoming committee or if we're the only lucky recipients."

"They were probably waiting to ambush us." Emery rolled his eyes and looked at his Keeper, whose brow arched. "What?"

"Their tactics are getting redundant. They've done this before."

"Well, redundant or not, they took us by surprise and now we're sitting on a mountain without a means of getting home."

Emery narrowed his eyes and tilted his head, assessing his Keeper. A dangerous grin tugged at the corner of his mouth. "Are you doubting my ability to get us home? I thought you had more faith in me, old man." He dipped his head, bringing his face close to Slade's. "We both have someone waiting for us to make it back safely. I don't disappoint those I care about, and last I recall, neither do you."

He watched as Slade's eyes hardened and his mouth slowly mirrored the grin that continued to stretch over his own.

"One way in, one way out."

Emery straightened up and rolled out his shoulders. "Keep your eyes peeled. Hope you can handle a rough ride."

Slade motioned to his leg. "I think I can handle the turbulence, dragon."

"Good," he rumbled on a stream of smoke as his dragon unleashed. He grabbed Slade in one claw, hooked his other into the rock wall, and began to scale the mountainside. *"There's a break up here. I'll lift you to spy over the crest. Tell me what you see."*

"Got it."

Pebbles and bits of rock pinked down the mountainside as he climbed higher. The wind picked up strength, whipping across their bodies. Clouds thickened and churned overhead, the first flakes of snow escaping swollen bellies of moisture. The taste of magic lingered on his tongue as the storm brewed with sudden fever. The chance of a safe reentry to The Hollow was dwindling as the Baroqueth built their attack strategy against his otherwise magicless self.

Emery angled his body parallel to the crest in the mountain break and lifted Slade. His Keeper gripped the jagged rock and pulled himself up. Emery adjusted his position until Slade waved for him to stop.

"Enough. I can see." With a grunt, Slade settled into position. *"One slayer in the valley. Seems to be the one responsible for the storm. No impressions. No thoughts. The veil is unmanned, at least physically."*

"They wouldn't leave a single man out in the open like that. The others are close by, watching him."

"He's the bait."

"He's the distraction."

Slade looked down at him. *"Distraction if the others are planning to blitz us. Bait if he's there to lure us out."*

"Old man, you think I don't know the difference? He's the distraction. They know we'll not attack him on our own. The others have eyes on that one. They hope we're stupid enough to focus on him in our escape and not pay much attention to their whereabouts. Any movement elsewhere?"

Slade turned back to his lookout. *"Use my eyes."*

Emery tilted his head. It had been over three decades since they'd made such a connection. Using a Keeper's eyes wasn't something done lightly or easily. It was a connection he and Slade had forged over hundreds of hours of trials and concentration. He wasn't even sure Syn and Gio held that connection, but then again, each dragon and Keeper had their own special attributes that others did not possess.

"You sure?"

To his surprise, Slade lifted a finger to his mouth, bit through the skin of his pad, and held his bleeding appendage out to Emery. *"Do it."*

Emery stared at the beading blood on his Keeper's finger. He flicked out his cleaved tongue as the drop fell, capturing the first and second drop before he closed his mouth and allowed the blood to stream down his throat. He closed his eyes as the blood burned through him, pulling at his essence relentlessly, drawing him into the powerful, pulsing bond. His dragon's essence wove through the glowing threads, penetrating deep into its core.

Within seconds, vision returned behind his closed lids as he found himself peering through Slade's open eyes, only using his dragon's sight instead of his Keeper's.

"We're going to start along the tunnel's wall. I need you to scan from the valley to the peak, so as not to miss someone overhead. Go slow, look at everything. I'll tell you when I see something."

"Got it."

Slade began the arduous chore of scanning the mountains, peaks and valleys and crevices. He followed Emery's instructions, scouring every inch his eyes could garner. Emery spoke only when he picked up thermal evidence of a hidden Baroqueth, and by the time Slade had completed the turn and snuffed Emery from his sight, Emery had formulated a plan.

Pulling Slade off the crest, he said, *"I detected five total, including the storm brewer. We're going to scale the mountain south of here, and come around the back. There's a plateau behind the veil's peak, which should hopefully give me enough time to build speed to break through the veil, but the ascension will be sharp and sudden, the descent reckless, and I'm going close to the mountain in hopes of using some of the geography as protection. If I can get you to the entrance, you'll be safe should I be hit. We'll be close enough to reach out to the others."*

Slade scowled, baring his teeth before he knocked his fist into Emery's shoulder. "Shut the fuck up, dragon. You have my daughter waiting for you back there, so you'd better not get hit."

"Aw, the sentiment is touching, but I didn't say I'd be dying today. I have every intention of returning to my lifemate, and returning with her father, preferably in one piece. But we know reality isn't always fair. Look at your leg if you need a reminder."

Though he spoke the worst, he refused to entertain any outcome other than breaking through the veil and finding Sera the moment he got back home.

Without waiting for Slade's retort, he began the tedious journey of maneuvering along the mountainsides without pause. He estimated an hour at a clipped pace, if he was lucky. The path to the plateau wasn't easy, coming with many descents and ascents along the way to remain undetected, shielding Slade from the freezing gales that strengthened every few minutes, the pelting ice and snow that slicked his scales and the rocky walls, and the sudden onset of bright blue lightning. Thunder rumbled through the sky, sending loose rocks tumbling down from their peaks. He pulled Slade as tight as he could to his underside, using his warmth to keep the chill at bay.

By the time they reached the plateau, the storm had turned perilous. The snow and wind made it difficult for his thermal vision to cut through, the icy conditions too dense for warmth to pierce. Opening his wings to shield Slade, he lowered his Keeper to the snow-laden ground, the gathering flakes a few inches deep, and reconsidered his plan.

The longer he waited, the less likely return would happen today.

"Em, this might be too dangerous. Maybe we should consider abandoning it today and finding a place to hunker down for the night. Come back to it tomorrow."

A hint of truth rang with Slade's observation.

"They'll be here tomorrow, and the next day, and the next

until either we get through the veil or they get us. The only reason I'm going to suggest we try now is because as blinding as this storm is for us, it's blinding to them as well. I can get to the entrance blindfolded. I just need a bit of speed."

Slade shifted his weight, leaning on his good leg and using one of Emery's talons for support. His Keeper mulled the logic over in his mind until, at last, he nodded once, lips pinched tight.

"What's the plan?"

Emery lifted his head. *"Coming from a different angle, Slade. I swore to you the day you bled into my dragonstone I would always put your life before mine. That vow remains to this day, and moving forward."*

"It's not about me anymore. It's about Sera. She comes before us both." Slade leaned back until Emery tilted his head to stare at his Keeper with one large eye. The man pointed a finger at him. *"I want you to listen to me and hear me good. If you must choose between saving me or saving yourself, you save yourself for the sake of my daughter and her heart. Do you understand what I'm saying?"*

A growl bubbled up from his chest. *"Slade—"*

"No! I'm dead serious, Emery. If you must sacrifice me to save yourself, *you do it*. I will *not* forgive you otherwise."

Spoken words, not through mindspeak, lent the punch Slade most likely hoped for. His dragon struggled with the ultimatum. He could not sacrifice Slade. He would not. What Slade believed was a move to save Sera grief should things go south would only hurt her more.

"Well, then." Emery clamped his claw around his Keeper and launched straight up into the storm. His wings battled against the wind, pulling higher and higher until he broke through the cloak of clouds to hover above the turbulence. He

calculated his positioning, how far off the wind had taken him, and repositioned himself where he planned to break through. *"Guess there's no room for error today."*

He dove, keeping Slade close to his chest, wings glued to his sides. He cut through the clouds, prepared for the battering of the storm as he bulleted down, down, down, using minimal movement of his wings to align him with the entrance to the veil. The less he moved, the harder it would be for the slayers to detect him. He had one chance to do this and survive. One chance to reach the veil and return home.

One chance.

Slade's rising panic infiltrated his body, but he cast it aside. His Keeper was so fast to sacrifice himself, yet here he was, tense as a stone and mind quietly cussing Emery out.

Almost there. Almost—

The first launch of a magical blast glanced off the mountain, dissipating in the storm. Its dark streak stood in stark contrast against the white of the snow. The second shot went by his right side. He spiraled, increasing his speed, calculating the tunnel, his angle, his next move.

A third blast barely missed his tail.

He wrapped his other claw around his Keeper, banked left, extended his wings enough to bring him level with the tunnel, and flew through the open mouth—

A blast struck him true on his underbelly, sending him into a tumble. He broke through the veil, but his massive form struck the tunnel's sides as he rolled at breakneck speed along the path to The Hollow and shot out like a rogue bullet into their world.

He slammed into something unyielding. Talons grabbed his wings at their bases, steadying him in the air until he was lowered to the ground. When his feet hit the ground, he placed Slade on his own two legs and pulled in his dragon.

He stumbled, a dull pain running throughout his torso. Upon closer inspection, a large bruise had formed over his abdomen from where he'd suffered the strike.

Cade released his hold on the base of his wings, allowing Emery to absorb the last of his beast and drop to the grass on his ass beside his ruffled Keeper. They both breathed heavily, each mentally replaying the events of their return, Emery imagined. Cade crouched down in front of them, arms slung over his knees, fierce gaze assessing Emery, then Slade, lingering on the gaping wound in his Keeper's leg.

"Ambush," Cade said without preamble.

Emery shrugged a shoulder. "Just some old friends wanting to greet us on our way in." Slade groaned and fell onto his back. Emery smacked his hip. "Look at you, old man. No longer the well-put-together rich boy. Honestly, this disheveled look fits you much better than all that stilted formal shit."

"Fuck off, Em. You damn near gave me a heart attack."

"Can't handle the ride any longer? I was seriously hoping you'd, um, how'd you put it? 'Strap me up and ride me right?'"

Slade's head rolled on the grass, lazy as hell but the glower he graced Emery with was anything but playful. Until a smile broke through his tight-lipped expression, followed by a roar of laughter. Emery joined his Keeper a moment later. Cade snickered and shook his head, smacking his hands on his knees and pushing up to his feet. He held out a hand for Emery, who gladly accepted, and together they hoisted Slade onto his good leg, slinging an arm over each of their shoulders.

"Emery? Is everything okay? Are you okay?"

He stumbled a step, but caught his balance, earning a curious look from Cade. He waved his leader's concern aside, but that sultry purr inside his head left his heart racing and his body hot.

"Everything's perfect, my darling. Some scratches and bruises, but nothing we can't handle."

"You had me worried when you didn't come through with the others—only to watch you tumble through that entrance completely out of control."

"Oh, love, what's an entrance without it being grand?"

Sera's sexy laugh suffused his entire being. He tamped down the urge to abandon Slade and Cade and return to the siren who was singing to his soul.

As her laughter tapered, a heaviness settled over their bond. *"Is Uncle Slade okay?"*

"He's not your uncle, flame. He's your father. And he'll be fine after a little spring water bath and some of Amelia's witchy salve."

"I'll be waiting for you to get home."

A secret smile teased his lips. *"I won't be long."*

CHAPTER NINETEEN

The sun took its last breath of the day before dropping below the horizon, leaving this magical world in a glow of purple and magenta rays. The birds chirped and sang an evening tune, while the soothing hum of water in the distance drifted on an everlasting breeze to the terrace—or something close to a terrace, with a roughly carved, belly-high rock wall and a floor of soft grass and patches of coarse dirt—where she waited for Emery's return. She'd sent Sky home despite her new friend's protests and insistence on staying so she wouldn't be alone. In the end, she convinced the willful woman to return to her lifemate with the reassurance she would be fine.

Emery had returned. Safely would be subjective, she was certain. The weight of worry lifted off her shoulders the moment she saw him burst through the tunnel like a burnished red cannonball with wings. Cade had caught him and broken the uncontrolled flight, but soon after, she lost sight of them behind another cut of mountain.

That was well over two hours ago.

Yet the golden tether beat in tandem with her heart, bright and strong. Her bond to her dragon held no essence of pain or suffering. If he hurt, he kept it to himself. The only thought for his delay was that her uncle—Sera knocked her forehead with the heel of her palm—*father* wasn't as fortunate as to bullet into The Hollow unscathed. She understood that even though they were lifemates, Emery held a duty to his Keeper. She was safe and sound, tucked in his home. If her father bore injuries, she'd expect Emery to tend to those first.

Still, waiting for him to return was, well, painful. She had tried to distract herself with a shower and choosing an outfit from several some of the women closer to her size had loaned her until she could get some clothes of her own. She didn't like the separation now that she'd embraced their bond. In a single evening, she'd become a dragon addict, craving him every second he was gone, unable to get enough of him when he was around. The air she breathed held no life as it did when he was near, her lungs stagnant and cold. Her heart bore an ache despite its healthy rhythm, a tear within a muscle only he could heal. Gods, the bond was amazing, intense, entirely consuming. On the flip-side, it created a new agony she'd never fathomed. One where she felt empty and perhaps undead, because she could still walk, talk, and function like a living person but held a darkness inside her until her dragon returned and filled her with light.

With a sigh, Sera pushed off her elbows from the rocky wall and turned, intending to go back to the main living quarters.

She paused.

"You're a sight to behold when you're all caught up in your thoughts. I couldn't interrupt." Emery ticked a finger toward the sky, his eyes flickering with fire as he drank her in from his casual stance against the mountainside, a foot tucked up on the wall. The blasted man had to stand there, shirtless, the sensual colors of a sunset palette painting over every delectable cut and curve of muscle. The dragon tattoo on his shoulder rippled with his muscles as he hooked a thumb on his belt. "The sunset casts you in this ethereal glow, and I want to do nothing more than worship my goddess for a hundred lifetimes. From the moment my eyes open in the morning to the moment I fall asleep."

"You're such a romantic dragon."

"I'm behaving right now."

Sera snickered as she crossed the short distance to where Emery stood, following her with his hungry gaze. He dropped his foot when she splayed her hands over his pecs, slowly tracing the deep curves with her thumbs. The muscles beneath his hot skin hardened to steel. She soaked in the temperature of his gaze, heating from a simmer to a boil, a feverish delight as her fingers played over his nipples before trailing down his muscled abdomen. His arms dropped to his sides, fingers fisting and flexing as she teased her way down, tracing his belly button, scraping a nail over the short black hairs leading into his jeans. Jeans that bulged shamelessly. She knew exactly what lay beneath, fell beneath the magic it performed on her body, and she craved it again. Craved *everything*.

Dipping her head forward, she closed her eyes as she brushed her lips between the valley of his pecs, followed by the tip of her tongue. A sharp intake of breath greeted her advance. His stomach cinched as she worked open his belt and curled her fingertips beneath the waist of his jeans. She didn't need to delve deep to meet the tip of his cock, already wet for her. She smiled against his skin and continued to flick her tongue and brush her lips in a path up to his neck.

Tilting her head, the tip of her nose brushing along his jaw, she whispered, "I've had to wait all day for you, but I'd wait an eternity to have you as I do now."

Sera flicked open the button on his jeans. She kissed his neck, open-mouthed, scraping her teeth gently against the throbbing pulse point. A rumble vibrated through his chest. He released a sharp breath, smoke creating a haze around her head as she worked her mouth away from his neck, along his chest, his stomach.

She lowered herself to her knees and gazed up into the feral beast of her intense dragon. His eyes erupted with flames, smoke curling from his flared nostrils and the corners of his tightly-pulled lips. His upper lip drew back enough for the stunning rays of the last remaining light to reflect off fangs. Her face warmed beneath his insatiable gaze. It merely burned hotter as she lowered the zipper to his jeans, tooth by tooth. Her lungs turned light, fluttered like a thousand wings.

"How well can you behave, my sweet dragon?"

As the zipper reached the halfway point, she lowered her gaze to the prize still hidden behind the fabric. Gods, how she'd wanted to do so much to him last night, but neither of them possessed the control to explore. Both of them gave in to their most primitive desires. Tonight, she'd not deprive herself of a taste. She'd not deprive herself of knowing this man who owned her soul and came close to possessing her heart.

"Do you want to find out?" he growled.

Sera tipped her head, pressed her open mouth to his jeans, and sucked along his cock through the material. The hiss that escaped him brought a small grin to her lips as she teased the base of his shaft with her mouth. A wave of raw pleasure washed over her, a sensation he experienced and shared with her, setting her aflame with an intense swell of delight. She moaned against the jeans, working the zipper down to the end as her body throbbed. She trembled as she pulled open the flaps of his jeans and gathered his cock between her hands. The scent of his arousal saturated her lungs and made her mind whirl with hard-pressed hunger. Oh, how she wanted to trace the veins along his velvety shaft, bulging from the strain of his engorgement. She did this to him, and it sparked an empowering sensation within her soul. His wide crown glistened, beads of moisture along the slit.

As one of those beads prepared to fall, she leaned in and licked it away. The salty essence slid over her tongue. Her mouth turned wet, thirsting for another taste. More of his flavor. With a hand wrapped around the base of his cock, another around his shaft, the man still had a few inches left.

Inches she wrapped her lips around and drew into her mouth.

"Fuck," Emery barked. Sera would have laughed at the control she held over him at this moment, but the taste of him on her tongue, the feel of him filling her mouth, the way his cock jerked in her hands, ensured she could think of nothing more than making her dragon yield beneath the pleasure she delivered. "*Seraphina.*"

"Mmm?" she moaned, releasing one hand to take him deeper. Her eyelids grew heavy as she tightened her lips and drew back to his crown, then sucked him to the back of her throat.

The powerful rush of blinding pleasure exploded outward from her core. It rocked her on her knees. Her body shook beneath the sensations she delivered to Emery, their bond engulfing her as she played his cock with her mouth, her tongue. Heat welled up between her legs, leaving her whimpering and rocking and reaching down between her legs—

Emery snatched her wrist and pressed her hand to his hip. When she looked up at him, her vision pulsing in time with her clit, he wore a carnal snarl. "I'm behaving. Now *you* behave. No touching yourself."

Oh, Gods, the pressure between her legs. The heat. The... the...immense...

Oh, Gods!

She undulated against the air, but she may as well have been riding ... something. Control fractured. Her body splintered. She dropped her head as an orgasm speared through her, crying out around Emery's cock before it slipped from her mouth as she lost her strength and sat back on her heels. She flushed, head to toe, the pulse between her legs relentless as it drove her higher and higher on this peak. The power of her orgasm left her in the clutches of madness.

Only when she began to come down, gasping for breath, did Emery lower to his haunches before her. He lifted her chin with a single finger, his thumb caressing her lower lip, back and forth. He leaned forward, his forehead a hairsbreadth from hers, his eyes an inferno of desire.

"The power of our bond. I didn't even have to touch you to make you come, love. Imagine what I'm going to do to you when I get you to our bed."

Sera had no time to react to Emery scooping her into the cradle of his arms and whisking her into the mountain home. She clung to his neck, residual tremors skating along her muscles as he beelined to their bedroom. He didn't bother closing the door before crossing to the ginormous bed and depositing her on the soft mattress in a manner not so unlike the night before. Tonight, she didn't try to scramble away. Instead, she lifted her bare foot to his cock and drew the top of her foot along the underside of his shaft.

"You're wicked." She lowered her foot to the bed, crooked her finger, and motioned for him to come closer. "So misbehaved, dragon."

A dark grin crested his handsome mouth. He stripped off his jeans in a blink and climbed over her. "I never said I was a saint."

"I never said you did."

Emery lowered to her neck and graced her skin with airy kisses. "Whose dress is this?"

"It's not mine, that's all that matters."

He chuckled. "Tell me."

She felt the cool edge of his talon before she could stop him from scooping beneath the thick strap at her shoulder and slicing through it. "Emery! Gabby—"

He captured her mouth with his, silencing her panic with a kiss that stole her breath and laid claim to her. His tongue possessed her. His breaths filled her lungs with the life essence she so dearly craved. Those lethal talons shredded the dress in a matter of seconds, then scraped down her exposed side from shoulder to hip, flicking over her nipple on their path. She cried out as goosebumps exploded over her body, her back bowing off the bed. He slipped an arm beneath her waist before she settled on the mattress, holding her against him, bridged as he tore his mouth from hers and ravaged her neck, her breasts, with starved kisses. His tongue swirled, lighting her on fire. His teeth scraped, nipped, plucking her nerves in a spray of spasms with each delightful tease.

When his mouth clamped over her nipple and sucked the beaded flesh between his teeth, she cried out, a wave of mindless pleasure heating her from head to toe.

He had yet to lay her back, his thick, muscular thighs spreading her legs wider as his superior form cocooned her beneath him. A prize, a possession, a treasure. For every pinch of his teeth, every scratch of his talons, he soothed the pain away until she whimpered and moaned. He breathed life into erogenous zones she hadn't imagined existed until his mouth played her like an instrument created solely for him.

He leaned back on his heels, caught her hips between his hands as he laved and kissed his way down her belly. Her face burned with pent-up desire. Her body trembled from his attention. He pushed her deeper onto the bed as he lifted her to meet his mouth as if she weighed nothing at all. He held her with easy strength, leaving her shoulders and upper back, arms and head the only parts of her body in contact with the mattress.

Gazing up the slope of her body to the man ravenously nipping and kissing the inside of her thigh, what she might have considered awkward and embarrassing with any other living man she found erotic and arousing with Emery. The way he held her, the position of her hips turned up to his face, his eyes glowing with flames around dilated slits.

He bit into her thigh until she cried out, watching her every second. He released her skin and licked the pulsing area, his tongue magic in the way it took the pain away, releasing a rush of moisture from her core. His lips curled. Lifting his head from her leg, he burned that hot gaze into hers. His nostrils flared and he licked his lips.

"I can taste your fucking juice from here, flame."

His fingers tightened at her hips, the tips of his talons delicatiely puncturing her skin, anchoring her where she was, suspended before him like a shameless delicacy, waiting for her master to take everything he wanted while shattering her existence. A balance. A harmony.

"Get rid of my panties and you can have a drink from the source."

Her brazen tongue made her flush more. He chuckled,

dipping his head and dragging the flat of his tongue along the wet patch of fabric separating her core from every wicked pleasure he offered. She hissed, pressing herself against his tongue as he crossed over her clit and lifted his head away.

"I love your taste, Seraphina. It's my own personal ambrosia, but I don't care for the hint of cotton. Be a good girl and pull those panties to the side for me."

"Take them off yourself."

His eyes flared, the faint curls of smoke rising from his nostrils. He arched a brow, lowering that insatiable gaze to her center.

"If you want me to suck your little clit, sweetness, you'll have to help." Without warning, he tossed her up slightly, enough to shift his grip to her ass, and squeezed the globes of flesh roughly. Gods, she wanted to beg for the bruises he'd be leaving on her flesh. She began to lift her legs to his shoulders, but he shrugged them off and shook his head. "I've got you at a perfect angle. Now, are you going to move that scrap out of my way? Or would you rather me turn my attention elsewhere"—he turned his head to her knee and feathered kisses over the inside—"like to your leg?"

Sera reached between her legs and hooked a finger around the thin fabric, soaked with her pleasure. His carnal grin made her pause. She enjoyed the way his impatience darkened those flames and morphed his grin from playful to ravening. This was the power she held over him, and she basked in the control.

Balance.

Harmony.

For he possessed the same degree of control over her, as she proved when she moved the fabric aside.

Feral.

That was the only word that described the glow in his eyes before he feasted on her body.

"Damn!" She squeezed her eyes shut as his tongue rubbed over her clit, mercilessly rocketing her to the stars, but he stubbornly left her at the brink, mind whirling, body tense, waiting for the coil to snap. That tongue slid inside her, probed her, fucked her as she knew he would when he claimed her. His talons bit into her ass, drawing more blood between rough gropes and squeezes, and every prick of pain ignited a hundred more levels of pleasure.

"Aw, flame, I can feel you squeezing my tongue. Are you about to come for me?"

His grip on her ass didn't allow her to move. She was at the sole mercy of her dragon as he tormented her into madness. "Emery!"

In response, he ceased his delightful attention to her core, dropped her to the mattress, and fit himself between her legs. He cut away her panties and with one hard, thorough thrust, he filled her with his cock, shattering her on a sea of stars as she gasped and screamed with ecstasy. He rode her steadily through her orgasm, capturing her wrists and pinning them to the bed beside her head. She tugged, pulled, writhed and thrashed, the torrential waves of bliss coming one after another, stronger, fiercer, unyielding.

His mouth clamped down at the crux of her neck and shoulder, his teeth aligning with his previous bite. His hips pistoned, refusing to let her body come down from her climax. Her mind was worthless beyond sensation, drowning in this dragon-made heaven.

"Let me claim you. Really claim you."

"Yes!"

Before the word fully left her lips, he bit. Hard, fast, deep. So deep the pain nearly cut through the pleasure.

Then, he sucked. Pulled at the blood he spilled.

And she lost her fucking mind.

The orgasm that claimed her exploded through the last, pulverized her body, blinded her with stark white against the back of her eyelids. A frenzy of nerves singing at a high-pitched frequency. The essence of separation from the physical while remaining in the presence of her dragon. She melted into him, became one with him, his thoughts powerful impressions of energy that saturated her in this state.

His growling roar filled the space around them. Fire poured inside her body, filled her in fierce jets, driving her higher and higher until she couldn't go any further, suspended at the pinnacle of bonding.

Somehow, some way, the air around her shifted. The euphoria began to subside. In the distance, she could make out the rapid beat of her heart. The closer she came to reality, the more she registered. The cool air across her damp skin. The breaths that failed to fill her lungs because all she could do was gasp. The heat that surrounded her, pulling her into an embrace she craved. Every limb shaking uncontrollably.

For a long while, she lay in Emery's arms, their legs tangled, his shallow breaths hitting the top of her head in rapid succession. Faint tremors wracked his arms, tremors he did nothing to hide. His seed leaked along her thigh, around his cock still fit snug inside her. The more she recovered, the more she recognized dull areas of soreness. Her ass. Her hips. A small spot along her ribs. Curiosity gave her the strength to open her eyes to slits.

She was met by a set of scratches over Emery's right pec, deep pink with spots of blood. Gingerly, she touched the injury.

Emery laughed quietly. "That's the most innocent of

marks you left on me, but you can do as much damage to me as you'd like, flame."

She leaned close, pressed her mouth over the marks, and brushed her tongue across the welts. The smoky essence of his blood teased her tastebuds and made her shiver with an unexpected degree of delight. She gently suckled the wound, drawing the tiniest bit more, and sighed. His arms tightened around her, and he leaned back, enough to catch her gaze. He considered her, his eyes having returned to the familiar whiskey color and brimming with awe.

"I sensed your wild side, Seraphina, but I would never have imagined you'd match my level of crazy."

She smiled, her lips weak and quivering. He sapped her of all her strength. "Until you, I didn't realize how much I enjoy crazy. Nor do I believe I'd like crazy if it wasn't with you."

"Well, you don't have to worry, because there will be no other than me, as there will be no other than you."

"Do you hurt, love?"

Sera shook her head, still fighting for breath as she clung to Emery. Her body began to settle, the convulsions of pleasure slowly subsiding. As the fog cleared from her mind, she entertained how Emery could be so rough yet so gentle at the same time. She wore another bite mark on her opposite shoulder, where those fangs once again broke skin and drew blood.

The experience of sharing not only his thoughts and his mind, but his body as he drank from her and brought her to an entirely new level of bliss consumed her in every way possible. She'd never have believed she could get closer to him than when he filled her up and held her close.

Oh, how wrong she'd been. And now, she'd crave that deeper connection every time they lay claim to each other. He was her addiction, and she wanted more and more.

She'd most likely be sore come morning—she already felt the gentle ache between her legs from his merciless plunder—but she would beg for more before she ever let a little bit of soreness keep them apart.

The Emery who showered her with romantic promises and poetic compliments turned to delicious sin in bed. She absolutely loved both facets of her dragon, and all the nuances in between. Emery was complex in so many ways, and she thoroughly enjoyed learning each level as the hours went by. Between their lovemaking, the tender dragon emerged, healing her scrapes and cuts with water he'd brought back from the springs after healing up her birth father. Some welts and tiny punctures she still wore, refusing to allow him to heal. She smiled at the sight of them. Claiming marks. They were from Emery, her lifemate, his marks, and she adored them.

Emery pressed up on his elbow and eased her forward, onto her belly. His fingers traced a tender area between her shoulder blades.

"Shit, flame. I didn't realize how hard I scratched you." He growled and hopped over her, off the bed, before she could stop him. She twisted her head and choked at the sight of his naked backside, the round globes of his ass as they flexed with each step. The cords of muscles along his back and those that stretched down his legs. The man was a walking sex god, mussed hair and all.

And even more so when he returned to her with a fresh piece of linen damp with spring water.

Sera pushed up on her elbows as he sat beside her and dabbed at her back. The water stung initially, but the sting subsided just as quickly. She watched Emery, his expression shadowed, the sharp lines taut, as he focused on tending to her scratch.

"It's probably no worse than some of the others."

Emery snorted. "Woman, I'm not one to shred up your beautiful body. I'd rather worship you than ruin you. You just make me lose my ever-loving fucking mind."

"Dragon, you've already ruined me, remember?" She rested her chin on a fist and smiled when his gaze finally cut to hers. "Call me crazy, but I enjoy feeling you lose control. Even if it means a few scratches and bite marks. One, they'll heal. Two, they're from you. Three, you're the only man ever who I'd allow to mark up my skin."

His upper lip began to pull back. He snorted and went back to tending her wound until he was satisfied with the results. When the linen came away from her back, she realized why he'd been angry with himself.

The cloth was saturated with blood.

He disposed of the linen in the roaring fire and returned to bed, falling onto his back beside her and tucking an arm beneath his head. "I'll be more careful in the future. That one's gonna take a day or so to heal completely. All I need is Slade catching sight of a wound on your body and he'll have my scales faster than I could fly off."

The mention of her father brought a weight on her shoulders she didn't care to bear. Not right now. But it would be a topic that couldn't go much longer without being recognized.

Sera sighed and twisted onto her side. Emery slipped his arm beneath her head before she lay it on the pillow and pulled her close, pressing several lingering kisses to the top of her head.

"I'd let him, too, you know. He could descale me from lips to tail if ever I hurt you."

"Then you won't have to worry about losing scales. I doubt he'd descale you for my sake, and I know in my heart you'll never hurt me."

A finger came up beneath her chin and lifted her head until she met his stern gaze.

"Seraphina, let me tell you a little something about my Keeper. Your *father*. The secrets he kept ran deep, but never did he mistreat you. From my understanding, he was more of a father than Nick ever tried to be. When we were returning this afternoon and were met by the Baroqueth firing squad, Slade started with the nonsense of sacrificing himself should it come down to only one of us surviving. It had nothing to do with him being my Keeper and protecting me, but to ensure you did not suffer the loss of your lifemate. To make sure I returned to you. There isn't much more a person can sacrifice for another beyond their life. I would give my life to save you, Seraphina. I would give my dying breath to see you safe, and so would your father. Safe and *happy*."

Emery's thumb came up beneath her eye and wiped away a stray tear that had burned across her eye and fallen free. His words struck a raw nerve within her soul. One she knew needed to be addressed. She'd suffered numerous blows the night before, all of which simply collapsed on top of her. She'd not taken the time she needed to sift through the debris and choose what would be rebuilt and what would be disposed of.

Emery was right. She knew he was right. Her biological father had always been more of a father than the one she'd grown up believing to be her blood. She just wished he'd told her sooner. That she'd learned the truth under different circumstances.

"You two need to talk, and I believe tomorrow would be as good a day as any."

Sera pressed her lips together to stave off the quiver in her chin. She nodded once. *"I know."*

His thumb swiped back and forth along her cheek. His eyes searched her face for something he kept to himself. There was no hint of desire or hunger, simply the unabashed concern of her tender dragon.

He shifted lower in the bed to bring his face level with hers. His thumb turned into his hand cupping the side of her face. He tipped her head closer until their noses brushed and their foreheads rested together.

"My sweetest flame. I adore you in so many ways. Your happiness will always be my priority, and making amends with Slade will give you that happiness, and then some. I never want you to live with regret because the opportunity to fix something is taken from you too soon."

Sera closed her eyes. "I hate how logical you can be at times."

Emery chuckled. "Well, that's a shame, because I kind of like you, despite driving me to the brink of madness."

Sera's eyes snapped open. She leaned back enough to meet his gaze straight on. "Like?" She laughed quietly. "Well, I'm glad at least that you *like* me."

"Ahh"—his hand slipped away from her face and his fingers pressed gently to her chest, over her heart—"because I *love* you more."

The very organ he pressed fingers over fluttered. Her own hand sought his, covered it, and flattened his palm over her chest. "In a day?"

"Lifemates, remember? Things happen a little differently for us. You took my heart that first night in the forest and have had it ever since. The instant my dragon sensed you, recognized you, knew you for who you were, I was yours. We have lifetimes to learn the tiny nuances of each other, but remember what I said. Our souls know each other on an unreachable level for anyone but us. The moment you took your first breath, I was yours and you were mine. And I would ask for no other than you, Seraphina, to be my forever and my eternity."

CHAPTER TWENTY

"Hm. Looks like both brothers enjoy using teeth."

Sera spun around, adjusting the shirt to cover the bruises on her shoulder. Warmth flushed her face despite Sky's coy snicker and lingering gaze on Emery's mark. When she stepped up to Sera, she hooked a finger beneath the collar of her jacket and lowered it to show off the scars of a bite mark very similar to her own.

"I won't lie"—she fixed the collar back in place, her mouth curling into a deeper, more devious grin—"Emery's always been the lighthearted, playful, big-kid type. I never suspected him to be the biting type. Or the kinky type, given the bruises on your wrists."

Sera gasped, checking her wrists as Sky laughed, a sultry sound that didn't leave her as embarrassed as she might have been had anyone else pointed out the ghost of bruises circling her wrists. Though the bruises weren't necessarily because Emery was rough, more that he had her shackled with his hand while she shattered over and over.

"Damn it."

"It's nothing to be ashamed of, Sera. We all have ideas of what happens behind closed doors. We all understand the bond creates this relentless, insatiable sexual hunger that can't ever be quenched. It's not just you. It's all of us. We're willing prisoners of a bond that creates a bunch of mindless sex addicts out of us, even the most timid of the group." She motioned blindly to the living space. "Guess my brother-in-law has one helluva dark side, which is interesting. Anyhow, Emery spent some time with Slade at the springs yesterday. Did he bring any water home? We can have those bruises gone in no time. Bite, not so much, since it looked like he broke skin and his saliva mixed with your blood."

"Yes, actually." Sera twisted back to the bedroom and wiggled her fingers for Sky to follow. Under her breath, she whispered, "Hopefully, there's some left."

Sera paused when she realized she wasn't being followed, observing Sky's rather awe-struck expression. Sky hesitated in the doorway to the bedroom, looking over the expansive room with wide eyes and a slack jaw.

"Is everything okay?" Sera glanced around quickly before returning her attention to the woman, who seemed to shake off the shock. She blinked, her turquoise eyes practically glowing. "Is there something—"

"No, no. I'm actually impressed by his décor. Now I see where all his effort went." Sky waved aside her concern and slowly stepped into the room, like she was stepping over a threshold she wasn't certain she could cross. Or should. "I'll be teasing Gabe later that I was in his brother's room."

"Oh, shit." Sera stared at Sky for a heartbeat or two, then burst out laughing. Sky joined in and came to her side, spinning in place to take in the room. "I don't want to see those two go at it. From what I know of your man, he'll pluck scales until Emery cries 'uncle.'"

"Those two might mess around, but they'd never hurt each other. Their blood runs thick and deep. Mess with one, you mess with both, and that's a scary duo to fuck with." Sky leaned toward her as Sera led her to the table with the bowl of spring water. Thankfully, it was still half-full. "As laidback as Emery is, I've seen the lethal glint in his eyes. Gabe doesn't hide his bloodlust or his brutality behind a mask like Emery does. I've always wondered about Emery's ruthless potential."

Heaviness settled in the air as Sky's smile faltered and fell. She took one of the torn pieces of linen from the table and dipped it into the water, squeezing out the excess into the bowl. She took Sera's hand and wrapped the bruised wrist in the linen, holding it secure with her hands. When she lifted her gaze to Sera's, pain sliced through her gaze. Pain that Sera somehow experienced as viscerally as she might had she suffered that pain herself. It wrenched at her heart and squeezed her lungs. She had to steel herself against the potency of Sky's emotions, which proved to be a challenge as she absorbed them seemingly from the air itself.

"I wasn't in the hotel room when the Baroqueth dealt the lethal blow to my mama. One of those bastards snatched me and tried to escape the hotel with me. Emery was watching over us while Gabe met up with the other dragons that night."

She sighed, lowering her gaze to Sera's wrist. Her thumbs smoothed over the linen, perhaps a nervous gesture. The air thickened as Sky's mood turned even more grim.

"My father owned a martial arts studio that he built up based off fighting techniques he learned from Gabe, and then taught me. I never realized that one of his private classes, a class I taught beside him then continued after he was murdered, was a group of civilians from this world. The dragons were transporting them back here when the Baroqueth attacked us at the hotel. Emery was left alone to protect Mama and I in a world that stripped him of magic and power outside his dragon. Gabe never sugar-coated things with me. For that, I'm grateful. I was forced to adjust to a reality hidden from me all my life, and quickly. Yet I didn't realize just how *powerful* the Baroqueth were until that night. The guy who took me paralyzed me with magic. No amount of training, skill, or self-defense could save me against magic in a world that takes our magic from us. He rendered me *helpless*. I can only imagine what Emery faced during that time I was gone. Alone with my mama, and me taken from his protection. Partly because I thought I could fight them and win."

Sky licked her lips as she busied herself with a second piece of linen and applied the compress to Sera's other wrist. Her skin paled slightly. Her shoulders curved forward, an unseen weight burdening her smaller frame.

"I know Emery enough to know he blames himself for Mama's death. I know it's a scar he can't heal. In his mind, he let Gabe down. He caused me to suffer grief he believed he could have prevented. *Nothing* could've prevented what happened. Gabe's spoken to him about it. He's assured Emery neither of us blame him. *I've* assured him." Her gaze bounced off Sera's for the briefest of moments. When Sera caught the shimmer in her eyes, she realized why Sky avoided her gaze. "I never blamed him, and never would. I know he took hits to protect her. He took hits protecting me. My capture was solely due to my reckless behavior. Mama was murdered because of circumstance. Had we been here, in The Hollow, she'd still be alive. But...I didn't realize that until I was here."

Sky shrugged her shoulder, a stiff movement followed by a tic at the corner of her mouth.

"Emery hasn't mentioned it to me, but from what I know of him, he would hold himself accountable for any ill befalling someone in his care, fault or not. It's who he is."

Sera wasn't sure how to step on this delicate path. She'd known Sky for a day, and anything else was based off what she'd learned from Emery. And yet, she felt a connection with this woman she'd never had with Jes. It went deeper than any friendship. As tough as the woman appeared, the fragility beneath the steel shell began to show through. She wasn't sure Sky meant for her to see it, or if she had developed a knack for sensing vulnerability in a person since coming to The Hollow.

"He's loyal, Sky. He's loyal in the very blueprint of his makeup. A loyalty like his doesn't come without burdens or scars. He knows he can't save the world, but when he loses, he hurts, and he hides it well. We would all hurt because we hold a sense of camaraderie, a sense of loyalty to each other, right? There are seven of us. Seven, that's it. If we can't build bonds between ourselves, we leave ourselves weak for anyone to tear us all apart."

"I've always kept people at arm's length. Never allowing them close. I never had friends because of these walls I've kept erected around me every day. Elena was the closest to a friend that I ever had, and even she remained at a distance." Sky finally lifted her chin and blinked several times, her bright eyes luminous beneath a sheen of tears that crept into her thick lashes. She scoffed and snorted out a laugh, shaking her head. "Sorry. You don't need to hear my sad story." Her fingers trembled, messing with the linens at Sera's wrists. "Let's see how these look."

"Hey." Sera turned her hands, releasing Sky's light grip on her wrist, and captured the woman's hands in hers. She tilted her head until Sky finally met her eyes, tears brimming along her lower lids. Her lips pulled tight, jaw set. "I want to hear it. I'll share mine. We're not without histories, right? There's nothing to be ashamed of when our pasts make us the women we are today. You've been through hell, and only a few weeks ago at that. Let me be here for you." Sera released her hands and caught Sky's shoulder. "Please. I'll be here for you. We're not just lifemates to dragons, you and I. We're lifemates to blood brothers."

Sky's chin quivered despite the fight she clearly put up to keep it steady. Those tears breached her lids and crept down her cheeks, pale skin flushed with grief.

"I miss them, Sera." Her voice shook, as quietly as she spoke. The first sob escaped her. She swiped at her face with the back of her hand. "I miss my dad. I miss my mama. I had just gotten her back and they took her from me for good. I've been alone all my life, even in a crowded room, I've always been alone until Gabe. I d-don't want to be alone anymore."

Sera's heart broke. Fractured and cracked open for the woman she gathered in her arms and held close as she cried on her shoulder. She squeezed her own eyes shut, batting back the sting of tears that had no right to develop, but she suspected were more from Sky's emotions than her own conscious mind. Whatever was happening to her, she'd have to bring it up to Emery. Perhaps it was some power that lay dormant in Colorado, activated here in a land of magic.

"You're not alone, Skylar," she murmured close to Sky's ear. "Solitude is a thing of your past. You have a tight group of women who will stand beside you, carry you through storms, lead you through darkness and bring you to light. We're a sisterhood, the seven of us. But know I can be a little more, if you'll let me. I can be a sister beyond the bonds we all hold. Grieve as you must. I'll be here for you, okay? For anything."

Time passed, the sound of Sky's agonized sobs muffled by her shoulder. Sera held her tight, smoothing a hand over her hair, being the shoulder she suspected Sky needed from a woman, not a man. The linen compresses had long ago loosened and fallen to the floor. Any concern beyond the suffering Sky expulsed and she soaked in faded.

Until the familiar essence of her dragon brought her gaze to the doorway.

There, in the shadows of the corridor, she detected his silhouette, watching in silence with no intention of interrupting. He simply observed, his presence a warmth that suffused her blood like a spiritual embrace.

"This is one of the many reasons I love you. Your heart, my sweetness. Big, pure, and utterly selfless." The shadows shifted as he disappeared on muted steps. His words hit her heart differently, brimming with adoration, pride, and contentment. He filled her with his love, filled her soul with the truth of his claim. *"I'll keep my brother busy until you ladies are ready to come out. We'll be in the living room."*

"Thank you."

She sensed his smile, but her mind remained quiet.

Sky's sobs tapered off a short time later. As they did, she dropped her head and used her jacket sleeve to dry her face before she lifted her chin with a sniffle. Her cheeks were deep pink, her nose red, and her eyes glowed like ethereal lights. Sera pulled the sleeve of her shirt over her palm and helped wipe a few stray tears from her jawline. Sky's lips quirked into a shy grin.

"I'm sorry," she whispered.

"Why? You've nothing to be sorry about. I've two shoulders, and one is still dry, so if you ever need it, let me know, okay?" When the woman's brow creased and her jaw finally loosened, Sera smiled, gathering her hands in hers. "I mean it,

Sky. I'm not just spewing words." She nodded her head toward the door. "We're a little more than lifemate sisters, right?"

Sky laughed, a breathy sound against the rawness her sobs had created. She squeezed Sera's hands in return. "Yes." She nodded. "Yes, we are. And I think we're going to build this up to be something unbreakable."

"We will." Sera released Sky's hands and grabbed a fresh scrap of linen, dunked it in the water, wrung it out, and handed it to Sky. The other woman thanked her as she wiped the spring water over her face. Sera watched in mild awe as any signs of her meltdown disappeared, then glanced down at her wrists. Her bruises had vanished. "Whenever you're ready, the boys are back."

Sky sniffed a couple of times, rolled her shoulders, cracked her neck—Sera refrained from cringing at the sound—and smiled. "I'm ready. You're going to have your first flying lesson today. Emery had his riding harness adjusted for you when you arrived. I think you're going to love this."

Recalling the brief memory of gliding through the sky, free as the wind, before she'd fallen asleep in Emery's claw, Sera couldn't agree more.

GABE LEANED INTO HER BACK, REACHING FOR THE HAND grips to adjust them down to Sera's reach. She tried not to notice how similar his build was to Emery's, especially as Emery gauged them with one fiery orb and his scaled lips parted in what she deciphered as a dragon scowl. The low-frequency growl that touched her mind supported her suspicions. She patted him alongside the row of spines she straddled, strung up in a leather contraption that sent her mind into a different realm of thoughts that had nothing to do with riding her dragon.

Well, maybe they did, just not the way she was about to.

"Woman, you'd better behave with those thoughts. I can easily turn this harness into something that'll fit the bed."

"Tell my brother to stay focused," Gabe whispered alongside her head as he adjusted the second hand grip. When she glanced at him, he winked, green eyes smoldering. "He's stewing like I did when he set Skylar up on my back the first time."

"I can hear him."

"He heard you," Sera said with a short laugh. She tried the hand grips, giving them a tug. Her feet, secured in stirrups, rested comfortably against the curves of Emery's dragon form. His scales—Gods, they were as big as her hand, if not bigger—exuded a consistent warmth that heated her from beneath.

Gabe sat back, wrapped one last strap around her waist, and cinched it snug. "Good. Now, this is your dragon-riding seatbelt. If you lose your footing or grips, you'll be secured with this so you won't fall. Once you become comfortable, you'll probably forego the belt. There's something that comes with the risk of riding without full security that adds to the excitement and freedom of flight."

"I'm not there yet, so dragon belt it is." She gave the strap an exaggerated pat. "I'm trusting you, Gabe."

Sparks spit from Emery's maw. Smoke plumed from his large nostrils. His serpentine neck maneuvered to lift his massive head in their direction. Gabe chuckled, swung his leg over Emery's spine at his back, launched off—

And transformed into another enormous beast before his claws hit the shelf.

Sky groaned. "Showoff." She tipped her head up, shading

her eyes from the sun with a hand. "How're you feeling up there?"

Sera shifted until she felt centered, ignoring Emery's continued glower. "Great!"

"Remember not to resist Emery's movement. Kind of like riding passenger on a motorcycle, but your resistance won't change the direction he goes. It'll just be uncomfortable for you. Become one with your dragon in the sky. You'll realize how easy it is. How natural."

"Become one. With me."

Sera pressed her heels into his sides. *"Already happened. A few times."*

Another spark-strewn snort and exhale of smoke escaped Emery as he swung his head away. *"I'm a dragon, love. Not a horse. Your heels are nowhere near my flank. Tongue-clicks and whistles don't work on me."*

Sera leaned over his back, alongside the short spines that followed the peak of his neck to the magnificent burnished red crest tipped with black, like his scales. He was a stunning picture of red and black ombre. Keeping quiet, she issued a few kissing sounds. *"How about that? Will that work? How about a cookie?"*

"Goddess, I'm going to punish you later."

A delightful shiver tread down her body. She grinned as she sat up straight. Emery tilted his head enough to catch her eyes with one of his. The reptilian slit of his pupil widened, insinuating exactly what he meant.

"I can't wait."

Sky couldn't have had better timing when she settled on Gabe's back and flashed Sera a wide smile. "There's nothing like flying, Sera. You'll learn really quick why Keepers often become addicted to flight."

"Ready, flame?"

"All my life, dragon."

Sera choked back a squeal when Emery dove off the shelf. The drop left her stomach light like the descent of a roller coaster, only for him to pinwheel skyward at a ninety-degree angle. She swallowed down a shriek, fingers fisted around the hand grips, knees digging into the diamond scales until her hips hurt. Every muscle in her body tensed, hard as stone. Wind hit her face mercilessly, and for a long while, she struggled to breathe anything more than a gasp. Her eyes teared up.

Inhale. Exhale. You know this, girl. Just breathe. *You're made for this.*

"Seraphina, relax. Listen to your own advice. And lean into me. Aerodynamics play a bit of a role here."

"You have to go and joke around, right?"

His deep, rolling chuckle filled her head and soothed away some of the tension that had strangled her stupid. She lowered her body parallel to his, allowing the powerful wind to curve over her head and back instead of beating her face. She focused on breathing, taking air deep into her lungs and finding none of the resistance she had only a few seconds before. As they climbed higher into the sky, the air filled her lungs with ease, her tension uncoiling.

"That's it, love."

She smiled against the wind. This was true freedom. True, exhilarating freedom. Emery banked right, then eased his wings out, slowing their ascent until they leveled far above the land.

"It's okay to sit up. Take in the view from this perspective. It's something else. You can also communicate with Sky through thought impressions. She'll pick them up."

"Nothing's a secret between us girls."

His snicker licked along her nerves with a delightful heat. *"Nope."*

Carefully, Sera pushed off his scales until she was upright, loosening her hold on the hand grips. She looked down, soaking in the view of a magical land filled with more vibrant colors than a color wheel back in the human realm. Trees cascaded over mountainsides, brilliant, blooming flowers spraying emerald green brush with bursts of color. She caught the shimmering reflection of water between copses of trees, creatures skittering along the fields or dodging through forest greenery. Birds dove away from the dragons as they approached, sending leaves flittering to the ground.

Off in the distance, she caught sight of a large expanse of water, and more mountains. *"Do you have oceans here?"*

"No. What you're seeing is a lake. There's a beach along the shore, surrounded by cliffsides and forests. It turned into a funerary site after the attack." Emery's large head tilted toward his brother and Sky, who glided slightly behind them. *"We held the funeral for Skylar's mother and father along those shores."*

"Oh." She glanced over her shoulder. Sky was adjusting something on her harness, but appeared at ease on her dragon's back without assistance from hand grips. At least she wore her dragon seatbelt. When she looked up and caught Sera watching her, she smiled and gave a thumbs-up. Sera mirrored her gesture and turned back in her seat. *"Where's this village I've heard about?"*

Emery eased them further right, then straightened out his flight path. As they rounded a mountain peak, her eyes widened at her first glimpse of a bustling, quaint village. Dirt paths wove between simple wooden structures, some at different levels of completion, others with wooden signs hanging over doors or smoke coming from chimneys. The fountain appeared to be a highlighted spot in the center of the village, despite ladders and stone at the base of the dry pool. It seemed to need a little more work before it was complete, but people still gathered around the large structure, eating snacks they'd bought from vendors set up around the fountain. Scents of seasoned meats and barbecue filtered through the air, making her mouth water. She was of half a mind to ask Emery to stop so she could walk the streets and taste the foods, but she wasn't ready to return to solid ground yet.

Civilians meandered along the paths, carefree and jubilant, from what she could see at this height. As they drew closer, Emery lowered them from the sky, gliding over the village like a low-flying plane. Excitement filled her, overflowed within her soul when she heard the civilians cheer as they passed, jumping and waving, shouting and laughing. At the end of the village, Emery pulled upward, and turned toward a mountainous area to the left.

"You once told me you weren't one for pomp and circumstance."

"The flyby was for you, flame. But it's always a treat for the civilians to watch dragons fly overhead. A longstanding tradition, in a sense."

She scraped her nails over his scales. In response, her dragon growled inside her head. *"So, you* do *like the attention."*

"Keep scratching at my scales and you'll find out how much I like that.*"*

"You're insatiable."

"You don't do anything to help the situation, which leads me to believe you're as ravenous as I."

She didn't argue his point. It was valid, utterly so.

Gabe glided up beside them. Sky waved, then pointed to her temple. Sera narrowed her eyes, confused.

"How're you doing? What do you think so far?"

Ahh, now she understood. Sky's voice didn't hit her the way Emery's did. It wasn't as clear or precise, but more like Gabe when he sent impressions to her mind for her to capture and decipher. Sera nodded.

"Great. Think I've got the hang of it now. Different when you're on top and not asleep," she passed back to Sky.

"You definitely look natural on his back."

Sky's reassurance left her brimming with completion. It lent weight to the rightness of how her life had turned. Twenty-six years of trying to fit in without being an imposition and she had finally found exactly where she was meant to be.

Two hours of sightseeing from the sky, along with a few stops—one to a cliffside field that Sky and Gabe used as a private practice ground, another to the far side of the beach, away from the funerary site—Emery led them back to the landing shelf of their mountain home. His landing was smooth, with not a jostle or jolt. She waited for Gabe to land beside them before she began her dismount. Her legs were weak from straddling Emery's back, reminding her of the handful of times she'd gone horseback riding over the years. Emery's large head came up to her as her feet hit the ground. She smiled, placing one palm on either cheek, absorbing the smooth surface of smaller scales and the warmth they emanated, and pressed a lingering kiss to the tip of his snout, between his wide nostrils. The scent of campfire and fresh air suffused her lungs, drenching her in contentment.

She would never be able to live without Emery. He'd become her world, her life, her everything.

"Thank you."

"For what, little flame? For not performing loops in the air?"

She snorted and shook her head, turning away from his playful glowing eyes, and began the task of releasing the harness from his massive form.

"For everything, Emery. For forcing me to accept what I kept resisting. For not giving up on me. For showing me what it means to be complete." She smiled more to herself than him as she tugged at the leather strap. *"Everything."*

She tugged the strap again when it didn't fall away, only to remember it was strategically looped over his spines. She was about to hike herself up onto his back when the dragon shrank and transformed back to the gorgeous man, harness draped over his shoulders. His midnight hair fluttered over his face in the light breeze, the waves making her fingers ache to tangle in them. He reached out and cupped her cheek, his thumb brushing over the corner of her mouth as he stared at her, eyes brimming with emotion. His emotions reflected those she kept close to her heart, the ones that made said heart speed up and leave her feeling faint.

Emery took a single step into her and pressed a tender kiss to her forehead. She closed her eyes, resting her hands on his chest, and reveled in the perfection of the moment.

"I love you, Seraphina." His voice was barely more than a whisper against her forehead, yet the deep, soothing baritone poured through her. "There is nothing I *wouldn't* do for you."

Her mouth curled. Raw, genuine truth rang from his declaration. A declaration that worked its way up her throat.

"How was your first real flight, sis?"

Sera held her breath, the words of her own declaration

nearing the tip of her tongue before Gabe's interruption. A subtle rumble through Emery's chest left her to wonder if he sensed she was about to respond to his love in turn, or if he was frustrated their tender encounter had been disrupted by his brother. Either way, it was a stark reminder they weren't alone.

Unhooking the harness from Emery's shoulders and dragging the long leather straps around him, she smiled. A heartfelt smile, because both Gabe and Sky appeared eager to learn of her first flight.

"After the initial shock, it was amazing. I'm looking forward to the next."

"You've a lifetime of exhilaration to experience."

Sky stepped in front of Gabe. Though she appeared controlled and calm, her eyes gleamed with excitement. "I'm going to the cliff tomorrow to work on cultivation and increasing my connection with the magic of The Hollow. I usually spend a couple hours a day enhancing my talents, and then an hour or so practicing in our gym. Gabe has an amazing gym for martial arts practice. If you'd like, you can join me. All the women and I get together three time a week to work on magic and self-defense skills, but if you're interested, maybe we can work together a bit more."

Sera's mouth had pulled into a giddy smile by the time Sky finished. She looked up at Emery, who nodded once.

"I'm not holding you back. Whatever makes you happy."

Sera bounced—actually *bounced*—on her toes and clapped her hands together. "I'd *love* to!"

Sky's tempered expression shattered into a happy grin. The smaller woman wrapped her arms around Sera in a tight hug, then stepped back. "Wonderful! Em"—she cut her attention to Emery—"could you bring her by around ten?"

"If she's out of bed."

Sera rolled her eyes. "I'll be out of bed, showered, and ready to go." She lifted the harness between them. "I should put this away. I'll be right back."

She draped the harness over her shoulder and started the daunting task of forming it into some semblance of neat loops to hang on the hook inside the entryway. Between grips and straps and foot loops, she managed to tangle herself in the harness more than not.

"You can string a person up good with this thing," Sera muttered, trying to twist the harness into something neat on her arm, catching herself as she stumbled over a loop that had dropped to the ground. She made it halfway to the entrance when the harness ripped from her hand, cinched about her arm, and wrapped around her other arm, binding them behind her back. It happened so fast she barely registered her predicament when Emery pinned her to the rocky wall, his massive form hovering over her like the most delectable threat she could imagine.

"I heard you, siren," he whispered, tugging the harness for emphasis. His eyes flashed with fire, hips crushed to hers. Those strands of hair she craved to twist in her fingers teased his sharp jawline. He drew his thumb across her lower lip, a painfully slow motion that left her gasping. "I'm more than tempted to see how you look in my harness and nothing else." He dipped his head close, his breath feverish against her lips. "But I set up something important for you to attend, so our experimenting will have to wait."

"Oh, you're brutal, dragon," she hissed.

His dark smirk fanned her fire into an inferno. "I'm not the one who entertained the idea first, though I'll definitely carry through with it. Just imagine how"—his finger dropped to her shoulder and drew slowly across her torso, between her breasts—"you'd feel bound in leather"—and back up, marking an X—"as I savor your delicious body."

"Hey, brother, don't be giving Skylar any ideas."

Emery blinked, the motion languid and slow, snuffing out the flames in his eyes. He drew in a slow breath—one she copied to cool her blood—took a single step back, and turned to Gabe, releasing his grip on the harness. He shielded her from his brother and Sky as she regained her control, fumbling with the harness as her face burned furiously.

"I'm sure anything you witness here is mild compared to what transpires between the two of you. *I* don't do blades."

Gabe's dark snicker raised the goosebumps along Sera's arms.

"Blades. Talons. Teeth. Brother, they fall into the same category when it comes to reactions."

She stumbled into Emery's back. Emery caught her in a gentle grip and gathered her beneath his arm. Sky's face had turned a shade of rose that probably competed with her own. Her turquoise gaze held Sera's.

"I told you, there's not much that's kept secret. They're shameless. But apparently"—she shoved Gabe in the arm, earning herself a wicked glower that was far more feral than frustrated—"these two have no sense of privacy, at least in the presence of their women." She huffed at Gabe. "Is nothing sacred?"

"Like you don't talk about it," Gabe teased, pinching her hip. Sky swung her arm, fending his hand off. Sera gaped as the two began to fight. Full-out martial arts moves that left her stunned, and awestruck, until Gabe caught Sky in a hold, hiding her from both Sera and Emery as he whispered against his lifemate's ear. Between Gabe's spread stance, she caught sight of Sky's knees buckling.

"Well, I have a feeling they'll be taking their leave now,"

Emery mused. When Sera glanced up at him, he shrugged. *"Fighting is their foreplay. And if I sense anything about this, they're about to finish things up at home."* Emery lowered his arm from her shoulder and slipped his fingers between hers, relieving her of the harness with his free arm. "Okay, lovebirds. We're heading in. Catch you later."

Emery pulled her away from the engrossed couple. He hung the mess of a harness on the hook as they entered their home and led Sera down the maze of corridors from the launch shelf to the main living quarters. The air between them sizzled with energy, wild and unspent. His fingers between hers tensed and relaxed, the subtle motion more telling than words of how hard he fought to maintain control. If this was how relationships between lifemates were, how the hell did anyone leave the bedroom?

"Ah. I think we've a guest waiting for our return."

When her steps slowed, Emery glanced at her. Her brows furrowed. "Who's here?"

"Uh-uh, flame."

He tsked as he led her down the last main stretch and into the living room.

Sera came up short, bringing Emery to a halt.

Slade's hand lowered from one of the antique pieces on the mantle and turned to them. Dark eyes glanced over Emery, then came to rest on Sera. Eyes she'd known her entire life, hosting warmth and kindness she'd always believed to derive from sympathy and pity.

She understood that look. Understood the hidden pain she could never name, until now. The secrets she'd learned he kept, and the evidence of regret etched in the fine lines that formed between his brows, that succeeded in cracking the strong, formidable Slade Rogue right before her eyes.

CHAPTER TWENTY-ONE

Unease knotted her belly. Squeezed her lungs. A wave of icy heat—because it was neither, yet both—washed over her muscles. She pressed her lips together, her gaze barely able to hold steady on the man halfway across the room, poised yet vulnerable. This was not the confident Uncle Slade who'd rescued her whenever she found herself in a situation her father didn't care to help with. Not the steel wall of a man who'd protected her when she couldn't protect herself. Not the tender man who'd told stories and drew chicken-scratch pictures of a world she had dreamed of since childhood.

No.

Before her stood a man who tread a thin rope he wasn't certain how to navigate, but his intentions were clear. Despite everything that had come to light, the one sure fact he did not hide was regret.

Emery's hand tightened around hers, drawing her out of her daze. Slowly, he led her forward, glancing at her every few steps. She didn't doubt she dragged her feet, even if she tried to look like she wasn't. Her legs grew heavier the closer they came to facing truths withheld from her all her life. Those dark eyes held no shield to what Slade thought or how he felt. Everything was there for her to see, to read, to understand.

As they came up to Slade, Emery's hand released Sera's and pressed to her lower back, guiding her forward. *"Give him a chance to explain. You'll find much solace in the truth."*

The pressure on her back ceased, but the familiar sense of calm and warmth flowed through her mind and infused her body. Emery's magic settled her riled nerves enough to clear her thoughts. The faint hum of energy teased the outer edges of her mind, a signal she realized must have been Emery and Slade communicating along their own telepathic link. She hadn't realized she'd pressed into Emery's side until he eased her around him and graced the top of her head with a lingering kiss.

"I'll grab a few glasses and some drinks," he murmured, giving her upper arms a gentle squeeze before he stepped back.

She gazed up at him, at the support and reassurance swirling in his eyes. He gave her strength when she lacked it. Part of her wanted to beg him to stay, but she knew this was between herself and the man who'd played the role of a doting uncle to compensate for not performing the role of father. Emery's mouth curled at the corners, a reinforcing grin for her only. Then he headed toward the kitchen, leaving her alone with a man she knew so well but felt like a stranger.

Swallowing down her nerves and a sudden dryness of her mouth, she worried her lower lip for a few long seconds, buying time before she leaped off this cliff into uncharted waters. To her relief, Slade didn't try for small-talk. He was never a pointless chatter type of guy, and filling silence with nothing of worth wasn't something he did during crucial encounters. *That* much she knew.

Fingers wringing tightly at her waist, she finally sucked in a slow breath and faced her real father.

For a brief eternity, they simply stared at one another, the silence daunting, suffocating, rife with energy. Her heart pounded in her chest, the rush of blood in her ears deafening. She shifted on her feet to hide the involuntary sway, but it didn't escape the man's keen eyes. He caught her beneath her elbow and motioned to the sofa.

"Sit, Sera. Please."

She complied. There was no point in trying to be stronger than she felt, which wasn't strong at all. Despite knowing this encounter would come sooner rather than later, she wasn't prepared. She wasn't sure she'd ever be prepared until it was over.

Emery returned as she settled into the corner of the sofa. Slade relieved Emery of the glasses filled with some fruit-infused water and handed one to her. Emery placed a pitcher of the same deep purple liquid on the coffee table, his gaze lingering on her as she drank. Slade took a seat on the sofa, keeping a comfortable distance between them. His eyes brimmed with sadness. As much as she tried to ignore it, she couldn't. His pain cut her deep.

"Sera?" She glanced up at Emery, whose brow furrowed in concern. As she lowered her glass, she offered him a faint smile and a nod. He brushed his fingers over her cheek before he left the room, this time in the direction of their bedroom. *"I'm not leaving you. I'll be in the bedroom if you need anything at all."*

"How're you adjusting to The Hollow?" Slade asked.

"Well. It's more beautiful than the stories."

"There's only so much a story can describe. This is a

place no number of descriptive words can portray and do it justice. It's a place one must see firsthand to completely comprehend the immensity and the beauty it holds." She watched from the corner of her eye as Slade shifted on the sofa and set his glass on the table. "Sera, I know there isn't an apology that can fix the mistakes I made. Nothing I say or do will change the last twenty-six years. What I believed to be in the best interests for both you and Nick was poor judgment, but I didn't realize it at the time. I can't turn back the clock or change the past. I can only atone for the wrongs I've done and hope to do well by you moving forward, if you'll give me a chance to do so."

Uncle Slade at his finest. A man who did not waste breath where it shouldn't be wasted.

Sera wiped the condensation on her glass mindlessly, watching the droplets fall from the bottom and splatter over the floor. The burn of his patient gaze needled through her head, the weight of his hope bearing down on her shoulders.

She sucked in a sharp breath and straightened her back. Dredging up her strength, she finally faced the man who'd flipped her world upside-down.

"Why?" Her single question broke the man's expression. She witnessed the single most immovable pillar of their small Keeper community crumble beneath her steady gaze, despite the turmoil wreaking havoc beneath her own surface. "Why didn't you claim me? Was it shame? Was it regret for fathering a child with someone other than your wife? Was it out of fear that I'd steal your dragon from your legitimate daughter? Was I a regret? A mistake? Why?"

His eyes widened and his lips fell apart on a gasp. She shifted back as he scrambled closer to her, desperation flashing in his eyes.

"Goddess, *no*. That can't be furthest from the truth."

When he reached for her hand, she drew back. He froze. "Sera, I would apologize to you until my dying breath. I would grovel at your feet for forgiveness if I knew it would change the past, but it won't. Your mother was my first, and only, true love. Long before Claire. Long before Nick. She and I had hopes and dreams that wouldn't come to pass until the one night that brought you into my life."

Sera sighed. "Wonderful. Not only did I take Mom from Nick, I took her from you, too."

She was shocked when her father grabbed her face between gentle hands and held her gaze steadily. "*No.*" He shook his head, strands of dark hair falling over his eyes. "I have *never* blamed you for what happened to your mother. It was Fate, Sera. Something no one could prevent, as tragic as it was. The one thing that kept me going was the moment I first laid eyes on you in that hospital. My heart broke with the loss of your mother, but you breathed new life into me when you looked up at me from that bassinet."

"Then why did you leave me with a man who hated me?"

"I thought I was doing the right thing. Nick was shattered. I hoped he'd find solace with you, believing you were his daughter. I had hoped he'd heal, but my hopes were founded in fantasy. I had every intention of remaining a steady figure in your life. Like I told you, your mother and I came to an agreement during her pregnancy that Claire and I would be an aunt and uncle. When things took the turn they did, Nick believed you were his, and I couldn't break the man more."

Sera laughed, a prickly sound, and twisted her head from his hands. She leaned forward to put her glass down and prepared to stand. He moved back a little, his hands falling to his thighs.

"You realize how ridiculous this sounds, right? You gave me up to a man who thought I was his daughter, a man who held contempt for me from as early as I could remember. You claim I breathed new life into you, yet you abandoned me to a man who wasn't my biological father, allowing me to grow up believing things that weren't true, experience things I might otherwise have been able to avoid. Aunt Claire knew. She knew I was yours. Your sacrifice to your Keeper friend seems a little steep, giving up a child you claim to have adored for the sole purpose of *hoping* he would heal."

She shoved to her feet and crossed to the fireplace, staring blankly into the calm flames. Then she spun around, hugging her arms around her chest, and glowered at her father as he stood.

"Do you hear how backwards this sounds? To me, you had the best of everything in your '*wrong*'"—she emphasized quotation marks with her fingers—"decision. I'm sure Aunt Claire finding out you had fathered a child with another woman didn't go over well. My mom's death probably made her happy. Then there was me. What to do with the bastard child. What would be the easiest way out of the mess you created, right? Nick was clueless that I wasn't his. It was perfect. You got to keep your happy little family while skirting paternal duties unless you felt the desire to step up and save the day, yes? I meant so much to you that you quickly handed me to another man to raise, and do a piss-poor job at it." Another sharp laugh, and a snort of disbelief. "I was *disposable*, in other words."

"Seraphina, you were *not* disposable—"

"Then why didn't you claim me as yours?! *Why*?! You knew! Aunt Claire knew! What held you back?! Jeslyn and I would have grown up sisters! *True* sisters! Not like now where she feels contempt for me because I'm fated to the dragon who we both grew up believing would be *her* lifemate, since I was made to believe my father was Nick Allaze and not Slade Rogue! I was subjected to Nick Allaze's hatred toward me for years because I *killed* his wife! Where does this leave me? I'm the one in the fucking center of this entire fiasco, and I'm the one who stood to lose *everything*! The only person in this equation who hasn't deceived me is Emery, the very person who shouldn't be mine, but Gods bless, is!"

Slade rounded the table, his expression growing stern. Only his eyes belied the agonizing battle he waged within himself.

Good. You deserve it.

"Because I wasn't in my right mind, Sera, and I know—damn it, *I know!*—I was wrong! If your mother hadn't died, I would've taken you both and—"

"It was *her* who meant more, not me, because you abandoned me when she died and your entire plan fell apart!"

"No!" He shook his head sharply. "It makes no sense, not even to me, why I made the decision I did, but I can't fix the past. I *can't*, as much as I want to. As much as I wish I could. *I can't fix it.* I did my best to fill in the gaps where Nick failed you. I tried to be a father under the pretense of being your uncle. Maybe I made the decision I did subconsciously to keep the peace. Between me and Claire and Nick. Why do you think I did everything I did? You had your own room in our home. I funded your college, your sports, your activities. I came to your games, your competitions. I supported you opening your business, helped you start it, sat with you for hours planning out a good strategy to make it thrive. I was trying to be a father without the title—"

"To fulfill your selfish desire to coddle your conscience for giving me to a man who *wasn't* my father. To play a misplaced hero."

The cold words spilled from her mouth before she could

stop them. Slade stared at her, his face unreadable, his eyes wide, unblinking. She huffed a breath.

"So, the day your perfect world came tumbling down, *this* would be your reasoning. You played the father without being the father. Ah, I get it. Always easy to fuck over the bastard child—"

"Enough!" He crossed the space between them in a matter of steps. He took her by her biceps and leveled his hard gaze on her. "I fucked up, Seraphina. I fucked up and there's not a day that goes by that I don't regret the decisions I made when it came to you. The only thing I don't regret is *you*."

"Funny way of showing it, wouldn't you say?" She twisted her arms up and shoved at his chest. "Let me go."

"Not until you hear me out."

"What more is there to hear? Every time you speak, you make it sound worse and worse. My mother was your true love. She's dead. As happy as you say you were when I was born, your decisions speak volumes. They *scream*. The sight of me probably tore you up as much as it did Nick, only in different ways. You couldn't bear the sight of me because your heart was broken. Nick couldn't bear the sight of me because I took his trophy wife. You left me with Nick in hopes he'd heal. Well, what about you? Maybe I could have helped *you* heal. Nick would've gladly tossed me in a dumpster. The only reason he didn't was because he held hope I'd be worth something to Rayze." She shoved at Slade's chest again, but he held fast. "There's nothing more to discuss. I think if Emery and Jeslyn ended up together, as we all thought would happen, you and I wouldn't be *having* this conversation."

"That's absolutely not true."

"Oh? It took twenty-six years." She smacked her hands against his chest and shoved hard. Her eyes began to burn and blur. "Twenty. Six. Years!" She punched at him again, her fists feeling like they were pounding steel. He barely moved. "And only because Nick found out and *I was there*!"

"Sera! Stop this."

He shifted his grip to her wrists, but she yanked and fought his hold as tears broke through the barriers and streamed down her face. She pulled at her arms, trying to break free of his iron hold as the familiar pain from the night everything changed—the night Nick would have gladly put a bullet into her body—exploded from the depths of her chest to every extremity in a rush of painful betrayal.

"Dear Goddess," Slade hissed.

She began to collapse, but Slade caught her, gathered her up and pulled her close. He embraced her, crushed her against him, arms holding her in a desperate hug.

"Sera." He pressed his cheek to her head, his hand smoothing back her hair as he rocked her on her feet. "Sera."

"Why couldn't you keep me?" she sobbed. "Why? Why only my mother?"

"I'm so sorry, angel. I'm so, *so sorry*."

She stopped resisting and wrapped her arms around his waist, crying into his shoulder. The pain she'd stored up tore through her, seeking release from its cage. The impending tsunami finally crashed, shattering any wall, any barrier, in its path. She clung to him—*my father*—the man who, despite all this truth that had come to the surface, had come to her when she needed a father most. Right now, without his strong arms holding her upright, she'd fall. Without his continuous apologies, whispers in her hair, against her temple, the betrayal would continue to rip into the fabric of her soul.

How long she sobbed, she didn't know, but the heat of Emery's presence, his magic in her mind, tempered her tears. That persistent embrace he'd provided in trying times. Her lifeline, her savior, the steadfast support she knew would never let her suffer alone.

As confused as she felt, caught in the vortex of a storm that whipped her around like a leaf, she could never refute one solid truth: Slade Rogue had been more of a father to her than Nick ever was. It made sense now. It didn't take the sting out of the knowledge that he'd never claimed her as his until his hand was forced. It didn't smooth the edge of betrayal.

The arms around her remained steady and strong. The hand smoothing her hair rhythmic and calming. Her cries tapered to shallow gasps, then even breaths, and only then did she press away from the supportive figure and wipe her face with the heels of her palms. Slade's hand lingered on her shoulder, his fingers relaxed despite the tension she sensed in him.

"You eclipsed Nick in every way when it came to parenting. I often wondered what it would have been like to be your daughter, seeing how you treated Jes. There were times I was jealous"—she guffawed, rubbing her tight cheek with her sleeve—"because I wanted what she had. Not the material things." She rubbed her lips together, regaining her bearings, and finally lifted her gaze to his. "I wanted a dad who would love me unconditionally. Teach me to ride a bike or climb trees. Bring me to daddy-daughter dances at school. Celebrate my perfect grades in school and my accomplishments as an adult. I wanted a mom who would do my hair and paint my nails. Bake cookies with me and read me stories. Help me find the perfect prom dress and put together a Sweet Sixteen birthday party. The closest I ever came to a mom was Aunt Claire. The closest I came to a dad was you, but you weren't always there. You weren't *present* like you were in Jes's life. My mom was dead, the stand-in father figure spent his time philandering with women, and my true father had his own family to occupy his time."

Slade's expression fractured, his dark eyes saturated with guilt and shame. His jaw shifted as he clenched his teeth, lips pressed tight. His hand dropped from her shoulder when she stepped back, falling listlessly to his side. Dressed in jeans and a fitted long-sleeve shirt, he looked far more humble, more vulnerable, than the Uncle Slade she'd known, with his fancy designer suits and straight-backed composure. The man before her looked no older than a decade her senior, at most, not a man in his fifties, but he held the wisdom and weight of decades of strife like an elder.

So unlike Nick.

She sniffled, lifting her chin higher. "You can buy a person everything in the world. Fill their homes, their lives, with gadgets and objects. It does nothing to fill them on the inside where it's most lonely. Where tangible items hold no value when there are gaping holes inside your soul. Where the structure to one's emotions is as fragile as filigree, but with a little nurturing, can turn to steel and weather any storm. Or just turn dark, cold, and numb." The corner of her mouth twitched, her fingers curling, hidden beneath the long sleeves of her sweater. "You made the choice to keep me at arm's length. You were a wonderful uncle. Admirable in how you treated me when I was not your responsibility. I wasn't blood, just the daughter of a friend you had a special Keeper connection with. You owed me nothing, and yet you gave me more than most would give blood family."

Pain etched her jaw as she forced back another wave of tears. Gods, the shame in his face, the gleam of moisture over his eyes. The agony he wore as plain as the sun shining through the glassless windows hit her through the heart. It twisted at her gut, burned through her veins, a pain unlike anything she'd experienced, and yet it wasn't her own. It belonged to a father who feared losing his child.

She lifted a finger and wagged it at Slade, her eyes narrowing. "And yet…yet I *was* blood this entire time, and in *that*, I was cheated." She lowered her hand and tilted her head. "Do you have any idea what it feels like to watch the man you believed to be your father turn a gun to your head and pull the trigger?"

Slade broke their gaze and turned his head away. His eyes squeezed shut, his face taut. His hands fisted by his sides, the muscles in his shoulders tense.

"Do you have any idea how it feels to have that same man, only a couple days before, put a threat in his words when he warned you to stay out of his way? To be told you are no daughter to him? To be reminded that you are the reason his wife is dead? That had it not been for me, the only woman he loved would still be here? Do you know how much that hurt?"

Damn these tears.

One snuck by her eyelids and trekked down her cheek. Slade lowered his head. That's when she caught the glimmer of the firelight against his own tears that crept down his cheek and disappeared in his beard.

She breathed a quiet laugh. "No. You don't. You never will. And I should never have had to suffer that pain, either."

"You're right." His voice, thick with strain, gravelly with emotion, barely reached her ears. "You're right, Seraphina."

Sucking in a deep breath, he lifted his head and turned to her. A broken man.

"You should never have had to endure any of the hardships, the torment, the neglect you did. I alone carry the fault for what you've suffered. I wish I could take it away. I wish I could fix it. I do. No magic in the world can erase the past."

He rubbed at his temple, a nervous tic she knew well. "You believe the decision I made was to ease my conscience, to have everything as it would best benefit me, but that's the furthest from the truth. I know it won't change how it looks, but at that time, in those crucial moments, I believed it was best for you to be with a man who believed you to be his daughter. Not because Dina passed. Not because I wanted my little family, as you put it. Your mother and I decided long before you were born that I would be your uncle and Claire your aunt. Claire wasn't exactly happy about it, knowing what she did, but she accepted the role, the title. I speculated the resentment that would come with me taking you in as my daughter. I suspected there would be disdain held over your head by my wife, and I didn't want that for you. Instead, I watched Claire love you like a daughter in her role as an aunt, not a stepmother. I wanted you and Jeslyn to grow up close, sisters as you are, and you did. I never thought Nick would be the one to heap such scorn upon you."

Another tear rolled down his cheek. He did nothing to hide it. Nothing to wipe away the evidence of vulnerability she'd never witnessed from him before today.

"So few are gifted the ability to see the future. I'm not one of them. My conscience was never clear after I made the decision to keep the truth quiet and leave the hospital without you. You were right when you said you can buy everything in the world but none of it matters when you're empty inside. You've seen my house, Sera. You've seen my attempts to soothe the void inside me. The only times that emptiness found some solace was when you were with me. I found peace in your presence, more than you'll ever understand. Watching you grow, witnessing the woman you've become. You're a beacon in the night, and no one can hold a candle to you."

Slade took a single step toward her, slow, cautious. The air hummed with hesitation. Sera stiffened. She might have even leaned away a tad, because he stopped.

"Sera, I'm not asking for you to forgive me for the past. That, I know, is too much to consider. I would never expect forgiveness to that degree. But if you can find it in your heart to give me the opportunity to be your father, to assume the responsibilities I should have held all along…"

His voice faded. The question was there, heavy in the air. An energy that teased her mind while it wrung her heart. Silence filled the space between them, broken only by the distant song of birds and the crackle of the fire. His eyes pleaded with her. His had always been a powerful gaze, but now, it threatened to shatter her resolve. Gods, what she'd do to throw everything to the wind, to forget it all happened, and go on like life was perfect.

But it wasn't. Her life had left scars that needed time to heal. Maybe not as deep as some of the other lifemates, but they were still scars, *her* scars, and still painful.

"They say hindsight is always twenty-twenty. We can't change the past. We can only learn and grow from our mistakes." Sera swallowed a lump in her throat as she formed the next question. "If you had to choose all over again, choose to leave me behind, would you? Would you choose one daughter over the other?"

Uncle Slade's jaw slackened. He blinked a few times, staring at her as if her question didn't register. Maybe it didn't. It was not a characteristic request of her, to give an ultimatum. Or maybe he hoped he'd heard it wrong. She was well aware what she asked bordered unfair, but so was life.

"What?"

"Uncle Slade"—he winced at the title she'd given him from the time she could talk—"your hearing is impeccable."

"That's not a fair question to ask. You're both my daughters."

"Yes. We were *both* your daughters, from the start." She huffed a snicker, a nasty sound that froze her own blood. A worrisome light flickered in his eyes. "Still, you *did* choose one over the other." She threw up her hand, stopping him dead in his tracks after he took a single determined step toward her. "Seems you wouldn't change things even if you could."

"If I had to do it again, I would have taken you with me. To hell with Nick. If I knew then what I know now, I would have done things much differently. If Claire left me because of it, so be it. At least I'd have had you."

"Shame it took twenty-six years and an unhinged madman for you to realize that, but I'm willing to bet I'd have been left with Nick Allaze all over again. Unless my mother had lived."

She burned those last words into him through clenched teeth, her gaze hard and cold. She watched the way the formidable man crushed before her, the consequence of her accusation. A few breaths later, she turned her back and left him to suffer the maelstrom of emotions they had brewed between them, seeking solace and peace alone on the terrace.

CHAPTER TWENTY-TWO

The low, resonant hum of magic flowed through him, a consistent spring feeding his suffering lifemate as she struggled with the emotions knotting up her soul. At times, he feared even his presence wouldn't be enough to keep the cracks in her strength together to persevere through the confrontation with Slade. His talons dug deep into the arm of his chair several times to keep himself grounded, seated where he was, and allow his beloved lifemate and his Keeper to work through this obstacle.

Slade's betrayal lanced deep. Deeper than he had initially realized, or perhaps feared. He held tight to a glimmer of hope that a few screams and cries would help mend the broken bridge between them, but in the end, the gap yawned wider than before.

Slade had reached out to him through mindspeak once, asking for his advice. He offered nothing, because this was of his Keeper's doing, and he had to figure out how to fix what he'd fucked up.

Now, sitting in one of the high-backed chairs in front of the fire in his and Sera's room, rapping the tips of his talons on the punctured arms, he listened to muffled steps approaching the room. He tempered the turmoil in the bond between him and Slade while continuing to feed Sera calming magic through theirs.

A knock preceded Slade's entrance. He didn't wait for an answer before throwing the door open. Emery ceased the rapping, retracting his talons, and slowly panned his attention to his disheveled Keeper as Slade approached in a handful of strides.

"Thanks for the help," he groaned, falling into the chair catty-corner to Emery's with a huff. He poured himself a healthy dose of whiskey from the decanter on the small table between them and threw it back in one gulp. Emery lifted a brow as Slade replenished his glass, only this time taking a small sip before lowering the glass to his knee. As his Keeper stared into the fire, Emery caught the sign of dried tear tracks along his cheeks. A vicious war waged within the man's eyes, one that he tried to bite back behind grinding teeth and stiff muscles. It heated the air around him, thrummed with potent energy seeking a single opportunity to flee its cage.

"I told you when we discussed today that I wasn't going to interfere. This is between you and Sera, not you, me and Sera. This is the product of your decisions. I wasn't there when this happened, and therefore, I have no business being involved in the resolution. The most I'll do is bring you two together, but you need to figure out how to resolve this. I'm curious, though, Slade—how much longer were you planning on keeping the secret had it not been exposed?"

Slade's head snapped toward him, his face a hard, unreadable sheet. Only his eyes bore the storm of emotions he tried to hide. Emery perched his elbow on the arm and rested his chin on his fist, steadily burning his gaze into his Keeper.

After a few moments, Slade released a sharp breath and took another hearty drink. "I don't know."

"Hmm."

"What?" Slade sighed and dropped his head back. "I don't. Every time I thought about telling her, I also considered how it would affect her. The older she got, the harder it got for me to bring myself to tell her the truth. I could give her everything as her uncle, and not destroy her. Turn a little girl's world upside-down? Turn an adult's world upside-down?" He lifted a hand and shrugged a shoulder helplessly. "Would there have been a good time? Destroy Nick? Destroy Claire?"

"Well, isn't that what happened in the end? And it was worse that Sera found out the way she did, rather than by your mouth. You knew from the beginning that making the decision you had would ultimately come to this. There is no easy way out of such a situation, and unfortunately, you're going to be bearing the brunt of her anger, because you betrayed her. Claire knew. You'd already reaped the repercussions from her. Nick, well, he's always been questionable." Emery released a breath as he rested back in the chair. "Quite honestly, she's right in that you made things sound worse the more you spoke. Surprising, coming from my gilt-tongued Keeper who can make the worst news sound pleasurable. I can understand why she'd think you intentionally abandoned her."

Slade opened his mouth to protest, most likely, but when he met Emery's gaze, he snapped his jaw shut and dropped his head onto his hand. Emery kept the silence as he focused on his glowing bond with Sera, nursing his woman as she ached. He yearned to go to her side, but there was a hint of resistance along their bond that kept him seated. She needed time alone, and he'd grant her that time.

"At this point, my advice to you would be to keep your tongue in check instead of trying to justify why you did what you did. Nothing you say will go over well, not after this grand exposure. She's my lifemate. Your change of feelings may be misconstrued based on our relationship, yours and mine, and not on the truth. She may take your change of heart based on the fact we're lifemates."

"None of my feelings have anything to do with you and Sera being mated."

"I know that. You know that. She does not. Nor will it be an easy task to try and convince her of such a thing. She's been betrayed, Slade. Hurt by those she trusted most. That's something that's hard to come back from. It tends to make people jaded and skeptical. You may have been a wonderful uncle to her, but you were a shitty father." When Slade cast him a toothy scowl, Emery chuckled. "Truth hurts, doesn't it?"

Slade smacked the tumbler down on the table, whiskey sloshing over the lip of the glass. "If I'm going to suffer the brunt of your displeasure, I'll figure this out on my own."

"It's not my displeasure, Slade. It's hers. Your *daughter's*. I'm merely reinforcing how she feels, which, in all honesty, she has every right to feel as she was the one who suffered the most because of your decision to skirt your responsibility as her father, regardless of the consequences of accepting her. You should have long ago dealt with the upheaval, and all of this would have been avoided had you only done what you had planned to do if Dina lived. Not only did you lose your true love, but you turned your back on your love child. She made a great point. You planned to take Dina and Sera away, but abandoned that plan when Dina died and left your child with a man who resented the air she breathed." Emery narrowed his eyes and tapped the pointed end of a talon to his temple a couple of times. Slade sank into his chair. "For just a moment, listen to that statement and tell me how you'd interpret it."

Slade cast his attention to the floor, his fingertips pressing into his jeans. Emery helped himself to a short pour of whiskey and swirled the amber liquid in the glass, allowing the firelight to cast it in a deep orange glow.

"Acting like a toddler about to throw a temper tantrum because someone calls you out on your mistakes doesn't look good on you, Slade. Never believed it was in your character to act like that." He took a sip of the drink, enjoying the subtle burn along his throat. A thin stream of smoke fled his nostrils as he exhaled. "My interpretation of that comment? You didn't give a shit about her."

Slade whipped an arm out, slamming it into the small table, knocking it across the floor. The crystal decanter and tumblers shattered over the stone, the liquid pouring through the bits and pieces of sparkling drinkware. He shot to his feet, his face twisted with anger and anguish, and roared, "That's not fucking true!"

Emery bolted to his feet, pitched his glass into the fire, and grabbed a fistful of Slade's shirt beneath his chin. He brought his Keeper close to his face, his vision flickering between dragon and man. Smoke curled from the corners of his mouth, twisted up from his nostrils.

"I know it's not true, but *she* doesn't," Emery hissed, keeping his voice low. "I *feel* your pain. She doesn't. I *taste* your regret. She doesn't. I am part of you. She is *not*. But I am part of her as well, and I know what is going through her head right now. She doesn't know what to believe, and you've given her nothing to prove what you say is true, other than a few tears. Impressive, I might add, since I've never known you to cry about anything. But again, *she* doesn't know that."

Slade grabbed his wrist with both his hands, squeezing tight. Desperation flared in his eyes. Determination set his expression.

"Then *help* me make this right, Emery. I want my girl back. I want my *daughter* back." He shook Emery's wrist, tightening the shirt around his neck. "I want her to love me as her father, not her uncle, and I'll do everything in my power to be the father I should've been from the moment she took her first breath."

Goddess, the sincerity was gut-wrenching. Watching the despair weave through Slade's eyes, wrenching open fissures that exposed the depth of his agony, stabbed deep into Emery's consciousness.

Slowly, Emery loosened his grip on Slade's shirt and retracted his arm. Slade released his wrist, smoothing a hand over the wrinkled shirt, but held his gaze.

Emery's mouth quirked. "I wonder which one you'd choose, or if you'd do the right thing and claim them both from the start if you had to do it again." When Slade's eyes widened, he waved his Keeper's shock aside and rolled out his shoulders with a nod. "I'll help you, but I'm not meddling to bend her to your favor, Slade. I know you wouldn't want that, but I'll do what I can to help her understand what I understand. What she isn't privy to. However, her decision will be hers, and hers alone."

"Thank you." His Keeper took a long, deep breath. The tension trickled away from his body, but his eyes glistened with a sheen of moisture that hadn't been there a few seconds ago. "Thank you, Emery."

"Whatever her decision will be, I expect you to accept it, whether you like it or not. Remember, this was your doing, not hers. She is the bearer of the consequences of your actions, or inactions." Emery leaned closer to Slade, his lips curling into a dark grin. "I will say this much—the shit she's gone through created one magnificent woman, and for that, I'm forever grateful. Jeslyn might do well to learn a few things from Sera, and I don't say that because Sera's my lifemate. It's simply an observation."

"Jeslyn has had it easy her entire life. Claire and I know that."

Emery straightened up with a chuckle. "Overcompensating again, huh?"

"I think our parenting techniques differed. I wanted to spoil one child because I failed another. Claire found it in her to love another woman's child, but Jeslyn was *her* daughter, and therefore would always come first."

"Mm. And how is Claire handling Sera being my lifemate?"

Slade shrugged, combing a hand through the mussed strands of his hair. He nudged some of the broken shards of crystal with his toe. "What she tells me is different from what she feels. These last few days haven't been good between us. She's been with Jax and Lauro's wives, and Saralyn has been keeping company with them as well. Mark offered me a place to stay until we figure things out." He motioned to the mess on the floor. "I'll clean this up."

Emery spread a palm toward the floor. Fire poured from his fingertips, catching along the trail of whiskey. The flames burned low to the stone, the heat intense. The crystal melted until it seeped into the cracks and spaces between the stones, and the whiskey evaporated, leaving the floor clean.

Flicking his hand, extinguishing the flames, he said, "No need." He brushed his palm on his jeans. "Think you forget we're back home where our magic and power are full force. I need to pick up some food from the village, since I'm not well stocked here. Let me check on Sera. I'll be right back."

He found Sera at the far end of the terrace, sitting on the stone ledge with her legs dangling over the edge. She leaned against the thick branch of a tree that had rooted in a crevice along the mountainside, its light pink blooms lending a subtle sweetness to the air. She played with one of the blooms she'd plucked, the petals large, nearly the size of her palm, velvety in texture. With each soft gust of the breeze, seedlings fell from the mature flowers on fluffy, palpus-like stems, some catching in her midnight hair, some floating around her, creating a perfect dreamscape with his woman as the focal point.

If only she was as content within her mind as she appeared to be on the surface.

Quietly, Emery approached her. The last thing he wanted to do was disturb her in this momentary serenity, and he had half a mind to turn around and leave her be, except for the whisper of loneliness he sensed, the desire for his presence.

She didn't startle as he stepped up beside her and lowered himself to the ledge, hip to hip with her. He dangled his legs alongside hers, following their rhythmic swing, and reclined back on his hands. For a long time, they sat there, the silence peaceful, soothing, knowing that she found comfort in his presence alone and words need not be spoken. She stroked the petals of the flower, her thoughts nothing more than a dull blend of the events that had taken place. Her tears had dried up. The fortress protecting her from suffering another blow swayed in its impressive stance, an unseen sign of internal conflict.

"It hurts," she murmured. Emery lowered his gaze from the distant horizon to Sera. Her lips pursed. A faint crease formed between her brows. "A piece of me wants him to hurt as much as I do, but I know that's childish. I also know he could never hurt the way he hurt me."

"Mm." He reached across her and cut another bloom from the branch with his talon, spinning it on the long stem. "A parent's pain differs from that of a child."

She lifted her head, the vulnerability in her eyes torture for him to bear. He offered a small grin and tucked the stem behind her ear, securing the flower in place. He drew his fingers down the side of her cheek, her neck, and slipped his hand to her nape.

"He bears the sentence of his own skeletons, and those are darker than you may ever wish to understand. I don't excuse his actions by any means, but remember, he is my Keeper. We have a bond, one you do not share with him. In turn, you and I have a bond, one much stronger and deeper, but one he does not share with you." He caressed her jaw with his thumb. Her wavering resolve buckled. "We all know we can't change what has already come to pass, but we can make decisions to change our paths to determine what we want in our future. You aren't the only one who hurts, flame. He does as well, and it's a pain that only a father can know, understanding how his poor decisions caused you strife. He is not without faults. None of us are. Only the Goddess above is perfect and pure."

"Do you think I'm wrong? Do you believe I'm over-reacting?"

Emery chuckled. "Love, I think you've handled this with more composure than I would've had I been in your shoes. I have a reputation for breathing flames, remember?"

Goddess, the quiet laugh and her timid smile breaking through the clouds in her expression sang to his soul.

"I believe you have all the right to feel as you do. But"—he lowered his head to hers, their noses brushing—"it's not something that should go on for long. We are not guaranteed tomorrow. We should make certain we live our lives and resolve conflicts when we can so we don't live with regret should something happen. I'm not saying to forgive him for the past, at least right now, but perhaps he can prove to you his words are true in that he wants to be a father to you. He's shown you love and support all of your life, as much as he suffered in his own grief over a situation he created for himself and for you. He definitely didn't articulate things very well just now, but Sera, he loves you more than you will ever know. I felt his sincerity in here"—he pressed his hand over her heart—"where you can't see but where he and I connect. A powerful inferno that burned through everything. Your father wants you in his life, as his daughter, not his niece. He yearns for a chance to show you his intentions, not to tell you his faults. And that's the Goddess-honest truth."

Her eyes closed, the weight of her internal battle slowly easing. He lifted his mouth to her forehead, pressing a tender kiss to her cool skin.

"You know, Sera, you wouldn't be the woman you are today had things happened differently. You wouldn't be the woman who burns bright in the darkness, glows in the light, and appreciates the life you live, and all that comes with it. You wouldn't be my Seraphina, beautiful, stubborn, selfless, loving. Perfect."

"He asked you to argue his point, didn't he."

"Whether he did or not, I wouldn't be wasting my breath on a topic should I deem it pointless. And this rift between you and Slade is not a pointless matter. It's a matter that affects you to your core, and I don't like to see you suffer when you don't have to."

Sera sighed, looping her arms around his waist and leaning into his side. She rested her head on his shoulder. "He's your Keeper. You hold a degree of responsibility to him."

"Yes. It's a bond. It's loyalty. But let me make this abundantly clear to you, Seraphina. You, my lifemate, the woman who holds my heart and the woman who I'd sacrifice my life to protect, come first over anything and everything. My undying loyalty lies with you first. Everything and everyone comes after you." He combed his fingers upward, sinking them into her thick waves as he held her close. "You have an opportunity that some of the other women would do anything to have. You consoled one of those women earlier. What Sky wouldn't give to have her parents back for even a day, and you have the opportunity to build a relationship with your father now. Slade will do right by you. I know he will."

"I hate the logic. It reminds me you're a couple hundred years old, and I thoroughly enjoy you, old man."

Emery laughed, squeezing her about the waist. "My stamina defies my age. As do my looks."

Sera scoffed, but the dreary energy that had taken up residence in her mind finally began to subside. "We'll have to put that to the test."

"At your earliest request, my love." Emery leaned forward, gauging the sharp drop from the ledge. "Ever wonder what it's like to fall from the sky without fear?"

She leaned back, her eyes narrowed, scrutinizing his sanity, most likely. "How is that a fearless endeavor?"

He winked. "You trust me?"

"I'm beginning to wonder if my trust is misplaced."

"Aw." He leaned into her, securing his arm around her waist. "That was a low blow."

"You want to jump off the ledge." She tapped his forehead. "I can see it in your mind."

He brought his mouth close to hers, breathing in her shallow breaths as he savored the flavor of her excitement. "I swore to you I'd never let you fall, didn't I?"

"A freefall excursion?" She must've seen something in his devious grin, because she wrapped her arms around his neck and delivered herself to him. "That's falling."

"It's exhilarating, and you'll never leave my arms." Without another moment wasted, he angled his foot to the side of the ledge and launched them off the mountain into a fall. Emery held her close, twisting so his body was beneath hers as she swallowed down a shriek, her eyes squeezed shut, head pressed painfully tight to his chest, legs linked around his. "Open your eyes, love."

"Batshit-crazy dragon!"

He roared with laughter, the wind cutting up against him, the scenery a blur as they fell, locked together.

"Release all your worries, love. Open your eyes."

To his delight, her eyes fluttered open in time to catch the last bit of the fall before he transformed into his dragon, shot out his wings as the ground barreled up to meet them, and lifted them skyward. He tilted his head to capture the sight of her small frame clinging to his underbelly, her arms barely spanning a fraction of his width, same with her legs, as he held her between his claws.

He reached the ledge and caught the edge with his hind claws, reining in the dragon to settle back at the spot they had fallen from. A wide-eyed Sera shuffled way from the ledge, a fist pressed to her chest, gasping for breath. The only giveaway that she'd enjoyed the stunt was the deep flush in her cheeks and the clarity that shone in her eyes. Her wild hair clung to the corners of her mouth, lay disheveled around her head, and made him hunger for her in ways she had yet to discover.

As he stalked up to her, she straightened her shoulders and lowered her fist. He captured her face between gentle hands, drawing her to her toes. "That, flame, is freedom. The freedom to choose to release the dark that hinders your future and rest assured you will be safe."

He took her mouth in a lazy kiss, a tender kiss, one that whispered of his restrained hunger while coaxing a gentleness from the depths of their bond. He tapered the kiss, reluctant to end it, but knowing damn well if he didn't, the rest of the day would be spent tucked in their bedroom. Instead, he witnessed the transformation of his hopeless lifemate caught in a storm to something strong and unyielding. Independent.

She wrapped her arms around his waist, her eyes smoldering. "Are you planning on making a habit of freefalls?"

"If you wish." His smile faded. "Anything you want. You will always be safe with me."

CHAPTER TWENTY-THREE

Slade scraped the heel of his palm against the ground, sending a wave rippling through the dirt on a powerful thrust of magic. Emery jumped over the wave, landing in a crouched position, preparing to counter the attack when he caught a dangerous glint in his Keeper's eyes. One that warned him this was a little more than a practice session to refresh their use of magic and fighting skills. A week of daily sparring during the time Sera spent with Sky to learn the basics of martial arts in Gabe's home gym and the fundamentals of casting magic in a world that allowed her to explore a dormant gift. Slade's skills, though rusty, were coming back quickly, his agility nearly what it had been before the attack.

Grass whipped around Emery's wrists, reinforced through braided blades. He growled, yanking back on his arms only to find his natural shackles unyielding, woven with a spell likely to keep him from easily breaking loose.

"I've meant to speak with you on a topic that's been crawling beneath my skin."

Emery's brows furrowed as he turned his gaze up to Slade. His Keeper worked his outstretched fingers, flickers of neutral-colored energy guiding the grass bands up Emery's forearms.

"This isn't going to hold me. Don't get careless."

"It'll hold you long enough for me to issue a single warning."

What in this Goddess-given world had he done now? That glint wasn't one of playful antics and sparring fun. No. That was a look of pure warning he bore into Emery's head.

"I've been meaning to bring it up, but you've kept kicking my ass—"

"Which I plan to do again. Just making you feel like you've got the upper hand."

Slade's lip pulled back from his teeth. He twisted his hand. The shackles shot up to Emery's shoulders. The ground at his feet fell out from beneath him, dropping him into a hole up to his chest. Roots latched onto his legs and waist, tying him down.

"Hm. Like riding a bike. All comes back to you pretty quickly, eh?" Emery taunted.

"You'd better not be hurting my girl."

Emery blinked. Slade's voice had a lethal edge that reflected the cold warning in his eyes and the hardened mask of his face. In his moment of disbelief, Slade tightened the roots around his chest, forcing a gasp from his lungs on a plume of smoke. He coughed, sparks spraying the ground in front of him. The drier brush around him smoldered.

"What the hell are you talking about? Who the fuck would I be hurting?"

Because he was honestly dumbfounded.

Dirt rushed into the hole, compressing around him. His scales cut through to the surface of his skin, protecting him from the pressure of the soil. It wasn't that he couldn't escape. He could in a heartbeat. He wanted to know what the hell had Slade's underwear in a bunch under the assumption that he was helpless.

That would be another lesson—reminding his dear Keeper that little could hold this dragon down.

"I saw the bruises." Slade growled as he crouched down a foot from Emery's bound hands. The blades of grass tingled on his arms, barely able to grip the areas where his scales had appeared. "And the fucking bite mark on her shoulder."

For a long moment, Emery simply stared at Slade, his wildly infuriated and overprotective partner in crime, agape. Heat pooled in his groin in that instant as he realized what had driven Slade to foolishly believe he contained a dragon in a hole in the ground of a world that fed dragons and Keepers their power.

Or that he was *hurting* Sera.

"Oh."

"Oh?"

Emery snickered, then laughed, which agitated Slade even more. Before the man could lay another magical blow on him, he cracked open the ground around him, broke free of the grass bindings, and launched out of his makeshift cell to stand beside Slade. His Keeper slowly straightened to his full height, extinguishing the thrumming energy wrapped around his fingers as Emery dusted off the dirt from his jeans and T-shirt. A strange flush burned across his cheeks, barely hidden by the rebel strands of hair that refused to stay tied at the back of his head.

"She may not care to speak with me, but I'm still her father, and you'd better be damn sure I'd protect her—"

"Hold up"—Emery threw up his hand, cutting Slade off—"and unknot your thong, 'cause you're coming after me for no reason at all."

"Emery," Slade snarled.

He groaned, but a grin teased his mouth. "I claimed her. She's my lifemate, after all. I really don't think she'd appreciate me discussing what happens behind closed doors with her father. That's, honestly, awkward. Even to me. I swore I'd always take care of her. She's safe with me. I can assure you, she never *hurts*."

Slade's anger shattered into a look of unease that painted his face a light pink. He cleared his throat a few times, rubbing the back of his neck as he dropped his head, creases forming on his forehead. Emery chuckled with a shake of his head, shifting on his feet in an attempt to adjust his thickening cock at the mention of his love marks on Sera's beautiful body. It made him crave to take her to bed, taste her from her mouth to her core and everywhere he could get his lips and tongue.

"If I do ever hurt her, I give you sole permission to pluck me scaleless and singe my flesh with acid as punishment. Spear me through the heart, because if I cause her pain, I deserve the torture. My woman deserves the universe and everything it offers, and I am hellbent on giving her everything I can to make her the happiest woman alive."

All joking aside, he spoke with raw sincerity, punctuating the truth behind each word with a hand splayed over his heart. Slade turned his face back to him. The man pressed his lips together, the flush of his cheeks still darkening his tanned skin. His eyes glimmered with a familiar sadness that had haunted Slade since the night their lives changed back in Colorado.

Emery clapped a hand on his shoulder, giving it a reassuring squeeze. "Let's steer clear of that topic, shall we? On another note"—he wiggled a finger toward the disturbed mound of dirt and uprooted grass—"you've forgotten little keeps us down, old man."

"You've a few centuries on me. I'd be careful who you're calling old."

Slade raked a hand through his dark hair, stubborn strands falling over his forehead again. He'd trimmed his beard shorter than before. His clothing remained more casual since returning to The Hollow, Slade opting for jeans and shirts—polo-type tops, T-shirts, and an occasional button-down—and a pair of boots Emery bought him from one of the civilians in the village. He'd had a few things commissioned for Sera, since leaving The Hollow for clothes shopping right now was out of the question, and couldn't wait to grab them for her on their way back home.

"Tired?" Emery asked.

Slade rolled out his shoulders and his neck, then checked his watch. Not that they followed any set schedule in The Hollow. He found his Keeper continued to address his expensive time toy more out of habit than necessity.

"We've been at it for three hours. Think we can call it a day and resume tomorrow. Didn't Cade want to speak with us this afternoon anyhow?"

Oh, shit. He'd almost forgotten about that. "Ah, yeah. Dragon and Keeper reunion at his place." Emery gathered up the harness from the branch he'd hung it from and tossed it to Slade. "We'll head back to my place. You can shower and change. I don't expect Sky to give up Sera before we leave."

"The two of them are hitting it off, huh?"

Emery smiled and nodded. "They're sisters, essentially. Sky never had anyone close to her, so it's nice to see her comfortable around Sera, and vice versa."

He released his dragon and settled close to the ground. Slade tossed the harness over Emery's back and secured the belts before climbing up and adjusting the straps around the shorter spines of his neck.

"Have you spoken to Jeslyn?"

It wasn't a topic he wanted to broach, but it wasn't something that would go away. Jeslyn was his Keeper's other daughter, therefore connecting her to Emery, whether he cared for it or not. His respect and loyalty to Slade would keep her in his favor, however light it might be.

"No."

"Claire?"

"Only if necessary. Whether or not the boys are trying to placate me or make me feel better about the situation, they've assured me Claire is going through a grieving period and should come around soon. At least their wives are being cordial. I haven't received a tongue-lashing from Saralyn, either. Hope that bodes well."

Emery curved his neck and tilted his head to get a better view of Slade. His Keeper focused on fixing the hand grips and cinching the top strap a little tighter, no longer the lighthearted man who had been strapping him up with ease and excitement.

"Things will work out, Slade. Give it time. If you want to come to my home, you know I have spare rooms."

Slade gave one final tug on a strap and patted his scales. He sat up and caught Emery's inquisitive eye, offering a halfhearted smile. *"I know, but I doubt I'm welcome in a home that doesn't solely belong to you anymore. Not until things smooth over between me and Sera."*

"They will."

The flight back to the peak was quiet, with Slade indulging his inner child with the love of flight. Emery refrained from any spirals or loops, allowing his Keeper the time to readjust to this excitement before resuming their old, crazy ways. In the twenty-minute flight home, Slade's mood had shifted from dreary and weighted to free and relaxed. Oh, the magic of flying.

And freedom.

He landed and gave Slade time to dismount before transforming back to his human form, shrugging the harness off his shoulders and arms and stepping out of the loops. Slade laughed, taking the leather straps and draping them neatly over his arm.

"The one thing that hasn't changed is how much flying can release burdens, if only temporarily." Slade hung the harness on the hook of jagged stone as they came to the entryway. "Nothing can ease the mind as much as the wind in your face."

"Better than some other things against your face."

Slade roared with laughter. Emery followed suit, knocking his Keeper in the shoulder. They made their way down the maze of tunnels until they reached the living area. Emery choked on his laughter. Slade coughed.

Sera and Sky both stared at them, glanced at each other, then back to Emery and Slade. Sera's gentle expression shifted, morphing into a mixture of emotion-woven facets. She caught her hands at her waist, her fingers knotting together. Thin strands of her hair were pasted along the sides of her face and the nape of her neck, those not long enough to remain in her ponytail. Her leggings showed off her long, toned legs, the cropped T-shirt exposing her flat belly and one strap of her sports bra. Emery swallowed down a growl, the scent of salt on her skin making his mouth water.

When her eyes landed back on Slade, she shrugged her shoulder and pulled some of her hair over the scar from Emery's bite. The move left him sour in his stomach, but he understood why—the same reason he'd changed topics only a short time ago when Slade revealed his discovery. Who the hell wanted to discuss their sex life with their parents?

That was one adventure he didn't care to embark on. And, apparently, neither did his flame.

"Were you planning on surprising me?" Emery finally asked, breaking the uncomfortable silence. He split from Slade's side and greeted Sera with a tender caress along her cheek, a chaste kiss to her lips, and a lingering kiss to her forehead. From the corner of his eye, he caught Sky scratch at her neck and turn away. "How was your practice?"

"Intense, but I'm learning a lot. My muscles ache."

"Why don't you soak in the tub for a bit? I'll get you set up."

The hesitation in her silence raised his curiosity. He leaned back, catching her chin as she lowered her head, and raised his brows.

"What is it, flame?"

Her gaze shifted toward Slade, despite Emery's shoulder standing as a barrier between them. *"Can I have a few minutes with him? Alone?"*

Emery refrained from smiling, brushing his fingers along her brow. *"Of course."* To Sky, he flashed a smile and pointed to Sera. "You better not work her too hard, or I'll be having a talk with Gabe."

Sky snorted, folding her arms over her chest. "Since when do I push any of the women beyond what they can handle? Sera can handle a lot more than the others." She leaned to her left and wiggled her fingers toward Slade. "Hey, Slade. Nice to see you again."

Slade plastered on a friendly grin. "Likewise, Skylar. Were you both heading back out?"

Emery moved from in front of Sera and urgently ushered Sky from the room. "We'll see you two soon."

Only when they were safely down the corridor toward his bedroom did he stop, earning a glower from his brother's lifemate. He pressed a finger to his lips. "Leave them be. This is a good thing."

"I sure hope so. I get the feeling their estrangement is fueling her during practice. She bent one of Gabe's kicking posts today. And yesterday, she manifested enough energy to cause a small boulder to explode." Sky leaned close to him and whispered, "I'm almost jealous, because she's adapting to the use of magic quicker than me. I shouldn't be teaching her. It should be the other way around."

Emery snickered, suppressing the swell of pride he felt at Sky's compliment. "I'm sure you remain supreme when it comes to sparring."

"I've had a lifetime of practice. Technique comes over time, but she's definitely gifted." She hitched her thumb over her shoulder. "Let me get back and shower. I know you guys have a meeting with Cade in a little while. Sera wanted to try some of the street fare in the village while you were busy, so I asked the other women if they wanted to join us for vendor snacks."

"I'm sure she'll enjoy it." He gave Sky a tight hug. "Thanks for taking her under your wing so quickly. You've made the adjustment much easier for her."

"Are you kidding? She's incredible, and I'm so happy she's yours, because that makes her the closest thing I've ever had to a sibling."

Emery snorted and stepped back. "What about me? What the hell am I then?"

Sky knocked him in the arm. "You're my silly brother who apparently hides some dark secrets. I might have to pick your brain one of these days. I have a feeling your bloodlust might be more potent than Gabe's, which is a frightening thought."

Emery grinned, the truth of her words reflecting in the mischievous shadows he sensed come over him. He winked lazily. "Something like that. He had to learn from someone."

She shoved at his shoulder before pressing to her toes and pecking his cheek with one of her sisterly kisses. "I'll come back in an hour."

"Want me to fly you home?"

She waved his offer aside. "We *are* neighbors. A fifteen-minute walk, at most, and it's a good cooldown."

CHAPTER TWENTY-FOUR

The awkward tension thickening the air tightened her nerves more than they already thrummed. This was the first day she'd crossed paths with Slade since their parting a week ago, and each day that went by chewed at her more and more. The last couple of days, she was on the verge of asking Emery to bring Slade back so she could settle things once and for all, but whether it be nerves or doubt, she'd always bitten her tongue and let it go another day.

At least now her decision was forced, and for the better.

She found it hard to look at him for long, her thoughts tangling in her head, matching the way her fingers knotted at her waist. Both times she'd seen him since arriving in The Hollow, his choice of attire leaned on the casual, giving him a far more approachable than the suit-clad businessman in Colorado. His gaze remained sharp, but cautious, yearning. The pain in his expression resounded in her chest. She didn't know a life without him in it, whoever he was, and wanted him back.

Slade. Uncle Slade. *Dad*.

Sera motioned to the kitchen. "I was going to grab something to drink. I'm sure you two worked up a thirst. Want something?"

"Sure. Whatever you have on hand is fine."

Her mouth twitched in a semblance of a small grin before she turned and disappeared into the kitchen. It wasn't until she grabbed two glasses off the shelf and one nearly slipped through her fingers that she realized how badly she trembled. Her stomach tilted, a subtle wave of nausea working its way through her gut. She swallowed, poured two glasses of water, and returned to the living space.

"Are you okay, flame?"

Emery's quiet inquiry soothed her riled mind, helping her to focus. *"I am."*

"I'm going to step out for a few. If you need anything, you let me know immediately and I'll be at your side."

His promise filled her heart with warmth. *"I'll be fine."*

She stepped up to Slade and held one glass out, unable to hide the tremor that caused the water to ripple. He took it with quiet thanks and caught her hand as she lowered it. The feel of his strong fingers around hers shattered the fragile barriers she'd built over the last week, releasing the vulnerability she'd tried to expel. Instead, she managed to find the strength to meet his eyes and see for herself the tenderness and love he held for her.

"You've nothing to be nervous about, Sera. It is me who should be nervous."

"You're not, though. I've never known you to be nervous."

The corner of his mouth lifted. "Don't take what you see on the surface at face value. I hide it well." He tilted his head toward the terrace. "It's a beautiful day. Want to speak outside?"

Sera nodded. She allowed Slade to lead her onto the

terrace, where they both settled against the rocky wall that was just taller than her waist, gazing out onto the sun-drenched land of untouched beauty. The breeze carried floral scents and a coolness that tempered the warmth. Sera rested on her forearms, cupping her glass between her hands. Slade mirrored her, sipping his drink in silence.

"Can you tell me what she was like?" Sera moistened her lips and looked at Slade. He lowered his glass and met her gaze. "My mom?"

"Of course I can. Anything you'd like to know."

"Did you know her well?" She played with the glass, trying to select her words so as not to trip over what she wanted to ask. "From being part of the group?"

Slade's gaze softened. "I knew your mother from the time we were kids. She was one of the most caring and selfless people I've ever known. Her heart was generous and warm, as beautiful on the inside as she was on the outside. She sacrificed her own happiness to please others, more times than not."

The weight on those last words piqued her curiosity. She watched him take another sip of water as his gaze returned to the horizon.

"She and Nick seem like polar opposites. How did they end up together?"

"Their parents were close friends and there was an unspoken expectation that they would marry."

Her eyes narrowed. His words held a degree of hidden meaning, explaining one thing while trying to hint at another. She didn't believe he did it intentionally, but something in her gut needled at her that the unspoken words would explain everything.

"You don't seem happy about how things turned out."

"Things turned out the way they did. She went along with

the marriage to appease her parents. Claire came into my life shortly after that." He released a long breath. "Your mother deserved the universe for everything she did for those around her. She deserved to be treated well. To be happy. Instead, she suffered in silence for years, miserable in a life she portrayed to everyone as perfect, and died before she knew what a happy life could be."

"She confided in you. That she wasn't happy. Why wouldn't she leave Nick, then?"

"Loyalty. Responsibility."

"But the two of you…"

Slade placed his glass on a flat area of rock and turned to her, resting his hip on the wall. His eyes were torn. "Your mother and I dated for a long time in secret before she confirmed her suspicions of the arrangements between her and Nick. She didn't want to cause contention between Keepers, families, and dragons. We agreed to keep quiet until we could figure something out, but in the end, she acceded to her parents' wishes and married Nick. Even Emery didn't even know about us. He didn't know who Dina was. Her family had no connections to Keepers or dragons. I'm not entirely sure how Nick's parents befriended hers. I met her one day when I was hiking along the mountain paths and found her lost in the forest. She had followed one of The Hollow creatures into the forest, believing it was injured."

Sera stared at him for a long while, his words playing over and over in her mind. The more they began to make sense, the more she saw Slade differently. The more she began to understand the turn of events.

"You loved her, but let her go."

Slade's sad smile tugged at her heart. "I did. It was all I could do. I loved her with all my heart and wanted nothing more than to be with her, but I wanted her to be happy, too. I prayed that Nick would be the man she deserved, but I knew in my soul he would never make her happy. He didn't understand love or commitment, but I had no say in the decisions made. So I let her go but always stayed close. Then I met Claire and things happened from there."

"Until you cheated on her."

He nodded once, his gaze lowering briefly. "Yes. I can't deny it, nor would I. What I did was wrong, but the circumstances around what happened are a bit more complicated. Regardless, Sera, if I had it to do all over again, I would have done things much differently. You are one of my greatest joys, whether or not you believe me. You've made me proud beyond words, seeing how you've grown and thrived." He reached up to her cheek and brushed his fingers over her skin. "You have so much of your mother in you. So much. She would have been so incredibly proud of you. She would have loved you with all her heart and soul, cherished you, adored you beyond words. We were both looking forward to a life together, with *our* child."

He lowered his hand and sighed.

"I've not made the best decisions in my life. Sometimes, I question whether I'm morally sound, even if Emery insists I am. I gave up the woman I loved and found peace with another. I planned to leave my wife and daughter to start a life with my first love and our unborn child. I handed you over to a man who believed you to be his." He chuckled and shook his head. "Had I been able to turn back time, I would have had you with Dina from the start. I love you and I love Jeslyn. You're both my daughters. You're both my blood. I love each of you for who you are as people. I wish, though, I had made different choices. Decisions that wouldn't have hidden truths. I often wonder how things would be if I fought for Dina and she didn't end up with Nick, but with me. I also know that had things been different, you wouldn't be Seraphina today. You would be someone different, and my heart is full because of the woman here, standing before me. Losing you, Sera, would break me as a man and a father."

Sera pressed her lips together. She'd cried enough over the last week; she refused to cry more. Not today.

"I don't understand why you gave me up. I believe your words but your actions conflict with everything."

"Do they, though? I'm not trying to argue that what I did wasn't wrong, but I never abandoned you. I took on a different role, but I never *left* you. It doesn't correct my mistakes, but I could never leave you." He rested a hand over her wrist. "If you let me, I will do everything in my power to earn my place as your father. I'll prove to you I can be your father, and should have been from the start."

Swallowing down a knot that had formed at the back of her throat, she looked away and drank her water. That knot bobbed a few times before it finally dissipated, taking the burn from her clenched jaw. She nodded slowly, considering his sincerity, trusting in Emery's assurance that despite all that had happened, Slade wanted to be her father.

She turned her wrist over and pulled her arm back enough for his hand to capture hers. His fingers closed over hers, a secure hold.

"Your dragon has a way with logic that can be utterly disarming," Sera said against the lip of her glass before she took another sip of water. Slade's chuckle drew her attention, and a faint grin to her lips. "Reminds me how old he really is."

"He's not my dragon so much anymore. But I agree. Don't let his carefree nature fool you. He's loaded with wisdom that could ground you before you realize what happened. Speaking of which…"

Slade released her hand and disappeared inside the house. Sera's brow wrinkled at his sudden departure. She watched the archway for a few minutes, waiting for his return, but when she remained alone, she turned back to the scenery. Despite the twisted decisions of the past, she had a clearer picture of how she'd come to be. What she thought had been a one-time fling couldn't have been further from the truth. The one thing that bothered her still would never have an answer, but despite being given to Nick at birth, both Emery and Slade made valid points. Truths she already agreed with.

Slade had never abandoned her. He might not have been in her life in the role of father, but he'd done more for her than Nick ever had.

Now, she knew the truth. Now, she knew her real father.

"Sorry." Slade stepped up beside her and rested a dark wooden box on the wall between them. Not so unlike the one from Nick's study that she'd become so familiar with. Her eyes widened and she glanced up at him, catching his smile and the excitement in his eyes. "This, angel, belongs to you. I may be his Keeper, but you're his heart. Nothing and no one will come before you in this lifetime, and I have no greater joy than to hand this over to your care."

"Emery's dragonstone?"

He laughed. "Yes." He held out a delicate key. "Go ahead. Open it."

Sera set her glass down and took the key. She quickly popped open the lock and lifted the lid. On a bed of black silk rested a breathtaking reflection of Emery's scales, melted and molded into a swirling design of black, red, and flecks of gold. The veins running through the stone pulsed, following an unseen heartbeat fed by the blood of Slade, and all the Keepers before him.

Slowly, she lifted the stone from the box and cradled it

between her hands. Heat poured through her, magic humming in her veins. This was how a living dragonstone felt, heavy with power, electric with energy. She sensed Emery through the stone, a visceral connection that ran parallel to their bond.

Slade chuckled beside her and shook his head. The pain and sorrow she'd witnessed in his face was extinguished by pure elation.

"He's scolding me for not warning him I was opening his box. He walked into a tree."

Sera burst out laughing, bringing the dragonstone to her chest and holding it close. "That's our dragon." As her laughter died, she lowered the stone back to the silk lining and closed the lid. "Whenever I held Rayze's dragonstone, there was always something missing. When I learned he was dead, I thought I understood why I never felt a connection with him. Then I learned the truth." She tapped the lid. "Emery's stone is alive. So different from Rayze's."

"What we feel with Emery's stone will be different from what we feel with another. The connection is instantaneous with the dragon you're linked to."

The brittle bases of her internal barriers blew away in the breeze. She wrapped her arms around Slade's waist and hugged him tight. His arms came up around her, their embrace one of familiarity from a time before all the turmoil. The embrace of a father, filled with comfort and love.

"I love you, Sera. I always have, and I always will. However you decide our relationship should be, my love for you will never change."

"We'll work through this. It may take me a little time, some adjustments, but we'll get to where we're supposed to be."

CHAPTER TWENTY-FIVE

The village was alive with people walking the packed dirt roads and pathways, working on half-finished buildings, setting up shops that were near completion. The scents of roasted meats and sugared sweets filled the streets, making her mouth water and her stomach growl. Gabby laughed, the willowy blonde keeping step at Sera's side as Briella and Caryssa took the lead. Sky lingered a few steps behind, going over self-defense techniques with Ariah and Kaylae, who was childless this afternoon.

"Maybe I can find a shop to replace your dress," Sera said to Gabby, glancing at one small shop with fabrics on display at the front of the building.

"Don't worry about the dress. Taryn filled my wardrobe when we first arrived here. I've got plenty of clothes, so if you need anything else, let me know."

Sera snickered. "I wouldn't trust a certain dragon with any more of your outfits."

"From what I've heard the others talk about, neither of those brothers hold regard for clothing." Gabby hitched her thumb over her shoulder. "I'm surprised Sky still has clothes left."

"Brothers." Sera rolled her eyes. She pinched the hem of her tight-fitting beige shirt. The airy, billowy matching beige pants flowed around her legs like a skirt. "I promise this one won't end up in tatters."

"That one looks really good on you, so make sure Emery keeps his talons to himself."

"Oh! Here's the vendor I was talking about. He makes these amazing sugar-coated fruits on sticks." Caryssa beamed, pointing to a simple wooden cart tucked beneath the shade of a few mature trees. She tugged on Briella's hand, who followed at her heels, twisting to wave them closer. Gabby linked her arm with Sera's and they hurried to catch up, the women surrounding the cart like a group of kids who had just received allowance. Ariah leaned in close to the shield that protected customers from the hot liquid bubbling in a bowl over a low flame. Caryssa said, "Oh, you have those juberries!"

The vendor, an older man with wrinkles at the corners of his eyes, laughed as he pulled one dowel filled with shiny deep purple berries from its place on a display rack. "I do, indeed, Caryssa. Taj told me you enjoyed them the last time you were here."

He held the treat out to Caryssa, who accepted the stick with a beaming smile. She dug out a small disc of gold from her pocket and handed it to the vendor, who tried to wave it away. She dropped it on the cart and turned to the group.

Holding the stick out to Sera, she nodded. "Try one."

Sera pinched the berry at the top of the stick, the sugar creating a hard, slightly tacky shell around the fruit, and pulled it off. She bit into the fruit and gasped at the explosion of sweet and tart, warm and cold. Juice poured over her tongue and a moan escaped her lips as she popped the rest of the bite into her mouth.

"Uh-huh. Right?" Caryssa helped herself to a berry. "I left enough for each of us to get a stick. Go ahead. Once word gets out he has the juberries, they'll be gone in a flash."

"Thanks, Caryssa. I'll get the next booth," Sera said, accepting the juberry stick the vendor held out to her. "Dessert before dinner." She tapped her fruit to Caryssa's. "I like the way you think."

"It's the way to go," Caryssa said, her mouth full. They shared in another laugh and continued down the smaller path that wove through a small, park-like area.

"This is a new addition to the village. I guess some of the civilians that were with Sky's father suggested a park, since many of them found a degree of comfort in parks while in the human realm." Briella pointed to fresh-planted flowers in the early stages of growth. "My mom and a couple of the other women got together and designed small flower gardens to follow the paths. They're going to be planting trees next week. I can't wait to see what it looks like as it matures."

"Don't forget the community produce garden they're putting together," Kaylae added, tapping one of the sugar-shelled berries before she pulled it off her stick with her teeth.

"I think they're putting that in a different location, but yes. There will be a community garden where civilians can pick fresh fruits and vegetables and contribute crops as well. There isn't much commerce here. The Hollow is based more off barter and favors. Trinkets of gold and jewels are always appreciated, but overall, what everyone has is shared."

"One hand washes the other, as the saying goes," Ariah said.

There were a few hums and nods of agreement. Sera couldn't help the grin that refused to leave her mouth. This was the world she'd learned about from her earliest days, and now she lived the fantasy she'd created in her head. Only this was so much more than her imagination could have ever developed.

"Ah! It's late enough for the meat sandwiches." Gabby pointed with her stick to a larger stall-like cart that was sending billows of steam into the air. The savory fragrance of roasted meats and herbs teased Sera's nostrils as they closed in on the vendor with a small crowd gathering for his goods. As they approached, the civilians parted for the dragons' lifemates, greeting them with enthusiastic waves. Gabby slowed down, her cheeks flushing. Sera took quiet notice of how she angled herself in a motion to hide from the crowd. Her unease was near palpable. Like she was suffocating.

"I think I'm going to wait for a sandwich. I'm still working on my dessert." Sera motioned off to her left. "I'm going to wait over there so I'm not in the way, if you want to hang back with me."

Gabby glanced at the vendor, then nodded with a small sound of relief. She followed Sera away from the gathering crowd. Sky cast them a curious look, slowing down a step from Ariah and Kaylae, allowing the two to join Briella and Caryssa in the line. She joined Sera and Gabby, playing with one of the juberries on her barely touched sugar stick.

"Everything good?"

Sera cast Gabby a side glance. Sky lifted her chin in understanding, biting into a berry and pulling it from her stick. Gabby shifted on her feet, rolling her stick between her fingers. Sera felt for the poor woman, who was older than she but withdrawn like a child. Her timid behavior outside the comfort of a practice session or one of the seven homes where they grouped pained her, a residual energy she picked up from Gabby. She didn't know the depths of the woman's abuse in the human realm, only that she'd suffered more traumatizing situations than anyone should ever have to. Emery had briefly explained to her all of the lifemates' histories, but when he spoke of Gabby, she experienced his empathy toward the once-broken woman.

In the course of a week of being in The Hollow, she'd learned her ability to feel others' emotions came from being here. Emery dubbed it her superpower. She secretly loved it and cursed it, especially when the emotions she absorbed hosted a canyon's worth of gaps because she wasn't up to speed on everyone's past battles. It could be disorienting at times.

Sky's shoulders straightened, her gaze lifting from Gabby to something over Sera's shoulder. Her expression shuttered, her eyes taking on a sharp edge Sera had yet to witness. In the same instant, the hairs at the nape of her neck tingled and an unsettling vibration plucked her nerves.

"Sera?"

Shit.

For a brief moment, Sera closed her eyes, pursed her lips, and gathered the turmoil that sprang to life in her chest. Emotions again, only this time, she would bet most of these were hers alone.

Slowly, on a controlled exhale, she turned toward the familiar voice. Jes had earned both her friends' attention already. It didn't make the sight of her half-sister any easier. At least she had the decency to appear regretful. Maybe even a little nervous. Sera observed her for a few heartbeats, noting her modest attire of linen pants and a pretty button-down blouse. No fancy jewelry. No curling iron waves or glittery accessories.

No.

Jes looked like the rest of them for once. She appeared humble.

"I, uh, saw you walking down the street. I was hoping to have a chance to speak with you."

Sky's steps were so quiet Sera didn't hear the woman move until she stood beside Sera. Although she appeared occupied with her juberry stick with only occasional glances at Jes, Sera felt her energy alive and vibrant, on full alert.

"This is Slade's other daughter, I presume?"

Sera tried to relax her back, but her spine refused to loosen. Sky's impression into her mind worked to reassure her, but failed. *"Yes."*

"Careful with her."

Sera spared Sky a short glance. Her friend merely plucked another berry from her stick, ignoring Sera's split-second silent inquiry, appearing aloof when Sera knew all too well that she watched everything like a hawk from beneath those long lashes and white-blond waves. Even Gabby shifted back half a step. She began to lower her head, but quickly lifted her chin, a gesture Sera'd seen her do multiple times. As if she'd remembered something and cast off her submission.

"After everything that happened, I believed I'd be the last person you'd want to talk to, even if the root of my creation is beyond my control." Sera tucked the wave from her cheek behind her ear and folded her arms across her chest. Jes's cheeks flushed, her gaze moving between Sera and her friends. "You realize that, don't you? That I have no control over who my parents are? Who my lifemate is?"

"I-I know that, Sera. It came as a terrible shock, realizing the game Emery played until you finally accepted him, and why it was you and not me." A sharp breath fled her lips as she nervously played with her hands. "I took my anger out on you, and I shouldn't have. Mom reminded me that none of us have any control over who the Goddess chooses for each person, especially when it comes to the dragons. I was"—she shrugged helplessly, her face falling—"angry and hateful and I should never have taken it out on you. He told me what you did. How you pushed him away for my sake, and suffered for it. It made me even more frustrated, because you've always been the one to make sacrifices for everyone else. Your arrest to save my ass. Sleeping in your shop so you wouldn't impose on Emery and me. Giving me your last few dollars to buy ice cream when we were kids and going without. Letting me have a pair of shoes that you loved simply because I *liked* them. Declining awards in school because you didn't want to overshadow me when your grades were always perfect and I struggled for mine. You've always been so much more than me, and when I heard Mom tell Emery she knew you were his lifemate, and he said nothing to deny it, I...broke."

Sera watched Jes crumble before her, shoulders hunching, eyes lowering, mouth pinched, knuckles white. A piece of her wanted so badly to run over to her and hug her tight, reassure Jes that she forgave her for everything. Her soul hurt having suffered the unspoken resentment from her best friend, her blood, and craved to heal from the wounds.

Her mind, on the other hand, took heed of Sky's warning. Twenty-six years of knowing Jes like she did, Sera knew she wouldn't come to anyone flaunting her faults. That was one vulnerability she would never divulge.

Unless The Hollow's changed her.

Maybe it had.

"Love, what's going on? You're upset."

Sera nearly snorted a laugh, but caught herself with a rub

of her neck and a glance at the cloudless sky. And here she thought she'd put up a mental smoke screen so he wouldn't worry about her while he was in his meeting. *"Fine, my sweet dragon. Jes caught up with us in the village. Took me off guard."*

"She's not—"

"No! She's trying to apologize, in Jeslyn's way."

The subtle vibration of a growl tickled through her veins. She pictured Emery stewing over this news, unable to leave his mandatory meeting.

"I'll bring back a juberry stick for you, as long as you be good in your meeting. I'm in exceptional company here. I know how to handle my sister."

"Only if I can watch you eat it."

She bit back a laugh and tried to keep the wave of heat from reaching her face. His rumbling chuckle in her mind assured her he knew he'd received the reaction he'd hoped for.

"Naughty dragon."

"Very."

"Sera, I'm sorry." Jes's apology brought her attention from her internal conversation to the external one. She lowered her gaze from the sky to Jes and studied her for a long moment. Her stomach knotted, an odd sensation rising in her. She wasn't sure if it was her or Jes, but either one, it screamed unease. Jes dropped her hands to her sides, her shoulders folding further. Her chin dipped. "I'm really sorry. You've always been like a sister to me, only to find out you really *are* my sister, and that's when I pushed you away." Her fractured gaze lifted again. "I don't like this. I hate it. Hate the distance. I want *us* back."

"*Us* may take time."

Jes nodded vigorously. "I know. I know that. But I'll do

everything to show you I mean it. I'll show you I'm sorry." She slapped a hand over her heart and raised three fingers in a Scout salute. "I swear."

Sera managed an uncertain grin. She should feel a world of relief with this impending reconciliation. Yet...

"I'll hold you to that," Sera said.

Jes smiled, her mouth quivering. She threw open her arms. "Can we hug on it? Like old times?"

"Of course."

She stepped toward Jes as her sister closed the gap between them in a few quick strides.

A commotion at the stall drew her attention. Caryssa stumbled, a dazed Briella swaying in her arms.

Like a switch had been flipped, Briella shook her head, her gray gaze icy clear, cutting to Sera. She opened her mouth, screamed, an arm reaching out in Sera's direction.

Gabby grabbed Sera's arm. Pulled, hard.

The world slowed. Slowed and grew hazy as she looked from her new friends to Jes.

Her sister's face, cold, hard. Filling her vision.

"Sera!"

Something sharp stabbed into her shoulder. Her eyes widened as she looked down, seeing a needle-thin blade in her flesh, a tiny trickle of blood escaping beneath the delicate gold handle. A handle strategically secured between Jeslyn's index and middle fingers.

She looked up at the woman who moments ago had apologized. Witnessed her resentment, hatred, in a white-toothed scowl and ice-cold eyes. Pain had yet to hit her from the stab, shock beckoning her to succumb. The world moved in slow motion, the sounds of screams, shouts, motion all a painstakingly slow, muffled blur. Gabby, tugging her arm. Sky, shoving Gabby away as she swung an arm to knock Jes away.

A soul-sucking jerk, pull, the sensation of her body being torn in multiple directions. Pain erupting throughout her entire being, piercing the barriers between physical and metaphysical. She threw back a head she couldn't feel. Arched a torso that wasn't even there.

Suffocating darkness closed in around her as she screamed into nothingness.

CHAPTER TWENTY-SIX

Slithering tarriness coiled around the golden glowing bond. The table talk dimmed as Emery followed that foulness, seeking its source. Gentle prods into Sera's mind left him without answers.

Until he heard her scream.

The screech of a chair startled him back to the present. Eyes watched him, several pairs of eyes from his brethren and surviving Keepers.

"Emery?"

Cade's authoritative voice drew his attention to the head of the table, where his leader watched him through a narrowed gaze, his face tense. Only then did he realize the screeching chair had been his, and he was the one standing, braced on locked arms and fisted hands against the table.

"Em, what's wrong?" Slade's carefully controlled voice filtered through his mind. One bright-burning bond while the other faded into shadows.

"No, no, no! Skylar!"

Gabe shot up from his chair, hands raking through his spiked hair. The promise of death cast his brother's face in a mask worthy of fear. He kicked his chair, sending it straight across the room to crack and splinter against the wall.

"Something's happened," Syn said, leaning forward, his fists at his temples, eyes squeezed shut. "Hold on."

Slade slowly stood, tilting toward Emery. "What is it?"

"Sera. I can't feel her. All I heard"—Emery thumped a fist to his forehead—"was her scream." To Cade, who had taken to his feet, he growled, "Are they here? Do they dare come back?"

"Briella said she saw Sera being stabbed, but by the time she realized her vision was about to happen, a woman had already stabbed her. Sera and Sky disappeared into thin air with the woman."

"Malla," Tajan hissed. Cade growled, his eyes glowing red fire as they cut to Tajan. Emery punched the table, once, twice. The wood splintered as his talons dug into the scales over his palms. He spun to Slade, his vision thermal.

"Jeslyn. She was speaking with her right before she screamed."

Slade's eyes widened.

"That's right."

The room grew silent, except for the sound of movement as everyone turned to the newest arrival. Emery clenched his teeth, his fists, fighting back the dragon as it reared and roared for release. His scales spread across his body, fire warming his throat and expelling as sparks from his nostrils.

He swung out an arm to keep his brother back when Gabe lunged toward the door behind Cade. Their leader folded his hands behind his back, but two tiny spheres of burnished red formed in his loosely-held fists. The brethren had all begun to converge, coming to stand alongside Cade.

Nick Allaze strode into the room, a dark smile taunting his audience. He kicked at the stone floor, his stance casual, at ease. His fingers played with a glowing black and blue stone, pulsing with live magic as he contemplated each and every one of them.

He pointed to Cade. "If you want to know what happened, keep your magic at bay. I feel its energy. Otherwise"—he shrugged—"you'll never know what happened to them and you'll lose your only chance to reach them."

Cade didn't vanquish the orbs. Instead, they morphed into something near invisible, except for a few white filigree threads. Emery knew what that magic was, and he'd love to see it put into action.

Those cold, dead eyes turned to Emery. Nick's smile grew. Every muscle in Emery's body hummed, nearing a breaking point. He wouldn't be able to hold back the dragon much longer. Not knowing Sera was in danger. Standing somnolent, waiting for a speech, wasn't in his blood.

"Would've been easier if I'd killed them both back in Colorado. I could've spared you this mess. Instead, you intervened. You and your nuisance of a brother."

Emery grabbed Gabe's arm this time, yanking him back. His brother breathed smoke and fire, his body already growing. Emery yanked at his arm, hard, and tugged Gabe behind him while shielding Slade with the width of his body.

"You've decided your best choice would be to collude with our enemy." Cade's gravelly voice resounded throughout the room, intense and thick. Magic wove through his words, whether Nick realized it or not. Emery watched as those filigree threads hidden behind Cade's back stretched spindly strands toward the doorway, creating a web seen only when the sunlight caught it at the right angle. "You know what happened to the last Keeper who turned traitor to our clan."

"This clan is nothing more than the Baroqueth by a

different name. We are one and the same. Our end goals are the only things that differ."

"And what would those goals be?"

Nick wagged a finger at Cade with a contemptuous snigger. He fisted his glowing stone in his other palm, tucking his hand behind his back. "Now, do you think I'm idiot enough to tell you that?"

"How long have you been scheming with our enemies?"

Nick considered Cade for a long moment.

Then, those dark, soulless eyes snapped to Slade. As much as Emery tried to shield his Keeper, the damn man defied him, brushing by to stand in front of him. Shoulders straight and chin high, Slade crossed his arms over his chest.

"Say it, Nick. Get it off your chest. Everyone here already knows, so say your piece and let Sera go."

Nick huffed, then burst out laughing. He curled over himself, roaring with laughter like a madman. Taj slipped past Cade, preparing to attack.

Nick threw up his hand from his back, presenting the pulsing stone. Taj came to a sudden halt. Cade's fingers flexed at his lower back. More threads of near-invisible magic wove along all possible exits, creating an unseen trap.

"Do you know what they want with lifemates?" Nick swung the stone toward Emery and Slade. His eyes could shatter diamonds, the hostility simmering in his soul. He leaned forward, conspiratorial, his smile evil. "They fuck those whores until they're broken and pregnant. The cycle continues until they're barren or dead. You fucked *my* wife, and you killed her—"

"You killed her long before she took her last breath. You strangled the life from a woman who wanted nothing more than to live. I *loved* her long before you *controlled* her. You, Nick, disregarded her loyalty, found your entertainment elsewhere more nights than you were home. I didn't kill her. *You did. I* did everything in my power to save her."

"By impregnating her with your fucking kid!"

"By reminding her life was more than what you showed her! If you want to continue this, we can, outside of this room. But we've been down this road. You threatened me at gunpoint, then turned the barrel on my daughter and aimed to kill. That I can't forgive, Nick, regardless of my mistakes."

Nick crept closer, his steps calculated, his face twisted with malice.

"Slade, watch your tongue. We need to know how to get to Sera and Sky before he loses his shit."

"I'm very aware of that. Don't try to protect me right now."

Emery growled, a low, resonant sound that echoed through the room. Nick's gaze flicked to him, then back to Slade. He kept his distance from Cade. Perhaps he kept a side eye on the big dragon-man as well, but not closely enough to notice how the web of magic their leader created began to slither across the floor, using the cracks in the slate as camouflage as they closed in on Nick.

"I don't want your forgiveness. Instead, I want to watch you suffer. I want to watch you break." His upper lip pulled back from his teeth. "Both of your daughters are at Darieth's mercy. Both of them will become nothing more than a vessel for his soldiers to fill with their seed and watch life after life pop out of them. They are *nothing*."

Emery's jaw fucking ached because of how hard he clenched his teeth. Something in Nick's gaze warned him of an impending strike. He slipped a little closer to Slade, grasping his shirt and holding it in a tight fist. Slade began to twist, but Emery nudged him, silently warning him to stay still.

"Don't bite, Slade. He's taunting you."

"However, he's willing to barter." Nick turned the stone over in his fingers. "If I bring back a dragon or two, he might consider releasing the women. If"—his eyes lifted to Emery and he winked—"you cooperate."

"What does he want?" Emery asked cautiously. He'd do anything to save Sera, but he wouldn't leap into the fire without a plan. They'd both end up dead.

"He wants a bit of leverage for the Baroqueth."

"Leverage," Emery repeated, glancing at the glowing stone. Was that their way to the Baroqueth hideaway? Was that why he flaunted the stone so freely?

"Don't make me throw your own warning back at you, dragon."

He might have laughed if the situation wasn't so dire. Slade rolled out his shoulders, tipping his head just enough for Emery to catch the half-glance in his direction.

"I've kept my cool this long. I'm not about to jeopardize Sera's safety."

"Any bartering will be done with me," Cade interrupted. He took one firm step toward Nick, his massive frame swelling to block out those behind him. "I'm the leader of this dragon clan."

"Leader," Nick scoffed. "You lost most of your dragons and half of your civilians! My dragon died under you! What kind of fucking leader are you?" Nick moved around the room until he came into view. His manic expression deepened. "And you, Slade. You want to save your daughters?" He pinched the stone between his thumb and forefinger. "This will get you to them. But when you get there, when you finally find your precious little girls, I hope you never forget this." His smile dropped, twisting into a serpentine scowl. "I enjoyed defiling Jeslyn as much as you enjoyed defiling my wife. Nothing like young flesh."

The strike of a viper.

Slade lunged.

Emery yanked at his shirt, pulling him back. Gabe bolted forward on a roar. Emery went after him, after Nick.

Nick laughed, wild, crazed. He tossed the stone up in the air. Reached upward to catch it.

Cade unleashed his magic.

The stone landed in Nick's hand as the filigree wisps whipped out toward him. They coiled in thin air where Nick vanished. Emery stumbled through the empty space, his grasping arms snapping closed around his own chest. Only a hollow echo of Nick's laughter remained. An ominous sound that brought the weight of the stifling silence onto his shoulders.

Slowly, he turned to Gabe. Slade. They stared at each other, at the floor where Nick should have been, at the fading wisps of magic that failed to capture him before he disappeared. The shock of failing to stop him, losing the only lead they had to where Sera and Sky had been taken.

Pressure built up in his stomach, filling the gaps in his chest. Pressure that started as a tap from within, growing steadily stronger and stronger with each beat of his heart until it beat at his insides and doused his world in red.

"Emery, Gabe. Come with me," Cade commanded, his voice allowing for no argument.

"I'm coming, too," Slade insisted.

"It's better that you remain here."

"Absolutely not!" Slade angled himself in front of Emery. "Those are my daughters!"

Cade considered him for a long moment. Emery battled back the desire to send the room up in flames. His thoughts twisted, filling with fragments of ideas and scenarios, but nothing of value. Gabe stood as stiff as a stone, no doubt fighting the same battles Emery did, trying to remain controlled when they both wanted to seek destruction and blood.

"Come," Cade said. "Step quick. We've not much time."

CHAPTER TWENTY-SEVEN

Sera stumbled as her feet hit solid ground. Pain shot through her shoulder, radiating down to her fingertips and up through her neck. She grabbed the small handle and yanked the needle-sized implement out, casting it to the ground as she shuffled on unsteady legs. For a moment, the world around her tilted, spun, then finally settled.

A room.

As she slowly turned, her stomach dropped and her heart thundered.

No, a cell.

She'd landed in a cell with a crude-looking bed on a questionable wooden frame, straw poking out of a torn and stained mattress. A small, lopsided table. A single chair. Two walls and a ceiling that appeared to be carved out of a mountain, not so unlike Emery's home. Only this room wasn't much larger than her bedroom back home, and was slatted with metal bars on two sides. One of those sides acted as a divider between her cell and a similar one where a dazed-looking Skylar struggled to get to her feet.

"Sky, you okay?"

Sky groaned, working her shoulders and neck to try and disperse the effects of whatever had just happened to them. "Yeah, yeah. I'll be fine. You?"

"Be better if I knew what the hell just happened."

Sera's attention didn't linger on her friend. Instead, she turned to the one responsible for this.

Jeslyn was coming around. She lay curled up on the floor, leaning against the metal bars in Sera's cell. She shook her head several times, rubbing her eyes, her temples. Her arms shook as she used the bars to pull herself to her feet.

"What the fuck?" Sky mumbled. The sound of metal scraping against rock drew Sera around. Sky's face pinched as she tugged on the bars, assessing where they disappeared into the ceiling. The shock had vanished, a fierce determination playing out scenarios to escape etched in the crease between her brows and the sharp glint in her eyes. "Where are we?"

Sera huffed a short breath through her nose and turned back to Jeslyn. The woman had managed to get to her feet, eyes wide, mouth slightly agape. Sera tilted her head, brows lifting, and crossed her arms over her chest. The slight movement sent a dull wave of pain through her shoulder, where a thin circle of blood was soaking through her shirt. She considered herself lucky that the weapon wasn't much thicker than a needle, not more than an inch in length, and that Jeslyn had terrible aim. It hurt, but it didn't impair her.

"I'd like to know that, too, Jes."

"I-I don't...I don't—" Sera grabbed her shoulders and shook her once, hard. Jeslyn shrieked, shoving at Sera's chest. "Stop!"

"Stop? Stop?!" Sera pushed her into the bars. "Look around you! Look!" She released one shoulder and jabbed a finger to the cell behind her. "Whoever you colluded with landed you here, too! Who is it? Where are we? How do we get out? I'll deal with the injury you caused later, but get us out of here!"

"I don't know how! This-this wasn't..." She shook her head, tears welling in her eyes. "I don't even know—"

"What did you do?" Sera leaned in close to Jes, burning the accusation of her question into the woman she had called a sister since she was a toddler. The same woman she had trusted, cherished, and sacrificed for. Jes pressed her back into the bars, looking for an escape from Sera, from the cell. Sera moved with her, parrying her every step. "*What. Did. You. Do.*"

Jes pointed a finger toward Sera's shoulder. "Y-you're bleeding."

Sera blinked once. Did she seriously just hear that right?

"Sera, we've got to figure a way out of here. Don't waste your time on her," Sky interrupted. Sera tossed Sky a glance over her shoulder as she stepped away from Jes. Sky glowered at the woman who was trying to shrink into the bars. "She obviously doesn't hold you in much regard if she planned a trap that would land you in Baroqueth territory."

"Baroqueth?"

Oh, fuck.

"Yeah. That type of magic paired with landing us in cells stinks of slayers. Sad they had to resort to the likes of her to accomplish this."

Sera snapped back to Jeslyn, grabbed her by the biceps and shoved her harder into the metal bars. Jes grimaced, a shocked cry bursting from her lips, followed by a flood of tears.

"What have you done, Jes?! Who are you working with? Why?"

"Why?!" She tried to bat Sera's hands away, tried to kick

at her shins like a child throwing a temper tantrum. Sera took a kick, but blocked her other attempts to free herself. The woman before her transformed from fearful to menacing in a blink, her whimpers melting into crazed laughter through tears that continued to pour down her cheeks. "*You*, Sera. You are the reason. You took *my* dragon. You! You took what was *my* right, *my* future, everything I waited for. You took everything that belonged to me because my father fucked some other chick and had *you*! *You ruined my life!*"

Sera snorted and shook her head. "That's as adolescent an excuse as I've ever heard from you, Jeslyn Rogue. Pointing fingers and laying blame on others when you know damn fucking well none of us have any control over our fate. And this, Jes, you've chosen. This, what happens here and now, will be on your shoulders and on your hands. So, you'd better pray that either we figure a way out of here or someone saves us, and you'd better plead for forgiveness, especially from our father."

Jeslyn's face smoothed into a sheet of ice that made the blood run cold in Sera's veins. Her tears, though at a trickle, might as well have been acid with how they burned with loathing.

"Who said I give a fuck about him anymore? You should never have been born. Had it not been for his one-night stand with your whore of a mother, you wouldn't be here and I'd have what is *my* birthright."

"Hold back, Sera. She's prodding you. That bitch is lucky I can't break through these bars or I'd have her twisted like a strung-up hog. She'd better pray I don't get my hands on her."

"She's not worth it, Sky."

"Nor is she worth the time you're wasting on her now and the thoughts I can see playing over your face. We don't know

when those beasts will come, or if something was triggered by our arrival. Our only chance is that our magic, the novice tricks we've been working on, should work here."

Sky was right. She wanted to pound a fist into Jes's face for the low comment about her mother. She obviously didn't know Slade had a relationship with Sera's mother years before he'd met Claire. She wasn't privy to that information, and certainly didn't deserve it.

"Now I understand what Emery meant by us Hollow folk holding deeper grudges than humans. Sad to realize that all our lives, you played at being my sister and when we found out the truth, that we *are* sisters, you turned into a snake." Sera shoved her to the ground and wiped her hands on her pants. Her scowl deepened. "But even a snake needs a handler when it's lost. Who is it, Jeslyn?"

"You're a fool. You've always been naïve." Jeslyn pushed onto her hip, braced herself with one arm, and made a circular motion with a finger at her temple. "An idiot. You never suspected a thing."

She chuckled, slowly climbing back to her feet. She dusted off her pants and lifted icy eyes to Sera's.

"Nick hated you. The only good you were to him was as a way to appease Rayze. A priceless gift to his dragon, who he adored. But with his dragon dead and the truth about you being discovered"—Jeslyn licked her lips—"what better way to get back at the same worthless piece of shit that burned us both than by coming together? Joining forces, in and out of bed—"

Sera barely realized the *thwack* came from the back of her hand hitting the side of Jeslyn's face until a dull burn spread up her arm and Jeslyn's head snapped to the side.

"Oooh, that had to hurt," Sky teased.

Jeslyn lifted her head, a thin trickle of blood at the corner of her mouth. The fury that boiled up in her eyes when she cast Sky a look before returning to face Sera barely compared to her own.

"You think that's something to be proud of? Sleeping with the man we thought was my father? And you run your filthy tongue about my mother?" Sera scoffed and stepped back. "You're disgusting. You're low, ugly, rotten. Nothing you do to the outside of yourself can hide your foulness, now that I see it. You're pathetic, and I pity anyone so blinded by self-righteousness that they can't even see how far they've fallen."

"Well, this has been an entertaining show, ladies."

Sera spun at the sound of the deep voice from beyond the bars. Three men appeared out of thin air in the dark corridor along the barred side of the cells. Three tall, muscular men in black leather from head to boots. Black hair, fathomless eyes flecked with silver that caught the single orb of light in the cell. Tattoos painted the sides of their faces and necks. The one in the center with his hair shaved, except for a small patch through the center of his head, had tattoos along the sides of his head. Mercurial tattoos that shifted and moved from deep silver to black, some rising from their skin, others remaining smooth.

The man on the right clapped slowly. The one on the left wore a malicious smile, his thumb playing at the corner of his mouth.

The middle one filled her with dread. With a face of angles that could cut like blades, eyes colder than hell, and an air of power she knew she couldn't survive, her heart suddenly sank as her fear rose.

Silence filled the space of their minds, their thoughts shielded from Sera.

These men must be members of the infamous Baroqueth.

Murderous sorcerers who had destroyed The Hollow and killed so many innocent people.

She cast Sky a sideward glance. Sky stood straight, her face unrevealing of her thoughts while her eyes observed. Calculated.

The middle man casually shook a finger toward Jeslyn. "You did well. Not only did you bring the one lifemate you agreed to hand over. You brought two."

He laughed and flicked his hand. The lock on the cell door clicked and the door creaked open a few inches. Jeslyn shuffled back, behind Sera. Sera eyed her escape, devising a plan as quickly as she could to get past the three men—

"Don't think about it, pretty girl. I can sense your adrenaline building. Save it. You'll be able to use it in a few minutes." He leaned toward the bars, his eyes glinting like hematite. "Trust me. It'll make it that much more fun."

Those words twisted in her gut.

The man who'd clapped entered the cell and crossed the short distance to where Sera stood. She lifted her chin and clenched her teeth, fingers fisting against her legs. She stared up into those soulless eyes, into a face that may have been handsome at one time, before the evil on the inside began to seep out through his pores.

"Do you know why you're here?" he asked. Sera remained silent, her gaze unwavering. She faced a monster she couldn't defeat, but she refused to let him see how badly her insides roiled. "Defiant. You'll be a fun one. Understand that your silence is short-lived. You'll be screaming until you're deaf soon enough."

He whipped up an arm. Black, smoky ropes of magic shot from his palm and fingertips, cinched around Jeslyn, and yanked her to him. She opened her mouth to scream, all evidence of her anger washed away with fear, but her voice never made it past a black rope that slipped between her lips. The man hoisted her over his shoulder and left the cell with a writhing Jeslyn. He disappeared into shadows a few steps later.

It had happened so fast. Too fast for Sera to try to intervene. One second, he was glaring down at her, the next, Jeslyn was bound and gone.

"Wait!" Sera lunged toward the cell door. The man with the patch of black hair blocked her, forcing her back into the cell as he advanced on her. She tried to sidestep him, but he kept a step ahead of her moves until she hit the pitiful table toward the back of the cell.

"Leave her alone!" Sky demanded, drawing the attention of the last man in the corridor. His toothy grin widened as he headed toward Sky's cell. *"I'll distract them. You have an open door. Get out and get help!"*

"Not without you."

Sera gripped the table and ducked to the left.

The man grabbed a fistful of her hair. Yanked her back. An invisible force knocked her knees out from under her. She dropped hard to the stone floor, pain blossoming up through her legs. The man forced her head up with a sharp jerk of his fist in her hair. She grabbed his thighs and tried to push away.

"Can't have that."

Brutally hot threads burst over her wrists, twisting her arms behind her back. She tugged hard, trying to loosen the magic manacles, but the harder she pulled, the deeper they cut. They could have been wire, had she not known better.

"Darieth wanted us to introduce you to your new home. We can't disappoint our leader."

Sera opened her mouth to protest, but the man pushed her face into his leather pants, over his cock, and thrust his hips. She balked, tried to turn away, the bulge of cock and zipper rubbing painfully against her mouth and nose. Her teeth dug into her lips. She fought against his hold, knocking her shoulders into his legs, scraping her knees as she scooted backwards.

"Behave and I won't be so rough. The first time."

He yanked at her hair again, setting her scalp on fire.

She heard Sky cussing from her cell, followed by the sounds of a commotion. She squeezed her eyes shut, swallowed back her pride.

Emery.

She waited until the man pounded his leather-clad cock into her face again. Opened her mouth wide.

And sank her teeth into his shaft.

The man stopped. Stunned, perhaps. She bit harder, deeper, and swore she felt his flesh give beneath the pressure of her bite.

He roared, snapping her head away.

Hair tore from her head when he ripped her off her knees and threw her into the stone wall. Her head crashed into the unyielding stone, her shoulder crushed into a jagged edge. Stars erupted in her vision. Her surroundings blurred, dimmed. Her legs gave out beneath her and she fell to the ground, her vision unfocused, darkening with each beat of her heart.

In the distance, she heard Sky screaming her name. Demanding she get up. When she tried to squeeze her eyes shut, a new level of agony exploded throughout her skull, strangling a whimper in her throat. Still, she listened to Sky's unrelenting demands. Kept Emery's image at the forefront of her mind. She wouldn't let these creeps take her down. Not like this.

Slowly, she pushed up on her hands, her head heavy between her arms. A stabbing pain attacked the shoulder that had hit the wall, nearly dropping her back to the ground.

A swift kick to her side knocked her down. She yelped, nauseating agony consuming her body. She curled up on her side, the motion inducing a brand new crushing pain as she tried to breathe. She coughed. More pain, taunting her into the arms of unconsciousness. A coppery flavor came up to the back of her throat, pooled inside her cheek.

"Emery." Her golden beacon in this nightmare. She had to fight. For him. *"Emery."*

She peeled her eyelids open enough to catch sight of the man she'd bitten curled over on his knees, cursing, punching the ground, holding his cock, his face deep red.

A second set of boots appeared behind the downed man.

She'd barely lifted her head off the ground when her body flew off the floor on a wave of air and slammed down on the table. The scream she'd been fighting back finally ripped from her lungs. She swore she heard her ribs crack. Definitely felt them grind as the remaining man twisted her on the table, spreading her legs at his waist. His hand clamped on her neck, hard, threatening, making it difficult for her to breathe. She pulled at his strong fingers, but her hand shook, weak from the beating. Her head throbbed, making it almost impossible to see, to gather her strength to defend herself. She felt her shirt pull at the back of her neck before she heard the distinct tearing of the material. Cool air flowed over her exposed skin.

The monster leaned over her, pressed against her core, hand groping her breast through her bra. His scowl glistened with spittle.

"The more you fight, the worse it'll be for you. Learn now, lifemate, you are nothing but our toy. You are nothing except a place to grow our sons and strengthen our race again. And each time we fuck you, it'll hurt. The more you scream, the more it'll hurt until you learn to like it."

His hand squeezed her breast until she cried out. His hand tightened around her throat as she gazed up at him through barely opened eyes. He was nothing more than a gray blur as her vision and her mind threatened to go dark. His cruel snicker left droplets of spit on her face. She weakly kicked at the backs of his legs, scratched at his arms. She coughed as he cut off her airway, blood spatter spraying over his skin. The sight of the bright red, the taste of fresh blood, slowed her fight.

Gods, did she have a punctured lung? Was she bleeding internally?

Was she going to die like this? Being tortured and raped?

His hand left her breast, grabbed the waist of her pants, and yanked.

A piercing scream filled the air. The table jolted. The pressure at her neck disappeared. She grabbed her neck, rolled onto her uninjured side, and coughed violently. Hard pieces of material drizzled over her, dust filling her nostrils. The table rocked again.

Gentle hands grappled at her shoulders pulling her upright. She resisted at first, whimpering from the blinding pain.

"Sera, Goddess, we don't have much time. I know it hurts. I *know*, but we've gotta run."

Sky.

She pulled Sera's destroyed shirt over her, covering her chest, fixed the waist of her pants, and supported her as she guided her off the table.

Sera swallowed a wave of nausea and the blood and bile rising in her throat. She squinted to see the fading cell. The floor was a wreck. Chunks of stone and rock spread over the surface. "What happened?"

"Magic."

Sera tried to glance over the room, but the slightest swivel of her head had her gagging. She clenched her shirt closed over chest, pressed a hand to her mouth until she could keep from throwing up, and allowed Sky to hustle her out of the cell at a fast pace, the woman's arm around her shoulders keeping her steady.

"I hope I don't lead us into the lion's den. The other guy took that wretched traitor in this direction before he vanished. I can only hope this leads to another hallway."

Sera slid her hand to her forehead as a dizzy spell took over. She stumbled into Sky, but her sister-in-law kept her upright without slowing.

"We need to work harder...when we get home. I failed... self-defense."

"Let's get home first."

Sera couldn't focus on the hallway except to notice that it was a row of cells. Many sat empty. The last couple were occupied by two women, both emaciated, naked, bruised and dirty, curled up on straw pads in the corner of their cells. Neither of them moved when she and Sky passed. Catatonic. The last woman's belly was swollen with child.

"Dear Goddess," Sky whispered. "We'll have to tell Cade about these women."

"Mm."

It was all she could manage to say without triggering another heaving episode. Each step rocked her stomach dangerously. Each breath ground her ribs to the point she couldn't take full breaths at all. Warmth tickled as it crept down the side of her face. She drew the tips of her fingers over a tender area above her temple. They came away stained with blood.

"Emery can't see me like this."

Sky shot her a sharp glance as they came to the end of the hallway. "He's the first person, besides me, who should see you like this. He'll make sure you're avenged." She craned her neck into the adjoining hallway, looked both ways, then jutted her chin to the left. "Let's try this way."

Sera swayed as they turned, smacked a hand to the wall, bent and vomited. Sky pulled her hair back while bracing her under her arms. The world spun viciously as she submitted to the demands of her stomach. The foul taste of blood and bile filled her mouth and nose. She grimaced through each contraction of her stomach as her ribs shifted. When at last she stopped, she gasped for air, feeling pressure along the left side of her chest from her broken ribs.

"I-I think I have a punctured lung. It's harder...to breathe."

"Fuck. Okay." Sky looked around. "Okay. Let's keep moving. Let's just keep going. We'll be worse off if we stay put. You'll get a spring water soak when you get home."

Gods, I hope I make it that long.

They had made it halfway down the hallway, coming upon an intersecting corridor, when Sera heard the distinct stomp of heavy steps pursuing them. Sky's hands tightened on her, the only sign of worry the woman expressed. She quickened their pace, but Sera couldn't push herself faster. She could barely catch her breath.

"Come on, Sera. Please."

"Go without me."

"Like hell. We do this together."

"Wretched whore!" The bellow echoed down the corridor. They both looked over their shoulders to see the man who had choked Sera sprinting down the corridor after them, his face twisted in rage. Deep blue and black magic formed around his fingers, bolts of silver and gray filling the growing spheres. "You'll suffer for that!"

Sky grabbed her shoulders hard and forced her into a jog.

Sera glanced back again to see the man closing in on them frighteningly fast. They couldn't outrun him. There was no way. Not in her condition. He pushed forward, then came to a sudden halt, pulled back his hands, aglow with magic—

Sera cried out as she twisted from Sky's grip and shoved the other woman forward with all her strength. Sky pitched onto the floor, skidding over the smooth material. Sera turned to face the Baroqueth, to shield herself from witnessing Sky's horror. If she could give Sky the chance to get back to The Hollow, to tell the others what had happened, she had a chance to survive. Sky was their best bet.

The Baroqueth's shoulders rolled forward, the force driving his arms, and those magic spheres.

Her feet flew out from beneath her. Sky cushioned her fall as the spheres flew over their bodies, barely missing them.

"We do this together, sister."

Sera stared up at the tall ceiling, with the rocky edges and shadows. The corridor was dark except for a light orb every few yards, but the orbs didn't provide much illumination. Even so, something moved up there. Crept along the ceiling, hidden in the deep shadows and craggy surface. She narrowed her eyes, not trusting what her mind processed or her eyes beheld. Sky tugged at her arm, but she couldn't move. She hurt too much.

"Emery, I'm so sorry. I never told you I loved you."

It was a reaper. She was dying.

Her eyes drifted closed.

"Death is here. But not for you."

CHAPTER TWENTY-EIGHT

*E*mery and Gabe separated the moment they landed in a small room doused in darkness. How Cade had a means of getting into the Baroqueth hideaway, he'd love to know, but that would have to wait. All he cared about was finding Sera and Sky, and getting the hell out of this place with them safe and sound.

In this secret place, with its cavernous corridors and rooms, floors of obsidian material that echoed even the lightest of footsteps, the golden glowing bond that had been smothered in shadows burst to life. Sera's lifeline, his guide to finding her. He instantly latched onto the light, forgetting everything, everyone to hunt down his lifemate. His dragon rumbled. Within the vibrant beams of life lay the masked pain she endured. Something had happened to his woman, and that something fueled the barely controlled rage ignited by her abduction.

"Let me know when you find her, Em," Slade reminded him.

"You'll know."

Emery sank his talons into the rocky, towering wall and

scaled it. These tunnels reminded him of their mountain homes, carved but rugged, with nooks and crannies throughout. He held onto his human form, allowing the black tips of his scales to cover his skin to camouflage him against the deep shadows and black voids of space. Slithering like a lizard high up on the walls, weaving his way through the stalactites once he reached the ceiling, he closed in on Sera, following the bond, absorbing her pain, trying to soothe her panic. He had no idea what had happened to her, the extent of her injuries. He couldn't get past the fog that surrounded her mind. It was impenetrable, which fed his panic.

His only flicker of hope was the understanding that the Baroqueth wanted the lifemates for breeding. They wouldn't kill the women, but that didn't soothe his raging nerves with the thought of another man laying a glance, let alone a finger, on his woman.

Someone is dying today.

He'd been crawling along the ceiling, following the bond, using his dragon's sight minimally to avoid detection by his fiery irises, for minutes. Eating up distance, but moving within this unknown maze.

A muffled bellow froze him. He tilted his head, focused on the direction of that voice, then twisted, retraced his path, and took a different corridor. Quickening his pace, he turned down another corridor, a third when a shrill scream filled the space.

Coming around another curve, he paused in shock as two blue orbs flew beneath him, dissipating against the walls in a plume of rock and dust. His attention shot to the source of the magic.

His dragon unfurled, but he kept the beast in check, rushing forward, following the ceiling. Sky hovered over his flame, speaking to her as he came closer. It took every ounce of control not to drop from the ceiling and destroy the slayer lunging toward the women.

He needed to stop him stealthily. He couldn't give away their position. He had no idea who might linger in the shadows.

Broken thoughts flickered along their bond as he approached. Nearly above her, he assessed her injuries while batting aside the dismal thoughts of failure.

Then, she saw him, but doubted her vision. He was about to reassure her when her whispered voice filled his head.

"Emery, I'm so sorry. I never told you I loved you."

Her eyes closed.

He released the rock, twisted to fall on his feet.

A sheet of black smoke shot over both women as the slayer reached them, and immediately cleared, leaving an empty space where Sera and Sky had been a second before. The slayer jerked around, looking for his prey, as Emery landed quietly behind him. All he saw was red, tasted fire, smelled blood as his rage unleashed.

The man had no time to fully turn and face his adversary before Emery punched his talon-tipped hand straight through his back, ripping through his spine, puncturing lungs, and grabbing a beating heart before his hand exited through the sternum. Blood soaked his arm, dripped freely to the floor. He leaned close to the doomed man's ear and whispered, "You take my woman, I take your life."

He yanked his arm back, dragging through wet organs and tissue, bones scraping along his scales. The slayer bowed, then folded to the floor as blood poured from the gaping hole in his body. Residual magic from his attempt to build a defense fizzled at his fingertips. Emery squeezed the quivering organ before it stilled, his talons piercing the chambers before he dropped it next to the slayer's face.

"Sera! Where are you?"

The bond glowed, but it was convoluted. He ran blindly through the labyrinth of this place, grappling at the bond, trying to figure out where she was as his mind stormed with panic and fury. His flame. She'd been injured. The blood on her body had been real. Hers. He recognized the scent, the lingering taste in the air. Her pain had been explosive as soon as he reached her. No magic he sent her could dull that pain she suffered.

Two Baroqueth hurried around a corner ahead of him.

Emery lunged toward them at full speed, claws spread, his own magic growing in his veins.

They shouted, raising their hands in preparation of an attack.

Emery released the dragon, transforming and filling the space of the corridor. He exhaled a stream of magic-infused white fire, engulfing the slayers and leaving no trace of them as the flames died out. The heat of his fire scorched the walls, patches of stone steaming with residual embers. He returned to his human form and continued ahead, stopping only when he came to a four-way cross-section. Each direction stretched into darkness. No rooms. No doors. Just open corridors and twisting tunnels.

He closed his eyes, calmed his dragon, his mind, and focused on the bond. His only true connection and means of finding his lifemate.

"Emery."

His heart thumped hard. His eyes shot open.

In front of him, where moments before lay a long, endless corridor, now stood an archway with a smooth black door. A strange haze edged the door, giving it a ghostly appearance. Slowly, he stepped up to it, stretched his hand out, hesitated for only a moment, then pushed it open.

The door swung inward on silent hinges to a small room empty of furnishings. The stark contrast of white and beige against black caught his attention. He rushed forward, dropping to his knees and sliding the remaining distance, gathering Sera in his arms. Sky sat back on her heels, blood staining her hair, skin, clothes. Her bright eyes held a frighteningly controlled calm that reined Emery in as he looked down at Sera.

Goddess, the sight of her destroyed him. He'd let this happen to her. The woman he had sworn to protect.

"Love, I'm here."

"Em, is everything okay? Did you find them?"

He'd all but forgotten Slade. At least his Keeper was with Cade. He brushed Sera's mussed hair away from her face, assessing the multiple scrapes and the growing bruise across her cheek. A gash along her temple had stopped bleeding, but plenty of blood caked her skin and her hair. His gaze roved lower, his fury growing when he paused at the faint red marks around her neck and the torn shirt. Her skin held an alarming pallor. Her eyes remained closed, her mind quiet.

"Yes. We'll be back soon."

"What happened?" He didn't trust his voice above a deep rumble. His words alone held a curse he feared to unleash. Fire thickened in his throat, smoke enhancing his inquiry. He lifted his gaze to Sky. "Tell me. Everything."

"Jeslyn was in on it. She and Nick. The two slept together to get back at Slade, she said, and they conspired to help the Baroqueth kidnap Sera. I was a bonus. We arrived in cells. She and I were split—"

Emery threw up a hand, pressing his face to his arm to stave off the desire to burn this entire place to dust. He took a few breaths, regaining control, then met Sky's worried gaze. A faint crease had formed between her brows.

"Will you give me permission to see it through you?"

Sky's eyes narrowed. "I don't understand."

"Give me your hand." When she extended her hand, he caught the back and cradled it in his palm. With the tip of a single talon positioned over the pad of her pointer finger, he said, "All I need is a drop of your blood and for you to open your mind to me. Should work even though we're not lifemates, since Gabe is my blood brother and you're his lifemate. I want to see everything that happened so I know how slow and painful my revenge will be."

"Of course, but I can tell you now, you'll be taking your sweet time and making sure they're brought back from the brink. Death would be too kind."

Sky didn't give him a chance to pierce her finger before she impaled her flesh on his talon. Blood welled up from the puncture, more than a few beads, and he quickly brought her appendage to his lips, drinking the earthy essence. He lowered her hand, holding the puncture tight between his fingers to stop the bleeding, and closed his eyes.

Her mind lay open to him, a theater of the events since the women's abduction. Everything rolled quickly, like a movie on a quickened speed. The village. Jeslyn asking for forgiveness. Briella screaming. Sky grabbing Sera and pushing Gabby aside as Jeslyn stabbed Sera in the shoulder with something…tiny. Falling into blackness, then finding herself in a cell, separated from Sera and Jeslyn. Sera and Jeslyn fighting. Three Baroqueth interrupting. Jeslyn being whisked away over the shoulder of one Baroqueth. Another trapping his woman, touching his woman, forcing her to her knees, her face—

"Easy, Emery. Easy."

His fangs pierced through his lower lip, the smoky metal taste of his blood coating his tongue. He pushed through the vile scene, Sky fighting the Baroqueth who had come into her cell to try and overcome her. But the nightmare continued when he abandoned her at the howling scream of his partner. The same slayer whose heart he'd torn from his chest, whose blood still coated his arm, damp and sticky, pinning her to a table, choking her, ripping her shirt, groping her breast.

Skylar, his beloved sister-in-law, unleashing magic that drained her of strength in order to try and save Sera. A crack sped across the cell floor, webs of cracks spreading up the walls and raining stone over the occupants. Sky escaped her cell—the door had been left open—and gathered Sera. They ran blindly, the blood, Goddess, the blood covering his sweet Sera. They ran until the dead Baroqueth caught up to them, and Sera couldn't run anymore.

Sky protecting her.

Then, that sheet of black he'd witnessed casting them in darkness, only to disappear and reveal the room they were currently in.

And...

Emery's eyes snapped open, glancing first at Sera, then up at Sky. "Malla?"

Sky pressed her lips together. She reached toward Sera's forehead, the gash.

"Sera's lung was punctured. She was bleeding inside from the kick in the ribs. I don't know what she did, she didn't tell me, but the bleeding stopped and the welt on Sera's cheek has gone down. She's breathing better now. I'd wager Malla healed her enough to get out of here." Sky let her hand fall away. "Sera said something her first day here, and I'm beginning to believe she's spot on."

"What did she say?"

"She suggested that Malla is really no different from us. A generation of females born to Keepers. Today is my first time seeing her, but she's not much older than us, Em. And the Baroqueth started from a rogue Keeper. I don't think she's an enemy. In fact, what Sera said makes a lot of sense. That she and Cade may be lifemates."

His chest suddenly felt light, like air had leaked out of his lungs and into his torso. He stared at Sky for a long moment, processing what she had just said. What *Sera* said on her first day in The Hollow. Hearing it put together, it shouldn't surprise him. There had been subtle hints all along, especially when it came to Cade's attitude in regard to the female Baroqueth. Her seemingly convenient timing when someone needed to be brought back from a dance with Death.

"Baroqueth aren't supposed to have healing capabilities because their magic went dark, and healing is of the light," he murmured, smoothing his hand over Sera's blood-caked hair. He brought her up to him and pressed a kiss to her forehead. "We need to find Gabe and figure out a way to get out of here. Try and reach him."

"How did you guys get here?"

Emery snickered as he readjusted his hold on Sera and climbed to his feet, cradling her in his arms. "Cade. Now I'm wondering what part *she* played in us having access to this place." He jutted his chin at her. "You stay behind me."

To his relief, Sky didn't try to argue and play fearless. She kept close to his left arm, but stayed behind him as they stepped out of the room and into the dim cross-section of corridor. The door slammed shut behind them and by the time they spun around, it was gone, revealing the corridor he'd first encountered.

"This place is like a living labyrinth," Sky muttered. "Gabe said he's close, not to move."

"Tell him to hurry the hell up. We can't stay in place for

long. We become too great a target." He cast Sky a look and raised a brow. "You both know that."

He gauged each corridor, mentally reaching out in hopes of sensing his brother as he searched for danger. The air hummed with energy, an electric warning that their time here undetected was coming to a close. They had to figure a way out of here, or find Cade. If he got them here, surely he had a way out.

Just as he was about to start down the corridor to his right, he felt the familiar heat and vitality of his brother. A few seconds later, Gabe dropped to his feet from the wall, retracting his talons as he grabbed Sky's shoulders and looked her over. It was the only time Emery had seen his brother crack and soften when it came to his lifemate and danger.

"Are you okay?"

Sky nodded, hugging him around the neck. "I'm fine. Sera is another story."

Gabe rested a hand on Emery's shoulder, his attention lowering to Sera's body draped in Emery's arms. He hitched a thumb in the direction he'd come from.

"You took off on raw instinct, brother. You get lost like that. We came from this way."

Emery started to follow Gabe and Sky down the left corridor.

The whizzing sound of a fast-moving object was the only warning.

He spun away from the open cross-section, in the opposite direction from Gabe and Sky. A rapid succession of smoky power bullets sped by them, embedding into different areas of the cavernous wall where the room had been a short time ago. Rock exploded from the sides, plinking and scraping, a cloud of dust thickening the air.

Emery pressed his back to the wall and looked across the

way, catching Gabe's lethal gaze. His brother's lips curled in a dangerous smile. Emery leaned toward the edge of the wall and pinpointed their pursuers.

The one at the front of the group of three made his blood thicken to lava. Carefully, he lowered Sera to the ground, propping her up against the wall. His hand caught in her hair as he guided her head against a small jutting piece of rock.

"I'll be right back, love. This bastard will regret ever looking at you."

He straightened up and rolled out his shoulders, the familiar heat of scales flowing over his skin. The attack had ceased, but pounding boots quickly approached, swallowing up the distance.

Cracking his knuckles, he snickered.

"Let's see how you like facing a merciless opponent."

CHAPTER TWENTY-NINE

*P*lumes of dirt and dust filled the corridors the moment Emery pushed off the wall into the open cross-section. The trio of sloppy slayers spit magic blindly, closing the gap between them with an uncoordinated blitz. Gabe spun out of his side of the corridor, Sky bolting across the firing zone to get to Sera. Emery leaped onto the wall, scurrying up as a line of smoky pellets followed close on his heels, blasting rock and obscuring his position further. It bought him time to get closer to the trio, a mere dozen or so feet away. He sensed his brother mirroring his actions across the way, dividing the slayers' attention between them.

One pellet harmlessly grazed his scales. He dug the talons of his feet into the wall and used it to catapult himself in an arc over the small cluster of men. The dust had become so thick he doubted the Baroqueth could follow him accurately as he twisted in the air and landed behind the group.

The three men spun, hands raised in preparation of an attack.

Gabe ripped one around, cutting his talons across his

throat. Emery landed a kick to the chest of the second, his gaze locked on his target.

The third. The leader.

Dead man.

He grabbed the bastard's forearm, twisted until bones snapped and he howled. He threw up his free hand, his power swollen and ready for release. Emery opened his mouth and breathed a skin-melting stream of fire at his arm, snuffing the magic as his skin charred and blistered until all that was left was bone covered in oozing, burnt tissue. The slayer's eyes went wide, so wide Emery thought they'd pop out of his head.

With two quick swipes of his talons, he severed the slayer's remaining hand, satisfied with the wet plop that followed as it hit the floor, and cut through the front of his pants.

He grabbed the slayer's chin, pinching his cheeks against his teeth until his mouth was forced open. The tips of his talons pierced his skin, leaving thin streams of blood trekking down to his jaw. His prey's eyes glowed with malice, tears, and fear. Sweat beaded on his forehead. Emery tilted his head, burning his fiery gaze into the Baroqueth's.

"*No one* touches my woman and lives to talk about it."

Emery cut his talons downward, hitting his target. The slayer stopped breathing, the pure shock plastered across his face brutally encouraging. Blood pulsed against Emery's leg from his devastating blow. The corner of his mouth twitched before it curled into a snarl.

The slayer's mouth opened huge, his shoulders pulling up on a deep breath.

Emery grabbed his weapon from where it dangled in the shredded pants and shoved the bastard's severed cock deep into his open mouth, lodging it at the back of his throat before he could let out his scream. He grabbed the slayer's head, slammed his chin upward, forcing the appendage deeper down his throat. His victim's eyes teared, his face turning purple as he choked on his own cock.

Leaning close, his snarl melted into a fierce smile. "How pitiful of you to force my woman's face into your crotch only to end up like this. Brings new meaning to the word cock-sucker, wouldn't you say?"

With a dark snigger, Emery watched the slayer buck and fight futilely, his broken and burnt arms useless, his body twisting and thrashing in desperation for air. The purple of his face deepened to maroon, eyes bulging, veins popping along his neck and head. The tattoos etched into his skin beat at a tempo that echoed his frantic heartbeat.

The Baroqueth fell to his knees. His eyes began to roll back in his head. Emery sighed, disappointed that he wouldn't suffer longer. With one quick swipe, Emery laid his throat open and shoved him to the ground. His body convulsed as blood pooled around his head. Within moments, he lay still, except for an occasional twitch, his eyes fixing on the wall.

"Uh." Gabe coughed as he stepped up beside him, his attention on the fallen Baroqueth at Emery's feet. "Damn, brother. I'd forgotten your brutal side." He crouched down and tipped his head, scrutinizing the Baroqueth's face for a long moment. "No, you *didn't*."

"Didn't what?" Emery used his boot to shove the slayer onto his back. "Don't tell me you wouldn't go this far if it was Sky." His jaw slackened in death, exposing the tattered end of his severed cock. Gabe slowly straightened up, eyeing Emery cautiously. Emery wiped his hands on his jeans. Goddess, he couldn't wait to take a shower. "He was so eager to have Sera suck him, I figured I'd help him do it himself. It was a nice gesture from me, wouldn't you agree?

He died happy. A memorable ending going into the hell realms."

Gabe shook his head, rubbing the back of his neck. Emery stepped over the remnants of his work and hurried back to Sera and Sky. He caught the look Sky cast him as he knelt before Sera.

"I told you he had to learn from someone, didn't I?" Emery asked Sky, guessing why he'd earned that look. Sera's forehead wrinkled as she moaned, head lolling against the rock. He captured the side of her face in his cleaner hand, sinking his blood-coated fingers into her equally bloody hair. "Sweet flame, I'm here."

"Well, the fuck deserved it," Sky said.

"He deserved more, but we're in Baroqueth territory. Haven't any idea how much time we've got before another wave comes." He dropped his head. *"Love, open your eyes. Let me know you're coming around."*

"I-I'm here." Her face pinched in a grimace. *"Gods, I hurt."*

"Can you breathe better?"

A few seconds ticked by. Finally, Sera opened her eyes, slits of cloudy gray that struggled to focus until they found his face. She nodded once, reaching up and wrapping her fingers around his wrist.

"Questions have to wait, Em. We need to get back," Gabe said.

"I know." Emery graced Sera with a chaste kiss, slipped his arms under her legs and behind her back, and stood. She rested her head against his shoulder, a hand splayed against his chest. "I'll follow you."

They hurried along the winding corridors, some pitch black while others were lit by an unseen source. Emery lost track of time as they hustled, but dread built in his gut as

Gabe led them down one corridor after another, and none brought them to Cade.

"Slade, did the room change? We can't locate it," Emery reached out. *"This place keeps shifting."*

"We haven't moved." Silence followed for a few seconds. *"We're going to try and find you."*

"You're better off waiting where you are. We have to come around at some point."

"You've been gone a while. We don't know how much longer we can stay under the radar."

"Um, yeah. Not much, considering Gabe and I just slaughtered six Baroqueth."

"Are you okay? The girls?"

"Everyone is alive. Sera was hurt before we arrived, but those responsible are no longer breathing." Emery came to a sudden halt when Gabe turned right down yet another corridor. He glanced left, the fibers of his Keeper's bond urging him to go down this particular corridor. He'd been so caught up with Sera, soothing her pain and discomfort, he hadn't paid attention to Slade's bond. Though not as strong as his bond with Sera, it was still a beacon. "Gabe, this way."

Gabe paused, considering him. "I think this way—"

"No. It's this way." He started down the corridor. *"Do me a favor and step into the corridor. Let me see if I can't get a better lead through our bond."*

"Got it."

The three of them hurried along, Emery tracing Slade until, at long last, he caught sight of his Keeper halfway down this newest corridor. They picked up their pace, closing in on their target. He could only hope Cade had a way out of here.

Slade's expression dropped the moment he saw Emery with Sera in his arms. He ran to meet them, falling into step beside Emery as he brushed his fingers over Sera's face. "Angel, what happened?"

"I'm okay," she rasped. Emery wished he could cover her up as she tugged her torn shirt more tightly over her chest, but the shirt he wore had more blood on it than Sera's. "I'll heal."

Slade looked up at Emery, who shook his head vaguely. Now wasn't the time to prod for details. He didn't think there *would* be a time for that.

As they rounded the doorway to the room, he caught a glimpse of Cade before the floor fell out beneath him. Sky shrieked. Slade grappled for his arm as they plummeted through black nothing. Sera pushed her face into his shoulder, her arm tight around his neck.

"Not again," she moaned.

His feet hit something solid. His knees buckled and he twisted to protect Sera as he fell. He managed to lower her to the floor softly, then spun and straightened up on his feet.

The room before him was vastly different from anything he'd seen in this place so far. In fact, he'd go so far as to say this room was fit for a high-ranking official with fine tapestries that depicted magic battles with dragons. A long wooden table set with lit candelabras. Fancy sconces lined the walls, bright blue-white orbs spreading light throughout the space, reaching every corner, every cranny, leaving nothing in shadow.

Emery shoved Slade behind him when he realized how bad their situation had turned. Gabe sidled closer, Sky behind him until she could drop beside Sera.

He'd take an ever-shifting labyrinth over a mock war room any day. The magic that thrummed in the air was ominous, a whispered warning he couldn't decipher. He wouldn't fool himself into believing he'd be able to use any magic here.

"I think we just fell into the Baroqueth officials' laps," Emery relayed to Slade. He cast a side glance at Gabe. His brother was busy taking in each detail of the space, his keen attention masked behind an expression of indifference. The room lay empty, all except the subtle ruffle of the tapestries and the sway of the orb lights and flames. *"This isn't going to be good."*

"Wonderful boast of confidence, Em."

"I'm being straightforward. We need Cade and a way out of here."

The curtains rustled as a gust of air swirled through the room. Emery assessed the direction of the air, following the path as it hit each tapestry, then pulled together in the center of the dais in front of them. A hazy cloud of grayish white formed. It dropped away, revealing the one person Emery least expected to see.

Nick, arms crossed over his chest, a dark scowl pulling his mouth taut. He looked over each one of them slowly, his dark eyes seemingly darker. Was that a fleck of silver in his irises? Had he given himself to the Baroqueth completely?

Emery refrained from making a smartass comment, even if it teased the tip of his tongue. If Slade and the women weren't here, he'd dance with the devil, but their safety came first.

"Surprised you found them," Nick groused. He leaned to the side, craned his neck. Emery shifted, shielding Sera and Sky from the traitor's curiosity. "Pity, because there are consequences to leaving the cells. They'll be punished once Darieth has you separated." Nick spread one hand to the room. "There's no escape, dragons. None. The only way out is by finding a portal, but they move constantly. If Darieth doesn't want them found, you will *not* find them."

Emery kept quiet. He had nothing to say that wouldn't

taunt this madman. Instead, he'd let Nick ramble. He'd learn about this place in these next few minutes, learn everything he could to better understand how this realm worked. Apparently, his brother was of the same mind, because Gabe continued his silent observation, sparing Nick a glance every few seconds.

Nick chuckled, that maddening sound scraping down Emery's spine. Darieth had to be close, if not already hiding behind magic in the room with them. Emery doubted the leader of the Baroqueth would allow a traitor Keeper the run of his version of a conference room. Not if the leader of these evil bastards held a modicum of pride. He suspected Darieth's pride swelled to maximum proportions. His might even be responsible for that low-resonant energy that made the top layer of Emery's skin tingle.

"See you brought your worthless Keeper with you, too." Nick rubbed his hands together. "I'll have fun dealing with him."

"Don't say a word, Slade."

"He's playing us."

"Yes, so don't let him."

Nick tilted his head in a creepy way that reminded Emery of a psychotic killer in a horror movie, his soulless eyes cutting to Gabe.

"Seems your brother has lost his tongue, Gabe. How about you? Terrence managed to get himself killed by humans." He laughed. "Humans! A non-mortal martial arts master killed by powerless creatures. I always thought you taught him well. Seems you failed him, just like you failed Ellie."

Nick's face darkened, cast in shadows built from within his body. In that moment, Emery caught the faint pulse of a small tattoo painted beneath his ear. His dragon growled, the vibrations felt in his marrow, but the sound outwardly unheard. It was an internal response, thankfully. He didn't need to give away his growing frustration.

Nick had gone Baroqueth. There was no coming back from that.

Nick chose to become their enemy. They held no mercy for enemies in this war.

Gabe seemed to be mentally speaking with Sky, most likely calming her, or vice-versa. His brother's shoulders tensed slightly, not enough for Nick to pick up, but Emery knew his brother well. The small nuances kept him on the alert.

"You'll fail your lifemate, too. All of you will. There's no stopping us. Not now. Your powers will be drained over time, and the women will all become a means to growing our army. When we do, there's no telling the glory we'll achieve. Conquering the human world. Conquering The Hollow. Taking over everything we wish."

With each minute they didn't respond, Nick grew more irritated.

"Nothing to say?" Nick pursed his lips and nodded, pacing a small line back and forth before them. "Okay. Maybe, this will get you to talk."

He snapped his fingers.

Another rotating swirl of gray-white air formed a few feet from where he stopped pacing. This time, when the cone absorbed into the floor, two Baroqueth were there. Between them, Jeslyn lay crumpled on the ground, her hair mussed, her clothes ripped, tattered. Bruises marred her arms, but her face remained untouched, except for dried tear tracks.

Emery immediately whipped his arm back, grabbing hold of Slade's wrist. *"Don't. Don't fall for it."*

"Emery, this is crossing a line."

"She crossed the line that landed us here. If I must remind you, take a look at Sera and what she's endured due to Jeslyn's collusion. She's lying right behind you. Then look at Jeslyn and tell me her injuries match up to Sera's. Something's off here."

Emery didn't spare him a glance, keeping his focus on Nick and the newest arrivals. Jeslyn scrambled away from the two Baroqueth, who quickly grabbed her by her arms and yanked her back.

"Daddy!" she cried. "Help me!"

"Emery!" Slade snapped.

"Wait! Don't complicate this more by running to her."

"She's my daughter!"

Emery steadied his breaths, but his grip on Slade's arm tightened. Gabe closed the small gap of space between their shoulders, blocking Slade's view completely. His brother wagged a finger at the two holding Jeslyn captive as the woman sobbed and screamed for her father.

"Aren't you going to save your daughter?" Nick taunted. "Or have you forgotten about her now that you have the other daughter back and she's your precious dragon's lifemate? Wonder how it would be if this one was Emery's bitch."

Nick stepped up to Jeslyn, grabbed her by the hair, and tugged her to her feet. Jeslyn whimpered, squeezing her eyes shut as Nick released her hair but wrapped his hand around her throat. He fisted her ruined shirt, his face alongside Jeslyn's.

"Why do you hide the coward, Emery? Let him prove himself. Prove how morally sound he really is." He tugged at Jeslyn's shirt, ripping the tattered pieces away and casting them to the floor. He turned his face into her ear for a brief moment. Emery's skin bristled as he heard the whispered warning. "She may not be a lifemate, but she'll be a great addition to the breeding program, wouldn't you agree?"

"Let her go!" Slade roared, ripping his arm from Emery's grip, shoving through him and Gabe. He stumbled forward. Emery caught his arm again, cut in front of him with a split-second glance at what caused Slade to falter.

Sera's fingers held fast to the hem of Slade's jeans. Her face twisted in pain, pain that blossomed inside his mind, but she tightened her grip, teeth clenched. "Dad, no—"

Whips of magic sparked alive. Tentacles wrapped around Sera and Sky and recoiled with them too fast for Emery or Gabe to intercept.

His dragon boomed as the beast tore through his human form. He lowered his neck, parallel to the ground, slinking back and forth as he assessed this turn of events. Gabe had transformed beside him, but he began to circle the group in the center of the room. Three Baroqueth, three women. Sera and Sky suspended a foot off the floor by coils of sparking shadow bands. He sought the source of the magic, the handler of this spell. Nick dropped his hand from Jeslyn's throat, knocked out her knees, and resumed his grip in her hair as she kneeled before him, covering her bare chest with her arms.

He had to get Sera down. He had to figure out a way to break through the bindings without hurting her more. The coiling magic was enough to keep her pain alive, the battle in her face to keep her suffering hidden agonizing to witness. He wanted blood. He wanted death. He wanted to torture these monsters.

He would, as soon as Sera was safe.

Slade came up to his shoulder. "What do you want, Nick? I can't give you Dina. I won't give you Sera. What the fuck do you want?"

Nick's dark grin twitched. His nostrils flared as he twisted his fist in Jeslyn's hair until her hands grappled at his forearm, trying to relieve the pressure. Her pitiful sobs echoed through the room.

"I want to break you, Slade Rogue. I want to chip your will away, piece by piece, until you are nothing. I want to watch as I kill you, day by day, torturing your conscience until you can't take it another minute. Then I'll drive you to the cliff's edge, breathe against your nape, and watch you plummet to your fucking death like you did to me twenty-six years ago."

"Emery, don't do anything crazy. Please. We'll get out of this. You and me and my father. Sky and Gabe. Jes. We'll get out of this, just please..." He dared to lift his gaze to Sera's. She stared at him, pleading with all her might. Despite everything, his flame kept Jeslyn's wellbeing in mind. *"I knew a life without you too long. I don't want to go back to that. I need you."*

"Love, there will be no other life than one where we're both in it." He smacked his front claw down on the ground in front of Slade when his Keeper stormed toward Nick. *"Stay strong for me while I temper your father."* To Slade, he growled, *"Stay* back!*"*

"Then do something!"

The smoke that plumed from his nostrils was not for Nick alone. When they got out of this mess, he'd have a long chat with Slade and remind him who their enemy was. Irrationality would get them killed faster than they could process.

"We. Need. Cade. I'm trying to bide my time until he can get here. We can't escape. We don't know how, not without Cade. So calm the fuck down, Slade. If you think I'll let them harm my lifemate or my brother's, you need to do some serious self-reflection."

"And Jes."

Emery snorted. Sure, he'd save the devil child, but not without consequence.

The two Baroqueth who'd come in with Jeslyn grabbed Sera and Sky by their shoulders and yanked them down to the ground, dropping them to their knees. Sera's face tensed. Emery tried his best to take her pain away.

"Are you through chatting it up along your mindspeak lines? You're wasting time and the boys here are overdue for some fun—"

A burst of energy brought Emery's neck away from the ground, his senses on high alert. Fire readied in his throat, prepared to attack as a small storm of black and blue clouds built behind their adversaries. He endured the heat of invisible electric currents trying to infiltrate his body, breach the barriers of his scales. Slade ducked behind his leg, using him as a shield as the storm mounted and mounted, growing until it stretched to the ceiling.

And vanished, revealing the source of its power.

Dread weighed down Emery's chest. There was no mistaking who this was. Tall, covered in tattoos, slithering with silver and black magic. He might have serpents living beneath his skin, for all Emery knew. His hair was shaved except for a thick patch on top, black hair tied up with gold coils before falling past his shoulders and disappearing behind a black cape made of material and midnight mist. Blue bolts of magic skittered across his skin.

Endless black eyes threated to steal Emery's spirit and smother it in a netherworld.

"Welcome, dragons. I hope your time here has been entertaining."

"W-who is that?"

Sera hadn't tried to look back to see their newest arrival. Sky, on the other hand, struggled to get a glimpse. Jeslyn cried on her knees, muttering nonsense, seemingly oblivious to the changes in her situation.

"Think we've been granted VIP tickets to meet the Baroqueth leader."

Sera's face paled until she appeared ashen. She must have shared the impression with Sky, because the other woman immediately stiffened and stopped trying to see who stood behind them.

Darieth Constantine.

Murderer. Monster. Madman.

He remained behind his men, but his presence commanded attention and bled warning. He wasn't here to play. He was here for a reason, and Emery worried that reason would end with them all falling victim to his desires.

"This is long overdue, wouldn't you agree?"

Darieth's expression didn't change a fraction. His face remained hard as stone, his eyes unforgiving and cruel. He stretched an arm out, splayed his fingers. Strands of what appeared to be electricity shot forward.

The three women all at once went stiff and started trembling.

Gabe lunged forward.

Emery grappled for him to pull him back.

Darieth cast a net of similar electrical threads around Emery's brother, slamming him to the floor.

"Gabriel!" Sky screamed, her voice breaking as her body convulsed.

Darieth tilted his head to Gabe's spasming form, but his eyes dipped to Emery. Pure evil glowered at Emery, threatening to snuff the fire building in his veins.

"I'm willing to make one request of you, since I'm not a bartering man. Your women will be treated with higher regard if you comply with my demands. If not, then they will be subjected to the worst kind of torture you can imagine, and I'll be sure you bear witness to their suffering before I kill you. You'll die knowing that they will suffer like that for the rest of their lives until I've deemed them of no use and put them out of their misery."

"D-don't-t-t a-agree-e-e-e."

Sera's telepathic voice shook with her physical form as the shocks strengthened. His body had drawn so taut, the slightest flick would cause him to snap.

"Slade, ask what he wants."

Slade spun around to look up at him. He cast his Keeper a short glance, then resumed his staring contest with Darieth. *"You can't possibly be thinking—"*

"All I want to know are the terms. I said nothing else."

Slade cleared his throat and emerged from behind his leg. "What are the terms you speak of?"

"They're not terms. They're demands. They're expectations. I won't settle for less, nor will I change my mind. The only thing that will change is how the lifemates are treated. You really have nothing of value in your possession right now to *barter*."

He pulsed the hand connected to Gabe's net. The magic threads flashed brightly, then fizzled, but not before his brother's body stiffened and bowed with the flood of electric shocks. He fell limp, a huff of breath releasing a thin stream of smoke from his nostrils as his eyes closed. Panic cut across Sky's face, despite her own low-frequency torture, and she thrashed in the bindings.

"Sky, stop. Stop, please," Sera begged, her voice quiet, but leaking into his mind.

"You may do well to listen to her...*Sky*." Darieth lifted his chin, his fingers moving methodically as he played with his magic. Sky listened, begrudgingly, her eyes glistening as she fisted her hands at her sides. "My *demands*, Keeper, are as follows. I want each dragon that remains living to bleed into the one dragonstone I have in my possession."

He raised his hand. Mist swelled from his tapered fingertips. When it poured over his hand and faded, a dragonstone perched on his fingers. Large, oblong, and old. What once gleamed vibrant red and gold and black lay in faded shades of those colors.

Dead.

Darieth released the women from his magic, came rounded his men and paused at Gabe's snout. He flicked his hand. Gabe's unresponsive figure transformed from dragon to man. Slade's eyes widened. Emery immediately reined in his dragon and put himself between Darieth and Gabe.

"No. Not my brother."

A sharp breath, perhaps a quiet snort, fled Darieth. The beast wore no discernable expression. He was as cold as ice.

"You only delay the inevitable. This was bound to happen, dragon. All your efforts to restore The Hollow and your civilians were in vain." Burning cold shackled Emery's wrist and yanked him forward on an unseen tether. Darieth's hand lifted, another invisible force spreading Emery's fingers. "I'll accept your offer first."

"Emery, don't! Don't do it!" Sera cried.

Emery tugged at his arm, fought the pull and the magic, trying to use his own power, to futile effect. That fire in his throat licked and burned as Darieth drew a short blade from his belt and nicked his finger. His dragon bellowed, but his scales wouldn't emerge to protect him. He felt them trying to break through a phantom wall, scraping and cutting, but unable to spread.

"Fire, dragon! Sky says now!"

Blinded by rage, Emery recklessly listened to his flame, exhaling the mounting fire from his chest.

Flames swept up from beneath him.

Gabe pressed to his hands and knees, flames pouring from his mouth as his body thickened and swelled in slow transformation.

The shackle on Emery's wrist released. Darieth reeled back, spun and cast a protective shield around himself. Emery lunged toward Sera as the coiled bindings vaporized. The two Baroqueth minions fumbled in the chaos, shielding themselves from the flames that stretched with Gabe's transformation. He caught both women and spun away. Darieth struck the spot with a force that shattered the floor where Sera and Sky had been not a second before. Emery shoved the women into Slade, who hustled them toward the only door in the room.

"Daddy! Daddy, don't leave me!" Jeslyn screamed. She fought futilely against Nick. Nick lifted her again, wrapping his arms around her, pinning her arms to her sides. Slade paused, turned to Jeslyn, his eyes torn. He dropped his arms from Sera and Sky as Jeslyn's hands tried to stretch toward him. "Daddy!"

Emery spun around, embracing his dragon—

And found himself staring at Darieth's fury in the form of an ethereal silver-tipped spear rushing at his heart.

A wall of faded blue exploded before his eyes. The air vibrated with the force of the power, knocking him back a few steps. Gabe stumbled, dropping to a knee. Darieth and the two Baroqueth tore off the floor. Their bodies pitched across the room, crashing into the wall.

The floor at his feet opened in a churning cloud of stormy gray and bolts of energy.

"Go!"

Emery whipped his head toward the voice and stared at the vision.

A familiar petite woman who melded and molded magic unlike anything he'd seen. One hand forged the offensive attack that now acted as a forcefield protecting them. It warped the air, made his ears feel like they would pop from the pressure, and stirred a metallic-scented breeze around them.

Or maybe that came from the portal she'd opened with her other hand.

Two forces of powerful magic induced by a single woman.

Darieth's daughter. Malla.

She snapped her head toward Emery, her eyes fierce, face tight. "Lest you wish to find out what he was about to do, *go! Get out!*"

Gabe had already gathered Sky, and herded Slade and Sera toward the portal.

Jeslyn stopped screaming, her glistening gaze breaking as she watched Slade embrace Sera before Gabe shoved him and the women into the storm. He caught Emery's gaze. With a single nod to each other, they struck out at Nick and Jeslyn, grabbing both, and pulling them through the portal before either could escape.

CHAPTER THIRTY

Sera cringed as Emery lowered them into the steaming hot spring water. Every cut, scrape and gash seethed as the water touched them, instantly beginning to heal her wounds, both inside and out. She snuggled against his chest, tucked securely in his arms, the water sloshing as he settled against the tub's side. For a long while, they soaked in silence, his fingers stroking her arm, his mouth resting against the top of her head.

There was no other place she cared to be than in Emery's arms. Despite the trauma of the day, his embrace washed most of it away. The heat of his skin. The strength in his muscles. The certainty of his presence. She wasn't ignorant of the severity of what had happened on the Baroqueths' turf. She'd nearly lost Emery, and that drove a fear inside her she never wanted to feel again.

She also understood that their escape would only fuel Darieth's revenge and determination.

For him, failure wasn't an option.

"How are you feeling, flame?"

"I have you. I'm complete." She tipped her head up and

caught his warm whiskey gaze. The scent of old blood resided on his skin, on hers, the faint taste of minerals lingering at the back of her throat. She couldn't wait to wash everything away. After she healed. "Don't you ever scare me like that again."

His eyes widened, mouth falling open, aghast. He shook his head, narrowed his eyes and tsked. "Excuse me, but I think you have things reversed. I got the whole report from Sky. I know what happened to you, and yet you minimize your injuries only because Malla fixed you up enough to stabilize you for an escape." He raised his brows. "So, would you have told me everything?"

Her cheeks flushed at the vile memories. She began to lower her chin, but he caught her with a single finger and half-shook his head. His gaze softened.

"You fought, and I'm so proud of you for fighting. You should be proud, too, because you were able to deter one assailant."

"And bear the brunt of his anger with a swift kick to the ribs that punctured my lung." She sighed. "I thought I was going to die. When I was laying on the floor in the corridor, I stared up at the ceiling and swore I saw something crawling overhead. I thought it was a reaper."

"Not sure if I take that as a compliment or not," he scoffed, but his smile grew. "Reaper to others, savior to you." He leaned close, lips brushing hers. "I thought I heard you say something before Malla swept you away from me."

Sera reached up and cupped his face between her palms. She kissed him slowly, indulging in the heat of his mouth and the possessive way his tongue slid over hers. Gods, she wanted an eternity like this, her and Emery, sharing these tender moments between ones of intense pleasure.

Drawing back, she stared shamelessly into his eyes. "I

love you, Emery LaRouche. I love you so much it hurts when you're not with me. I love you so much that I no longer know who I am without you. My heart aches when you're not near. My soul cries when we're separated, yearning for your return. I was foolish to push you away, because now, I would do anything to keep you as close to me as possible."

He traced her lower lip with a single finger. "You aren't foolish. You were never foolish. You did what you did for selfless reasons. Just like you shoved Sky away when that Baroqueth attacked you in the corridor. You are selfless and self-sacrificing, for which I have a few words to share. See, I'm self*ish*, and I don't want you sacrificing yourself for anyone. You're mine, Seraphina." His hands slipped beneath the water to her waist and tugged her flush against him. The only way to get closer would be for her to straddle his legs and fill herself with him. "*Mine*. I don't share. Anyone who puts a finger on you will regret it."

She shuddered at the thought of what Sky had told her when they'd landed back in The Hollow, in a field in the middle of nowhere. It took half an hour of flight to get back to Cade's, where Emery and Gabe dropped Nick and Jeslyn into the hands of their dragon leader.

"So I heard." She tucked her head beneath his chin and traced the dragon tattoo on his arm. "Detachable penis?"

Emery shrugged. "Think it was still too kind of me."

She smiled to herself. She knew, no matter what, Emery would keep her safe, avenge any wrongs committed against her, and die to save her. She only hoped he knew she'd do the same for him, and that motivated her to work harder at her skills in magic and martial arts.

Never again would she let herself fall victim like she had today.

"I don't think I've ever seen someone so self-controlled

as you today. I felt your discord, your dragon beating at the doors, but you somehow stayed in complete control. It helped calm me." Sera drew her fingers across his pec, lingering to experience the strong beat of his heart. She closed her eyes, utterly complete. "Have I told you I love you?"

"No." He chuckled. "I'm afraid not. So go ahead and tell me. Confess this love you have for the dragon cradling you in our tub."

Sera laughed. "Silly dragon. I'll confess loud and proud until the end of time."

They soaked until the water cooled. Emery lifted her from the tub and gently placed her on her feet as he drained the cloudy, red-tinted water, rinsed the tub, and filled it again with water from the faucet. This time, he scooped her up and lowered her into the hot water alone. She slipped completely under the surface, scrubbing her fingers in her matted hair until it began to loosen, and resurfaced. Emery had pulled up a stool and settled behind her, pouring shampoo into his hand. He took up the task of washing her hair, his fingers working into her scalp, soothing her to the point of nearly falling asleep.

"I want to bleed into your dragonstone, Emery," she said quietly as he took his time rinsing the shampoo from her hair. He didn't falter at her confession. The corner of her mouth lifted. "I want to take that final step with you."

"As soon as I'm done pampering my beloved flame."

"I would've thought you'd jump at the opportunity."

His hands slipped down to her shoulders and began working out the knots in her muscles. She moaned, tipping her head to allow him easier access.

"Neither one of us is going anywhere tonight. Whether it be this instant or an hour from now, you'll bleed into my stone and bind us together forever. What I want is for you to heal."

She took in a slow, deep breath. The ache in her ribs had faded to a nuisance more than pain. The laceration on her head was nearly gone, the persistent headache and dizziness barely detectable. The cuts on the inside of her cheek were nowhere to be found. Any other injury she'd sustained—she couldn't even remember all of them—held no place on her body. The spring water worked its miracles, and Emery's fingers and hands worked their own unique magic.

"I'm almost there. I really wanted to clean all this blood off me and curl up in your arms in our bed." She looked back at her delightfully naked dragon, her gaze lingering on the blood stains splattered over his neck. "You still have some specks on you."

"Mm. You first. I'll shower when you're done." He smiled, leaned over, and captured her mouth in an upside-down kiss that left her breathless. "You're an awfully delicious distraction, you know that?"

Her gaze lowered to the evidence of his burning arousal. "I'm not the only one."

His massaging fingers paused, the lightness of his expression turning feral. "If you want to lay together in bed, be sure to wear layers of clothing to keep my hands off you, siren."

Sera twisted around, folding her arms on the edge of the tub. She rested her chin on her hands. "I never said the *only* thing I wanted to do was curl up in your arms."

Emery closed his eyes, sucking in a controlled breath, and released a flutter of smoke. When he opened his eyes, they burned with fire. "Woman."

She pointed to the shower. "Hurry up, dragon. Otherwise, I might fall asleep, and you'll be blue until morning."

Emery rushed to the shower, knocking over the stool in

his dash to fulfill her command. She settled back in the tub with a giddy smile and washed her body with one of the scented soap bars on the glass caddy. She couldn't help herself, staring at Emery as he scrubbed away the blood and remnants of their encounter in the Baroqueth world. How his muscles flexed and moved, creating a fluid landscape of mouthwatering eroticism. He was her fantasy come to life. Her everything.

Her perfect.

Tonight, as they lay in each other's arms, she would bleed into his dragonstone, completing them entirely.

CHAPTER THIRTY-ONE

The moon sat high in the sky when a faint zing along his skin triggered him awake. Emery opened his eyes and carefully stretched a hand toward the bedroom door, connecting with the inlays of magic throughout his home. It didn't take long for his visitor to trip another warning. Emery gently worked his arm from beneath Sera's head and slipped out of the bed without waking her. He pulled on a pair of flannel pants and silently left the bedroom, following the path to the living room.

Standing before the fire, Cade waited patiently, hands folded behind his back. Emery gauged his stance, the faint lines of tension deepening his cheeks. His hair had been tied back in a careless knot at his nape, uncharacteristic of his leader. In fact, if Emery dared to think it, Cade appeared disheveled.

Combing a hand through his hair to pull it away from his face, Emery said, "Malla rescued us."

Cade nodded once. "I'm aware." He released a heavy sigh and faced Emery. The fire in his eyes wasn't as fierce and bright. Emery wondered what he had encountered in his own escape. "You found it in your heart to bring Jeslyn and Nick back."

He scowled. "I would've left the traitor Keeper, but he'll be held accountable here. He'd run rampant like an unaccompanied toddler if I left him behind. After what happened, I wasn't letting him off."

"And the woman?"

"Slade assured me he would take care of his child. She came back with us because of my loyalty to Slade. And Sera implied in her own selfless way that Jes not be left behind, despite everything that woman caused my lifemate. I only hope Slade stands his ground and ensures she's punished accordingly."

"Jeslyn's actions won't be overlook. She caused unnecessary injuries and could've gotten people killed. I spoke with Slade before I came here. He asked me if I would agree to return to Colorado. He believes a suitable punishment is exile from The Hollow, considering she cannot be trusted with the people here. He has offered to get her started with a small house and will aid her in starting a business or getting work, whichever she chooses. But he confided in me he can't forgive her for the dangers she brought upon us, herself included. Even as a father, he won't condone her behavior, love or not."

"She and Nick were in it together from the night Nick learned the truth about Sera. I heard him whisper to her in that war room to play along until they had us in captivity so they could reap their revenge. By that time, though, I think Jeslyn had realized her mistake to collude with Nick. Unfortunately, her part in the entire fiasco had already dealt unforgivable damage." Emery straightened up. "I'm glad he's exiling her. It's fair punishment for a woman who's been spoiled rotten all her life to try and figure things out on her own. But what about Claire?"

"He gave Claire the option of returning with Jeslyn or staying here. He doesn't want to separate Claire from her daughter, so he's leaving it up to her. I'm not sure of her decision, or if she's made a decision yet." Cade stroked his beard, tucking his other fist beneath his elbow. "Until I can get her out of The Hollow, she'll be under house arrest. I've set up a perimeter around their property that is sensitive solely to Jeslyn. She can't go more than ten feet from the house in any direction. I've also asked Amelia to place wards within the home to detect Baroqueth activity, should they have a tracking spell on her. The other option was a cell in my dungeon, next to Nick. Which brings me to the reason I came in the middle of the night."

"I thought you'd decided to take up raiding our pantry. Sadly, I don't have much here."

The corner of Cade's mouth lifted. "We need to upgrade your abode, but that's for another time. I wanted to ask if you're up to"—his eyes narrowed, those flames darkening—" making a special visit with me. See how our friend is getting along."

Emery's lips peeled back in a lethal smile. "Oh, I'm game."

Deep in the belly of Cade's monstrous mountain residence was the place where nightmares called home. A small maze of alcoves fitted with magically imbued bars that created cells of different shapes and sizes. Some had enough room for an occupant to stretch out across the ground. Others were small to the point where a grown man would have to hunch or curl up to fit.

No one in their right mind would dare lay on the ground. Not when the crevices and cracks were hideaways to a number of insects and reptiles unique to The Hollow, more specifically, the dungeon. Poisonous creatures. Carnivorous creatures. Serpents that took joy in gnawing out eyes or chewing holes through flesh like Swiss cheese. Bugs and worms that burrowed deep beneath the surface of the skin until they reached the organs and began their feasts, causing a slow, agonizing death from the inside out. Stones stained with bodily fluids from previous residents, down to the decaying remnants of prisoners that had become fodder for the bottom dwellers. The stench alone could scar one's sense of smell and send one into a heaving fit.

The dungeon was a living, breathing, palpable nightmare. Everyone knew it existed, few ever got to see it, none wanted to be in it.

Cade lit the torch across the winding walkway from the cell they'd stopped before. Firelight cast the pitiful accommodations beneath a soft orange glow. A thin layer of straw was the only luxury offered.

Not that it mattered.

Cade had strung Nicholas Allaze up with spell-imbued shackles, his toes barely brushing the straw beneath his feet. Emery noted the strain on his shoulders with a small dash of pleasure and wondered how much longer he could bear his weight pulling on those ligaments and tendons. The man looked feral, his eyes wild, his lips pulled back like a rabid creature. His tousled hair clung to dried sweat along his temples, forehead. He'd been dressed in jeans and a T-shirt when Emery and Gabe snatched him back to The Hollow; Cade had long since stripped him of every ounce of clothing, and dignity.

This cell. Oh, this cell.

If Emery recalled the stories correctly, this particular cell housed a vicious reptilian creature that took its time devouring prey one nibble at a time. Its bite sent painful venom through its victim, the sensation like acid washing the underside of the skin, or so rumor had it. He'd have to ask Nick when his chosen fate came out to take its first bite.

"Like the setup, Nick. Fitting for one of your…stature," Emery ridiculed. Cade pressed his palm to a pad of iron and stone. A lock released and the cell door squeaked open. Emery glanced at Cade, who simply nodded for him to enter, then lounged back against the wall across the walkway with his arms crossed. Emery slid into the cell, the faint tingle of the spells, wards, and magic that kept prisoners in teasing his skin. "You appear comfortable."

"Fuck off," Nick spat.

Emery tsked. "That's not very hospitable of you. I came to keep you company. See what I can do for you." He exaggerated his perusal of Nick's neck, and the single tattoo. "Oh"—he flicked his talon up—"you've got a little something on your neck. Let me"—he sliced through the skin of the former Keeper's neck, cutting out the tattoo and cauterizing the wound with a burst of heat. To his displeasure, Nick barely flinched—"get that for you."

"You'll have to kill me to break me, dragon. I won't give you the satisfaction."

Emery straightened up, dragging the curve of his talon along Nick's jaw. The blasted man glowered at him, unfazed. He turned his finger so the tip of his talon hooked in the fleshy area behind his chin. Nick clenched his teeth, his eyes narrowing as Emery pressed deeper into his flesh, hooking him like a fish from the bottom up.

Nick's tongue pulled back as Emery's talon broke into his mouth. His breathing picked up, sharp, shallow. Blood oozed down Emery's talon, his finger, until it reached his hand. A single drop fell from his knuckle to the straw.

"Let's test that, shall we?" Emery grinned. "The last man I killed shortly before we landed in your presence ate his own cock. The one before that had his heart ripped through his chest. Quick deaths, considering what they did to Sera. But you?" A rumble accompanied his deep chuckle. "Your sins are far worse than theirs, and I have plenty of ideas in mind for you."

With one swift motion, Emery yanked his talon from Nick's chin, cleaving his jaw in half. The traitor's eyes went wide, and he released a scream that filled the dungeon and echoed down the walkway. His eyes moved frantically, bouncing between Cade and Emery. A subtle glance over his shoulder and he knew Cade wouldn't stop him. His leader's eyes were locked on Nick, a lethal grin shifting his beard and mustache. He flicked his own talons in casual waves, the click methodical.

Perhaps it would become another layer of torture tonight.

Emery found the click relaxing.

"That's for my Keeper." He brought his bloody talon to his mouth and drew it across his tongue. The sour taste riled his dragon. "A complimentary gift before we begin. After all, once the *glacha* scents blood, he believes it's dinnertime." He stabbed his talons into Nick's flank. The man thrashed and bellowed. The first sign of tears crested his eyes when Emery fished for his kidney, twisted the organ, and tore it from his body. Nick's eyes rolled back into his head, tremors wracking him from head to toe. "Aww, Nicky. The night's still young. There's so much more to look forward to. Surely you're not breaking already."

CHAPTER THIRTY-TWO

The air had taken on a characteristic chill that accompanied the predawn hour. The first signs of day painted the horizon navy blue by the time Emery was through delivering his punishment. Cade almost pitied the man, had he not turned traitor and brought harm upon those under his watch. Alas, there was no sympathy to be had for a creature such as Nick. He chose his path and reaped the rewards, only in this case, he reaped his own suffering. Emery left him barely alive, torn, tattered, bloodied and dismembered. When Emery finally backed out of the cell and closed the door, the *glacha* had caught whiff of the blood and come to investigate with a tiny nibble at one of the three remaining toes on Nick's foot.

By the time he made his next round at dusk, Cade expected to see a lot less of Nick Allaze hanging from the shackles. He'd be surprised if a heart still beat inside his chest.

"I'm in for another shower before Sera wakes up." Emery considered the blood coating his arms. "That certainly hit the spot."

"Go get some rest." Cade sealed the dungeon entrance with a flick of magic that hid the door beneath a façade of cavernous rock. His prisoners could scream until their vocal cords wore out and not a soul would hear. "I have some things to contemplate after these events. I'll be calling a meeting later this afternoon."

He followed Emery up the circular stone stairs that deposited them in a tunnel beneath his homestead. Here, the air still stung with a frigid edge and moist dirt lent a comforting scent. Two more levels to get to his lowest live-in space, and they would have a few more minutes of walking to reach his home.

Cade dug into his pocket and pulled out a handkerchief. He handed it over to Emery, who accepted it with a quiet thanks and started the daunting task of cleaning drying blood from his fingers and nailbeds. Despite the silence, tension stirred between them. Thankfully, Emery busied himself with his hands for the remainder of their trek.

As Cade opened the doorway to the path leading up to his launch shelf, Emery hesitated. The young dragon lowered his hands, the handkerchief balled up in his fist, and faced Cade. His brows furrowed, a light of genuine curiosity swimming in his eyes.

"When I found Sera and Sky tucked in a room in that Goddess-forsaken labyrinth, I learned something that I haven't been able to brush off."

Cade went on guard. The first slither of his dragon roused to the impending inquiry. He already knew what Emery wanted to ask: How did he get them to the Baroqueth headquarters? It had been a lingering thought in the air he'd caught from Slade and Gabriel as well.

Emery ticked a finger, the furrow of his brows deepening. "Actually, the more I think of it, the more I wonder if Sera is right. She has a way of unraveling things that we can't because we're so involved in the events of the present. She somehow manages to keep herself a half-step outside the box for a better understanding of what goes on around her."

"You have a keen lifemate, Emery. Whether she knows it or not, she is an empath, and with that comes rare qualities in the position she holds beside you."

Ah, yes. He'd picked up on Seraphina's gift the first time he met her. Her heartstrings turned to feelers, reaching for those around her to understand their emotions, absorb their turmoil, and allow them a moment of peace while she processed their feelings within herself. He doubted she grasped the significance of her capabilities, especially the magic woven within her gift. A gift that could turn into a burden if not managed appropriately.

Emery smiled, softening the dragon's features. Sera brought him the joy he had witnessed in each of Cade's dragons at the discovery of their lifemates. With their happiness came his contentment.

"I'm aware, which is why her disclosure weighs that much more." His smile waned. "Malla rescued us. If she is truly the daughter of Darieth Constantine, then she turned traitor to her father, and those consequences are immeasurable. We're all aware that Briella had a vision months ago that centered around her and an impending war with the Baroqueth. After yesterday, I understand there is no diverting this war. And yet, it goes a little deeper, doesn't it?"

Cade folded his arms over his chest and tipped his chin up, gauging Emery for a long moment. Right now, he'd rather address the curiosity of how he transported them into Baroqueth territory than linger on this tedious path.

Emery glanced over his shoulder, toward Cade's home. "How did you get back?" His attention returned to Cade, unwavering and suspicious. "I didn't see you before we went through the portal."

He chose his words wisely. "I wasn't far behind you."

Emery watched him, unblinking, picking at his expression, no doubt. He gave little away in his words, deliberately vague. His dragons had their lifemates to concern themselves with. He, on the other hand, had an entire race and a world to protect.

"That's it?" Emery asked, a hint of skepticism in his voice.

"That's it." Cade motioned to the tunnel. "You should go, before the sun rises and your woman wakes alone. I doubt she'll be pleased to find your side of the bed empty and cold, especially after her trauma from yesterday."

"One thing about Sera? She's resilient. She also likes to put puzzles together. Before I go, answer one more question for me. After that, I promise I'll leave you in peace with sagging wings and my tail between my legs." Cade arched a brow, his only gesture for Emery to fire away. "Briella saw Malla at the center of a war. Sera reminded us that Baroqueth are nothing more than rogue Keepers. If you connect the dots, Cade, it begs the question; is Malla a lifemate?" His eyes darkened. "*Your* lifemate?"

That had been the last thing he expected. Instead of offering an answer, he simply said, "I'll make the rounds tomorrow with a time to meet. For now, we both have had a challenging day. Give way to speculation, Emery, and obsession follows, especially when your mind is rife with bloodlust and running with conspiracies."

Emery rolled his eyes. "As convoluted an answer as ever." He clapped Cade's shoulder. "Thanks for allowing me to indulge in my bloodlust. Quenched the thirst I've harbored since the night he pointed a gun at Sera's head."

Once Emery was out of sight, Cade closed the door and headed through the tunnels to his private wing. Unlike those he oversaw who'd rather have their homes set up within close quarters, he preferred rooms to be separated by a few levels or corridors, for good reason.

He came to the last tunnel in the north end of the mountain, a solitary tunnel with a single door at the end. Casting his thoughts into darkness, his approach into silence, he quietly called forth a spell that worked across his fingers and jumped ahead of him to the intricate design of a disk-like lock. The door eased inward on silent hinges for him to enter without pause, and closed at his back, engaging the lock once more.

A quaint room, warm from the ever-burning fire in the large fireplace, set up with all the necessities to make one feel comfortable and welcomed.

He hesitated a breath, holding his defenses in place, then allowed the lure of the woman on the oversized bed to draw his attention. Alluring, stunning, the epitome of beautiful. A small, delicate woman who appeared fragile and helpless in the sea of blankets, but who held a world of strength and power. Even in her unconscious state, he tasted the energy radiating off her, a sweet nectar that conflicted with the roots from which that energy blossomed. It caressed his skin, a subtle siren's song he shut out with fierce determination.

Dainty gold wristbands fitted against her pale skin, imbued with powerful spells to contain her magic. He couldn't take chances, not when it came to the lives of his dragons and their women. The Keepers and the civilians. His people depended on him, trusted him, to keep them safe and protect them from their enemies.

She was an enemy.

His dragon rumbled in his mind, a warning of his misplaced accusation. Or the beast's perceived accusation.

Until he knew Malla Constantine's intentions, she was a danger. She was a threat. She may have saved Gabriella and Dorian, released Briella and Tajan, provided *the key* to open the portal to Baroqueth headquarters, healed Sera and nearly sacrificed herself to help the team escape yesterday, but he was no stranger to deception and betrayal.

Betrayal was an old friend of his. He and the bastard had shared in hours of flight and laughed over mead while a blade hid behind its back, waiting for the perfect moment to strike.

Cade Fenryn knew betrayal all too well, from someone he had trusted with his life, and nearly paid the ultimate price. He, the oldest living Firestorm dragon, had a thousand years' worth of experiences.

Of *secrets*.

When one leader falls, another rises from the ashes of the first.

His honored guest winced in sleep, tempting him to infiltrate her mind, to see her dreams, her nightmares. No. He would not. That boundary was set, too intimate a line to cross. Too risky. Fate had been set in motion, whether he liked it or not, but the end result would be controlled by him, and him alone.

He was Firestorm. He was power. He was *indestructible*.

After all, the ashes of his predecessor were no other than his own.

Betrayal failed in its ploy to destroy its dragon, and created a true beast.

THE END

Watch for the highly anticipated conclusion, *Blaze of the Firestorm, The Firestorm Dragon Chronicles,* coming soon!

ABOUT THE AUTHOR

Born and raised a Jersey girl with easy access to NYC, Kira was never short on ideas for stories. She started writing at the tender age of 11, and her passion for creating worlds exploded from that point on. Romance came later, but since then, all of her heroes and heroines find their happily ever after, even if it takes a good fight, or ten, to get there.

Kira resides in Central Florida with her husband, four children, two bunnies, two cats, and black lab. She works full-time as a nurse when she's not writing or traveling between sports, other activities, or her characters' worlds.

Kira loves to hear from readers! Find her at:

Website and Newsletter: www.kiranyte.com
Contact: kiranyteauthor@gmail.com

Made in the USA
Columbia, SC
17 June 2024